BRIGID OF IRELAND

A HISTORICAL NOVEL

CINDY THOMSON

MONARCH
BOOKS

Oxford, UK & Grand Rapids, Michigan

First published in the UK in 2006 by Monarch Books
(a publishing imprint of Lion Hudson plc),
Mayfield House, 256 Banbury Road, Oxford OX2 7DH
Tel: +44 (0) 1865 302750   Fax: +44 (0) 1865 302757
Email: monarch@lionhudson.com
www.lionhudson.com

Distributed by:
UK: Marston Book Services Ltd, PO Box 269,
Abingdon, Oxon OX14 4YN;
USA: Kregel Publications, PO Box 2607,
Grand Rapids, Michigan 49501.

ISBN-13: 978-1-85424-747-6 (UK)
ISBN-10: 1-85424-747-6 (UK)
ISBN-13: 978-0-8254-6112-5 (USA)
ISBN-10: 0-8254-6112-X (USA)

British Library Cataloguing Data
A catalogue record for this book is available
from the British Library.

Printed in Great Britain.

Dedication

For Michelle. Keep searching

Acknowledgments

God, in his wisdom, sent many people my way to help make this book a reality. My agent Les Stobbe was instrumental in making connections for me. Tony Collins at Monarch is owed thanks for taking on the project. Prayer partners included Scott and Dawn Brown, Cris Carnahan, Lori Colopy, Holly and Gregg Graham, Diane Harper, Robin Kane, Teresa Richardson, Tessa Stockton, and Marsha Weiner. Critique help came from Tricia Goyer, Sharon Hinck, Becky Miller, Jacquie Stevanus, Barbara Taylor Sanders, and Donna Wyland. Jan Eckles helped me understand the sightless when I wrote about Brocca. Most helpful, my husband Tom cheered me on without ceasing. If not for his willingness to do laundry, cook dinner, and place occasional bouquets of fresh flowers on my desk, I may never have finished. Thank you all. Isn't God grand?

Glossary of Irish terms

ath (pronounced: AH) – ford of a river

bodhran (BOD-run) – hand-held goatskin drum often played with a stick

Brehon (bre-HOON) – judge of the ancient unwritten Irish laws

crannog (CRAN-uk) – ancient Irish dwelling or fort built on an island

curragh (CURR-akh – "kh" as in Scottish "loch") – a boat made of animal skins on a wooden frame

maimeo (MAH-mo) – grandma

mamai (MAH-mee) – mama

ogham (AW-gum) – early Irish alphabet in the form of notches inscribed on memorial stones; a stone bearing such writing

Samhain (SOW-in) – ancient Celtic celebration in early November to mark the beginning of winter; elements of the festival remain in All Soul's Day and Halloween

seanachaidh (SHAN-a-khee) – wandering storyteller

seanathair (SHAN-a-hir) – grandfather

seanmhathair (SHAN-va-hir) – grandmother

Tuatha De Danann (TU-a-ha day da-NAWN) – lit. "Children of the Goddess Dana"; the pre-Christian gods of Ireland

Names – pronunciation guide:

Aine (AWN-ya)

Ardan (AR-dawn)

Brocca (BROCK-sha)

Cu Chulainn (koo HOO-lin)

Dubtach (DUFF-akh)

Eoghanachta (YOO-an-akh-ta)

Geall (GYAWL)

Maire (MOI-ra)

Prologue

"Does it bother ye? Being a slave, I mean?" The aged druid guided Brocca's way while she rode horseback through the rocky slopes spanning the southern part of the Irish isle. He was her new master now.

Brocca gazed down into the man's frosty blue eyes as he traipsed alongside the horse.

He glanced away. "Just wondering."

A chilly midday mist coated Brocca's eyelashes. She wiped away the moisture and patted her large belly. How should she answer? Her lot as a slave would soon cost her dearly. Didn't the old man know?

The child within her bounced with every hoofbeat, but riding was far easier than stumbling along a rugged trail. She thought of her previous master. How could he have been so heartless to force her to leave Leinster while she was expecting his child?

Brocca took comfort in one thing. If this druid, her new master, had meant to be cruel, he would never have allowed her to ride.

Brocca clutched the mare's blond mane and cleared her throat, causing the druid to glance back at her. She swallowed hard, hoping to steady her voice. "Nay, it does not bother me to be a slave. Patrick taught that if one accepts baptism in the Lord's name, one may dwell on the promise that long-suffering for Jesus will result in a reward in heaven."

The druid shook his cloaked head, aiming his words at the ground. "I do not understand ye Christians."

Their conversation waned as they plodded through mossy fields. The druid's statement hung in the air like fog in a gulch, and Brocca thought once or twice she'd explain. But just as soon as the words were about to come forth, she closed her mouth tight. Every explanation she could think of paled against the backdrop of what her former master had planned.

The horse whinnied. The druid patted her nose. "That's right. We're almost home."

They approached a dense grove of budding trees, and the druid's voice rose above the chatter of rooks roosting there. "Tell me about this Patrick."

A welcome distraction. "He had a glow about him." Brocca leaned forward as the horse suddenly picked up its pace.

The stubby man ran alongside until he finally persuaded the animal to slow. "She knows we're close. Knows a warm barn and a feast of hay await her, she does."

Just beyond the grove Brocca spotted Cashel, the high point occupied for many years by various kings and used as a lookout. Just a rocky patch topped with green turf, yet so important to men who sought to control other men. The man she spoke about, Patrick, had visited that same hill, even baptized a royal poet there.

"Ah, I see." The druid rubbed his milky beard. "'Twas magic, then. Patrick – a sorcerer, was he?"

Brocca smiled. Truly, this pagan knew little of the Holy Spirit. She lifted her head to breathe in the dampness, filling her lungs as much as the growing babe would allow. "Patrick? Nay, man. He did not use any magic. He had the glow from our Lord."

Her new master arched his snowy eyebrows. Brocca knew that talk of serving only one God sounded foreign to his ears. One day she'd explain, perhaps even introduce this druid, whom pagans called a priest, to Patrick. There was so much to tell about the holy man who roamed Ireland preaching the good news of Jesus the Christ.

But now her body ached. The child within her was too large to move about any longer. Brocca knew the time of birth was drawing near. Winter had been long and hard, but spring, and her baby's arrival, approached.

The druid urged the mare through saplings and down a lane toward a thatch-covered cottage. Smoke bellowed from the house's roof, beckoning them with the promise of a warm turf fire. Brocca accepted the druid's wrinkled hand as she wiggled down from the horse's back.

He tipped his head toward the dwelling. "Go on in, now. I've got another slave maiden in the house who'll serve ye some broth."

Brocca lowered her chin to her chest and waited a moment while the old man led his horse into a tiny barn. The cries of cattle echoed off the stone-speckled hills. That barn would be her domain. Her purpose was to tend the druid's dairy.

Brocca feared the worst part of her relocation. Before she left with the druid, she'd pretended not to hear her former master's words. But she *had* heard. His pronouncement still echoed in her head. She held her hands over her ears, trying to drown out his voice. "The unborn child has not been sold," he'd said. "When the time comes, he'll return to me in Leinster."

Brocca rubbed her swollen belly. Tears filled her eyes as she turned her back to the dairy. Perhaps the child would not be a boy. She breathed a sigh of relief. That cruel man would likely reject a girl. At least she hoped he would. Brocca wrapped both her arms around her middle and stepped slowly toward the house, longing to hold on to what she feared would soon slip away.

The wind brought the smell of spring to her senses – warm dirt, moist grass – and she pushed the thought of parting with her child to the hidden places of her mind. Pulling her colorless shawl over her head, she followed the smell of mutton broth.

After a few mornings of forgetting where she was when she awoke, Brocca adjusted to her surroundings. Then one day, just as she had settled into a routine and convinced herself that nothing would come between her and her baby, a dark figure approached the house just after milking time. Brocca scooped up her buckets and padded toward the kitchen as quickly as her large body allowed.

"Cook," she puffed, out of breath, "a man is nearing." Brocca trembled, fearing the baby's father had sent someone to take possession of his offspring.

The cook never looked up from the black pot she was stirring. "A prophet from the woods, that's all, dearie. Calm yourself. He's just come to speak to the master. Does that often. Ye spook easily, don't ye?" She grunted and lifted the kettle from the coals, sending sparks dancing across the dirt floor.

Brocca let her shoulders droop. The man entered, welcomed by the old druid, and Brocca immediately noticed the stranger's eyes. They were probing, curious; windows to the man's thoughts. He was searching for something.

The druid motioned to stools near the peat fire. "Come, sit."

Brocca kept busy with her butter churn while she listened in on the conversation. The prophet was common, but his presence still bothered Brocca. Was he here to steal her child? His glare landed on her, and she looked away.

"That girl," the prophet said to the druid, pointing in Brocca's direction.

She dug her fingers into the wooden butter paddle, desperately trying to focus on her task. The man's gaze disturbed her, and the child within her seemed to endeavor to free itself. She blew a puff of air, and a crimson strand of hair resting on her forehead stirred. *Not yet, darlin' child. The time has not come. No one can take ye when yer not born yet.*

The druid waddled toward her. "My dairymaid. Bought her from a laird up in Leinster."

The visitor rose, leaving the snug fire to get a better look at her. The man Cook called a prophet was as mysterious as a mountain pass when he leaned over her. Brocca bit her lip. Why had the room grown so hot? The paddle seemed to stick, and push as she might, it wouldn't budge. *Why doesn't he leave? Vanish back into the dreary forest?*

She sensed the prophet bending over her, although she tried to ignore him. He crept so close that their faces nearly touched. Brocca stole a quick glimpse. He parted his dry lips to speak. "Special, the child this one will bear. Could be a blessing or a curse. Fate will tell." He backed away, his voice pitched high like a cackling hen's. "The child is not to be born within the house." He waved his cloaked arms toward the doves roosting in the beams and boomed, "But not to be born outside."

Such nonsense. The child poked Brocca from within, and she rubbed down the spot where the baby's tiny limb bulged. Her child *was* a blessing. But what about the prediction of the birth? What could it mean?

The man droned on, as if in a trance. "The child will be born at sunrise tomorrow."

"Oh, splendid!" The druid smacked his leathery palms together. "Her state has kept her from carrying out her duties effectively. 'Tis good the baby's coming so soon."

Brocca covered her mouth with her hand. *Long-suffering.*

9

Reward in heaven. She clung to Patrick's words and prayed to God for strength.

Before the next morn's sun crested the new grass on the surrounding hills, Brocca had dismissed the odd man's prophecy. She completed the milking and shut the stone barn door behind her. The cook needed her delivery of milk to thicken a special first-day-of-spring stew.

Brocca breathed deeply while she toted two wooden buckets toward the house. They were filled to the brim, and Brocca watched the milk run up to the top of the bucket and then recede back again with every step she took.

She halted, freezing in her tracks. As gently as she could, she set the buckets down, and then took another breath. How strange. The baby seemed to have moved away from her lungs, and the discomfort she had experienced the day before had subsided.

Brocca leaned down to retrieve the buckets' rope handles, and then gazed up at the sky. She admired the pink horizon and remembered to thank God for the new day.

She continued, the rain-soaked soil squishing under the thin soles of her shoes. Brocca lifted her mud-caked foot and stepped onto the stone threshold. Her other foot refused to follow. Being precariously out of balance, Brocca lost her footing and plunged to the ground. A sharp pain shot up her middle like a thousand daggers. Brocca's bloated body had landed half inside the house and half outside.

In that position Brocca's daughter came forth, the dropped buckets providing a baptism of milk for the squalling baby, whom Brocca named Brigid.

CHAPTER

"NI HEASPA DO DITH CARAD.
THERE IS NO NEED LIKE THE LACK OF A FRIEND."
OLD IRISH SAYING

Brigid would never forget that day. Yet the memory of her mother's face and the sound of her voice were fading like the sun-bleached pebbles she plucked from the water's edge.

"Hush now. Bear up, child," she remembered her mother saying as she was led away.

Ten summers and childhood innocence had caused her to forget the details of their separation. Even so, she recalled the smells: her mother's hair, heather-scented from her home-made soap; the stench of cattle pulling the wagon her mother rode on; the aroma of cabbage cooking in her father's kitchen. Brigid couldn't stomach a meal of cabbage since. One whiff sent her running outside, clutching her stomach, tears running down her face.

But her mother's face? She couldn't remember it. Brigid squinted her eyes and gazed out at the clouds skimming the Irish Sea. The white drifts took on images. Brigid tried to discern them, imagining each one a face. Was her nose long? Her hair curly?

"Hurry along, lass! We've got to finish our chore and get

11

back to Glasgleann. The master wants his supper," Cook called, holding a string with several fish attached.

They'd been gathering all day – she, Cook, and Brian, her father's coachman. Brian, an excellent fisherman, had been allowed to drive them to the shore. Brigid's father had a taste for fresh fish, eels, and clams, so Brigid and the others had been chosen to do his bidding.

Brigid gathered the clams she'd dug and plopped them into an open-weave basket. "Coming."

She stowed her catch in the back of the flatbed wagon, then clambered inside. Cook filled several wooden crates with her strings of fish and then covered them with flat lids.

Brian secured them by pounding wooden pegs into the top. "No fear of losing the treasure on the rocky ride home."

Brigid watched the young man work. Brian's face was as red as hot fire coals. His pale skin reflected the summer sun and trickles of sweat dripped from his wispy beard. At his feet, five bags wiggled. She knew he'd been successful in his eel hunt, and she wanted a peek. "What did ye catch?"

Brian struck the last peg with his hammer and loaded Cook's fish. "Ye mean in here?" He pointed at his feet.

"Aye, in there. Caught a dog, have ye?" Brigid stuck out her tongue and pulled her hands to her chest, doing her best puppy imitation.

He threw one bag onto her lap and she jumped to her feet. The sack hit the wagon floor with a thud. The creature inside was still alive, wiggling frantically. "Should I take a look, then?"

"Nay!" He sprang up and snatched the bag.

Cook laughed as she crawled in to sit beside Brigid. "Brian fears he'll lose his catch. What would the master say then?"

"I do not fear the master." Brian seized the bag and untied the rope. He reached inside and pulled out an eel, black as the ocean's depths. Brigid nodded her acknowledgment, and Brian stuffed the creature away.

12

Cook held up a sun-scorched hand. "Fear the one who holds yer future."

Brian took his place in front and leaned over to pat the horse. "I do that." He made the sign of the cross on his chest.

They trundled back toward Glasgleann, the estate her father had named for its green valleys, and Brigid tried again to picture her mother. Was her hair red? Her eyes blue? Or were her mother's locks golden like her own? Perhaps her eyes were green, matching Brigid's.

"Cook? Do ye remember my own mother?"

The old woman gazed at her. "Why would ye be asking such a thing?"

Cook was much older than Brigid's mother. She had to be. She had grandchildren, lots of them, running about her skirts while she baked brown loaves of honey-sweetened bread in Glasgleann's kitchen. Cook's daughter helped out in the dairy. Brigid rubbed the back of her neck, burnt by the sun during her clam digging. Why had Cook's family been allowed to stay together? They were slaves, same as her.

Brigid noticed Cook glancing up at Brian who was busy guiding the horses. He hadn't heard them. The old woman fingered her linen apron, smoothing out the wind-driven wrinkles. She spoke, and Brigid had to lean in close to hear. "I suppose 'tis no harm to tell ye a bit. Seeing as yer father cannot hear us."

Cook squeezed Brigid's arm so tightly it turned numb. Brigid was stunned and tried to wiggle free.

Cook kept up her grip. "But promise ye'll not repeat what I tell ye, Brigid."

"I'll not. I promise."

Cook let go and Brigid rubbed the red impressions left on her skin. She stared in surprise at the woman, who had never treated her so harshly before.

Cook's eyes narrowed and her voice lowered to a whisper. "If ye ever heeded me, child, do it now."

Brigid nodded. Her eyes blurred, her heart raced. Her voice caught in her throat and she forced out the words. "Tell me, did she do something wrong to be sent away?"

"Ah, child. 'Tis a shame, it is, ye being apart. Yer father had a wife, still does, though she doesn't live at Glasgleann."

"What? I have never heard of this."

Cook tapped Brigid's hand, and Brigid pulled away, fearing she'd squeeze too tight again. "Ah, lassie. That's not something we should be talking about."

Brigid's chest ached, as though something had been cut from her. "But please, I have to know."

Cook silently stared down the grassy trail ahead of them. Her lips moved, as though she were about to speak. Then the old woman bit her lip and gazed at her lap. She turned sharply and looked directly at Brigid, pulling the girl's face into her open palms. "Dearie, Brocca was with child and our master's wife would not have it. She urged him to send yer mother away." Cook's dark eyes glowed. "Master cares about his wealth. Would not lose two good slaves, so he sent for ye." She released Brigid and held a wrinkled finger to her parched lips. "Even though the mean, old wife lives elsewhere, we cannot speak of this at Glasgleann." Cook pressed her lips together. She meant what she said.

Brigid rubbed the back of her neck again. The story was confusing. "When she and I parted, were we not at Glasgleann?"

"Aye. Yer dear mother dropped ye off. She had to return to her master in Munster." Cook stole a quick glimpse at Brian, and then motioned for Brigid to scoot to the rear of the wagon.

They nestled themselves between crates and spoke in mumbles. "I once lived with her in Munster? I don't

14

remember it." The smell of the catch was starting to distress Brigid. Or was it the thought of that terrible day? Brigid massaged her queasy belly through her dull linen dress.

"Are ye sick, dearie? Should I have Brian hold up?"

Brigid didn't want her discomfort to end the conversation. "Nay, please, tell me more."

"We should talk about something else. The dairy. Ye've been doing a fine job, Brigid."

The miracles. They could talk about that later. "Did she look like me?"

Cook slumped crossly against the wagon's side. "Stubborn child. Ye always were." Her words were sharp as spear points.

Why was she trying to deny Brigid the only connection she had to the one person who truly loved her? Cook had many family members. She couldn't possibly understand what it was like to be alone.

Cook blew a puff of air, sending a gray curl bouncing on her forehead. "I believe she did look like ye, some. Though her hair was more auburn." Cook's face brightened. "Her eyes were pools of sea water, like yer own. Yer both beautiful lasses." Cook squeezed Brigid's hand, but not too tightly. That was her signal that their conversation was finished. They'd had many talks in the ten years since Brigid had been motherless. It was Cook who had first taught Brigid about Christ. Together they had traveled to hear a man named Patrick speak to the masses. Brigid always wondered how they'd been able to get away that day. Why had her father allowed the trip?

That journey six months ago had been life-changing. Brigid still remembered Patrick's face, one she'd never forget – kind, warm, friendly. And his message. He spoke of a love that was available to all. Brigid desired such a thing – Dubthach certainly didn't love her – and so she had embraced the Christian faith that day. Cook and Brigid, and a few others at Glasgleann, nurtured their beliefs by discussing Patrick's

15

teachings in the evenings. Sometimes the other servants mocked them; sometimes they listened.

"My mother? Did she know the One True God?"

Cook kept her eyes on the road. "Hush, now. We can't be speaking of her any longer. 'Twill make yer father angry, it will." Cook blinked her dark eyes. One corner of her mouth turned into a grin. "Aye, child. She does. She truly does." Cook's eyes watered as she turned away, pretending to survey the countryside.

Streams of tears stung Brigid's sun-scorched cheeks. She brushed them away with her rough linen apron. Brocca did not follow the pagan beliefs of most people. The thought was comforting. Brigid longed to discuss Christ's teachings with her mother. She imagined them sitting around an evening fire, hand-in-hand, chatting happily. Brigid could almost feel her cheek against her mother's auburn hair.

After they returned to Glasgleann and unloaded their catch, Brigid continued her daydreaming. She told the cows that her mother loved the Lord God. She whispered a story to the chickens, telling them how she and her mother would one day recite the twenty-third Psalm to each other. She returned to her butter churn in the main house and barely noticed Cook's steaming pots of food. Her heart was full of hope.

Then she heard her father's voice.

"Oh, Cook! Boiled eel, roasted clams! What a delight ye've prepared. Like a feast for a king." Dubthach clapped his hands and then proceeded to tear into the meal like a wild wolf. He was seated at the kitchen's planked table with a feast spread before him. His lone chair was centrally positioned, allowing easy access to all the platters.

Brigid eyed him from her corner of the keeping room. Whatever he didn't eat would be split among the servants, but that was not what concerned her. The man who had torn her from her mother's grasp was chomping away as though nothing had happened. He was ancient, nearly as old as Cook. He professed no belief in any god. He was heartless and greedy.

Dubthach slopped ale down his short beard, but he didn't seem to notice. His blackish teeth ripped flesh from the clamshells. "Well done, Cook. I must send ye to the shore more often." He glanced up at Brigid. Though she was his own daughter, he treated her like a common servant. "I hear ye've been making a great deal of butter, lass. And the chickens under yer care produce twice as much as anyone else's. Tell me, just how do ye do the things ye do?"

Brigid looked at him, and a wave of disgust washed over her. How could he possibly be *her* father? How could this man have touched her sweet mother? She shrugged her shoulders. He wasn't worth wasting breath for.

CHAPTER

"ALWAYS REMEMBER TO FORGET THE TROUBLES
THAT PASSED AWAY. BUT NEVER FORGET TO
REMEMBER THE BLESSINGS THAT COME EACH DAY."
OLD IRISH PROVERB

"Brigid, how did ye get away without a beating?" Cook grabbed
Brigid by the arm as the two marched toward the dairy.

"He can't hurt me, Cook. Not any more than he already
has." Brigid wiggled free and ran ahead, her feet digging into
the damp dirt path. The wind whistled past her ears, but all
she heard was the sound of her mother's voice, clearer than
she'd ever heard it before. "Bear up, Brigid. Take heart. Bear
yer lot." What could her mother have meant?

Brigid shoved the barn door wide and flung herself onto a
pile of hay. The animals' smell soothed her. They asked nothing from her, gave all they had to give, and would never take
anything back. If only people were the same.

Cook marched in after her, nearly hysterical. "Why didn't
you answer the master? Don't ye know, lass, we'll all suffer for
it? Could ye not think about us?"

Brigid sat up, pieces of hay sticking in her hair and
between her fingers. "Think of others? Is that not what I *have*
been doing? I make sure the hungry get what they need from
our dairy. I get up at dawn and return to my bed long after the

chickens roost. I work for the master, not myself. How can ye say that?" Brigid trailed off into a long sob that reached the depths of her soul.

If she had expected sympathy, she didn't get it from Cook. "'Tis time ye learned yer place, Brigid. Ye do what yer supposed to because yer a slave. 'Tis a far better lot than joining the starving masses wandering the woods with the wolves." She stomped out of the dairy and shoved the door closed, leaving Brigid alone in the dark.

"She doesn't understand," Brigid said to the cattle, the doves in the rafters, the chickens, and to God, if he was listening.

Brigid longed to stay there, with her face buried in the hay, but she felt a strange urging to return to the house and seek Dubthach's forgiveness. She hated the thought, but at the same time, she knew she had no choice. Cook was right. She was a slave, and slaves have their place. If she continued to act with disrespect, Dubthach would exact a punishment on them all, fearing some sort of rebellion. Brigid couldn't bear being the cause of it. She had to go back.

Evening had cast its black cloak. Brigid couldn't see her feet so she concentrated on making her way toward the dimly-lit turf-topped house. She rammed her toe into a tree root, causing a shard of pain to shoot up her leg; but thankfully she didn't fall. When she reached the house and cracked the door open, all was quiet.

Brigid's father had wanted an explanation. She sighed, tapping her fingers on the rock wall of the kitchen. He was still sitting at the table, examining parchment record books by candlelight. He looked up at her. His jaw was set. The old man dropped his writing instrument and curled his fists into balls.

"Dare to come back, did ye?" He shoved his round gut away from the table. "I'll not have such disrespect from ye, Brigid. The others will think I favor ye simply because ye were born to me."

Brigid gulped hard. Her own hands tightened under her apron. He never favored her. Never. "I'm sorry." She hung her head to keep the repulsive man from reading her true thoughts.

Dubthach was still for a moment, then slammed his fist on the table. "Very well. I'll accept yer apology. For yer penitence, ye'll have extra chores all week."

"Aye, sir."

"But ye'll have to do something for me first. I want an answer to the question, lass. How is it ye produce so much in my dairy when others do not?"

She linked her fingers together and squeezed, bringing her hands up to her lips. "The poor will always be with us." What she said surprised her more than it did her father.

"Aye. That's what I always say." Dubthach narrowed his eyes and stared. Brigid was uncertain whether he wanted to hear the explanation or whether he just liked the calming rhythm of her voice. No matter whether it was midmorning or suppertime, the slothful man could nod off quicker than a dragonfly darts.

She began. "Well, ye do have fine animals in yer barn. God has blessed ye with that. The cows are healthy indeed." Noting that he was being lulled to sleep, she kept up her rambling. "I hear the sheep are fine specimens also. And bearing young every spring. Just yesterday, Brian said..." She continued her banal observations for several minutes more until Dubthach's head folded down to his chest and great breaths of air pushed through his wrinkled lips. He was asleep.

Brigid lowered herself onto a tree stump chair. Her father took pride in his possessions. For an Irishman, healthy chickens and livestock meant wealth. When things went well he was bearable, she had to admit. But life was uncertain, something a slave knew well and a laird only remotely understood.

If a wolf would happen to steal into the barn and kill some of the herd, Dubthach would erupt into a rage lasting longer than a December night. Wolves hunt. They eat chickens; they devour calves. Didn't the old man know that? Why should he be surprised? Did he think he could invoke some magical power to hold the forces of nature at bay?

Brigid rose and stepped away from the fire. The old man would likely doze there until dawn. She lit a twist of straw from the candle dripping on the table. She'd need a wee bit of flame to light her path to the maidens' quarters.

Outside, there were no shadows, no moonlight. She heard movement near the house, but assumed the noise she heard was from the birds roosting in the oaks for the night. Brigid tiptoed, as if she feared she'd wake the fairies. Of course she didn't believe in such things, but in Ireland you had to be ready for anything. Patrick had said that, having come from a land across the Irish Sea, although Brigid didn't fully understand what he meant.

A voice from behind startled her. "Excuse me, miss. Might ye have a wee bit of food for a poor lad?"

She crouched low to the ground, as if she could hide herself. *A fairy?* Couldn't be. She managed to turn on squatted legs to see the form of a thin boy staring down at her. He came into the glow of her torch, and she saw that he was wearing tattered clothes. Wisps of raven hair stuck out beneath his gray felt cap, too large for the lad's wee head, but he was a boy just the same. Not a fairy at all.

Despite Patrick's warning, she hadn't been ready. The unexpected encounter made her search for words, stuttering in the process. She'd helped beggars before. That's what had started Dubthach's interest in how she was feeding the poor. But they had never come around in the dark of night before.

The lad's dejected, deep-sunken eyes convinced her she'd have to think of something. Whispering a quick prayer beneath her breath, Brigid ordered him to wait outside the barn door while she went searching, praying all the while.

21

The moon finally made an appearance, just as her torch was dying. A beam of light pushed its way in through the cracked door, illuminating the cow's mud-colored face.

"I know 'tis not time for yer milking, but supposing ye'd give me just a wee bit for the poor lad outside?"

Was that a nod from the cow or was she seeing things? Brigid ran for the wooden bucket she'd placed by the feed sacks when she milked earlier. To her delight, the cow did indeed have more to give.

"Now what about ye chickens?" Brigid eyed the red-feathered birds who'd also been disturbed by her presence. They clucked about the barn floor as if trying to avoid her suggestion.

"Come on, now. Have ye no compassion for a starving lad?"

The chickens lighted on their nests and clucked their ear-shattering agreement. "Oh, God, don't let them wake Dubthach - or worse, the foxes." Brigid retrieved two brown eggs and a white one with yellow speckles.

"Thank ye kindly, God's creatures." She put the treasures into the pocket of her apron and poured the milk into a tin dish. Then she headed carefully for the barn door, ever mindful of the gifts she held.

After squeezing through the opening, Brigid greeted the lad with the best smile she could muster. She'd better warn him. "Do not be coming here again at this hour. If the master does not chase ye away, the wolves will."

The door to the main house crashed open. "Brigid, are ye there?"

"Hurry! Don't come back!" She shooed the boy away into the woods and shuffled over to the house.

"Ye fell asleep... I mean ye were tired and all... and I thought I'd leave ye alone."

"Enough of yer rambling. Was that another beggar I saw?"

No use to pretend otherwise. "Aye."

"Tell me how ye did that trick? How ye got milk and eggs when the animals should not have had any to give?" Dubthach could see in the dark like an owl.

"'Tis not a trick. I just..." Brigid stumbled for the right words. Her master thought he'd found the secret to worldly wealth. How could she ever explain the wonders of God to a man like him?

He waved his cloaked arm toward the house. "Come back inside. Sit. There's a trick here and ye'll teach it to me." The round man waddled back through the oak door, barely able to squeeze his body through the opening.

She followed him inside and lit two tallow candles from the smoldering peat fire. She placed them on the table next to the candle stump left from Dubthach's earlier reading, and a circle of light filled the center of the keeping room, leaving the outer edges in darkness. *Like Patrick's message in Ireland*, she thought.

Dubthach blinked his eyes. He stood and motioned toward the cupboard. "Bring me some tea."

Brigid winced as she lifted the kettle off the iron hooks hanging over the fire. How did Cook manage? Brigid was efficient in the dairy, but the kitchen was unknown territory. She carried the hot pot over to the cupboard just as Cook bustled in the door.

"Ye'll burn yerself, darlin'. What are ye doing?"

"Getting tea for the master."

"Och! Why did ye not carry the mug over to the fire instead of the other way 'round?" She snatched the kettle from Brigid and plopped it down on the dirt floor. Then she marched to the cupboard and fetched a mug. Cook poured steaming liquid into the mug and returned the pot to the fire, refusing Brigid's offer to help.

Brigid put her hands on her hips. "I'm not a child."

23

Cook ignored her, served Dubthach his tea, and turned to leave. She stopped short at the door and motioned for Brigid to come near. "I'll be in the field first thing in the morning with Alana. Meet us there after yer done milking. Brian needs help with the plow."

"But what can I... ?"

"Needs lot of hands, he does." Cook winked at her.

"Fine, then."

"Now, on with it!" Dubthach raised his mug to his bristled face. "Tell me the secret."

Brigid lowered herself onto the stump seat. "Once again I coaxed extra milk and eggs from the animals in the barn, but this time there was more than enough for three."

"What? There were others with that lad? Tell me about that. How... ?"

"Standing near the forest's edge. I saw them when he ran away. Those pleading brown eyes and miry little faces melted my heart. They're starving, they are."

"As ye said earlier, the poor will always be around."

Why had she said that?

"Yer too soft, Brigid. Thought ye'd be more like... "

"Like you? Turn them away?"

He raised his hand to her. She cowered back, expecting a blow. He had never hit her, but he was an angry man and she feared him nonetheless.

He lowered his hand to his lap. His full lips turned into a grin. "Ye'll tell me the secret and I'll be patient until ye do."

"We feed the barnyard animals well. Shouldn't we also share with the poor?"

"A woman has no mind for business."

I've a mind for the Lord's business.

Brigid was tired. Her bed, and hopefully sleep, awaited her. She grabbed her cloak from a peg near the door. "Here's what I did. Here's the answer to yer question."

24

Dubthach wrinkled his forehead and flicked his fingers back. "Go on. Tell it now."

"I prayed. That's what I did. Here's what I said: 'Lord, what will all those hungry children eat?'" She was shouting, but she couldn't help herself. "'Can the woods bring forth enough wild berries to quiet their hungry cries? If they do have parents to feed them, I know their folks likely don't have work and will provide no more than hard biscuits. Give me a way, Lord, to help them.'"

"All those words?" Dubthach ticked off his fingers as if trying to remember exactly what she had said. "Which ones are the magic ones? Which ones make the chickens produce, the cows give more milk, make the butter sweeter and more plentiful?"

Brigid rolled her eyes and pulled the door open. "That's what I said. I'm off to my bed."

CHAPTER

"WHICH OF YOU, IF HIS SON ASKS FOR BREAD, WILL GIVE HIM A STONE?"
MATTHEW 7:9

Brigid approached the others the next morning. Brian tinkered with the plow. Cook and Alana watched.

Cook's neck strained like a goose's to look at her. "What was that all about last night?"

"The miracles in the dairy."

Cook grabbed Brigid's shoulders. "Did ye tell him, then? Did he listen?" She released her grip.

Brigid shook her head. "Yer right. He didn't listen. Was only concerned about his wealth. Thinks my prayers contain magic words that can be used by anyone to conjure up milk and eggs."

Brian shook his head and lowered his hammer. "Shall we get to it?"

Prayer time. That's why she had been summoned to the field. The four of them were the only Christians at Glasgleann, and they snatched moments here and there for prayer and support.

Alana recited a verse from the Psalms, one of many she had memorized. Cook's granddaughter had a mind as sharp as needles. Her recollection of verses recited by travelers was a blessing to their little group.

"One day I'll learn to read and write," Brigid promised. "I'll bring the Word of God here to all of ye and teach ye to read it for yerselves."

Brian chuckled. "Lairds, gentry – they're the ones who learn to read. Not slaves."

They didn't understand. Everything they had learned came from listening to stories. Brigid longed for more, ever since she had seen a page of manuscript shown to her by a traveling Christian monk. Dubthach knew how to read. Wasn't she his daughter? Why then shouldn't she learn?

That night Brigid lay awake, unable to capture the peace of sleep. She thought about the miracles God had allowed her to perform. She also wondered about her mother.

Puddin, Brigid's pet cat, lay on her chest, purring loud enough to wake the chickens had they been nearby. Brigid nudged the cat away and rolled to one side. The moon outside her window cast a faint glow on her face.

Why had God given her the ability to perform miracles? Brigid was thankful she could help people – that was her heart's desire. But she was no more special than anyone else. Was she?

Brigid pondered her conversation with the master. Why had she said that about the poor always being with us?

The room filled with the soft sighs of sleeping slave women. They'd worked hard and they welcomed sleep. She had labored also, but her dreams were held back by unanswered questions.

Brigid pulled her linen sheet over her face and turned away from the moonlight. Squeezing her eyes tight did nothing to calm her unsettled heart.

Where was her mother?

Brigid awoke the next morning and knew she hadn't slept long.

"Get up, lass!" Cook called. "Brian and the master have already left."

Brigid had nearly forgotten. Dubthach and Brian were riding to the shore that day to meet a merchant ship. Dubthach insisted on doing his own bartering. He didn't trust anyone.

His absence meant she was free to ask Cook about her mother. "Coming!" Brigid yelled out the window to Cook who was working in her herb garden.

She pulled a fresh tunic over her undergarment and splashed water from the room's basin on her face. She was dragging a comb made of bone through her tangled tresses when Cook appeared in the room.

"Think it's time to be lazy when the master is away, do ye now?"

Brigid was stunned. "Why, nay. I just didn't sleep well last night."

"Suppose being the master's daughter gives ye some privilege." Cook snapped a laundered apron off the wall of hooks and tied it about her waist. She took two steps toward the door.

Brigid blocked the doorway, hands on hips. "I'm a servant, same as ye."

Alana pushed in under Brigid's arm, followed by three golden-haired siblings. "Maimeo, are we making the honey bread now?"

"Aye, off with ye!" Cook shooed her clan out of the sleeping room and turned to Brigid. "If ye think yer the same as me, yer mistaken. And remember what I told ye yesterday. Mind me, Brigid. The master's wife has ears all over Glasgleann."

Cook shut the oak door and Brigid felt the vibration run

28

right through her. Cook was right. They weren't the same. The master's eldest servant was privileged enough to have her family near.

"Where's my mother?" Brigid whispered to the mice she heard running inside the walls. Her legs felt like day-old porridge. Throwing herself down on her mat, Brigid wept into her hands.

Brigid found Alana hovering over a mixing bowl when she arrived in the kitchen. The lass greeted her with concern. "Are ye ill, Brigid?"

"Nay, I'm just... well, tired is all. I came to fetch my milking buckets."

"Mamai's already done the milking, Brigid. Come, help us bake."

Alana's brothers and sisters scurried about the room, pulling at Cook's skirts. Hearing Alana speak about her mother and call Cook, her grandmother, "maimeo", was more than Brigid could bear. "I have some mending to do. And I have to check on Puddin. She's due to have kits any time now."

Brigid's excuse satisfied Alana and she returned to kneading dough. Brigid paused a moment to watch Alana and the others. Cook pulled back the shutters, letting streaks of sunlight fill the dank kitchen. Without the master to spoil the mood, the kitchen servants were relaxed and cheery.

Brigid hastened outside. *Behind the barn.* Puddin, if she had given birth, would probably be there. The sunlight gave way to clouds and a mist began to fall, coating Brigid's clothing with moist beads that would soon dampen more than her spirits.

"Puddin, are ye there?" She inspected the birches behind the barn and found no trace of her cat. Just as she was about to head into the barn, a likely place for a mother cat to give birth on a rainy day, someone grabbed her arm.

"Ouch! Let go!" She recognized the fellow. He was a common slave who worked for her father. A shepherd.

"Want to know about the master's old woman?" He grinned at her with a full mouth of white teeth, very unusual for shepherds.

She has ears all over Glasgleann. Brigid knew she had to heed Cook's warning. "I don't believe I do." Brigid flung his hand away and moved toward the barn door.

He blocked her path. His boots were covered in sheep dung, and a blade of grass hung from his lips. He pulled it loose and pointed it at her. "I hear ye've been asking why yer mother was sent away."

The man's black eyes bore into Brigid's soul. Hearing someone speak about her mother brought her to tears.

She looked away. "Where'd ye hear that?"

"Oh, I heard, that's all. Was that old woman that did it. Course, the master allowed it. Sent yer mother away, he did."

"I know that. 'Tis no concern of yers. Leave me be."

"Suit yerself, lassie. But Cook won't tell ye everything." He slipped off into the forest like a brown snake.

Why would that man leave his sheep to come tell Brigid what she already knew? No, Cook wouldn't tell her about that old wife, but what did it matter? Odd, he was. She knew others like him, always spreading gossip to feel important. Was that what was happening? Were all the servants talking about her now?

Brigid's head throbbed. She didn't care about some old wife her father had once had. Dubthach wasn't capable of loving anyone but himself, and he'd probably cast his wife away, just like Brigid's mother. No, that woman, whoever she was, was not to blame. It was Brigid's deceitful father who had separated her from her mother.

Brigid glanced around the dairy. Hungry people would visit soon. Surely there was more to give away than just extra milk and eggs. She rushed back to the main house, birds cluck-ing at her heels.

Cook's family was busy chatting in the kitchen. Dubthach's dishes were just out of their sight in a large cup-board that towered over Brigid's head. The cupboard door was slightly ajar, so she wouldn't have to risk having the door creak and draw attention. Brigid's heart pounded as she fin-gered the serving pieces. She kept an ear to the happy conver-sation in the next room as she tried to be as invisible as possible.

"Why is Brigid sad, Maimeo?" a child asked.

"She misses her mother."

"She has a mother?"

A boy chided his sister. "Yer lame. Everyone has a mother."

"Do not."

"Aye, they do."

Cook scolded them. "Hush now. She does. Can't remember her much and that's what makes her sad."

They went back to their baking, as though Brigid's plight was not worth wasting too much time worrying over. They'd never know what it was like to be motherless. None of them.

Brigid examined the cabinet's contents. Several pieces of silver intermingled with the everyday tin dishes and wooden utensils. Why shouldn't the beggars have the best? She slipped a bowl, two mugs, and a delicate vase from a shelf and tiptoed outside, not bothering to close the cupboard.

She curled the dishes under her apron and glanced around. If someone saw her, she'd think of something, say she was polishing them.

The people were there, next to the dairy barn, as always. Two lads and a bent old woman. Brigid ducked inside the dairy, promising to return. No one would miss the silver. Dubthach had plenty.

Brigid gathered what she could. The animals were always generous. Outside, she found the poor folks glancing around as though a wolf might pounce on them any moment.

"What's this?" The old woman patted Brigid's out-stretched bundle.

"No less than what ye deserve. Take it."

Toothless grins spread across their faces as she handed them the silver serving pieces filled with the farm's bounty. She had placed a daisy in the vase and presented it to the woman.

"Master must be away," she heard the old woman say as the threesome shuffled back into the forest.

Brigid went about her chores as usual and at the end of the day Brian and the master returned. By the following morning Dubthach had discovered what she had done, and his roar of rage set the crows to cawing. He bellowed her name.

Brigid wiped cream from her fingertips as she hurried from the barn. What would he do? Beat her? Or something worse? She found her father standing planted in the main hall, arms folded, spittle on his lips.

"We're going to see King Dunlaing." She hadn't expected that. Dubthach's cheeks were crimson. His eyebrows bent into a point above his nose.

Brigid's hands quivered. "Now?"

He spit his words. "Aye, now."

"Are ye having me jailed?"

Dubthach laughed. Brigid couldn't imagine what was funny.

"Suppose I could; though how would that benefit me?"

It was always about *him*.

"I can't be having ye give everything I own away. Would surely gain me more to put ye in his service."

"But I beg yer pardon, sir. I didn't give all our food away.

The chickens still gave enough eggs for us, and the cow provided more than enough milk." Perhaps he hadn't noticed the other things she had taken.

Dubthach gritted his grimy teeth. "'Tis not the milk and eggs I'm talking about. 'Twas not enough for ye, was it? We're going. I'll have no more talk about it." He pointed to the wagon outside. Brian was absent, making her feel even more nervous.

Brigid hung her head. What had she done? She gazed at her mud-caked skirts, forming a plan that would stall for time. "If I'm to go to the king, sir, I must look my best." She hoped Cook would be in the servants' quarters. Maybe she'd tell her what to do.

Dubthach paced, rubbing his gray whiskers. "I suppose I don't want the king thinking he's getting inferior goods."

Goods? If she hadn't known before, she did now. Her father had never loved her.

"Go on, lass. Hurry up, now. Every minute yer with me ye cost me something."

Brigid ran from the house. The morning mist wet her face, mixing with tears she couldn't control. If he didn't want her, why didn't he sell her back to her mother's owner? Why must they go to the king?

"Cook? Brian? Is anyone out here?"

Only the swallows answered. Where was everyone?

Brigid entered the maidens' room just as a thought sent a shiver of terror from her head to her feet. *Is he going to have me killed?*

CHAPTER

"DO NOT WITHHOLD GOOD FROM THOSE WHO DESERVE IT, WHEN IT IS IN YOUR POWER TO ACT."
PROVERBS 3:27

While Brigid was pulling on fresh woolen stockings, she heard a voice. She whirled to face the door. No one was there.

She called into the barren hall. "Who's there? Cook?"

No answer.

"Yer his servant, Brigid."

Her mother's voice. How could it be?

Brigid peeked through the wooden shutters covering the small window in the slave maidens' quarters. Just beyond Cook's herbs stood her father's rig. There was no one there. Dubthach was waiting elsewhere. The voice was either in her head or God himself spoke to her.

Brigid dropped down onto a straw mat. Until now she had long forgotten the words her mother had whispered into her ear the day they separated.

Brigid blinked back tears and inhaled. The musty smell of the damp room made her nose itch.

She tapped her fingers on her head. She had been so young when they separated, but she wanted to remember everything. Now what else?

Her mother's voice rang so clear that if Brigid hadn't known better, she would have thought Brocca was in the room. "Ye must remember yer a servant, darlin'. Patrick says the Lord expects us to obey our earthly masters. We'll be getting our reward when our life on earth is over. The only father ye must concern yerself with is yer heavenly Father."

There was something else. She curled a strand of hair around her finger as she tried to remember. *Patrick!* Mother had mentioned him. When had *she* met him?

Brigid chewed at her fingers. She and Cook had seen Patrick just a few months ago. Could it be there was another time Brigid had met the holy man? Could she and her mother have gone together to meet Patrick, and she was too young at the time to remember it now?

Brigid changed quickly into a fresh linen tunic. She tied a new bodice around her middle and smoothed back her hair with her hands. She had not done wrong by caring for the Lord's people. God was really in control, not Dubthach. She'd hold her head high when she met the king.

Brigid joined her father at the reins. He whipped the horses more fiercely than Brian ever did. The old man was silent. Brigid considered jumping out of the wagon and making a run for the woods, but what good would that do? She could never go back to Glasgleann.

Glasgleann. Cook. Brian. Alana. She'd never see them again, and they might never learn why. Would they blame her for taking the silver? She wanted to explain, but she couldn't. Ever.

A raven cawed overhead. Brigid cupped her hand against the sky just in time to see the bird's wing-tips. The birds had no fears, no concerns. God provided for them. Didn't the Scriptures say so?

Lately everything she'd learned seemed as snarled as the

ball of yarn that Puddin played with. Would God provide for that cat in Brigid's absence? Or would he punish Brigid forever for stealing from a greedy man? Brigid's mind wavered from fearing the man who'd hurt her the most, to trying to understand her father's reasons for getting rid of her.

They'd never been hungry. God had even provided a surplus when she handed out food to the starving. She was doing the Lord's work. Couldn't her father see that?

The wagon wheels labored along the lumpy road. Brigid clasped her hands around the small railing surrounding her seat. Father was in a hurry to be rid of her.

The smell of moist heather filled her head. On any other day she would have enjoyed a ride in the country. In the distance, gray spots speckled the edges of the road. As they drew closer, those specks took shape and she saw they were people. Common folks, hoards of them, stepped aside as they jolted down the road. Their sad eyes and outstretched hands spoke to her, silently saying, "Help me. I am no different from you. God made me too."

Brigid's eyes puddled with tears. She scolded herself for being selfish while people suffered. She was far healthier than those poor souls. Being a slave was the next best thing to being a laird. Slaves had food to eat, clothes to wear, and a place to rest their heads at night. She prayed God would forgive her disobedience. She had not been thankful for what she had.

Her thoughts drifted to Brocca. What about her? Was she still a slave? Was she even alive? Could she be among the discarded people, reaching skeletal arms toward the rich and privileged? Brigid searched their faces. Was there one resembling her own? Dull eyes stared at her above shadowed cheeks. The people seemed to float together, an island of grief, a collection of bones.

Brigid covered her mouth and gasped against her sweaty palm. Cook, Brian, and Alana had not been able fill the void in

Brigid's heart. Just like the unfortunates, she longed for a parent who loved her.

"I must share what I have with them," she vowed under her breath.

The morning's vapor gave way to warming sunshine. They drew near to the hilltop castle, and the beggars dispersed. The king's army kept them at bay, she was sure. The muddy roads gave way to grassy splendor, and streaks of sun burst through the alabaster clouds. Despite the inevitable discipline she was sure to receive after they gained audience with the ruler of Leinster, Brigid calmed as her tears dried in the sunlight.

They traveled on in silence through the rolling plains. Dun Ailinne appeared on the horizon. The ruler could look down from his castle, so near that hill fort, and gaze upon the common people in the distance.

The wagon lurched forward and the little mound in the distance grew larger. Brigid soon made out the regal dwelling against a sky that was as blue as royal robes.

At the limestone pillars of the entrance, her father barked orders. "Wait here! Don't ye move."

Brigid sat still, exhausted from her thoughts. She closed her eyes to rest. Moments later she was jolted by a voice. A man in tattered clothing approached.

"Excuse me, miss? Have ye a wee bit of food for a starving man?" The man's face and hands were terribly disfigured with swollen lumps – leprosy. He shifted back and forth on painful feet.

Brigid's throat was dry. What could she give the wretched man to ease his misery? She was miles away from her dairy. Slipping her hands beneath her cloak to check her apron pockets, she found them empty. She searched every corner of the wagon. An object under a green woolen blanket seemed to beckon her as it gleamed in the bright light. She scurried to the rear of the wagon as the hungry man eyed her, his delicate eyebrows arched.

There was something cold and hard beneath the blanket – her father's sword. When she pulled out the blade, the sword's gem-encrusted handle reflected sunbeams, casting colorful specks on the wooden-planked wagon floor. The weight of the thing surprised her. She had never held a weapon before. She lost her balance and had to drop the sword to the wagon floor to keep from tumbling over the side.

Her actions were misinterpreted. The man jumped back, holding up his arms.

She reached her free hand toward the beggar. "I mean no harm. I've no food, but ye can take this." Brigid lifted the gleaming sword over the edge of the wagon. She offered it to the pitiful man handle first. The leper stared at her for a long moment, then grinned, the expression briefly lighting his disfigured countenance.

"Thank ye kindly." The fellow scampered off with his treasure.

Her father returned just in time to see the man melt into a crowd of beggars standing behind a border set-up and guarded by the king's soldiers.

"Thief! Catch that man!" Dubthach pushed a few peasants aside, but neither he nor the guards could find the fellow.

Brigid leaned over the side of the rig and held her arms out toward her father. "Oh, nay! He's not a thief. I *gave* him the sword."

Just over her father's shoulder Brigid spied King Dunlaing, and she sat up straight. He wore a puzzled look as he stood under the arched gateway of his stone castle. The ruler of Leinster bore a beard speckled with the first gray hairs of age, and his sapphire eyes smiled at her with an approving wink. He seemed to think the gift she had made was some kind of joke. He approached the wagon and two servants

followed him, carrying the king's trailing robe on their out-
stretched arms. Brigid's father bowed in response to the king's
approach, but the ruler's eyes never left Brigid. He tapped his
golden scepter on the ground and then held it up to her as she
sat frozen on the wagon's seat.

"Touch it," one of the servants whispered. "It means yer
granted audience with the king."

Brigid had never spoken with him before, knew nothing
of royal procedure. She was just a slave girl after all. Her mind
drifted to Queen Esther in the Holy Scriptures. Alana had
recited the story more than once. Esther had been given permission to speak when the king held out his golden scepter.
Brigid stretched her hand, and gently brushed her fingertips
across the tip of what looked like an elaborate golden walking
stick. She had not been asked to disembark the rig, so she
stayed seated.

The king nodded briefly in her father's direction and he
also touched the scepter.

"Why do ye seek to sell her?" the king asked.

Brigid's father drew a long breath, seemingly measuring
his response. "Dear king, she takes my things and gives them
to worthless men. Ye've just witnessed it."

Her father's words were daggers in her heart. *Worthless?*
No one whom God Almighty had created should ever be called
worthless. Dubthach thought her mother was worthless. He
thought *Brigid* was worthless.

The king spoke again with an unfaltering voice, confident
from years of settling disputes. "Why do ye do this, lass?"

Brigid returned the king's stare, peering back at him with
an intensity that matched his. She spoke without hesitation. "I
tell ye, sire, if I were ye, with all yer power and wealth, Christ,
knowing what he'd blessed me with, would expect no less of
me."

The king hung his head. "She's far nobler than I." King

Dunlaing nodded once more at Dubthach. "From this day forward she shall be her god's slave alone. I remove her from yer service, and I will not take her into mine."

No one spoke for what seemed like an eternity.

"What are ye waiting for, lass? Ye heard the king. Be on yer way." Dubthach waved at Brigid but didn't return her stare. "Better to have ye far away from Glasgleann. Even if I get no compensation."

The king and his attendants disappeared back into the fortress. Only the masses of people at the edge of the woods remained.

The hearing was finished. This was the end. She was really being cast out. She should have heeded Cook's warning. She should have listened to her mother. God knew she had not been grateful and now she would pay. Dubthach hadn't plotted to kill her, but he might as well have.

Brigid lifted the hem of her skirt and stepped down from the wagon. Just as soon as she was clear, Dubthach whipped the horses and thundered off toward Glasgleann, leaving a trail of dust. A crowd of people surrounded her.

"Yer kind Brigid, aren't ye?"

"We've heard how ye give away food. Can ye give us a wee bit?"

Fingernails scratched her arms. Hands pulled at her hair. Her cloak was ripped from her, and then thrown back when they found it held no food.

"Ye've got nothing!" they taunted.

Nothing. They were right. She was alone, unloved, and now she had nothing to give.

CHAPTER

"IF ONE FALLS DOWN, HIS FRIEND CAN HELP HIM UP. BUT PITY THE MAN WHO FALLS AND HAS NO ONE TO HELP HIM UP!"
ECCLESIASTES 4:10

Brigid broke free of the masses and ran aimlessly across the open meadow. She glanced over her shoulder and saw the people disappearing into the woods. "Nay, wait! Where are you going? I need help."

No one answered. She couldn't help them. They wouldn't help her.

What about the king? Brigid hurried back toward the limestone gates. "Sire? May I come in? I've nowhere to stay the night."

A guard appeared. His red beard was barely visible beneath his headgear. She couldn't see his eyes. "Off with ye! The king has no use for ye."

"But please, can I not come in for one night? Will the king not show mercy to a traveler?"

The guard laughed and lifted his helmet to spit. "What? And have the whole lot of them filling every corner of the castle?" He spun on his heels and disappeared back into the fortress.

What now? She glanced in the direction the people had

gone. They went somewhere. There must be a camp nearby. Those people likely begged from all the king's visitors. The sky was graying. A wolf howled.

Brigid found a group of peasants huddled around a fire, attired in ill-fitting, shaggy clothing. Her tailored clothes and shoes, although standard for a slave, made her stand out like a fox in a sheep pen.

"Whatcha doing here?" an elderly woman barked. "Did yer husband kick ye out of yer home?"

"Wait a minute," a man, likely her old husband, said. "Heard there was a slave let free at the castle. Ye must be her, aye?"

Brigid stepped back from the fire.

"Ye'll not be eating our food," someone snapped.

Brigid sniffed. They were cooking a wild boar on a spit. She had been too distraught to notice at first. "Nay, I don't need food. Just shelter."

A middle-aged man with a bare circle of scalp surrounded by black hair answered. "The trees offer shelter. Have ye made yer offering?"

Pagans. She had forgotten for a moment that there'd likely be no Christian charity in this group. "I worship the God Patrick teaches of."

The balding man sniffed. "Oh, do ye now? Well, I hear tale Patrick has passed on."

Hushed voices spread around the ring of people. Nearly everyone at Glasgleann had heard of Patrick, even the visitors. Some thought he was a druid, but he was widely respected.

Brigid pulled her cloak up against the sudden chill and stepped forward. "How do ye know this?"

"Heard it from the abbot up in Dunshaughlin."

A woman pushed Brigid toward the fire and wiggled around her. Her eyes watered, and she drew a hand to her mouth. She addressed the man who had spoken. "Donal, are ye sure 'bout this?"

"Aye, Maire. As sure as rain, I am. All those Christians up there are moaning and grieving. Seems they don't believe in the next life."

Brigid listened carefully. The focus was now off her, and she wondered if some in the crowd might be Christian after all.

The woman, not much older than Brigid, exchanged places with some of the men so she could converse with the balding one who had given the news. Brigid followed as closely as she could.

"Christians believe in the next life, Donal, but not in the Tuatha De Danann."

The others backed away, their eyes wide. The woman was speaking about the supposed tribe living beneath the surface of the earth and in the depths of lakes – pagan beliefs.

The man answered. "Aye, Maire. But if they'd be wise to the Tuatha De Danann, they'd know their beloved Patrick was not far away, nor are any of us from the Other Side."

Maire and Donal were the only two left standing near the roasted boar. Talk of the spiritual Otherworld had chased the rest into the shadows. Maire and Donal didn't seem to notice Brigid so she remained close. Clearly Maire was either a Christian or a sympathizer.

"None of us is far from death, aye, true enough," Maire said. "We have hope in Jesus that we'll be reunited with Patrick one day in heaven."

"Heaven is for birds."

"'Tis not the sky I speak of. 'Tis a far better place."

"That so? Well, then, tell me why they're all carrying on so 'bout his death."

Maire poked the meat with a stick to test its progress.

"The work's not done. We, all the saints, know we must carry on for him and it will not be easy."

We. The woman had said "*We*." She was a fellow believer! Brigid tapped her on the arm. "I am one who mourns Patrick and will help carry on for him."

The woman turned to her. "If it is truly yer desire to do the Lord's work, ye may stay in my house. But not for long."

Brigid didn't ask questions. She followed Maire into the deep woods – the darkness shrouded their surroundings. Before long they arrived at the door of a small thatched cottage.

Maire whispered, "My husband's not a believer, lass. Ye'll not be able to stay long. 'Tis a wee bit crowded. We all sleep back to back. But I can offer ye some broth, unless ye want to bargain with the others for meat."

"Yer so kind. Broth is fine."

Brigid held her breath when they entered. Human sweat mixed with smoke from an ill-vented fire created a rank odor that made her cover her mouth with her hand. There were mounds of sleeping bodies, covered in thin blankets. She had to step over them to reach the fire ring.

"They're sick." Maire took a scoopful from the kettle over the fire and held a mug out to Brigid.

"Thank ye." The broth was watery and contained but a few slivers of turnips. Cook's mutton broth would be only memory now. While Brigid sipped, Maire prepared a place for her on the floor.

"Sit here by the fire. I'll give ye some mending so my good husband knows yer worth yer keep."

"Aye, I don't mind at all." Brigid lowered herself to the floor and studied the person closest to her. In the faint glow of the fire, she thought the face she stared at might be stricken with leprosy.

Maire drew a piece of cloth up around the sleeping

person's face. "Don't look. And don't be speaking 'bout it. 'Tis my own sweet Aine. If my husband finds out she's been stricken, he'll throw her out, no matter if she's his own flesh."

"I understand." Brigid understood all too well.

The door crashed open and the sleeping bodies groaned.

"Stop yer whining! 'Tis only by my woman's good graces yer out of the weather."

Clearly the master had arrived home.

"Ye'd better have yer rent now or out with ye!" He glared toward the fire where Brigid busied herself with the mending Maire had just thrown into her lap. "What's this, Maire? We've no more room."

"Dear, 'tis only for a few days. And she's helping out, see?"

He grumbled in a way that reminded Brigid of Dubthach. She could not stay under the roof of another man like that for long.

By the time Brigid woke the next morning, the boarders had left, as had the master.

"He'll be back for supper." Maire had freshened up and she looked lovely for one so poor. Her raven hair was pulled away from her face and held in place with two combs made of bone. Her dress, though ragged, was clean.

Brigid struggled to tidy up with the bit of water Maire had brought her. She splashed it on her face and ran her fingers through her hair. "What will ye do about Aine?"

"I... don't know. I prayed God would send the answer. She's only six summers old now. I... I think she's supposed to go with ye."

"With me? I don't know where I'm going myself."

"Go to Aghade. My brother's a monk there." Maire removed a leather bag from a cupboard and placed a folded tunic inside. Then she tucked in some parchment bags of grain.

45

Brigid was only nine summers older than little Aine, maybe ten. She'd never traveled other than going to the seashore. Not that she could remember, and certainly never alone. "But I don't know how. I mean... I've never been there."

"'Tis not hard. Travel by day. I'll tell ye where the landmarks are. Please, Brigid. Otherwise my Aine will be turned to the wolves."

Brigid sighed. She was looking for help from Christians and instead she herself was called to service. But leave a little lassie to the wolves? Of course she had to help.

"Please, Brigid. God will direct. If ye believed in Patrick's words, then ye'll do this for his people."

For his people. The words still rang in Brigid's ears when she left the cottage with Aine bundled at her side. Patrick was not Irish, but he, like her, had been a slave on this isle. Long after he was freed, after his formal training with the church, he had returned because the voices of the Irish called to him in a dream. Brigid clearly remembered him saying so when she visited him with Cook. He was speaking to hundreds of people that day, but perhaps he had really been speaking only to her.

CHAPTER

"HE WHO LOSES MONEY, LOSES MUCH; HE WHO LOSES A FRIEND, LOSES MORE; HE WHO LOSES FAITH, LOSES ALL."
OLD IRISH SAYING

"Don't cry, child." Brigid knew no words to comfort little Aine. She herself had been forced to leave her mother when she was such a young lass. The similarity in their situations made Brigid shiver. This young one had a heartless father as well.

Maire had given Brigid directions to head south and follow the river Slaney. At the ford, she was to cross and keep her eyes on the horizon. She was warned the forest would be thick, but if she looked, she'd find the habitation.

"Hurry along, child. We must not be on the road after dusk." The sun was still high, thankfully warm, but Brigid knew the hours would slip away like so many grains of sand in her fingers. If they didn't reach the monks' shelter by nightfall, they'd have to fend for themselves in the forest. Something she had never done before.

A voice from beside the path rang out. "Yer kind Brigid, are ye not?"

A cackle of people popped from the woods. "We've heard tale ye can produce food from nothing at all." They circled

Brigid and the sick lass, chanting to their gods and reaching out their arms.

"I've nothing to give. Please, leave us."

"Ye need nothing, lass. We know what magic ye can produce. If only ye will." A man with a face like weathered bark jutted his finger toward her and joined the others, surrounding her like hawks closing in on mice.

"They must be mad from hunger," she whispered to Aine who had begun to whimper and hide her face.

"Give us some bread."

"An egg will do."

"Have ye no pity?"

The people's demands evolved into curses and pleas to their gods to rain down troubles.

"Nay, please! I'll pray for ye. I can do that. God will provide what he pleases." Brigid could not pry Aine from her side so she pulled her down to the ground with her. Rocks in the path cut into her knees as she cried out, "Merciful Father! See these yer starving children. Feed them with earthly food and with living water. If any desire, let them ask about yer kindness."

The pagans' chants quieted. Brigid continued to pray with her hands on the hood of Aine's cloak. When she opened her eyes, the people were gone. Why? Brigid's eyes lighted on a fragment of bread, then another. Had God fed them? "Oh, praise the Father."

"Brigid? My hands. Look!"

Brigid brushed Aine's black cloak away from her arms. "Dear one! Ye've got no more marks."

The girl lifted her head. She had no signs of the disease that had plagued her. "Oh, praise the Father even more! Ye can return to yer mother."

Aine collapsed into a heap on the road, sobbing. "Nay, Brigid, I cannot."

Brigid scooped the wee one into her arms. "Why not, child? Yer healed. Yer father will welcome ye."

"He'll not. And my mother has sent me off. I must work for my uncle as she said."

"Oh, nay. I'm sure she'd want ye... "

"There she is!" A rustling arose from the forest.

Brigid pulled the girl to her feet. "We must go. Climb on my back. They've brought others."

Even carrying a child, Brigid outran the masses. The people were emaciated and could not keep up. *The poor will always be with us.* The truth was sad enough. Perhaps there was not enough food in all of Ireland to satisfy those who roamed the wilderness.

Much later Brigid stopped to rest. "When we get to Aghade, I'll send word back to yer mother about yer healing. She can come for ye. I'm sure she will, Aine."

The girl's hair was dirty and matted. Brigid couldn't detect its true color. "Would ye like to wash in the river, child?"

"Well, I'm not sure if... well, my mother has said there are no gods in the river who'll hurt me."

"Of course not."

"But my father... he says beneath the rushing water live the gods of the Otherworld."

"The Tuatha De Danann."

Aine's eyes became as large as goose eggs. "Ye believe it, then? And still ye ask me to wash?"

"Ah, nay, dear Aine. I know most believe there are frightful spirits under the waters. There's evil all right, but not in the river."

"Where, then?"

"In the hearts of some men."

"Men?"

"Aye. Some women also perhaps. But ye've nothing to fear

from washing the filth from ye in the river. God created the river. 'Tis not evil."

Aine smiled, revealing a simplicity that only children possess. The lass was beginning to trust her. Brigid watched as the child lumbered off toward the water.

"Careful, now. Do not wander too far off."

"'Tis not deep, Brigid. Up there I can see a place to cross."

The ford. Praise the Lord. They'd made it.

The habitation could be seen through the trees, but as Maire said, one had to look. The series of buildings built from fallen trees looked at first glance like shelters for pine martens or weasels. They so blended into the landscape that Brigid wondered what the monks were hiding from. There were so many people who needed to know about the love of Jesus. Why had God's people obscured themselves in the woods?

"My uncle's name is Cillian. He reads words out of marks. Mother said he'd teach me. I need to stay with him, Miz Brigid – so I can learn. Please don't send me back to my mother yet."

"Ye mean he writes?" Brigid longed to learn also.

The lass, her brown hair still damp, shrugged her shoulders. "I believe so. Anyway, he's going to teach me."

"Cillian. Aye, 'tis as yer mother told me. Said I'm to put ye into his service for a time. Is that what ye want, child?"

"Aye. To learn to speak those marks and to... write, as ye said. My mother says I can become wiser than any druid. Says my uncle has God's words on parchment."

The rude huts were only paces away. Brigid was not sure how to introduce herself. The monks would not be expecting her or this child. She had no choice, nowhere to go. Surely men of God would not turn them out.

Just as they were about to approach some men huddled in the center of the settlement, Brigid stopped short. "They might be praying. Let's wait." She pulled Aine over to a pile of chopped wood. They sat and waited. Minutes passed, but the men did not move.

Aine leaned in to whisper. "How much longer?"

"I don't know, little miss. Prayers can take as long as one… "

A gray blur of fur streaked in front of them. Without warning a wolf leaped into the clearing. His eyes were wild and spittle dripped from his long white teeth. Aine let out a scream and the monks faced them and gasped.

Brigid pulled the lass behind her and held out a hand toward the animal. "There now. What have ye come looking for? Has a hunter scared ye?"

"Woman!" a monk shouted. "Are ye so crazy as to talk to a wolf? Philib, man, fetch the spear."

"Nay. There's no need." Brigid kept her eyes on the animal. "He's frightened, that's all. Can ye not see that?" The wolf lowered its eyes to the ground and stepped toward her like a camp puppy. "'Tis fine now, wolf. Yer safe here."

"Safe? Are ye mad?" The monk who had spoken earlier stood with the others near a fire. He reached for a torch to light, all the while keeping his eyes on the wolf.

"Someone's hunting him. Hide him in yer dwelling."

The monks looked at each other.

Brigid stared at the one who seemed to be in charge. "Ye'd better do it now before it's too late. If the wolf feels cornered, he'll tear us all apart."

"Do as she says," he ordered.

The men held open the pelt door of one cloister, and the animal ducked inside.

The one called Philib waved his hand in front of his chest. "Now what?"

Hoofbeats held off the answer. Four riders emerged from the woods with painted spears. "Seen a wolf?"

"I've seen many," the head monk answered.

The men rode off in pursuit of distant howls. As soon as

they were out of sight, Brigid released the animal. He disappeared as quickly as he had come.

The head monk marched up to her. By his thinning hair she judged him to be in his fourth decade of life. "Now I must ask, young woman, who are ye to have such rapport with the creatures of the wild?"

Aine answered. "Kind Brigid. She's bringing me to my uncle Cillian."

The monk knelt beside the girl. "And ye've found me, Aine."

Brigid and Aine were treated to a fine meal of boiled beef – a gift from a visitor, they were told.

Cillian poured ale and then reclined on a straw mat. Other monks busied themselves with manuscripts in their private dwellings. "My sister vowed the day that little Aine was born that she'd send the girl to me for training. Seems that day has finally come."

"I was sick, uncle."

"Oh?"

Brigid explained. "She had sores, boils. It was pitiful. Her mother sent her to ye to hide her from her father."

Cillian reached for Aine who scuttled to his side. He brushed back her nearly-dry golden-brown tresses. "I see no marks at all."

"Brigid prayed for me, uncle. On our trip here. There were terrible hungry people who pulled at our cloaks." Aine went on to detail their adventure as though she were a bard with a harp entertaining a crowd with legends and song. That one had the gift of storytelling.

Cillian cast Brigid a long look while speaking to his niece. "Seems this young woman has healing gifts from our Lord, along with the ability to tame wild animals."

Aine giggled. "Aye, she does. Can she stay, uncle? Ye can teach her to read marks, too."

"I'd be pleased. We've got an empty dwelling suitable for ye both."

CHAPTER

"YOU NEVER MISS THE WATER TILL THE WELL RUNS DRY."
OLD IRISH PROVERB

Brigid took the opportunity to ask a question when she helped serve the evening meal. "Why have ye hidden yerselves here?"

Five men, ranging from Cillian's middle age to as ancient as the oaks, sat around a rock that served as an outdoor table. They didn't eat from a communal bowl. Brigid thought the monks had odd manners.

Cillian didn't look up while he heaped stew prepared from yesterday's beef into each monk's wooden bowl. "How old are ye, Brigid?"

"Sixteen springtimes, I'm told."

"Doesn't yer mother remember?"

Brigid had no desire to talk about her mother. She hoped her travels would bring her to mother's doorstep one day, but the details were too painful to relate to strangers. "My mother is not with me."

He looked at her in surprise. "I'm sorry to hear that. Where are ye from? If ye do not know why we have concealed ourselves, yer certainly not from nearby."

"For most of my years I lived with my father up north. In the territory of King Dunlaing." Brigid cut a loaf of brown bread and followed behind Cillian, serving each man a slice that Aine topped with a dollop of honey.

Cillian sat with his brothers in the Lord. "I'll tell ye, Brigid, since yer too young to know."

One of the brothers gulped down his food and stood. "I care not to hear it again." He hurried to his hut.

Cillian followed him with his eyes. "'Twas not so long ago there was a raid very near here."

Brigid was curious. "A raid?"

"Not of cattle, mind ye, but of workers for the Lord." Cillian ate, slopping his bread into the stew the way Brigid had seen Dubthach do.

"Two of my brothers were killed as they gathered peat for the next season's fire." He swallowed hard and reached for his ale.

Brigid stretched out her hand to comfort him, but he pulled back sharply.

"They seek to kill us, those devils! The kings are powerless against druids who evoke evil spirits."

Brigid sent Aine off to ready their sleeping hut since she'd eaten earlier. Children should not hear such terrible talk. The monks were probably not used to caring for children.

After the wee one scampered off with an armload of fleece for covers, Brigid whispered, "But God is more powerful than druids."

Cillian's eyes spread wide, his nostrils flared. "Don't speak of things ye do not understand, lass. Ye may have grown into a woman, ye may think yer wise, but ye've never been through the worst."

He had no idea. What could be worse than losing your mother?

He was quiet for a moment, and then, after he finished his meal, settled into a slump like a hibernating bear and told the story while she ate. "The brothers were opening a new peat bed. Hard work, that, ridding the bog of grasses and such. They'd been laboring most of the day not too far from here, just to the east. Takes a short time to walk there if yer donkey's not in a foul mood." He gazed at the clouds overhead. "'Tis a bog soiled by blood now. We won't go there. We use wood we cut from the forest to warm us through the winter." He scratched his orbed belly through his brown linen cloak – the color of a peat bog. He smelled like one too, earthy and damp.

Cillian's voice grew louder and tight. "Druids in robes, looking like winged gulls, swooped in, waving swords like warriors. Curse those druids! 'Tis not their role to take up weapons."

"You saw them?" Brigid had heard many tales about the cloaked men pagans called priests, poets, and prophets, but she had never laid eyes on one.

"Nay, not me. But Philib, the brother who left as I began to tell ye 'bout it, witnessed the whole attack."

"How awful." Brigid wondered how witnessing such unprovoked violence would affect someone. Now she understood why they hid.

"Did ye send for the king? Did ye have the druids arrested?"

The remaining monks gathered up the dishes and disappeared from the dining rock. Cillian stood and looked down on her, making her uneasy.

"Ye may be sixteen springs, soon to be seventeen since the winter's now breaking, but ye know nothing of the world, miss." He slapped his foot on the rock and withdrew a small knife from the leather laces of his boot. "This is justice, should I ever see another druid. No king will stand up to those devils. They fear their curses. They should fear God."

"But the Bible says justice is the Lord's."

He rammed the knife into the dirt next to the dining rock. Brigid gasped and knocked over her wooden bowl of broth. She hurried to wipe up the spill with her apron, but he held her back.

"Listen to me, little lass. I am the Lord's servant. If he wishes to use me to enact his justice, so be it." His voice seemed to shake the branches above their heads. Was he really hiding? Or was he lurking in the woods, hoping for an opportunity to avenge the monks' murder?

She turned away from his angry expression. "I... understand. I do."

Brigid hastened to her sleeping quarters where Aine slept secure under fur blankets. *Lord, why am I here? This man is no better than Dubthach. He says he's a Christian, but he seeks revenge for his own pleasure. Are Aine and I safe here? Is it worth staying here just to learn to write?*

Soon Brigid had her answer. The poor, the lonely, the hungry, had found her. And she now had something to give them. She was living with Christians, so it seemed, and a worker for the Lord always gives to the poor.

"Here now," she said to a fellow. "Take these eggs to yer wife and let her cook them over the fire. Tomorrow I'll fetch ye some cream from the monks' dairy."

The poor soul's face was covered in grime, but his eyes were sprite and excited. "'Tis so kind of ye. The monks rarely give away their food. Only twice a year on feast days."

"Feast days?" She could barely believe what she heard. Did the monks follow pagan feasts? Perhaps they were not what they seemed.

The beggar blinked. "Aye. Ye know, the Christian feasts? The celebration of yer god's birth and death. Falls on the breaking of winter and the breaking of spring. Well, thank ye again." He crept under the brambles surrounding the monks' gathering of log huts and then disappeared down the road near the river, in the direction Brigid and Aine had come from.

The pagan feasts occurred at the times the fellow

described as Christian feasts. Dubthach had allowed the pagans working for him to build large fires and celebrate in their own way. Sometimes they wore repulsive masks and drank ale far into the night. Their chants drifted into the window of the maidens' quarters where Cook and Brigid retired.

Cook had never let Brigid witness the pagan rituals, although once she spied Dubthach scurrying out to join the dancing, singing, and drinking. She had been curious, but Cook insisted that Christians should never take part.

Brigid wondered how Christians celebrated such feasts. She returned to her chores. Since she was an experienced milkmaid, Cillian allowed her charge of the monks' dairy in return for food, shelter, and occasional instruction in writing.

She freshened the rushes scattered on the dirt floor of the dairy. The monks thought such comfort inappropriate for an animal shelter, but Brigid believed in making all God's creatures comfortable. Besides, she thought of the place as her home.

She finished the task and contemplated the beggar's words. *Christian feast.* He'd said something about the Christian God's birth and death.

The door flew open and Aine entered, looking bright and alert in the new dress Brigid had made her. In the months they'd spent with the monks, the little lass had grown enough to need new garments.

"'Tis time for instruction, Brigid."

Brigid hung her broom on a peg on the back of the door. This was worth all the trouble. "What do ye think we'll learn today?"

Aine lifted the lid of a butter churn and stuck in her finger. "I expect we'll be copying words from a book by Luke. Uncle says that has the story of the Lord's birth."

Oh, joy! Maybe she'd get the answer she was looking for. Despite how gruff the head monk was, he was an excellent teacher. He seemed to delight in reading the Latin words to his scribes as they labored to copy text. He would pause and instruct the girls how to write down the stories in Irish. In this way Brigid learned both writing and, best of all, reading the Latin text of the Scriptures.

"I've been wanting to hear 'bout our Lord's birth." Brigid shooed Aine from the cream and nudged her out the door. "Seems like a long while since I heard the stories at Glasgleann."

They entered the scribes' room like spiders to avoid distracting the men who wrote. Brigid loved that hall, the only building built outside the tangle of oak trees. It sat on the riverbank with a row of windows strategically placed high on the wall to take in the expanse of sky left unobstructed by trees, thanks to the river. Sunlight burst through the windows and danced at their feet.

"Over here." Cillian waved them toward a shrouded monk who sat hunched over a tilted table. He moved his quill so deliberately that sometimes it seemed as though he was doing nothing. They watched for a time, taking in the beauty of his scratched marks.

"I'll read it to ye first, so as ye'll know what ye'll be writing later," Cillian explained.

Brigid gulped. The privilege of what they were doing was lost on Aine, who dropped to the floor and squirmed at her uncle's feet, but Brigid understood. Stories were passed on from generation to generation by listeners who in turn went on to tell the stories again. Druids, priests, monks, and common people all educated, inspired, and entertained others in that fashion. Brigid was sure that the pagan feasts included storytelling. And so far, all that she had learned about Jesus Christ her Lord came from the speech of others. Now she was learning to read the recorded texts for herself.

Brigid recognized some of the Latin words as she followed

Cillian's reading of the monk's work. She even jumped ahead: *ut cognoscas eorum verborum de quibus eruditus es veritatem.* "So that you may know the exact truth about the things you have been taught," she translated aloud.

"Brigid! I'm amazed ye learned so quickly." Cillian was staring at her with his lower lip drooping.

"I am so sorry if I've disturbed..."

"No matter." Cillian beckoned the monks back to their work.

From that point on, Cillian, finding Brigid a rapid learner, gave her special attention. She was allowed to visit the monks' transcription hall daily. She learned that events important to Christians were being celebrated at the time of pagan feasts so that Christ's teachings would be heard.

The man no longer frightened her. She began to understand Cillian's mission. He stayed close to the people, gained their friendship. Let them discover for themselves the miracle of Jesus by observing him.

"I never asked these men to stay here with me," he told Brigid one day. "They came because they chose service to God. We have become a kind of clan here. After I returned from a journey to Rome, I brought manuscripts for my own study. They wanted to examine them, and before long we produced all these pieces."

Brigid had counted the cubbyholes in the walls – twenty-one. Each compartment held four or five rolls. Each roll could cover a dining table. Yet Cillian told her the monks had only been transcribing for a few years.

"They have begun copying them a second time," he told her. "One day, when it's safe, I'll return to my Christian brothers across the sea and borrow more manuscripts."

Brigid thought the mission these men were undertaking was more valuable to Ireland than they probably realized. God had given them the desire to transcribe for a reason. Just like the biblical writer Luke said, "So that you may know the exact truth about the things you have been taught."

She decided to dismiss Cillian's outburst on the day she met him as out of character. He had probably just been upset remembering the slaughter of his brothers.

Brigid became so comfortable in her new home that she began to think of it as hers. And just as she had done in Glasgleann, she gave away what she could to the poor. God continued to provide, just like he always had, and, unlike Dubthach, Cillian tolerated her charity.

After two springtimes passed, Brigid realized Aine would never be going home to her mother. The fact didn't seem to bother the girl. She loved her uncle and he doted on her.

Still, Brigid missed Cook and the others. And the longing to find her mother never left, some days rising within her like a hunger that hadn't been satisfied for days. She had mastered the art of reading and writing, at least with the manuscripts in possession of the monks. The day was coming, she knew, when she'd need to move on in order to find more challenging work, and, she hoped, God would direct her path to her mother.

One morning Brigid headed to the bog. She had volunteered to cut peat since the monks wouldn't step foot near the place and she longed for something new to occupy her. She was also curious and knew that one day she'd venture farther than the bog.

She had been given a donkey, a tool for the cutting, and a large basket woven from the strongest rushes. "The bricks have to dry, of course," Cillian had said. "But bring back whatever ye can, and we'll set them up here. Ye don't want to linger there long."

She passed a lovely grove where a young lass labored among the fruit trees.

"Are ye Brigid?" the girl called from within the branches. "The one who lives with the monks?"

"Aye, that I am." Brigid left the donkey on the road and joined her among the trees. They both stood there admiring the glorious harvest. "God has blessed ye with such bountiful land."

"Well, the gods are appeased, I suppose. One never knows what may happen tomorrow."

Brigid noticed the girl was dressed in new garments – no holes. Her honey-colored tresses were neatly combed and her complexion as clear as a baby's. "Who owns this beautiful patch of land?"

"'Tis all mine." The lass spread her arms and twirled around. Her tunic and apron floated out to form a cloud around her. "I've a cow too, but shush. Don't be telling anyone."

"Why not?"

"I am grateful the gods have blessed me, Brigid, truly I am. I've heard 'bout yer god. How different he is. The druids speak 'bout the spirits in the woods, the god of the sun and the sea – but I'm wondering if that's not how it is at all."

She pulled a piece of fruit off a branch and handed it to Brigid. It tasted sweet and sour at the same time. Juice dripped down her fingers. The lass took an apple for herself and they ate together.

After they finished, the lass wiped her hands on her apron and headed back to picking her harvest. "But I've got to look out for myself till I figure out what your god wants of me. I've got to hide what I've got till then, just in case I need it. That's why I asked ye not to tell anyone."

The lass seemed unsure. Perhaps she was ready to convert to Brigid's faith. Cillian had tried to be a light for many years, but it was a light that glimmered softly. Brigid thought perhaps her example, along with Cillian's, was taking hold among the people of the woods after all. She went to the lass and touched her arm. "Well, then, do ye know what the One True God wants ye to do?"

The girl dropped to her knees and twisted Brigid's skirts between her hands. "Oh, I want to know! Please tell me."

"'Tis simple. He wants ye to share yer apples with the starving ones in the woods. Ye have plenty for yerself."

The girl pulled her hands back. "They'll take it all, then come after the cow. I'll be starving then. Can't ye see that? I'll have nothing to offer any god." She began to pace. "I'll get guards to protect the apples. I'm sure the king will send them. He doesn't want to anger the gods."

"Have ye not heard me, lass? There are no gods to appease in the woods. There is only one God. And he wants ye to... "

The girl left Brigid standing there talking to herself. She didn't understand. Brigid kicked at a fallen apple and squeezed her fists tight. "Oh, God, these people must learn. Curse this orchard so it produces no more fruit."

The girl turned toward her, eyes wide, and then disappeared inside a whitewashed house.

Disgusted, Brigid returned to the donkey and resumed her march to the bog. Late in the day she set off home, mumbling about the wet, nasty job, and how her shoes were forever ruined by it. She pulled and shoved the stubborn beast. He disliked the heavy load. At the sunlight's last glimmer she entered the settlement. The monks were waiting for her, lined up in a row like a king's order of guardsmen.

Philib stepped toward her. "We heard what ye did to Deirdre's trees." He frowned.

"Who?" Brigid dropped her turf bundles near the base of the dining hall hut. Then she remembered – the lass with the apple orchard.

Cillian suggested the men return to their chores.

Why are they so angry? I've returned with fuel from a place they

63

will not go. And I'm miserably wet from it, too. Brigid noticed Aine in Cillian's shadow. "Hello, lassie. How was yer day?"

"Go on, now." Cillian pushed the girl toward the dairy. "I need to speak to Brigid alone."

The girl obeyed. She was now more under his authority than Brigid's.

"'Tis not that they aren't grateful for yer gift. But Deirdre came to us wailing about a curse ye put upon her apples. The trees have all withered and her apples are full of worms."

Brigid started to giggle, then stopped at Cillian's expression.

"If ye be cursing people's well-being, then yer no different from the white-cloaked devils. Don't ye know? Have ye been sheltered from the world? The pagans believe apples are connected to fertility. With her crop destroyed, she believes she'll never marry. Never mind what she could have gotten for those apples."

"What she could get? Why those apples could feed... "

"Brigid, those apples can buy cows, goats, sheep. Ye had no idea, did ye? Ye never had to buy beasts." He shook his head like a rebellious horse. "The starving would not have eaten the fruit. 'Tis too valuable. With apples ye can buy livestock. With livestock yer rich."

"I do know 'bout dairy animals, sir."

"Oh, woman! There's so much ye don't know. And ye've got power from God without wisdom. That's a dangerous thing."

"Oh, I assure ye, sir, that if the trees died, God had a reason for it. He likely sent a plague that caused the crop to fail. Growing fruit is difficult. Has that not happened before?"

"Aye, but not right after a woman has ordered someone to appease God with gifts of fruit."

"Appease? I used no such word. I only told her that God expects us to share what we have."

"Like you do?"

64

A frigid breeze from the direction of the river slapped her cheeks. "Aye, like I do."

After that, every time Brigid attempted to help someone or give a bit of advice, the monks questioned her. When she tried to convince a young woman who came to her complaining of ill treatment by her husband that true beauty comes only from God, the monks accused her of trying to keep all women unmarried.

"But yer not married!" she barked back to Cillian.

"I am God's servant. I've dedicated my life to spreading God's Word. Have ye not learned that, Brigid?"

The bulge around his ankle from his hidden dirk loomed large. Brigid feared his anger would turn to rage against her. She clasped her fingers together to keep from shaking. "Aye. Ye do wonderful work for the Lord. And ye've been more than kind to take me in."

"Then ye'll heed my words. Ye may not favor a husband for yerself, but ye'll not be telling other women to disobey their husbands. The Lord sanctions marriage." His words sounded like a mortar full of grain grinding underneath the pressure of a pestle.

"I meant no such thing. I just wanted to tell her the Lord thinks she's beautiful."

He stomped off, leaving her to wonder what the change in the wind was really bringing.

Moments later a streak of white caught her eye. Standing at the edge of the woods with a gnarled walking stick stood a man, clothed in a white cloak. He smiled at her, and she heard the faint whispers of the monks who had gathered at the dining shelter's one window. "*Ardan.*"

CHAPTER

8

"THERE'S NO NEED TO FEAR THE WIND IF YOUR HAYSTACKS ARE TIED DOWN."
OLD IRISH SAYING

Cook made more noise than was necessary. She slammed down every pan she could find, making the table rattle against the stone floor. She sighed as loudly as she could. Dubthach was in the room.

"By the gods, woman, what are ye doing? Trying to make my head feel like there's chickens fighting in there?"

"If yer head feels that way, 'tis yer own doing. The whiskey barrel's nearly empty again."

"What?" He glanced toward the door. "Brian? Where is that man?"

"I already told him. He said no more will be ready for a week."

"Suppose I'll be going to the merchant ships, then. Tell him to be ready tomorrow."

Cook was in no mood to discuss the master's growing need for intoxication. Ever since Brigid was sent away, she had tried to talk sense to the man. He had made a deal – now he was reneging.

Cook felt trapped. She would have run after the lass

herself, but she couldn't leave her kin behind in Glasgleann. Her grandbabies were too young for her to abandon them, and her knees were too old for wandering the rocky hillsides. Still, she had promised Brocca she'd watch over Brigid. That's why she sent Brian weekly to check on the lass. But Cook's conscience poked at her. She had not done enough.

Dubthach had to answer for sending that girl away. Cook slapped down her cooking utensils and gave her master her full attention. "Ye made a deal."

"Is this 'bout Brigid again?"

"Ye know it is." She shoved the lid down so hard on the iron pot hanging over the fire that a pain shot up to her elbow.

Dubthach huffed. "Ye know Brian speaks to the monks every week. Brigid is doing exceptionally well."

"But the deal ye made with the druid was that I'd be with her."

"How was I to know that she'd turn out to be a thief – and ye would turn out a magnificent cook? 'Tis better that I'm rid of her and still have ye to feed me. And don't be thinking of running off. Not at yer age. I'll have ye whipped, and ye might not survive it."

Cook glared at him, the bag of hot air. "Ever since my dear husband died ye've threatened me with that. Have I ever tried to leave?"

"Nay. But there's that blasted trip to the seashore. I could take that away if ye don't stop yer nagging. Hmm, 'tis getting close to time for that again, nay?"

"Take it away? After what the druid said?" It was wicked of her to bring up that harmless curse. But Dubthach feared such things and because he did, she had been able to see darling Brocca over the years. Sometimes only at a distance, to protect Brigid from the agony of parting with her mother again, but even so it did Cook's heart good to see that

Dubthach's former slave was thriving. "Ye should remember, man. The druid expects Brigid to go on that trip."

"'Tis no concern of mine now."

"It is not, now? Well, I hear that the druid himself will be at the seashore this year. I'll just have to send him to Glasgleann to visit ye."

Dubthach's face drained of color. "Ye can't if yer not there to see him."

"Whether I'm there or nay, he'll find out and come looking for ye."

The master exhaled and chuckled. "That druid was aged when I first sent Brocca away. He's surely dead by now."

A voice bellowed from the doorway. "I saw him yesterday." They turned to see Brian standing at the door, a blade of grass stuck between his teeth. He whistled to break the silence.

Dubthach marched over to the door. He was a head shorter than Brian, but he tried to stare him down nonetheless. "How can ye be sure it was him?"

"He told me he was Brocca's master. Asked me to give ye this." He opened his fist to reveal a small leather cross. The one Brocca had always worn around her neck. "He said she couldn't come this year and he was there in her stead."

Dubthach snatched the cross away. "I'll not be dictated to by my slaves, hear me? Troya will have something to say about this."

Cook nearly collapsed onto the floor. Her legs felt like a newborn calf's, and the room was suddenly hot.

"No need to tell yer old wife." Brian's eyes pleaded.

"Well, if the druid is going to curse me, I've no other choice."

Cook knew she was wailing, but she couldn't stop. "Nay! That darlin' child! Think about her for once. Troya will kill her!"

"Ye listen to me." Dubthach shook the cross in Cook's face.

"I have tried all these years to provide for that child. She returned my goodwill by stealing from me. She's a curse, that one. Just like the prophet said at her birth. Ye know what the druid said 'bout that."

"Nay, nay," Cook wailed on. "She's a blessing. A blessing."

"A curse, she is. If that druid comes 'round, I'll have no choice but to inform Troya that Brigid still lives."

Cook didn't hear Dubthach leave. She covered her face with her hands and wept.

Brian tried to console her, but his voice trembled in unison with her hands. "We'll think of something. Something will come to us, ye'll see."

She pulled herself to her feet. "Brian, ye've got to go back to Brocca's druid. Talk to him. I've failed my mission. May God have mercy on me."

"Not yet." Brian's ruddy face drew up into a thousand wrinkles of worry. "I'd best be getting over to talk to that monk Philib. If Troya finds out where Brigid is, the monks will need to protect her."

He swung the door open to leave and four of Cook's grandchildren sailed in. "Maimeo, what shall we do today? Is it time to make butter?"

She didn't want to worry them, but when they looked at her, their faces fell silent. She shooed them toward their mother who was weeding the herb garden, and then she hurried to catch up with Brian. Since Dubthach was likely headed to the closest neighbor for a drink, he wouldn't notice she was gone till morning.

CHAPTER

"BUT YOU KNOW, O LORD, ALL THEIR PLOTS
TO KILL ME. DO NOT FORGIVE THEIR CRIMES OR
BLOT OUT THEIR SINS FROM YOUR SIGHT."
JEREMIAH 18:23A

"Greetings." The man in the white cloak approached Brigid. "My name is Ardan. I am a druid commonly working in the house of Dunlaing."

At first Brigid was speechless. She wasn't sure whether to fear the man because of the stories Cillian had told her or to welcome him because he was affiliated with King Dunlaing, the ruler who had granted her freedom.

"I realize the monks here do not welcome me, but I came to see Brigid. Ye must be her."

Thinking about Cillian's dirk hidden in his boot, she looked around for him. He wasn't in sight. She took one step toward the druid, in hospitality. "I am Brigid."

A shuffling sound came from the dining shelter. Brigid wondered if the brothers were taking up arms or falling to their knees to pray.

"Why have ye come to see me?"

Ardan walked toward a tree stump, his white robes trailing behind him like thin ribbons of clouds on a summer day. He held his walking stick tight in his hand, though he had no infirmity that she could see. He sat down and laid the stick across his lap. "Tales of yer works have spread among the people. At first they thought ye were a miracle worker, spreading charity. But now it seems the fox has found another burrow."

Cook had once told Brigid that druids spoke in puzzles. Now that she'd actually met one, she knew it was true. "What do ye mean?"

Grunts came from the monks, but they were obviously not going to emerge from their hiding places. The druid didn't seem so dreadful to her. She knew he had no real power. Even if he caused her harm, God would protect her soul from the ones Cillian called devils.

"Let's just say that ever since ye cursed that apple orchard, people have been saying yer, hmm, less than kind… perhaps even some kind of witch. Even a druid would not do such a callous thing."

"Outrageous! I always tell them I do the things I do in the name of the One True God." Brigid's voice was louder than she meant it to be, but she didn't care. "If God chose to curse that apple orchard, then it was to be."

Ardan stood and circled the stump – a pagan ritual, she assumed.

"Ye may be right. But… think about this: how will ye be able to help the people at all if they choose not to trust ye? If ye really want to spread the work of Patrick's god… "

"He's my God too. And yers if ye'll let him be."

He chuckled and his dark eyes narrowed. "As ye say. But if that's yer intent, ye'll need to prove yer god's charity and goodwill toward the woodsfolk."

"How?"

When he stepped close to her, she heard the monks thump against the shelter's door, likely straining to hear the rest. Cillian could not be in there with them. Not after the way he had once vowed vengeance against druids. It was probably just as well.

"There's a woman who's having a difficult time birthing a baby. No one will help her because the Tuatha De Danann stand outside her door, ready to snatch the baby away."

Brigid took a step back. "Nonsense. The dead cannot take a life."

Ardan smiled, and she was convinced he was sincere. She really did want to help the people and he seemed to want that also.

He circled her once again, tapping his long walking stick on the ground as he went. "Yer the only one who does not fear them. Yer the only one who can help."

She reached out to touch the stick. "Take me to her."

Night drifted in as she followed the druid. His white attire illuminated the path, but at times he traveled so fast Brigid feared she'd lose him. She shouted at him, "Why are babies always born at night?"

He didn't answer. A fox scampered across her path, shining his yellow eyes at her before sliding back into the woody landscape. The creature was not startled by their appearance. Animals have keen senses, seem to know when things are urgent.

She pulled her cloak over her head and shivered against the sharp late-summer winds. Why at night? Would she arrive back at her barn before milking time? With babies there was no telling. She knew that, from the few times she'd assisted with births before. Some bairns were quick, and some seemed to be so reluctant to make their arrival that they reminded her of how tenaciously stubborn the human race is.

"Here it is. The MacFirbis home. I can't stay with ye, Brigid. There are others who need my help tonight."

She watched him drift into the woods until his white

cloak appeared gray in the distance and then disappeared. She hesitated a moment before knocking. What should she say?

The door to the minuscule cabin swung wide and MacFirbis met her. The man glared at her with wild eyes, slipped his coat over sagging shoulders, and ran into the woods.

"Wait! Where are ye going?"

Too late. He was gone. Men weren't usually much help during birthing anyway.

Brigid peered around the cabin. A mound of blankets told her where the expectant mother was. "Where's yer maid?"

"They've all left me," the woman answered from the blanket pile.

Just as Ardan said. They all feared an invasion of the dead. If they were that frightened, it could only mean the mother was in grave danger.

The cabin was dark, cold, and vacant, except for the suffering woman.

"Are the pains bad?"

The woman grunted. She was curled up on the floor in a corner. The labor had progressed so that the woman could barely manage to speak. Brigid had seen it before.

A shriek followed, rattling dishes on the shelves. Brigid set to work building a fire. All the while she sang softly, hoping to calm the terrified woman. But as she lit the candles hanging from the rafters, Brigid was met with a horrifying sight. MacFirbis's wife had a scowl that would terrify the mightiest warrior in Ireland, even the legendary Cu 'Chulainn. Her hands were covered with blood and in her shaking arms she was cradling a still child.

Brigid breathed deeply, asking God for strength. "Please, darlin', let me hold yer child."

The woman cowered and hissed at Brigid.

Brigid crossed herself. "Oh, God, do not let evil into this

house tonight." She tried again, pulling ever so gently on the woman's sleeve. The woman softened and allowed the bundle to be taken from her.

Brigid rushed to a bowl of washing water left beside the fire pit. A warming blaze illuminated what she held in her arms. The wee bloody face was so thickly coated that the baby's mouth was hidden. Brigid dipped her hand into the lukewarm water and cleansed the child, a girl. She slid her fingers over the child's mouth and pried the babe's lips apart. The tiny face was blue, but the child's body was still warm from her mother's womb.

Her mother wailed from the corner.

"Don't be afraid." Brigid hummed a tune she remembered hearing the monks sing. The notes were cheery but not loud. The words were about hope in dark times.

With as gentle a hand as she could muster, Brigid cleared the baby's nose and then stopped her singing to breathe into the child's face. Suddenly she felt a hand on her shoulder. The woman was starting to recover. Perhaps Brigid's praise to the Creator had calmed her.

The baby coughed and Brigid and the new mother laughed out loud.

"What is that song ye sang?" MacFirbis's wife took her cleansed infant into her arms to nurse.

"A song to my God." Brigid steadied herself against a wall.

The hours passed, and the room transformed from a deep, dark cave into a brightly-lit home of joy. The rising sun shone tiny ribbons of light through the house's wooden doorframe.

"There's something familiar 'bout yer god. Something familiar 'bout ye. Do I know ye from somewhere?"

"Well, I've been living with Cillian's monks in the woods for the past two winters."

The woman kept stroking her baby while staring at Brigid. "Yer name, lass?"

"Brigid."

Her eyes widened. "I knew that name once. Dubthach's slave child."

Brigid stiffened. She had thought she was a long way from Glasgleann. She hadn't thought it likely she'd meet someone who knew Dubthach. "Seems ye know me. Did ye work for him?"

"Work for him? I say not. I do thank ye for saving my child's life. Though many thought that ye yerself died at yer birth."

Brigid pulled a three-legged stool to the fire and urged the woman to sit with her baby. "Now why would anyone think that?"

"My mother believed so. Before she was Dubthach's wife, she was my father's. When my da' died, she remarried. My aunt raised me, but I visited Glasgleann one summer. My mother never set foot on the place after yer pregnant mother left, and so she believed what Dubthach told her, that ye did not live. I knew better, of course, I'd seen ye myself. But I kept quiet. There's a woman there that people call Cook?"

"Aye, there is."

"Stern one, she is. I was afraid of her when I was a child."

"Afraid of Cook?"

"Aye. I met a shepherd boy there, I did." Her face took on the look of a mischievous child. "We spent many hours together in Glasgleann's meadows." She blushed. "I told him that my mother believed ye dead, but I told no one else. Cook threatened to throw me into the bog if I told my mother."

"I don't remember ye."

"Suppose not. Cook sheltered ye in that dairy. But I was there, nonetheless." She regarded her in the growing firelight. "So, Brigid still lives and she's near."

Dubthach's old wife. Why could Brigid not escape that story? "Did yer mother send my mother away when she was expecting me?"

"That's the way I heard it. Dubthach told her the baby, named Brigid, had died at birth. My mother said she was so jealous of Brocca that she would have killed the baby had it not died."

Brigid wasn't sure what to think. Did the old woman still harbor such feelings? A long time had passed.

"Where's yer mother now? Why is she not living with Dubthach if she loved him so much?" Brigid couldn't imagine any woman feeling possessive over that loathsome man.

"Love him? Nay. 'Twas an honor price she wanted."

Of course. The laws provided for such things when a person's honor had been sullied. That woman should be seeking it from Dubthach, not from her.

Brigid thought it best to avoid her. "Where does she live?"

The infant suckled at the woman's breast, distracting her.

"Yer mother, woman," urged Brigid. "Where is she?"

"A brisk horse ride from here."

Brigid's pulse quickened. She stood and rubbed her fingers over her face. Before she could stop them, the words spilled out. "That woman sent my beloved mother away. Dubthach wouldn't permit me to stay with her. I have lived my entire life without my mother because of her. I am the one who deserves an honor price!" She trembled. Her ranting caused the infant to wail.

MacFirbis's wife quieted the baby and then whispered, "If I were ye, Brigid, I'd run as quickly as I could back to the monks. My husband went to fetch my mother, and if she learns yer alive, she'll be quick to call for her honor by having yer head."

"But King Dunlaing would never allow it. He gave me my freedom. He respects my God."

"King Dunlaing? He has nothing to do with it. My mother has been petitioning that druid Ardan for two decades to produce an honor price for her."

Ardan? The monks were right not to trust the druid. She'd been tricked. Brigid grabbed her cloak and headed to the door.

"Wait! I want to know that God, Brigid. He spoke to me as ye sang and rocked my wee one."

Was it a trick? "What did he say?"

"He said, 'Learn that song. Trust me.'" Tears came to the new mother's eyes. "And, 'Save Brigid.'"

MacFirbis's woman patted her chest and cooled her eyes with a wave of her hand. "I couldn't believe it when I heard those words. I didn't even know it was Brigid herself who stood before me."

Brigid bit her lip. "That song is of praise and a plea for refuge."

Brigid forced the words out, though her heart raced, sensing imminent danger.

Praise be to the Lord my Rock,
who trains my hands for war, my fingers for battle.
He is my loving God and my fortress,
my stronghold and my deliverer,
my shield, in whom I take refuge.

Brigid prayed with the new mother. When she turned to leave, the woman stopped her once more.

"May God deliver ye, Brigid."

"Where is she, then?" Cook's voice trembled. She and Brian had ridden all day to get to Aghade where they met Philib beside the river.

"The white devil came to get her." Philib was on his knees praying to God for protection.

Brian pulled him to his feet. "What are ye mumbling 'bout? Tell us where Brigid is, man."

The monk pulled away and flung himself back to the ground. "Oh, God, shield us from the Evil One."

Cook motioned to Brian to return to the horses. "Something bad has happened to drive him mad. We'd better get to the habitation right away."

Cook's old bones complained about the riding, but her fear for the life of the girl she had sworn to protect overruled her body's protest. A small fire led them to the monks, who were huddling together praying. They heard the horses and embraced each other as though they expected an army to come to slaughter them.

Brian rode in close. "What's going on here? Where's Brigid?"

One monk stepped forward and lowered his brown hood. He was nearly hairless from his circular head to his chin. "I am Cillian, tutor to Brigid."

A girl trailed after him.

"Where is she?" Brian jumped down from his horse.

"Ardan, Dunlaing's druid, came for her just as night was falling. I had gone for my evening walk. Had I been here, I would have taken care of that white-robed devil myself. Without me, my brothers were unsure what was safe to do. They assure me the druid did not harm her and led her peacefully away. Please, come to the fire."

One of the brothers helped Cook off her horse. His hands were shaking. None of the monks would return her gaze. Had Brigid been killed? Oh, why had she allowed Brigid to go off alone with Dubthach to see the king that day? She'd worried constantly since then. She should have come looking for Brigid herself after that, instead of sending Brian. He was just a young lad who knew nothing of the evil that could take root in the fear of the unsaved.

Cook warmed herself by the fire and tried to steady her trembling hands and listen to the monk tell about a time when white-robed druids had attacked his fellow monks. He explained that ever since that day they'd hidden themselves as much as possible. When Ardan came seeking Brigid, they knew they'd been exposed.

Brian wagged his head. "Don't be foolish, man. Ye've been here for years. Everyone knows where ye are. If the druids meant ye harm, they'd have come for ye long before Brigid arrived."

"But the massacre. What of that?" Philib emerged from the woods, still shuddering.

Cillian went to him and offered an arm. He escorted the monk to the fire and Brian continued. "When ye first came, the druids feared ye. Thought ye'd take their powers. It was a shame what they did, but I don't think it has anything to do with this. Where did Ardan take Brigid?"

Philib piped up. "To the MacFirbis house to help with a birth."

Brian smiled. "Well, then. Ye see? 'Twas nothing sinister."

Cook tapped her forehead. "MacFirbis. There's something 'bout that name. I've heard something 'bout that clan." It was important. She knew it was. *Please God, let this old woman remember!*

The monks were calmed by Brian's pronouncement and headed off to their beds. The little lass followed too, slipping into a tiny hut. Only Cillian was left to aid the visitors.

Brian towered over the monk. "Do ye know where the MacFirbis home is?"

"Aye, but I don't trust that Ardan. How can he be any different from the other druids – if it were not he himself who brutally killed my brothers in the Lord?"

Cook interrupted. "I think I remember something, Brian. MacFirbis is relation somehow to Troya. I just know it."

Cillian's eyebrows shot up. "Troya of Bran Coill?"

"Ye know her?" Cook's stomach tightened like a rock in a

sling. She could not control the quiver developing in her lower lip.

"Not really. I heard some folks call her a witch. So that's what Ardan has to do with this."

Brian headed to his horse. "What do ye mean?"

Cillian pulled his cloak back over his head as though he was trying to distance himself from the revelation. "Ardan, the druid, and Troya, the druidess. People say they work together to coax evil up from the waters. Word has it that Troya was so evil her own husband kicked her out."

"Dubthach!" Cook didn't know how she had managed it, but she was on her horse before Brian had time to mount. "Point us toward this druidess, monk. We must save Brigid from her clutches."

CHAPTER

"GO N-EIRI AN BOTHAR LEAT.
MAY THE ROAD RISE TO MEET YOU."
OLD IRISH BLESSING

Brigid praised God that the MacFirbis woman had given her a horse and told her which direction to ride. Brigid's first foolish thought was to confront the woman called Troya, the one who had separated Brigid and Brocca. But good sense won, and she fled for her life. The monks' habitation offered little protection, so she headed toward Munster where Dunlaing's dominion ended. A woman traveling alone would not be required to pay admittance to the province. Sometimes being female had its privileges.

God is good. Her mother was somewhere in Munster.

By midday Brigid figured the threat was past. No one, as far as she could tell, had followed her. The landscape was less rocky now. A high patch of green grass topped by limestone boulders stood before her. She stopped to admire the steep ascent when a horse and rider appeared on the road behind her. Her horse sidestepped until she successfully wriggled his head toward the encroacher. She chastised herself for being careless.

A young lad, not a white-robed druid, was gaining on her. What could he want?

"Greetings!" he called out.

Brigid shifted in her saddle and the reins in her hands turned slippery with sweat. "Who are ye?"

She sat as still as stone until he drew near. A wooden pole attached to his saddle carried the flag of the Leinster king. What was Dunlaing's messenger doing out here?

He brought his spotted horse nose to nose with hers. "I've come to bid King Aenghus of Munster greetings from the great King Dunlaing who approaches one day hence. Tell yer people, good woman!"

He thought she was a citizen of Munster. She would not correct him. "Dunlaing? Are ye quite sure?"

The fellow chuckled and rode off toward the rising hill, the blue and white flag flapping in his wake.

Brigid gazed in the direction the messenger had come. The king's entourage was one day behind. Had Dunlaing followed her or did he have business with the reigning king? She wiped her clammy hands on her tunic-covered thighs. If Dunlaing was coming, would he bring Ardan, the king's druid, and Troya, Ardan's cohort?

Her body felt like a bag of rocks after riding through the night and half the day. Her sides ached, if not from hunger then from the excitement of being free enough to decide where she'd go and where she'd lay her head.

She'd best avoid the king's residence and trust God that she followed the right path. She'd find shelter and food and move westward again in the morn.

Brigid dropped from her horse and led him at a leisurely pace. Dunlaing and his attendants could not find her today. Both she and her horse were glad to be free from the jarring rapid escape.

Wait a minute.

She looked again at the rise in the land. Its prominence seemed to signify importance. She cast her gaze to the top of the hill. A rock barrier surrounded it. Would Dunlaing come in peace? Better to be hidden in the woods.

The smell of charred wood mixed with the sounds of harps and drums indicated a gathering was nearby. She tied her horse to a sturdy elm and headed toward the revelry.

Brigid blended with a crowd of people who had gathered to hear a man tell a story. She soon ascertained, however, that this wasn't the usual spinning of a yarn. The storyteller was a simple-minded fellow who had trouble forming his words. His frustration was apparent in his flushed cheeks and bulging eyes. His eyes darted around the crowd. He spotted her and pulled her to the front.

"P-p-lease, miss, tell it for me!"

She struggled to understand him but finally determined that he had gotten himself into a plight at the king's residence and needed help.

"Best we not be fooling with that king," one woman said.

Brigid turned to her. "The king from the clan of Eoghanachta? I have heard from the people in Leinster that he is a Christian."

The woman cleared her throat. "Whether Patrick baptized the king of Munster or nay, 'tis of no concern in this matter. This fool," she pointed to the stuttering man, "runs from the visiting king."

Brigid reached for the woman's hand. "Dunlaing?"

The man's face went white at the sound of the name. He nodded, but would say nothing more.

The gathering started to break up, looking for fresh entertainment. Some left to dance, others crowded together for warmth around the fire. But the man would not let Brigid leave.

"They'll k-k-kill me cuz I k-k-killed the king's fox."

The man clutched her arm with the grip of a wolf's jaw. She patted his hand. "Why would the king bother with a fox?"

"'Twas his pet. Did tricks. I di... di... didn't know."

Brigid tried to ignore the perspiration dripping down her back. Although she wished to avoid Dunlaing, this poor man needed help and none of the woodsfolk would do anything. "I'll go with ye to see the king tomorrow. I know King Dunlaing. He'll listen to me."

"Thank ye much. P-p-please come with me to my brother's home. Name's Liam. He'll p-p-put ye up there."

While the shelter and dinner of lamb's leg was more than Brigid had hoped for, she pondered the wisdom of the offer she'd made. The royal druids from Leinster might come to Munster, might even be with Dunlaing at that very moment. But was it right to worry about her own safety when someone was in danger and she had the power to help him?

Liam, the master of the house, was a Christian. He had offered prayers before dinner. Liam's family was large. Brigid's spot to sleep was the only one left, near the door, but she didn't mind. He was kind and truly worried about his brother. His eyes pleaded like the starving people she was accustomed to helping. "My brother is a good man, Brigid. Why this king comes, we do not know. There was a bloody battle one moon ago and my brother fought for our king. We thought peace had returned to our land. Now a messenger brings news of another king's approach." Liam paused, looking toward his brother who was busy ripping meat from a drumstick with his teeth. "He may be a simple man, but he knows right from wrong. He would never have taken revenge on someone's pet."

Brigid lifted a tin pitcher engraved with frolicking deer and poured cider for herself. "We'll make Dunlaing understand. How did your brother encounter Dunlaing when he has not yet arrived?"

Liam gulped his own cider then leaned back in his chair and crossed his arms. "My brother was hunting yesterday a half day's horse ride from here. The king, Dunlaing, had his fox traveling with his band. No one could have known he had such a pet. I'm praising God that the king allowed my brother to return to his family to make arrangements. He ordered my brother to appear at Cashel in two days. It was no use to hide in the hills. We'd be found, I'm sure. We'll see the king, but I'm fearing what he'll ask. There will be an honor price, and for a king that will be most all my cattle. With the size of my family, I can scarce afford it." His face paled. "If I do not pay it, the king can ask for my brother's life instead."

Brigid leaned her elbows on the table. "He seems to be a fair king. I'm sure he won't…"

"I'd feel better having ye there to speak on our behalf, Brigid."

What could she say?

She held her hand to her forehead. *A half day's ride away.* Of course. Dunlaing had set up camp at a respectable distance to allow for the announcement of his arrival. She turned to the accused man. "I must ask, does this king have a resident druid?"

Liam's brother shrugged his shoulders.

Liam rubbed his thumbs along his pale whiskers. "I heard no mention of one, not from my brother or from the other hunters there." He turned toward his wife. "Have you, darlin'?"

The mistress of the house paused from her task of covering children sleeping on the floor. She whispered, "I've heard of no druid present, though I have heard tale he employs a wicked one. The man's traveling apart from the king, as druids do. He's not around at the moment, so I hear."

Liam grinned. "The wife knows all. The way the ladies talk."

Brigid gathered up her dishes and prepared to take them outside for washing. She nodded at her host. "I appreciate the information. It will make my task much easier."

The next day Brigid boarded a wagon driven by Liam and filled with his family, including the unfortunate brother.

Chilling winds kicked in clouds from the southern sky. She snuggled up with three children under a woolen blanket. Their little faces gazed at her until they could contain their curiosity no longer.

"Where are ye from?"

"Do ye have a husband?"

She told them she was just passing through, and they questioned her on that too. She changed the subject. "Can anyone tell me something about this pet King Dunlaing had?"

"Aye." A boy about ten years old stood up. "I was with my uncle when I saw him first."

Liam's wife pointed her finger at him. "Sit down, child."

The lad plopped to the wagon bed. "The fox could do tricks, run to and fro, leap in the air and twist itself full circle before landing on the ground."

"Aye, aye!" the children chorused, clapping their hands together as though they could envision the performance.

Brigid held up her hand, and they quieted. "Suppose we could find another fox. I wonder if we could satisfy the king with a replacement."

The simple man nodded his head and motioned for his brother to stop the rig.

Liam retrieved a spear from the wagon's side. "Catching a fox is no easy task, but my brother always amazes me. Seems God replaced what he's lacking in words with his hunting skills."

"Don't kill it!" Brigid wiggled free of the children and joined the men outside the wagon.

Liam wagged his head. "We should be able to corner it. These woods right here hide a fox den. Seamus, come with us." He stopped short and tapped his fingers on his temples. "What are ye going to do, Miz Brigid? Teach a wild fox to do tricks in one day?"

"I'm not exactly knowing what I'll do." Brigid often didn't

have a plan when she decided to help someone. Matters always had a way of working out. "I just trust the Lord."

The boy sprang up from his corner of the rig and trotted off with his father and uncle, snickering as he went. The hunters hustled toward a wooded area. Seeing that Brigid hesitated, the children started in again.

"What's yer name?"

"How old are ye?"

"Do ye know how to spin? My mamai's got a new loom."

She smiled at them. "I'll tell ye later." Brigid hoisted her tunic above her ankles and hurried after the men.

The hunters seemed to know just where to go and were soon standing around a fix earth, just like they said.

Brigid snuck close to Liam. "I don't think it's necessary to frighten the animals."

Seamus spoke. "Shush. What do women know 'bout hunting?"

His father pulled him aside. "Seamus, ye don't know anything 'bout this lass. If yer smart, ye'll keep quiet till ye do." Liam turned to Brigid with his finger over his lips. "Think ye can nab one?"

"Let me try." She scooted close to the opening in the rock. She muttered not words, but soft sounds.

A red paw emerged, then disappeared. She continued. Seamus sighed loudly. Moments later a full-grown fox poked his head out and blinked in the filtered sunlight. He curled up in Brigid's cloak and she drew him to her heart. He was warm and reminded her of Puddin.

The hunting party traipsed back to the wagon in silence. Seamus had to be tugged along by his uncle. The boy's jaw hung open like the mouth of a slain boar.

The Eoghanachtan king's castle was under construction. A guard stopped them just short of the stone ring encasing it.

The fox trailed Brigid as she approached the gangling man who gazed down at her.

"What's yer business?"

"A fox for King Dunlaing. Has he arrived?"

The guard snapped his chin upward. "He has. If ye have a gift, ye can leave it with me."

"Oh, nay. 'Tis important I speak to him myself."

"Ye have business with him?"

Brigid sighed. Had she not said so? She bowed her head slightly. "Most certainly. Tell him Brigid of Glasgleann brings the fox he lacks." Dunlaing knew she didn't live at Glasgleann any longer, but he'd recognize the name.

Before long, Brigid, Liam, Liam's brother, and the fox were granted audience. They stepped round masons hammering loose blocks of limestone as they followed the guard.

The visiting ruler entered the makeshift hall in the same manner he had approached Brigid many years before, with purple robes flowing and his scepter stretched out before him. He pointed it at her and she touched it.

"Ah, Brigid. I do remember ye. Yer father sought to put ye in my service some time back."

"Aye, King Dunlaing, and ye gave me my freedom instead. I am forever grateful." She bowed, expressing sincerity.

He seated himself on an armchair, too ordinary for a king. "What brings ye to Cashel?"

"I could ask ye the same."

He laughed so hard Brigid thought he'd split the laces on his royal robes. "War is not a matter to be discussing with a lass like you. Unless ye've become a warrior, and I see no weapons." He bobbed his head as though looking for a shield and spear that he knew didn't exist.

It was enough of a distraction to keep Brigid from explaining her presence in Munster.

She opened her arms wide then folded them at her waist. "I've brought the king's fox."

"So I've heard."

The animal peeked from behind her skirts. She held her breath and prayed, believing God wouldn't let the poor simple man be punished.

Dunlaing squinted. "Aye, looks like him. Mine did tricks. If this is an acceptable replacement for my pet, it will fetch like a dog."

A servant produced a yarn ball, and Dunlaing threw it under the red curtain cloaking the doorway. The fox dashed after it and squeezed under the fabric. The animal returned shortly with the ball between its pearly teeth and then dropped it at the ruler's feet.

"Amazing. What else can it do?"

Brigid forced a smile. "'Tis a pet fit for a king. I have yet to be entertained by its games, but if it pleases ye, I beg ye to hold nothing against this poor man who killed the fox that ran through yer camp earlier."

Dunlaing glared at Liam and his brother. "We shall have a test. If the animal fails, the man who drove his spear through the heart of my pet will meet a similar fate. However, if this fox does everything I expect, then I accept that it truly was a mistake, and I'll not hold him responsible." He snapped his fingers and the fox jumped into the air, twisting itself into a ring so that its snout and tail nearly touched. Before it reached the ground, the animal straightened out and landed on its feet.

The king gathered the fox onto his lap. "'Tis him, 'tis him! He's been restored from the dead. Go now!"

Liam didn't want to take chances. He whisked them away from Cashel quickly. During the journey the children had more

89

questions, blurting them out at once like jabbering seabirds fighting over bait.

Brigid patted the head of Liam's eldest. "Seamus, why don't ye tell them what happened."

The effusive lad happily obliged while she gazed at the woods they trotted past.

She thought she spied a red fox near the area where they'd captured the one they brought the king. Had the fox escaped the king?

"Aye, I've seen her, that Brigid of Glasgleann." Dunlaing slammed his fist on the arm of his ill-carved chair.

Ardan stood in front of the king, hoping not to reveal too much delight in the news. His assistant, Troya, stood in his shadow. "Do ye know where she's staying?" Ardan tried desperately to motion Troya away, but she wouldn't oblige.

Troya pulled on Ardan's walking stick. "We've got to find her."

Dunlaing groaned. "Did ye have to bring yer apprentice with ye, Ardan? I've plenty to worry about without that woman causing a ruckus and disturbing the ruling king." He motioned to Troya and she stepped hesitantly forward, dropping her mangy ash-colored head toward the ground. Dunlaing pointed to the door. "Make sure he doesn't spot ye on yer way out."

Ardan knew the king's remark would throw the old woman into a rage.

Troya popped her head up and pointed a crooked finger at the king. "I am a druidess and a poet of satire. Kings should fear me. Listen to me."

Ardan pushed her away again and whispered, "Wait for me outside."

A guard helped with the request.

After she was behind the red curtains and rock walls,

Dunlaing muttered, "Why do ye keep her, Ardan? She's no poet, and no one fears her satire. She's a sham."

"She still learns, king."

"She's as old as my seanmhathair. Take up a younger apprentice."

Ardan said nothing.

King Dunlaing accepted a cup from a servant, sniffed at it, then threw it to the dirt floor, slinging golden liquid across one stone wall. He rocked on the flimsy chair. "I have to live in these conditions while this king's house is rebuilt. And if that were not enough, that Brigid woman comes to insult me."

Ardan could not believe his luck. "She was here?"

A servant retrieved the cup and backed out of the room.

"She visited with the intent of returning my pet fox. Or so I thought. She deceived me, that one. The fox left my presence almost as soon as she did."

The complaint was petty, but the king had information Ardan needed. "How long ago was that, king?"

"Yesterday. Enough of that. What news have ye?"

Ardan sped through tales of warring clans as rapidly as possible and returned to Troya.

The old woman paced beside their horses. "I've read it in the stones, Master Ardan. I know the time has come. Once the honor price of blood is paid, the gods will be pleased and I'll have trouble no longer."

This pleased Ardan. Long ago he'd found an unsuspecting companion who held a grudge against Brigid. He had allowed her to think he would restore her honor, though he never expressly said so, and she had no idea what he was really going to do.

Ardan circled Troya, meditating on his schemes. If his original plan had worked, Troya would have found the lass at her daughter's home and plunged a dagger into Brigid then. But it hadn't worked and as a high druid, he could not do it himself. The gods expected druids to obey a strict code of behavior. He needed someone else to commit necessary but unseemly deeds. He'd done it before when he hired beggars to dress in white robes and terrify the monks. And successful, that was. Those men had done little to advance Christianity since.

Troya shifted from one foot to the other and hissed, "Why do ye do that marching around? Makes my head spin."

"Silence!" His pacing habit helped him compose his words and served to unnerve those watching. He delighted in the experience, thought it more delicious than a harvest's first fruits.

He continued to pace around the old woman and think. This Brigid, the one a passing prophet once spoke to him about, had received the prophecy of being either a curse or a blessing. And now she had become a Christian with works and deeds, not in word only. Her power was so great that her god obeyed her command of destruction. She'd already cursed an apple orchard and seen its red fruit shrivel like beached salmon. Her displays of power had to cease. He paused and brought his fingers to his chin. If not extinguished, then perhaps such power could be used for his purposes.

Ardan tapped the old woman's shoulder with his walking stick. "Ye'll have the honor ye deserve, and the gods will know. They bless those who have high standing among men."

Gullible woman. Her bitterness had caused her to be rejected by the master of Glasgleann, opening the door for Ardan to use her. Things were going well. Eventually, Brigid would be eliminated by Troya's hand and King Dunlaing would have Troya executed.

Troya grinned. Her mouth contained few teeth. She bowed in front of him. This was almost too easy.

"Troya, at times it is a burden that I am the only one in all of southern Ireland who understands the skirmish that must take place – a conflict not resolved with swords on a battle-field, nay."

She cocked her head and wrinkled her thin nose. No matter. He alone understood. This struggle was for the hearts of the entire Irish race. He had to be clever and timely to assure that everyone would do as Troya did – bow to him, the leader of all the druids, and not to the god of Patrick and Brigid.

He remembered the prophet's words. "Brigid, the one born to Brocca, shall be Ireland's curse or blessing. I cannot predict which path she will follow."

The prophet couldn't predict. That could only mean that the woman's actions would determine her fate. Ardan pondered the meaning and circled his apprentice once more. She stared with questioning eyes which he ignored.

A blessing was Christianity's way of saying that belief in their god would overtake the island; but a curse – that was something for a druid to command.

CHAPTER

"HOPE DEFERRED MAKES THE HEART SICK,
BUT A LONGING FULFILLED IS A TREE OF LIFE."
PROVERBS 13:12

When Brigid returned from delivering the fox, she thought it best not to stay so close to Dunlaing, and bid an affectionate farewell to Liam, his brother and his family. Ardan was Dunlaing's druid and he was after her. Besides, she wanted to head west toward her mother. All she knew was that her mother belonged to a druid in Munster, but somehow she'd find her.

Meandering through the countryside and around rocky outcrops and clusters of forests, she kept her eyes toward the setting sun. She attempted to collect all the bits of information she had in her mind and make sense of them.

Cook had said the druid treated her mother well. How could she know?

Brigid slowed the horse to allow herself time to think. She remembered that strange shepherd who had surprised her at Glasgleann. He'd said Cook had not told her everything. Brigid smacked her hand on her forehead. MacFirbis's woman had spoken of the love of her youth! They had to be one and the same.

94

Brigid shook her head thinking of how impulsive she had been, running off so fast. She should have gone to see Cook before leaving. Now she'd have to manage on what little information she had.

Her mother knew Christ as her Savior. Brigid breathed deeply in that promise. *May God lead me to her.*

The air was moist, chilly, and fresh. There were no fires nearby, and thus no people. Brigid loved people, but being alone with her thoughts and prayers would certainly help her decide what to do next.

What else could she remember? She halted her horse and slipped down from the saddle. "C'mon, horse. We'll think on this as we walk." Perhaps traveling on foot would help shake the webs from her memory.

She and her mother had both heard Patrick teach. Many Christians learned from Patrick's teachings so perhaps that wasn't so unusual after all.

She sighed and patted the horse. "I'll name ye Geall, which means pledge, because the first time I met ye I vowed to ride ye until I found my mother."

A drizzle fell, threatening a downpour. She'd have to find shelter. Brigid cupped her hands to keep the rain out of her eyes and surveyed the horizon. Something dark jutted up from the ground. Curious, she made her way toward it. When she reached the object, she was disappointed to find it was a just a rock, not the door to a shelter.

"What ye search for is not on that stone."

The voice behind her made her scream out. She spun around and gaped at a pair of frosty blue eyes peering out from under a rain-soaked dove-white hood. She let herself breathe again. Those were not Ardan's dark eyes.

"Whoa, now. Ye'll scare yer horse, ye will. Didn't mean to startle ye. My name's Bram."

She backed away to have a better look at him. "A druid?"

"Who else would ye expect to see at a druid's stone?"

"A what?"

"Druid's stone. See those marks there?"

The rain pelted the surface of the rock, making it difficult to see anything. Brigid rubbed her thumbs across scratches in the stone. Along the edges of the rock there were several carved marks, lines really. They varied in length and seemed to be gathered in groups. At unpredictable intervals the marks seemed to break free from the others like dandelion seeds bouncing away from a stem.

She shook her head. "'Tis not Latin."

The druid agreed.

"'Tis not Irish either."

"What an intelligent lass to discern so. Come, I'll give ye shelter from the rain."

"Wait. Are ye associated with a druid named Ardan or his druidess assistant?"

"Certainly not. I am not any king's druid either. I am Bram, druid of the island Ennis Dun."

The druid led Geall past the strange stone and into a grove of trees. The branches above helped sieve the rain a bit, but Brigid was still damp and uncomfortable. They stopped just outside a shelter of sticks and animal skins.

"This is a camp I just built, but it's dry enough. Please." He motioned for her to enter while he tied up the horse.

Inside, a tiny fire was smoking within a ring of stones. Brigid had to duck, but when she sat down the shelter seemed large enough. She noticed a bag of rolled-up parchment tucked at the back of the hut.

"So ye know how to read, do ye?" The druid entered behind her and stoked the fire with logs. He sat across from her with his back to the bundle of parchments.

"A bit. A monk named Cillian of Aghade taught me."

The firelight made the druid's face glow, a face that was

anciently wrinkled. His pale hands barely showed themselves under the thick white cloak he wore.

He motioned to the fire. "Warm up a bit. Then drape yer cloak over the twigs near the smoke."

He had rigged a clothesline in the tiny space. The man seemed quite comfortable living in the woods. Where was Ennis Dun and why had he left there? More disturbing was what he'd said to her when they first met, that she wouldn't find what she looked for on that stone. "I do know how to read, druid, even if the meaning of your stone writing has eluded me for the moment."

"Well, like I said, that stone is for druids."

She rung the water from her cloak and draped it over the clothes rope. "A secret language?"

"Suppose ye could say that, aye."

She glared at him. Was he part of a scheme to turn her over to Troya? "Why did ye say what I'm looking for is not on the stone? How do ye know what I'm looking for?"

"'Tis a druid's business to know such things."

Such druid talk was maddening.

"And druids are brothers? Of one mind?"

Bram shook the rain from his cloak, flinging drops of water over the flames that sizzled in complaint. He hung his garment next to hers. "There is a code we live by. But nay, lass, I would certainly not say one mind."

"This makes no sense. Cook says druids speak in riddles. I wish ye'd just tell it plain."

He waved his hands over the fire, crossing them several times. "I am very old. I have time no more for riddles. This Cook who says this 'bout druids, who is she?"

"Cook of Glasgleann. She raised me ever since I was separated from my mother."

The druid's eyes grew round like a cornered badger's. "Glasgleann? Up in Leinster?"

"Aye. Dubthach is master there." Why was she telling him so much? She couldn't stop. She'd had no one to talk to all day but Geall the horse.

The druid's face brightened. His lips turned into a grin. "'Tis you! I thought it might be, I did."

More puzzling words. "Do ye know me?"

"Aye, I'll say I do. I snatched ye up from the ground the day ye were born. Yer mother, Brocca, birthed ye right on my doorstep. Yer all grown up now, but I can see in yer eyes it is you, Brigid."

She could hardly breathe. She held her hand to her chest and gasped.

The druid drew her into his arms. "A blessing. Tell me ye've become a blessing. Ah, dear child."

She wriggled free. "Yer my mother's master? The druid who purchased her from Dubthach?"

"Aye, that I am."

"Praise be to God!" Brigid jumped to her feet, bumping her head on the roof of the shelter. Her hair stuck in the branches and she squirmed.

"Let me help ye."

"Nay. Just tell me. Where's my mother?"

He helped anyway, gently freeing strands of hair from the grip of the twigs. "I told ye I'm the druid of Ennis Dun. Moved out there a few summers ago. Too many people near Cashel now. A druid needs peaceful retreat. That's where she is, Ennis Dun." After the last hair was free, he returned to the fire.

"Then she lives?"

"Oh, aye, indeed."

"Why don't ye free her?" Brigid resisted the urge to grab the old man by his tunic laces and make him confess to the sin of keeping mother and daughter apart.

"She would be worse off without me. It would be shameful to set her off alone."

Tears flowed without warning down Brigid's face. "She wouldn't be alone! She knew where I was. She would come and get me. Why would that be shameful?"

A wolf howled not far away.

"Quiet down now, lass. Ye'll be calling all the wild animals to us now that the sun has set. There's more to tell ye."

"Then tell me."

The druid Bram stroked his bony fingers over his chin. "She's better off staying put because she's blind."

Brigid held onto her chest again as if she'd have to hold in her pounding heart. "Ye said she was fine."

He smiled again. "Being sightless doesn't mean one is not well, my dear. My eyes are old. They don't see as well as they used to. But I get along fine. I have traveled for so many years that I scarcely need them anymore to make my way. Yer mother's that way in the dairy. She functions well there, she does."

"I must go see her. Does she ask about me?"

"She does, and I tell her yer well."

"Ye make up stories."

The druid's lips pressed into a thin line under his whiskers. He grabbed a stick and flung it into the fire – revealing for the first time an emotion other than gentleness.

"I'll forgive ye for that insult, young Brigid. Ye know nothing of druids."

She gritted her teeth and then let her anger go. "Ye mean druids don't make up stories?"

"I told ye druids lived by a code, nay?"

Her cheeks grew as hot as sun-baked stones. "Ye didn't tell me what that means."

He drew his withered fingers through his long mane of snowy hair. He might be impatient with her, but no more than she was with his ambiguous talk.

"One thing it means is that druids are truthful. They do not make up stories."

The only other druid she'd met was Ardan. While he had failed to tell her everything, what he did tell her about the pregnant mother being alone and needing help had been factual.

"Why a code? What does it matter?"

Bram's eyes were red-rimmed, and he tried to smother a yawn. She would get little more information from him that night.

The old man rubbed his weathered cheeks. "I will tell ye this: druids understand the spiritual world. They train for many years and learn from elder druids. They read the ogham writing like ye saw on the stone. They travel over many roads and talk with many people. If they were to make up stories or cause physical harm to those they meet, the gods would take revenge because the druids are…" He paused and closed his eyes. "They are spiritually tuned."

Brigid wanted to tell him that the One True God already knew what druids did, and what any man or woman did for that matter. But Bram *was* very old and his fortitude for the day was spent. Tomorrow she could ask him about curses and other druid activities, but right now there was one thing she had to know. "Will ye take me to see my mother?"

He lay down and pulled a woolen blanket up to his shoulders. "Ah, young Brigid. I was wondering when ye'd ask." With his eyes closed, his breathing took on a rhythm.

"Bram? Ye'll promise me, please? Will ye show me where she is?"

He grunted and bent one eyebrow over a squinted eye. "Ah, child. I will take ye, but I have to drop in on a bishop first. Ye'll go with me, aye?"

"I'll go, just so long as ye take me to see her right after."

She grabbed a blanket for herself from underneath the parchment rolls.

He whispered. "By the druid's code, I will."

A stick, the druid's walking stick, prodded her side, awakening Brigid. He spoke like a scolding mother. "Hurry along. One must not tarry in this territory."

Brigid rolled over onto her back. There were trees above her head. How had he taken down the camp without her noticing? She must have been exhausted from her travel. Knowing that she'd soon see her mother prompted her to rise. She popped out of her covers and rolled them up.

The old man had everything packed on his back.

"Let my horse carry that for ye. Do ye not have a beast yerself?"

Bram let the bag drop from his shoulders, and she carried it over to Geall.

"Once, long ago, I did. I'm so used to traveling without one now. Don't suppose I could even mount a horse anymore."

Bram was old indeed, and his legs were short but strong from much walking. His gait was straight and confident.

Brigid shook her finger at him. "Nonsense. Ye can do it, and I'll help. We'll travel much faster that way. I'll help ye up first, then I'll get on."

What sounded simple took many attempts. Bram's legs were hearty, but his arms weren't. He was not able to pull himself up far enough to reach the horse's back.

"Maybe if I get on first. Then I can lend ye an arm." Brigid mounted and gripped the horse's mane with one arm and held out the other to the druid.

His eyes grew round. "I don't think this will work."

She was sure it would. "Let's try."

He grabbed on to her arm, hiked one leg and then slid down to the ground with a thud.

"Oh, dear, are ye hurt?"

He twisted his head back and forth. "Nay, but I told ye it would not work. Yer as weak as I am, ye are. I'd better walk." He rose with the help of his walking stick. The fall had shaken him. He moved about like a tethered ox and seemed to carry as much weight.

She glanced around. Was there something he could stand on? "What about that druid stone? Could ye put a foot on it and walk yer way up?"

He peered at the upright stone, then back at her. He winked. "Let's try."

Brigid led Geall over to the rock and the druid hobbled behind. She got as close to the stone as she could. Bram gritted his teeth and pushed one leg up the rock. When he was high enough to reach her, she lunged with all her might and he bounced up onto the horse's back. How they kept from falling headfirst back on the rock, she didn't know.

"Yer quite clever, lass." Bram secured his walking stick by weaving it through his bag's laces and then they were ready.

Day was just arriving, bringing golden hues to the dark sky. Bram instructed her to travel through the forest but to keep close to a well-traveled path leading north. "There's thieves on the road. We may still meet them, but this way we won't be seen from a distance."

"I never saw any thieves on my way here, just beggars."

"That may be, but yer in the wilds of Munster now. And on this particular road, they're one and the same."

"They're just hungry, then." Why was she the only one with compassion for the people?

Steering the horse through the underbrush was laborious. The road would be much easier. Why hide?

The druid grunted behind her. "Hungry? Perhaps they are. But they do not work for their food, nay. They choose to steal it from others, sometimes killing them in their effort.

Ye've much to learn that Dubthach has not taught ye, young one."

Someone *was* out to kill her. Ardan and Troya were more of a threat than any beggars they might meet.

"Tell me about this secret druid code, Bram. Does it pertain to curses?"

He was quiet for a long time. His silence worried her. She pulled the horse to a stop and dismounted. "I'll go no further until ye speak the truth of it."

He smiled down at her. "I cannot lie, but neither can I reveal any sworn secrets. If ye will not travel on with me, I'll go alone."

She smiled back. He was old and feeble. She was young and strong. "As ye wish. But ye'll have to get down first."

"Ye'll help me."

"I'll not."

He sat there a moment, staring at her. Then he cocked his head to one side. He lifted his robed arm and placed his finger to his lips. He whispered, "Quiet. Get back on the horse. They're coming."

"Who... "

"Now!"

The sound of running feet filtered through the trees and Brigid threw herself back on the horse. Within moments men dressed in black hoods were visible on either side, carrying spears. Geall bolted and carried them past the bandits, who turned to pursue them.

Brigid steered the galloping horse to the road.

"Nay. To the left! Get to the left." Bram's squeaky voice was pitched high.

"Why?"

"Just do it!"

Brigid urged the horse off the road and into a riverbank. The river wasn't deep, but rocks in the bed caused the horse to

103

stumble a few times, threatening to send them sailing off headfirst.

She called over her shoulder. "Hold on!"

"I'm holding on to ye, but it's yer job not to get us thrown off. Steer him through that crag."

Up ahead she spied the rocks he spoke of. The druid knew the land better than Brigid, and those men meant to stab them and steal the horse. Given the choice of trusting a druid or facing death by impalement, she'd take a chance on Bram.

When they reached the rocks, she guided the horse up a narrow path. She could barely catch her breath. "They had no horses. They can't catch us now."

"Keep going."

The sky seemed to grow closer and the air thinner. Brigid's chest throbbed. She could only imagine how the flight must have jarred the old man's bones. "Let's stop here."

"Nay, we're almost there, we are."

The rocks gave way to a high plateau, invisible from the ground below. A cluster of stone buildings clung to one side of the cliff.

Quick breaths did little to help Brigid regain her strength. "Please, let's rest a moment." It was cold at that elevation. She thought she'd be warmer on the ground and dismounted.

"As ye wish." Accepting her hand, the old man carefully wiggled down from the horse.

Brigid stomped her feet on the ground, trying to warm her toes.

"Here, take this." Bram offered a woolen blanket from his pack.

She thanked him. "Why are we here, Bram? A druid visiting a Christian bishop?"

"I'm here to ask him to leave." The old man led the horse to a frosty stream for refreshment. "I'm sure it's warmer in his house. Shall we go?"

"Not till I get some answers. What know ye of Ardan and his apprentice?"

"Ah, stories people tell, that's all. I live on a far-off island."

Brigid padded over to the stream where the horse drank, his nostrils snorting warm air. She tossed the blanket over her shoulder. "Ye travel much. Ye told me."

"Aye, all druids do. Still, I have never met him or his student ye speak of."

"But ye have this secret code. Something all druids know."

The horse finished drinking and they headed to the building. Brigid measured her steps, making them painstakingly sluggish.

Bram blew air into his fist. "Ye make it sound as though I'm plotting with Ardan. Not all druids follow the code, and to those who don't, I owe no allegiance."

"Are ye saying Ardan does not abide by the code?" They were getting close and she had to know.

"I have no proof, nay, but I hear he lacks the virtue of... truth."

Brigid wrung her hands. "Please stop weaving mysteries. What do ye mean by 'lacking truth'? He lies? 'Bout what?"

The druid drew his white hood over his head, leaving a few pearly curls peeking out. He blended into the stark bald rocks like a wood mouse in a pile of twigs. From within the depths of his thick cloak, he spoke. "Truth doesn't change. Ye can't bend it to please yerself. Talk is that's what he does. Ye can't trust gossip, unless ye hear it from other druids, dear. I trust what I heard. If ever there were a judgment for that man, I fear... "

"Bram, welcome! I see ye brought a visitor." A man half Bram's age, but twice Brigid's, appeared at the threshold of the stone house.

Brigid whispered into Bram's hood, "He already knows who ye are and yer asking him to leave?"

He motioned her away. "Bishop, meet Brigid, formerly of Glasgleann."

"Welcome, welcome. Come in and eat. I've broth on the fire."

They trailed in after him. The house was cavernous and nearly bare. Pegs on the walls held utensils and clothes. One finely crafted table and matching chair shadowed the central fire ring. A lone cross, devoid of embellishment, hung on the wall opposite the door. If the bishop had any parchments of Scripture, they were housed elsewhere.

The bishop hoisted two stools from the corner and they all sat, the bishop on the chair, and the visitors on stools.

Brigid's weary legs and empty stomach overruled her reservations and loosened her tongue. "'Tis so cold up here. Why do ye live on this rock, sir?"

He handed them tin mugs. The smell of lamb stew caused her to further abandon her manners. She gulped the whole thing down and he refilled it. She realized what she had done and her cheeks turned hot. "I'm so sorry. I forgot to give thanks to God."

The bishop turned his ruby bulbous nose toward Bram. "Have ye brought me a Christian?"

Bram shifted and crossed his knees beneath his tunic. "Not meaning to. Found her on the road here and she needed help."

Brigid set her mug on the bishop's polished table. "'Twas not exactly that way. He found me, aye. I was traveling along and..."

The bishop rubbed his large nose with his finger. "No matter. I'm glad yer here. And what brings you, Bram? Just stopping off on your way somewhere?"

Bram finished his broth and rosy color returned to his pasty cheeks. "This is my destination, bishop. I came to speak with ye."

106

Now that he'd warmed up, and she had too, Brigid took their cloaks and hung them on the wall hooks.

The holy man waved a thick hand at the druid. "Speak, then."

Bram smiled and studied his palms before coming up with a simple inquiry. "Why did ye come here?"

The bishop sucked in a long breath. "I told you before. The church in Rome sent me. Must we go over this again, Bram? I'm to bring Christianity to this part of Ireland. We have spoken of this many times."

Bram leaned forward, one elbow on his knee. "The gods whisper to me, Bishop. I hear their words in the breeze, I do. 'Tis dangerous for ye. Ye should sail back over the sea. No one here will listen to ye anyway, and I'm warning ye to save yer life."

The bishop held a hand over his gut and laughed the way someone does when nothing is funny. Although Brigid didn't believe in Bram's gods, she felt insulted for him. He was trying his best to save this man from the blood-hungry men they'd encountered earlier on the road. As far she could tell, the bishop was alone up on the crag.

She had an idea. "Why don't ye join the monks? Yer all Christian brothers."

Again the bishop snorted. "The monks are isolationists. I am an official church representative. This is how it's done in Christendom. I come and ordain priests; they set up churches."

Brigid scooted her stool closer to the holy man. "But pardon me, bishop. Cillian the monk has been to Rome. He has brought back..."

"I know, I know." The bishop's face was red-hot. "They're Irish monks all the same. I have been *sent* here..."

This time Bram did the interrupting. "Aye, by the church. We've heard that." He licked his lips. "I do not understand it,

I don't. We are Irish. We welcomed ye when ye first set yer sandal on our shores. Why do ye seek to disrupt our connection with our gods?"

Brigid tried to grab his arm, but it was too late. The druid was standing, intending to leave.

The bishop stood also. "I have been sent here to convert... " He stopped and shook his head, giving up.

Bram glared at the plump man. "Dear bishop, would ye be granting us some supplies before we leave? We've a long trip back."

Brigid remained between them like a cornered hedgehog.

The bishop grunted. "I'll walk you out. That's all." He grabbed his cloak from the back of the door.

Brigid glanced quickly at Bram. He had been insulted yet again. She retrieved their own outer garments.

Bram fingered the sleeve of his cloak. "In Ireland, sir, we consider it the gravest insult to be refused hospitality."

The bishop thrust his shoulders like a rooster. "I've shown it. I gave you broth, and I'm escorting you out. Please, dear druid, don't waste my time by coming back."

Bram gazed at the floor a moment then lifted his eyes toward the bishop. "I would not ask this of a poor man."

Brigid wondered at what Bram said. She hadn't seen any riches, but then the druid was acquainted with the bishop and she wasn't.

Bram held out his hand to the holy man, but the bishop did not offer to assist him. Bram pointed at the wall cross. "I do not wish to see yer blood shed, sir. Not the way that god of yours was."

Brigid made the sign of the cross on her chest, as did the bishop. Apparently her mother's master knew something of the Savior.

Bram turned back to the door where the bishop was waiting. "That's why I came, it is. To warn ye."

The bishop held onto his large gut again. "I need no warning, druid."

Bram nodded. "Brigid, hang his cloak back up for him. We do not require escort."

Brigid took the thick black garment, slung it on a hook near the window and hurried out the door ahead of the druid. What the exchange meant, she wasn't sure. She was still hungry and chilled, but she would not require the druid to remain with such an inhospitable host and she was eager to reunite with her mother.

Bram and the bishop hustled after her. "How'd ye do that?" Bram asked.

She turned to face the men. "What?"

The bishop rushed to her. "I'll get you a wagon and some bread and cheese. Will that do for your journey?"

She was stunned. "Aye, that would be excellent."

He scampered off toward an outbuilding and Bram stared at her. "Ye hung his cloak on a sunbeam."

"Yer daft. Of course not. I hung it on a hook."

"A sunbeam, I tell ye."

Even after they were back on the road, Bram kept insisting she'd performed some kind of miracle and that the bishop had been so amazed he bundled up more than what he'd offered and sent them off with warm blessings. Brigid didn't understand. She was sure there had been a hook near the window, although the sun streaking through had blinded her a bit.

Bram clapped his fingers together. "I think I need to learn a bit more 'bout yer god."

CHAPTER

"...LET YOUR LIGHT SHINE BEFORE MEN, THAT THEY MAY SEE YOUR GOOD DEEDS AND PRAISE YOUR FATHER IN HEAVEN."
MATTHEW 5:16

Ardan soon learned that Cook and Brian sought him, so he convinced Troya to return to Leinster to distract them.

"I'll take care of that young one," he'd assured his elderly apprentice.

Tracking down the lass had taken some time. Finally, he rooted out some wanderers who told him the girl and an ancient druid had headed up the crag to see a bishop. Ardan threatened one of them with a curse. The fool became Ardan's hostage and led him up the path to the bishop's dwelling.

They arrived too late. Brigid and the druid had already left.

Overpowering the holy man hadn't been difficult. The pitiful bishop was shaking against the Roman-fashioned chair Ardan had tied him to. "I've told you everything, druid. All I know is they headed to Ennis Dun. That's where Bram lives."

Ardan's guide, a weak man with a weak mind, cowered in the corner. When Ardan approached the man, he shrieked.

Ardan smiled. "I'm not going to harm ye. Not so long as ye do what I command."

The chicken-hearted man bobbed his head. How perfect. Ardan had chosen his collaborator well. He returned to the bishop and lifted the bound man's chin with his walking stick until he met Ardan's gaze, his eyes still watering from the beating he'd received. Ardan lowered the stick and demanded information.

"Why were they here?" Ardan suspected Brigid had converted a fellow druid, this Bram, to her god. If that were the case, he'd need to know before the bishop met his end.

"He came to ask me to leave."

"Brigid. A Christian, is she not?"

"I believe so, why?"

Ardan slammed his stick to the floor. "I'll ask the questions. This druid... was he in agreement with Brigid's religion?"

The bishop swallowed hard. "No. He asked me to leave. He said no one would listen to me in Ireland."

Ardan smiled. Ah, the druid *was* his brother. Soon Brigid would be trapped like a fox in its lair. He'd bring her back to Troya who would kill the girl in King Dunlaing's territory. Ardan would make sure all the clans knew that Brigid had been a Christian preaching false beliefs. Then he'd proclaim Troya a nefarious witch driven by the Tuatha De Danann and he, the king's high druid, would be acclaimed as the one who had defeated her and brought her to justice under the king. Even King Dunlaing would bow to his authority over the spirits then.

Ardan picked up his stick and prodded the man's belly. "Living alone here, are ye?"

The bishop swayed back and forth in the chair, attempting to avoid Ardan's teasing. "Yes."

Foolish foreigner to cloister himself like this.

Ardan backed away. He tossed a chunk of peat on top of the fire to ensure it was smoldering properly. "Why was the lass with him?"

"I don't know."

The fire was hot enough to boil water. Satisfied, Ardan spun to face the prisoner.

"There's more, aye? There's something 'bout her ye haven't told me." Ardan didn't know if the bishop had more to reveal, but he often used the tactic to squeeze information from timid folks. The questioning had always been remarkably successful.

The bishop hung his head. "She performed a miracle." He glanced back at Ardan. His voice shifted in tone. "She hung my robe on a sunbeam. I don't know why it would matter to you."

It mattered. Brigid was becoming powerful enough to sway minds. When she ran from Troya, she'd somehow linked up with a druid. But the lass could not hide from someone like Ardan. He would not lose the battle. He needed to hear no more.

"Come over here." He gestured to the weakling in the corner.

Ardan stuck a torch into the fire pit coals until it burned yellow-hot. A druid could cause no harm, and he wouldn't. He turned to leave, handing the torch to his accomplice.

"It couldn't be helped if an accident occurred." He glared into the meek man's eyes until he was certain the fellow understood. "Tragedies happen all the time, especially in Ireland. The bishop should have understood that before he settled on our isle."

The bishop wailed from his chair. Portly as he was, his efforts to hobble the chair across the floor were useless. Despite a struggle, he couldn't free himself. Ardan knew how to tie knots. His father was a fisherman.

Ardan paused for a moment, watching a spark drop from the torch and fall to the rush-covered floor. Then he marched out the door. Soon, the murderer followed, his hands shaking and his face pale as ashes. Smoke started to emerge from the open door as the fire took hold.

"Off with ye!" Ardan squeezed a piece of Roman silver he'd rescued from the bishop's pocket into the man's palm.

As Ardan picked his way down the rocky slope on one of the bishop's horses, a stronger animal than his own, he heard a dull thud come from inside the house, followed by mounting screams. Once the bishop toppled himself, he'd never rise again. *Well, one less Christian to worry about.*

Wagon tracks were easy to spot on the muddy road. Ardan quickly determined which direction the druid and the lass were headed, and then he turned to a higher road. It was rocky and more difficult to navigate, but soon he'd be able to peer down on them and observe Brigid's actions from a distance.

He'd wait until the druid reached his home before claiming the lass. If Ardan managed things well, he could gain the allegiance of all of western Ireland. Yes, patience was in order. The brother who now had Brigid would surely help Ardan with some provisions for the return trip and perhaps even recommend a new apprentice to replace Troya. The plan was good.

"How surprising that the bishop was so generous. Bram, do ye know what's back here in the wagon?"

The druid was busy directing Geall, who was not accustomed to pulling a wagon. Brigid was glad to let Bram drive since she had no idea where they were headed.

Bram spurted words between commands to the horse. "Why don't ye tell me what's back there?"

"Apples, cheese, chunks of brown bread. There's even salted meat. And look here." She produced a gold chalice and held it up for him to see.

Bram huffed. "Wealth from the church, I suppose."

"The church?" Brigid thought only kings possessed such things.

"Aye. That church over the sea that sent Patrick here. Christians, I'm talking 'bout."

"Well, I'm hungry. Would ye have a bite?"

Brigid toted the food to the front of the wagon. She offered a prayer of thanksgiving and then shared the meal with her new friend. "How far to Ennis Dun?"

"Two days, likely. Would be much longer without the wagon. That is, if we don't get waylaid by beggars."

"Beggars? We've plenty of food. I'll feed them. Tell me, will the road take us all the way?" She munched on an apple much more tart than the one she had tasted in that foolish woman's doomed orchard, the one she'd visited while living with the monks. She handed Bram a chunk of cheese.

The food crumbled in his beard as he ate, and he flicked the mess away. "Oh my, we cannot get to an island on a dirt road, we can't."

She giggled.

"The journey will be difficult. There are many rocks to cross before we reach my raft."

"Ye've a raft? For the horse also?"

"Aye, but the wagon will have to stay on this side."

"I've never been to Ennis Dun. Do ye like it there?"

The druid sighed. "Of course ye've not been there. Not many have. It pleases me to live there because I'm not bothered. The place is my refuge after traveling among the poor and the privileged. Giving spiritual counsel, ah, 'tis hard work."

"Aye." She pretended to understand. Funny how this druid reminded her of Cillian's monks.

"But ye should know," he continued, "the weather's not always favorable." He reached behind her and snagged a slab of dried meat from a rush basket. "Is there anything besides food back there? Any more church gold? We should be prepared for bandits."

Brigid scrambled to the back and lifted blankets. "'Tis as

114

though he used this rig for storage. There's pots and pans, fleece blankets, a barrel of ale, more gold cups... "

"More gold, ye say? How many pieces?"

"I don't know. Seems there's a bag of them."

"Praise the gods. We can purchase our safe travel if need be, Brigid."

"There's only one God needs praising, Bram. He provides all our needs."

"Aye, praise yer god. And hope that the god of the sun keeps shining on us. 'Tis rain we'll be headed into tomorrow."

Ardan's vantage point was perfect. He could watch the old man and Brigid travel along the road and still be unobtrusive high on the cliff. The trees swallowed his shadow. He shed his white cloak, bundling it into his saddlebag.

He studied Brigid's small figure scrambling around in the rear of the wagon, uncovering items. In the sun's glint, he determined that the stash included several cooking pots. Wait. What was that? Something incredibly brilliant nearly blinded him when the sun bounced off the object.

Ardan strained to determine what it was. His eyes stung with flashes of white light that he hoped would soon abate. He rubbed his face, but by the time he was able to focus, the lass had covered the bed's contents with blankets and joined the druid at the reins.

Ardan would be patient. He'd waited nearly all his forty-two summers to achieve his place among the druids. His father had been wise to send him for training at a young age. Now he'd gained the privilege that comes with experience. The right to lead.

He allowed the wagon and its occupants to leave his sight. They were headed toward a druid stone. He'd examine it after they left and determine what the order of druids in this region had to promise him.

Brigid gazed at the clouds while they traveled. The day was fair. She couldn't imagine rain moving in anytime soon. Her thoughts wandered to the day she, Cook, and Brian had gathered at the seashore. She had examined clouds like those she saw now, trying to see shapes in them that would remind her of her mother. Today she had no clearer picture of what Brocca looked like, but it didn't matter. Her heart's longing would soon be fulfilled. She would be in her mother's arms soon.

"Has my mother been a good servant for ye?"

Bram's wrinkled lips curled up. "She's a milkmaid. Takes good care of what I need, she does. I think I told ye that."

"Humph. Well, can ye tell me what she looks like then?"

Brigid kept questioning the druid until he pleaded with her for rest. She took over driving while he dozed in the bed behind. He hadn't told her much. Brocca was thin with dark red hair. And she was blind.

Brigid was so overwhelmed by thoughts of her mother that she almost overlooked a huddle of beggars at the edge of the road. She stopped the wagon. The druid didn't wake.

"Take some cheese." She handed out all the food the peasants could stuff in their aprons and carry under their arms.

Her voice woke Bram. "What are ye doing, lass? Did they threaten us?"

She filled the last beggar's hands with dried meat and then returned to the reins before answering. She whispered so the poor people would not overhear the druid's insults. "Of course not. They're hungry, that's all. I stopped to feed them."

"Ye did what?" As fast as his old legs could carry him, Bram returned to the front. "We need that food! Ye only stop if someone points weapons at ye. Have ye the sense of a stone?"

"I'm doing my Lord's work by feeding the hungry."

Bram snatched the reins and maneuvered the wagon at a quick clip. "We'll be at the end of the road soon. The rest of the trip will be on foot. We'll have to make do on what we already filled our bellies with and tote the gold cups along with us. Ye didn't give those away, did ye?"

"Nay, just food."

"Ah, good. We'll likely meet many beggars, we will, and we'll need to pay them."

Brigid groaned. "I thought ye were unlike Dubthach. He was going to sell me to the king just because I gave things away."

Bram chuckled. "I'll not be selling ye. Here, 'tis different from Glasgleann, Brigid. Holding on to possessions until we must part with them, that's what we do to save our lives."

"But yer a druid. Doesn't yer position offer ye some privilege?"

He tightened his hands on the rope reins. "Not among thieves."

"Aren't people afraid ye'll put a curse on them or something?"

He laughed out loud. "Only Dubthach believes that. And I only threatened him to assure yer safety."

Brigid's head swirled like the dancing leaves around them. "Ye threatened Dubthach? Why? When?"

The druid dropped his voice low. "Oh, dear. I've said too much, I have. Yer mother will explain."

Brigid was about to question him more, but they'd reached another of those peculiar standing stones and Bram stopped the wagon.

"Wait here. Keep yer eyes on the surrounding woods while I read it."

"Nay. I want to learn to read it. Teach me."

Bram's clear eyes turned gray. "Ye'll stay here, I say. Becoming a druid takes many years of training, it does. A druid's language will not be shared without guidance from the gods." He hurried away.

117

What could he mean? The old druid was not nearly as protective over the first rock she saw, the one where she first met him. He'd said the lines represented something only druids understood. Not only did druids speak in puzzles, they apparently also read them.

She watched at a distance as Bram knelt beside the stone. He examined it beginning at the bottom left side. He ran his gnarled fingers over the marks, stopping every few moments to gaze at the trees that dropped their leaves like fox-frightened chickens shedding their feathers. Bram spat into his hand, sprinkled dirt on top and rubbed the paste onto the stone. What message could be so important? What was he reflecting on? What bizarre ritual was he performing?

Bram returned, but he did not acknowledge her inquisitive stare. Instead, he studied the trees, held out his hand toward the horse, and then drove on.

"What was that all about?"

He didn't answer.

She tried again. "Words that are written down tell stories. That's what I learned from Cillian the monk."

Still nothing.

Brigid had forgotten what she said until several moments later when the druid spoke. "Just stories? Is that all the monks are writing?"

A sharp wind blew from the south, bringing the smell of the ocean. She shouted an answer while retrieving a blanket from the back. "Nay, not just stories. Other things too."

Bram didn't respond until she returned to the seat next to him. He seemed to be unsettled since he studied the stone. More serious. He touched her hand with his. He was cold. She covered them both with the blanket.

He winked at her. "What other things do they write?"

"Do ye really want to know?"

"I do."

118

"Why is it fine for ye to know 'bout that, but I am not to know the druid's language?"

Bram's words sounded rehearsed. "A druid has a responsibility that can only be handled with years of training. The language, 'tis more than mere stories, even more than mere words." He pulled at the blanket with one hand. "I could teach ye, aye, but I've not enough time before the gods come for me." He smiled at her and wrinkles darted from his eyes like spokes on a wheel. "But stories... aye, we *can* share stories. Ye tell me yers. I'll tell ye mine."

A mystery, but perhaps learning some of the druids' stories, and pointing out the errors in them, might help Brigid reach him with the stories of Jesus.

She lowered her chin. "You first."

Bram began explaining about the branches of the oak tree and the mysteries they held. Just then a band of men lunged into their path.

Ardan saw the bandits and was torn. Should he rescue the druid? Druids have vast spiritual connections. Helping him might appease gods, but if the gods were responsible for the attack, Ardan's help would only bring trouble upon himself. Still, if he did nothing and Brigid was killed, his plan to use her and Troya to bring honor to himself would be ruined.

He looked down at his drab clothing. He was in disguise. No one would know who he was. A battle of wills raged in his mind. He was not a warrior. But a druid *can* defend himself.

While he debated, three aggressors shoved the lass and the old druid to the ground. They ransacked the wagon. What was that they held? Ardan squinted. His horse lost its footing, sending pebbles down the cliff toward the altercation. His presence was revealed. He'd now have to play the part of rescuer. The decision had been made for him. "Stop, thieves!"

The three men looked up, their eyes as round as full

moons. They saw him climbing down the cliff, bearing a dagger, and darted off into the woods.

The old druid struggled with his walking stick as he got to his feet. "Well, good man. Ye've certainly come at the right moment."

"Glad to help. Are ye hurt?" Ardan offered a hand then pulled it back and covered his mouth, pretending to shield himself from dust the tussle had stirred up. Hopefully, Brigid wouldn't recognize him.

Brigid stood brushing the road from her cloak. "Nay. No harm done. Bram?"

"I am well. We owe ye for yer help, sir." He reached into a bag and pulled out a golden goblet.

Ardan had never seen anything so luminous. He examined it closely, turning his back to the girl. The piece fit the curve of his fingers. The ornamentation circling the base was unlike anything he had ever seen. "Roman."

Brigid tapped his shoulder. "Excuse me?"

Ardan held the cup in front of his face. "Oh, I was just thinking to myself. This looks foreign. Where'd ye get such a lovely thing? From the merchant ships?" Ardan realized he'd been so caught up in admiring the piece he'd nearly forgotten his mission.

Brigid tried to look at him so he tilted his head away. She tended to the druid instead, flicking grime from his cloak as she spoke. "Nay. 'Twas a gift. One might not be enough to buy some new clothes. Bram, shall we give him another?"

Another? Ardan stared at the old man. "Well, I was just trying to help, that is all."

The old druid stepped forward. "I could use yer help when we get to the bay. This lass is on her way to see her mother. They have been separated since she was five seasons old."

Ardan stretched his tunic over his mouth, as if he were cold. It didn't appear that Brigid recognized him. As the old man mentioned Brigid's mother Ardan noted the sorrow in the girl's eyes. He'd trained himself to search for a person's weakness. Knowing such things was often advantageous. Brigid pulled on the edges of her cloak and glanced over her shoulder at the western horizon. She longed, ached, for her mother. It was clear.

The old druid pulled him aside. "'Tis an extremely important pilgrimage, ye see."

Ardan smiled. "Aye, I do see."

"If ye'd agree to help us, I'll see to it that ye get five of these exquisite cups. We'll be needing to get to my crannog with our possessions."

"Five? Kind of ye, sir. I'd be most happy to be of service."

A fortunate occurrence. Now Ardan would have Brigid cornered out in the bay.

He'd proceed slowly. If he sensed the old man would not be amicable to the scheme, he'd keep up his masquerade as a commoner and keep the gold vessels as a reward. Then he'd kidnap the lass during the Samhain. That all-important festival was approaching, a time when everyone dressed in disguise and the dead walked among the living. In that setting no one would know what had happened until it was too late.

"May I ask that ye carry on ahead of me and I'll catch up? I need to make a few arrangements at my home first," Ardan lied, returning the gold cup to the leather bag Bram had pulled it from.

CHAPTER

"ALL SINS CAST LONG SHADOWS."
OLD IRISH PROVERB

Ardan retraced the wagon's path until he arrived at the clearing bearing the ogham stone. He'd never seen this particular one. Since the ancient druid had intently studied it earlier, it had to have significance. If the druid was keeping something from him, Ardan wanted to know before he himself was cornered in the bay.

There were no other stones in sight. Having only one to interpret would make his task simple. A raven swept overhead, casting a long shadow over the stone on that unusually sunny autumn afternoon. The markings were not decipherable without adequate sunlight.

"Off with ye!" Ardan waved his walking stick at the bird hovering above his head. *What was happening?* With his robed arms billowing wildly, he must have stirred the ire of the tree gods. Leaves dropped with a sudden whirl of wind, bouncing up and striking his face.

The world around swirled, and Ardan lost his balance. He came crashing down at the base of the stone, striking his head against it. Warm trickles of blood dripped from his forehead onto the marks engraved on the stone, but his head hurt too much to make sense of it. Then all went black.

"Where do ye think he is?" Brigid cuddled close to the druid for warmth.

"I've been wondering myself, I have. Not likely a poor man would pass up the chance to get his hands on those goblets." Bram halted the horse.

"What's wrong?" Brigid glanced around for more robbers. The wind dislodged leaves from their treetop homes, but neither man nor animal was in sight.

"He said he was going back to his home, aye?"

"That's right."

He whipped the reins against the horse and started again, this time at an urgent clip.

"Bram, what is it?"

"We've been deceived, we have. If the man were going home, he'd have asked for one goblet in trust, left it for his family, and returned post haste."

"What do ye mean, deceived?" Brigid had to hold on to the side of the wagon to keep from being flung out. "Maybe the bandits caught him. We should go check. He might need help."

Bram wouldn't listen. The rig didn't travel fast enough for him so he stopped to hurl out everything he deemed unnecessary. With much effort, he tossed away the barrel of ale along with the pots and pans. He left only the sack of gleaming cups then scurried back to take up the reins.

Brigid stared at him. What had scared the man so? Bram gazed toward the horizon, ignoring her. What had she gotten herself into? Was this old druid mad? How did she know he really had her mother on his island?

On an impulse she leapt from the wagon, hitting the ground hard and scraping her face on fallen tree branches.

Bram halted a short distance away, scrambled down from

the wagon seat, and shuffled back to her. "Who's the daft one now?"

Her cheek lay in a paste of bloodied dirt. Her lungs refused to expand. She gasped, filling them with little pockets of air. She saw him creeping toward her, and she backed away on her knees. "I don't know ye. You may be the one who's a deceiver."

Bram reached out his hand, the color of sun-bleached shells. "Child, I want to help ye, I do. It's been hard for ye, living with Dubthach. Come. We've not much time."

Brigid dismissed his hand and scrambled to her feet. She was sore, scratched, but not hurt too badly. "How could ye know what my life at Glasgleann's been like? Some magical sense ye have?" She mocked him but couldn't hold back.

He shook his wispy hair loose from his hood. "Oh, I know, I do, because I've seen ye since that time you and Brocca were separated. And I've talked to Brian."

Brigid felt dizzy. Words stuck in her throat as she gasped for air to push them out. "Tell me how... how did ye see me? And Brian?"

"I will tell ye, but please, get back in the rig. Got to hurry." He handed her his walking stick.

The wind blew harder, stinging her raw cheeks. She'd have to go with the druid. If there were a chance her mother was on that island, she had to find her. The druid spoke oddly and was easily spooked, but putting up with the old man would be worthwhile if it meant she'd get her mother back. And certainly her mother *would* explain everything.

Her side ached as she pulled herself up to the wooden plank seat. She fingered her facial wounds and noted the rawness. Her fingernails were caked with dirt. What would her mother think? What would she say? It did seem idiotic to jump from the druid's wagon to save a poor man who was nowhere to be seen.

The druid snapped the reins against Geall's spotted back.

"Hold on. The gods are in the wind and they speak of danger. Long ago I built the crannog for times like these. We'll be safe with the servants, but we've got to hurry to make it before dark." His voice battled to be heard above the howling wind. A storm gathered on the horizon.

Before long the landscape changed. The terrain was so rocky that the wagon was of no use. Bran shouted directions. "We'll leave the wagon here. I'll tie the horse up under that rock shelter and come back for him later." The wind brought sheets of rain, coating the rocky earth with a shiny black film. "Take the bag!"

Brigid cared little about the treasure. She longed only for her mother's arms and a seat near a snug turf fire. She grabbed the sack anyway and threw it over her back. The metal inside thumped along her spine as she walked over and around slick, wet boulders. Bram, his white cloak providing a contrast to the darkening sky, seemed to navigate the rocks like a lizard as he carried his own pack.

"Hurry, now," he called back to her. "The water's rising, it is."

Brigid couldn't answer. She had to will her feet to take every difficult step. The rain hit harder, beating her shoulders like a drum. Finally, she forced out some words. "How much farther?"

Bram pointed to the hollowed-out base of a large tree. "We'll stop here just a moment – to rest."

They ducked beneath the finger-like roots. The ground was damp, but at least they were spared the constant splatter of angry raindrops. She tossed the bag of goblets outside the shelter.

"Let me look at ye." The druid nudged her chin upward and she gazed into his wintry face. He pulled a bundle of linen from his pack, dislodged one strip and patted her face with the cloth. "When we get to the crannog, I'll fetch some herbs for a poultice."

She didn't care. "My mother cannot see my wounds unless ye tell her."

He blinked, pulled his hood up, and waved his arm. "Keep going. Down this cliff I've a raft."

They darted back into the storm. The rain was sharper than before – splintered shards of ice. Brigid grabbed the bag of goblets and held it above her head like a shield. They skidded down an embankment where she spotted the raft hauled up on the beach, waves lapping close. Darkness descended, taunting them.

"Will we make it?"

Not answering, he dragged the raft down into the rising surf and pushed her onto it. Was this the same old man who earlier had not been able to mount a horse? Brigid wondered what kind of fear could drive the man to ignore his physical ailments, the hostile weather, and her foolish jump from the wagon, in his haste to return to the safety of his island fortress.

Rudely awakened by rain pounding his face, Ardan rolled to his side. He drew one hand up to his forehead and patted the throbbing spot. Moist warm blood mixed with the pelting rain. *The gods are angry.*

He pulled himself to his feet. Raising his peasant's hood did nothing to shield him from the damp. He retreated to the woods for shelter and slipped his tall frame under a brush pile. He had to have passed out for some time. The last he remembered, the sky was clear.

Ardan tore a strip from his undergarment, material that was of better quality than the rags he had been masquerading in. He tied it around his wound, pulled the soggy cloak over his head, and went searching for his horse.

By the time he found the mount, the weather had turned dreadful. Sleet was the worst climate to endure outdoors, and he knew that if the old druid lived closer to the coast, the conditions would be worse there. Knowing he had finer clothing stowed inside the bag he'd strapped to the horse, Ardan searched for a dry refuge in which to change.

The frozen rain fell faster and harder. "Come, now," he whispered to the anxious horse. "We'll find a cave if we keep moving. The rocks are plenty to the west."

Ardan closed his eyes, calling upon his spiritual sense to guide him. In the end, it was the horse's sense that found the way. The animal stepped gracefully through a carpet of mushy fallen leaves and bits of tree bark until he led Ardan to a tiny opening in a rock wall. "Good boy." Ardan patted the horse's nose.

Night was falling. Because the woods were wet and the tree branches coated in ice, he could not strike a fire. Ardan reached into his bag and gripped his warm woolen cloak. He shed his drenched clothing, including his undergarment, before pulling on the welcome cover of his own druid clothing. He wiggled his fingers inside the sack like a blind man and pulled out his sheathed ceremonial weapon. There was not even enough light inside the cave to reflect the normally gleaming surface of the solid gold sickle.

Welcome morning light illuminated the cave, but the air remained chilly. Ardan spotted the horse just outside the cave, munching happily on grass that was near enough to the rock's opening to escape the frost. Ardan rubbed the night's sleep from his eyes, and his thoughts drifted back to the events before he passed out the previous day.

The ogham. He'd gone back to the stone to read its message. His fingers wandered to his sore head. Just a scratch. In his mind's eye, Ardan saw the stone dripping in blood. His blood had filled in spaces in the carving, making it decipherable. He'd have to return today before tracking Brigid and her protector.

The commoner's clothing that had been damp yesterday

was now frozen stiff. No matter, he didn't really need it. He pulled his decorative embellishments from his bag. He normally reserved them for ceremony, but today they'd serve to remind anyone he might meet that he was a powerful druid – powerful enough to be endowed by kings with gifts from the craftsman's hand. The smith's first offerings were his, the best gold, bronze, and silver available.

He wrapped a massive metal collar around his neck and fastened it with a bit of chain that hung at the ends. He clasped two bronze bracelets decorated with rare trade enamel inlay around his wrists, although no one would likely see them there, and the coldness of the metal made him shiver. It was the presence of the objects that was most important. He draped a scarlet belt around his waist and then hurried outside to join the horse.

Ardan quickly realized he'd need the warmth of a fire to melt the ice from the druid stone. Besides, he was hungry and the gods who'd been displeased with him yesterday would require a sacrifice to ensure the journey would continue unmolested.

Ah, the druid's prerogative. He'd almost forgotten. He pulled a rock from his cloak pocket. A fisherman had given it to him, saying that it came from the bottom of the sea. A fire rock, he'd called it. Interpreting the will of the gods to the common people, as well as to the king, had proven advantageous at times.

Ardan dug under the frozen surface of the forest floor until he found several pieces of dry bark. He returned to the stone with the fire rock, the bark, and a small dagger he kept tied in the laces of his shoes. Using his tools, he managed to create a ribbon of smoke that gradually transformed into a little flame. *Praise the god of fire.*

Fortunately the wind was still. Ardan snagged two unsuspecting doves from their feeding at the base of an elm. He sacrificed them with his golden sickle, raising them in homage to the sky.

After he feasted, he attempted to read the stone. Its surface had been sufficiently warmed by the fire. Traces of blood stuck in spots but most of it had been washed away. He rubbed the grease from a dove carcass over the writing. Pleased that his craftiness had produced results, he studied the lettering from bottom to top.

Just as he'd hoped. The stone did not merely repeat some clan's genealogy, as many such writings did. The purpose of this stone was to open doors to hidden knowledge. Secrets a druid of his standing needed, but was sometimes excluded from by those who were jealous of his importance.

The gods had smiled on him. If he had never fallen and shed his blood on the stone, he might not have seen the message within the message. For without the hidden marks, the stone seemed to be a common marker, telling a traveler how much farther to the next druid gathering. But when he uncovered the concealed marks, the true meaning was clear.

> The passageway opens here,
> At the Samhain's midnight.
> A candle shown from stone's east side
> will mark the way to the one
> whose birth was prophesied.

Brigid. The coded message spoke of the young lass he sought. The gods had heard his request. At the festival where the dead mingle with the living, he'd be able to snatch Brigid and deliver her to Troya. Once Brigid was dead, the knowledge of the god who threatened to overrule Ardan's gods would die with her. The Others approved of his plan.

CHAPTER

"THE SEEKING FOR ONE THING WILL FIND ANOTHER."
OLD IRISH SAYING

Torchlight in the distance guided them to the crannog. Brigid hoped her mother had preceded them. "Is there someone there?"

"I've always got a man posted to tend to things. I'll call the rest." Bram handed Brigid the pole he used to guide the raft and grasped a bullhorn that was secured to the side of the vessel. He took in a long slow breath from inside the shelter of his deep hood and blew two short calls through the horn followed by one long blast. Then he sat down on the wet raft logs, exhausted.

Brigid felt the craft's edge with her fingers. "Is the raft safe?"

He blew puffs of air that clouded in the cold. "This weather's been a test of its worthiness, it has, and it shows no signs of stress. Don't worry, lass. We've made it safe, we have. My household will soon find us."

She struggled against the wind-driven waves to navigate with the help of the steering pole, but thankfully the little island was near. She glanced at the old man. "Yer spent. Would ye like me to blow the horn?"

He shook his wet hood. "Nay, the watchman heard."

A soft sound echoed Bram's call from the dark island. Brigid listened as it grew louder. "He's calling yer servants, then?"

"Aye. Yer mother will come."

When they reached the fortress, a shadowy figure dressed all in black met them, lending a hand and securing the raft. They scrambled over stones and up a steep path to the gate. Inside the picket walls they made for the largest shelter, and once inside, traded their soaked outer cloaks for dry blankets the caretaker offered.

"Oh, a fire!" Brigid headed for the central stone ring and shivered as her body detected the warmth. Her eyes watered for a moment, but soon she was able to take in the surroundings. The hut was simple, encircled by sleeping cots and baskets of what she hoped was food. There had to be more shelters in the compound. Perhaps her mother was waiting in another. "My mother, Bram?"

He blinked the smoky fire from his own eyes. "Soon." He turned to the servant. "Man, have ye put water on for tea?"

The servant scurried to his duties, preparing an herbal tea and a meal of dry bread and cheese. When they'd had a bite, Bram tended to Brigid's wounds.

He dampened some pulverized herbs with a bit of the tea and dabbed at the scratches. "Healing already. Ah, to be young when yer body does what it should."

She pulled the cloth away to have a look. "Pine needles? Comfrey?"

"Ah, ye know yer herbs. Some of that, aye. Ground up last summer. Should do fine for yer scratches."

Brigid endured the pampering for a while and then asked again. "Bram, when will I see my mother?" A dark thought crossed her mind. "Is she in danger?"

The caretaker tipped his head toward the pelt door.

131

Bram leaned toward her. "Someone's coming." He rushed to a corner and gathered his druid prophecy sticks. He hummed and chanted something Brigid couldn't understand and then tossed the sticks on the ground near the fire.

Foolishness. Brigid joined the servant at the doorway and listened. The sound of a boat lapping through the waves grew closer. The wind had died down and the patter of frozen rain ceased. The man hurried out of the hut and she followed.

"Who's there? My mother? That old beggar looking for his gold cups?"

The man answered her with a stern look. He climbed to a lookout, paused, and then slid down quickly. As she looked on, he departed the fortress walls and skidded down an incline where a curragh cramped with torch-bearing visitors waited. Bram joined Brigid at the entrance to the crannog and rested his hand on her shoulder.

She turned to look into his pallid face. "Not enemies, I assume?"

"One can never be too careful."

Brigid wanted to ask him what he was running from, but a tiny woman dashed toward them, stretching out her arms. A man followed close behind with a torch, picking her up every time she stumbled. The woman's face was radiant as she cried out Brigid's name.

Bram pushed Brigid forward. "Go to yer mother."

Brigid's feet froze. She'd longed for the moment, but now she couldn't budge, couldn't believe it could be true.

Brocca came to her and enfolded her in thin arms. "Ah, my Brigid! How I have longed for ye all these many seasons." She squeezed Brigid and wept.

"Maither." The word felt odd coming from Brigid's lips. It was a term others used, not her. Brigid felt herself being bustled into the shelter by the small wave of visitors.

After they had all collected inside, Bram introduced the

others. Although they were all his servants, they seemed to be his friends as well. They laughed, hugged, and smiled much like the peasants in the woods who held equal standing among themselves.

Brocca ignored the others and clung to her daughter. Everyone seemed to understand that the reunion was something special. Brigid and Brocca received attention as though they were royalty.

Brocca ran her hands over Brigid's cheeks. "What happened to ye, darlin'?"

Bram stepped forward. Brigid had not yet found her voice. "A fall from a wagon. Nothing serious. I've treated the scratches."

Brocca squeezed Brigid's hand. "Well, then. I will look after it also."

Brigid couldn't breathe. The close proximity of people and the smokiness of the fire that had been stoked to prepare food, made her gasp for air. She shook the hands off her and ran outside. The sleet had changed back to rain, and she welcomed the feel of it on her skin. Voices came from the hut, but only Bram followed her.

He urged her under the overhanging roof where the rain couldn't wash away her tears. "When ye seek something so long, 'tis sometimes impossible to believe 'tis true when ye find it."

Brigid swallowed. "A wise druid saying." She kicked at the mud sticking to her shoes. "I wanted to find my mother. I wanted to ask her questions. I wanted to be the one to care for her, yet she tends to me. And... I don't know her, Bram." Tears washed down her face like the rain dripping off the hut's roof.

Bram encircled her with his cloak. She leaned her head against the smallness of his shoulder. "It has been many years, child. Yer memories of yer mother are those of a child, yet ye no longer are a child. What ye needed then, ye need no more.

That's what's troubling ye. She will understand. I will speak to her." He pointed toward a smaller shelter. "Go there. Ye'll find turf for a fire and warm pelts. I'll confer with Brocca, and she'll join ye there later. I'll send some venison stew."

"Oh, thank ye, Bram!" How she wished that this man had been her master instead of Dubthach.

"Wait." He reached up to remove a torch from an iron pocket near the door where it had been protected from the rain. "Take this with ye and get that fire started. This will be a bitter cold night."

Brocca heard his footsteps approaching. "Bram. My sweet child – where is she?"

"I have sent her to the sleeping quarters. We will eat, talk, and then later ye'll join her there."

Brocca bowed her head. He was her master, and although she hated the thought of being separated from Brigid, even for an hour, she acknowledged his authority. He had said they would talk, and there was much to discuss with him.

The other servants busied themselves with food preparation. Brocca's work was done for the day. She had closed up the dairy just before the horn blast sounded. Bram only used the horn to signal danger and summon them to the crannog. But long ago they had agreed that if he were ever able to pry her darling Brigid from Dubthach's clutches, he would signal Brocca with a long horn blast. When she heard it, her heart had nearly leapt from her chest.

Brocca had known Brigid's arrival could come at any time. Brian, Dubthach's coachman, had told Bram of Brigid's exile.

"She seeks her mother above all else," Bram had told her after his last visit to the Christians' biannual seashore gathering.

Brocca scooted closer to the peat fire, letting the warmth dry her tears. Bram had much explaining to do. Where did he find her daughter? What danger had brought them to the crannog? There had to be a reason why they gathered there instead of meeting at their dwelling. And why did the girl seek solitude now?

Someone tucked a mug of herbal tea into her hands. She thanked the server and lifted the tin cup to her lips. Soon the smell of thickening stew wafted to her nose. *Oh, Brigid.* The poor lass. She must be terribly hungry.

The sound of harp music told Brocca the cooking was nearly finished. Bram's footsteps neared again.

"We will talk," he said. "But in hushed voices. The gods are angry, they are."

Brocca had humored his talk of pagan gods for far more years than she wished. She and some of the other servants had attempted to talk to Bram about Patrick's teachings, but while he was willing to accept the existence of another god, he would not abandon his gods for the One God, the Creator.

Brocca reached her hand toward him. "Why do ye say the gods are angry?"

His woolen cloak touched her legs as he seated himself beside her on the rush-covered floor. "The Samhain approaches. I have read the new ogham in the clearing. Druids from far off have placed it there. Wise men, they are, who have traveled from Leinster. I met them briefly during my wanderings. They left after marking the stone, but the message is important – a message concerning knowledge."

Brocca had become the old druid's confidante in recent years. Perhaps her blindness had made her the perfect listener. "What does any of this have to do with my daughter? My arms ache for her so."

"Patience, Brocca. Ye'll be with her soon, ye will. But first we must speak about the Samhain."

Brocca took in a deep breath and released it slowly. The pagans' holiday, a celebration that she had once enjoyed, was

135

becoming a burden. More and more people were seeking to have the future revealed on that occasion, when the veil between life and death was thought to be lowered. "Only the One God knows the future, master."

"Ah!" His cup hit the dirt floor; it was evidently empty because she felt no splatter of hot liquid. "The gods reveal their plans to me. I heard them just this afternoon on the journey here."

She resigned herself to hearing the pagan tales. "Very well. Tell me of the ogham."

Bram leaned in close and whispered, "I will tell ye the message, but ye must promise not to reveal it to anyone before its time."

She snorted. "Of course not."

"Not to yer daughter."

"She'd have no use for it."

"Ah, but yer wrong. On the way she begged me to tell her the message. Seems she's learned the writing and reading of the Romans from monks in Aghade."

"Monks?" The news surprised Brocca. She realized Patrick had established several areas in the east where some were faithful to the Word, and that some men had dedicated their lives to serving Christ; but writing?

"That's right. I cannot tell her, nor anyone save you, 'bout the message."

"Riddles. Yer becoming like every other druid in Ireland."

He moaned. "And I am to believe ye met every druid on the isle?"

Of course she hadn't, but she had traveled before she lost her eyesight. He'd allowed her that, but she had to admit he was far more familiar with people from distant provinces than she was.

He drummed his fingers against something hard, his druid sticks likely.

"Something is truly bothering ye, master."

"Aye. And ye'll be better off for knowing, but she won't."

"Tell me, then."

"The Samhain's in two days' time. When the time of the dropping of the veil comes, the stone instructs the holding of a candle near it, to lead the way to the passage."

She pulled the woolen blanket a servant had brought her up to her shoulders. "What of this?"

"The stone says the passage will lead to someone – someone important whose coming was prophesied."

"Ye know I don't believe in such things."

He continued on anyway. "There's a stranger in the forest, there is."

"That's why ye fled? To get away from the stranger?"

"Aye. Believed him to be a beggar, I did. Brigid thought so too."

"How do ye know he's not?"

"He did not return to claim a cup of gold I offered. He sought information 'bout us."

Surely the old man was a bit paranoid. "How do ye know he'll not return? What makes ye think he wants information more than bread?"

"I know ye think me a foolish man, Brocca. But hear me out. I felt the wind speak to me, saying, 'Hurry. Hide the lass.'"

"Brigid? Hide Brigid?"

"She was the only lass with me, woman. Danger and fear swept over me like a March wind."

Brocca could not escape the possibility that God himself had sent his Spirit to protect Brigid. Bram must have sensed it.

"And the writing, the ogham?"

"I must return to the clearing at midnight of the Samhain. See for myself, I must, this one it speaks of, and discern the future. Other druids will be there to do the same. If evil is present, I must bring good to battle it." Bram's voice cracked. He was old, older probably than the rocks.

"Nay. Yer not strong enough, Bram." She called him by his name, cherishing the friendship between them. "I'll go."

At last Brocca entered the hut where Brigid was waiting. Her tears flowed freely. The girl's footsteps rushed at her and her arms encircled Brocca, the embrace she so longed for.

"Oh, maither! I'm so sorry for the way I behaved when I first saw ye. 'Tis just that I've waited so long and..."

"And I was not what ye expected. Don't worry, child. I am still the maither who has loved ye since I first felt yer movement in my womb."

Brocca's daughter cried loud enough for Brocca to hear her pain. Brocca lowered herself to the ground, urging Brigid to sit with her.

"I am not the same, maither. I am grown. I have seen and learned many things. Still, all I ever wanted was..."

"Shh, now. Aye, ye've grown. And thanks to Cook."

"Do ye know her?"

Brocca was stunned that Brigid hadn't realized the connection. "Aye. She's been yer protector all these years – the condition allowing Dubthach to take ye from me."

Brigid was still. The news must have surprised her. Brocca heeded Bram's warning to let the girl come to her in her own time, ask questions when she was ready. The silence stood between them like an unstirred pool.

At last Brigid spoke, and she asked about the woman Brocca trusted most in the world. "Cook came with me from Munster, and my father made ye return to the druid's service?"

"That's right."

"Why would Bram sell Cook? He only owed Dubthach one slave."

"He didn't sell her. She was free." Brocca reached out to touch Brigid's cheek.

The lass didn't turn away. "This makes no sense." The muscles in Brigid's cheeks tightened.

Brocca took Brigid's hands into hers. "I will explain it all to ye, darlin'. Bram gave Cook her freedom so she'd be able to watch over ye."

"But she isn't free. She's a slave in my father's household."

"She is, but she went willingly. Dubthach, being somewhat greedy, welcomed her as a servant. Truly, he had no other choice."

"Ye don't know that cruel man like I do, maither. He'd not take anyone in lest it suited his purposes." Brigid rose.

"Please, sit down."

"Nay, I'm going to... tend the fire."

She had built a roaring flame from wood rather than turf. The fire crackled – Brigid was feeding it more fuel. Brocca thought to correct her, but then realized that the process of building the fire allowed Brigid time to contemplate all she was hearing.

Brocca raised her voice to be heard over the popping firewood. "No one understands how cruel that man is better than me. He whisked away my only daughter when she was but five springtimes old."

Brigid whispered. "Aye, I'm sorry. Ye must hate him."

"I did for a long time. I'd watch ye from a distance at the Christian gatherings."

Brigid dropped back down to Brocca's side. "What? At the seashore? Ye were there when I first heard Patrick? Why did I not know?"

Brocca stroked her daughter's hair. It was long and smooth as silk. "It was all arranged. Cook was to come care for ye; Brian was to give me messages concerning yer welfare. And in return, yer father allowed these things to avoid a curse."

Brigid leaned into her. Her damp hair smelled smoky. "Everyone knew things I didn't." She sat up straight. "A curse?"

Brocca laughed. "Bram pretended to threaten him with a curse on his cattle and boils on his skin."

Brocca thought this truth would amaze her daughter, but Brigid's tone turned bitter. "Why did he not threaten him with a curse if he did not return ye to me?"

Brocca reached for Brigid but her hands came up empty. "'Tis the druid way of things, daughter. And, the truth is, it was God's way too."

Brigid's voice escalated, seeming to rise to the roof hole with the flames of the fire. "It was not God's will to separate us! And what of this druid's code? 'Tis meaningless." Brigid kicked the dinner pot, sloshing venison stew over the dirt floor. "Oh, I've ruined the meal!"

Brocca gathered the broom she knew was in the northeast corner. "No matter. I was not hungry anyway. But perhaps ye'd like to return to the main building to get more."

"Let me do that." Brigid reached for the broom.

Brocca held up her hand. "I'm used to caring for myself."

Brigid took the broom from her hands. "Now that I'm here, maither, I'll do yer work. I don't know why we were separated by foolish pagans, but I'll make up for it."

Brocca returned to the fire, soaking in the comfort and searching for words that would help her daughter understand their situation. "Bram may be a pagan, daughter, but he's wise."

The swooshing of the broom ceased and Brigid joined her. "How can a pagan be wise? He may be kind, but he does not accept Christ's teachings. He clings to the old way of things. He speaks to gods he believes to be in the forest and in the wind. He reads mysterious druid writing but will not share its secrets with me. Oh, maither, I have learned to read and write

140

marks. Stories are being written down instead of just shared near a fire. One day all will know what Patrick taught even though he has died."

Brigid's last words hit Brocca like a rockslide. "He has died?"

"Aye. I heard the news from some Christians I met while making my way here."

Brocca's eyes moistened. "I am so sorry to hear he will not be preaching to the lost. I myself had hoped to hear him again this year at the seashore." She smiled. "And I thought that was where I'd see ye again, darlin' Brigid. But then the accident. Bram would not allow me to travel."

Her daughter's smooth young hands gripped Brocca's palms. "Was it a horrible accident, maither? Do ye prefer not to speak of it?"

"I will answer whatever ye ask of me, daughter. 'Twas horrible, but I have no more pain."

Brigid sighed, her breath sweet like apples. "How... what happened?"

"An accident. No one meant for it to happen. The maids were mixing herb potions for healing. I was curious since I have never done this. I was looking over their shoulders when the concoction exploded like waves hitting rocks. The hot liquid splattered into my eyes. When the pain eased, my sight did not return."

"I'm so sorry, maither. And I regret I was not here to help ye. I do not understand the arrangement. How could it be wise for us to be apart?" She paused and pounded her fists together. "Cook once told me that my father's old wife, Troya, sent ye away."

Brocca gasped. "Cook told ye that?"

"Aye, though she did not want to tell me. She made me promise never to mention the woman's name at Glasgleann. Why, maither? What concern is she to us?"

141

How could Cook do this? Tell Brigid about Troya's existence? Bram had warned everyone at Glasgleann to be careful about what they revealed to Brigid. She felt trapped. How could she avoid telling her daughter what evil lurked in the shadows, waiting to pounce on her like a wolf on a hen?

Brocca sighed. "There is much we must discuss, darlin'. But now I am tired. We are together. Yer safe. Bram's demons seem not to have arrived this eve. So, shall we sleep, daughter?"

Brigid agreed, and Brocca was pleased to avoid Brigid's question for the time being. She would pray silently for wisdom, and hope that God would show her how she would attend the druid ritual on the Samhain in Bram's place, explain to her daughter about the dark woman Troya, and plan for the day when Dubthach would come looking for them, accusing Bram of being a false druid and claiming an honor price for all he had lost in their arrangement. Those events were as inevitable as tomorrow's sunrise and she must prepare, somehow.

CHAPTER

"IN IRELAND THE INEVITABLE NEVER HAPPENS
AND THE UNEXPECTED CONSTANTLY OCCURS."
SIR JOHN PENTLAND

The next morning the house of Bram moved off the crannog. Apparently, he believed the danger had passed and whoever had been following them was pursuing no longer. Brigid was pleased. Now she could see the dairy for herself and take up her mother's work.

Brocca led her to the small stone building. It seemed familiar. "Have I been here before, maither?"

"Well, not this particular one, but Bram's former dairy was nearly identical. Ye'd sit on a stool in the corner and question me while I worked. Ye'd say, 'Why does the cow give us her milk? Why does it take so long to make butter?' My, ye were curious. But I hear ye were a fine dairymaid at Glasgleann. I guess those questions helped train ye even at a young age."

Brigid spied a child-sized stool in the corner of the dank dairy and supposed it had been the one she had sat on many years ago. She just wished she could remember.

The following day, preparations for the Samhain began in earnest. While the pagan members of Bram's household gathered firewood and prepared special feasts, Brigid went about the day's chores as though it were no special season.

Brigid's mother had not answered all of her questions, but there'd be time for that. Right now Brigid's head ached from all the troubling new information. She'd need to sort it out later, but for now she was glad of the distraction of the festival. Bram's servants had been staring at her and whispering, and now at last that had ceased.

"Ye can come with me if ye like," Brigid told her mother, "but I'm doing yer chores in the dairy. Yer so thin and weary. I will get the work done quickly so we can help the others cook."

Brocca agreed to wait for her at the outdoor fire, waving a slender arm in her direction. Brigid's mother's hair lacked luster, much like the women's in the forest. Hadn't she been fed well?

The druid's dwelling was not in a clearing as most estates were. His home blended into the woods like part of the wild landscape. Pagans worshipped trees, believing gods lived in them, and Bram probably held some kind of belief that kept him from cutting down any wood. A pagan carpenter at Glasgleann had once told Brigid that he would only work with wood from fallen trees. He wouldn't cut any down. Bram probably held the same superstition.

Dodging first one oak and then another, Brigid made her way to the stone entry door of the dairy. Finding it slightly ajar, Brigid entered. While she went about her mother's tasks – milking, sweeping the barn – Brigid thought about how Bram had been surprised to hear about her willingness to take her mother's place. Just as she was pondering that, he appeared in the barn. Deciding that he was supervising the work, Brigid joined some maids making butter at one end of the sun-dusted dairy.

He ambled straight for her, tapping his walking stick on

the dry packed ground. "Why indeed would ye slave for me, child?"

"Not for you, but for maither." Brigid ignored him and focused on her work. She removed the creamy curds from her butter churn and placed thirteen piles on a table board, as she always had at Glasgleann.

Bram hovered over her work. "Lass, most of my servants set aside the extra for themselves. Is that what yer doing with that large pile in the middle of twelve smaller ones? Ye cannot take more than yer share just because yer doing the working for yer mother, ye cannot."

Brigid paused, brushing a loose strand of hair from her eyes, trying to weigh how to react. The old man's question was potentially insulting. She fought the urge to shoot back a rude remark of her own but instead raised her eyes toward heaven. Perhaps he meant no insult. Bram didn't know any better.

Brigid pointed to the piles of butter. "There were twelve apostles of my Lord. The thirteenth pile is for Christ. There are twelve people who will come to buy yer butter today, but that large pile is neither for me nor my mother. I will not deprive my God of what is rightfully his."

The druid approached to examine what she'd removed from her butter churn. "My dear, ye got all this out of just one churn, did ye?"

"Aye."

The druid glanced over at the other maids' work and saw that they had not produced as much. He eyed the workers who delivered wooden containers to the maids who in turn filled them with the fresh butter. "We never had such bounty before, Brigid. Yer mother has told me 'bout this god of yers, and I believe we ought to give back to his children. Just as he's given to us."

Brigid helped load the wooden vessels onto a wagon, intending to go join her mother at the cooking fire.

"Wait!" Bram called after her. "I have another task for ye."

Brigid sighed. Her arms throbbed from the butter churning. She turned around. The druid retrieved the largest butter container holding the ample share – Christ's portion.

"Take this out to the road. Feed the poor. And take a cow, too. Keep it for yerself."

Bram's generosity swept away Brigid's voice. He urged the vessel toward her. "Please. I want ye to take it."

She smiled, searching for words.

Bram's winter eyes sparkled like ice crystals. "'Tis Christ's portion, not mine."

Brigid sucked in her lips as tears filled her eyes. He understood. Her mother, a Christian, had reached this druid. Such things *could* be done.

Bram tottered after her and they reached the fire together. Brocca turned when they approached, seeming to recognize her master's footfalls.

He tapped Brigid's mother softly on the arm of her cloak. "Brocca, yer daughter has worked long enough for ye. Done the labor of several maids in just one morning, she has. I must reward her."

"Reward the work of a slave?" Brocca's faint eyebrows arched.

"She is a free woman, and so too shall you be."

Brocca jumped to her feet. "What are ye saying, Bram?"

"I'm giving ye yer freedom. I'll make it official tonight by sending a messenger to declare such on my behalf to King Dunlaing."

Brigid stepped between them. "Dunlaing? Why not the king of Munster?"

"The agreement at yer birth was made under King Dunlaing. He and his ruling class of druids will judge your status."

Brigid helped her mother sit down and then joined her.

She twisted the hem of her tunic between her fingers. "Bram, what if they won't allow it? I mean... what if they have reason to... dislike me? Will we need to be present when the request is made?"

The old druid sat with them on the ground, handing the butter container to a servant for safe-keeping away from the fire. "Brigid, I am sure that yer actions have been virtuous, but the judgment of others is not always wise, nay. Man's thinking cannot always be trusted, but ye need not fear that. There is little ye understand of druid ways."

In the firelight, Brigid noticed the wrinkles on the druid's face and the milky color of his hair. His time to walk on earth could not be much longer. She feared her problems unfairly weighed him down. What he said made no sense.

He seemed to read her mind. "I am old, very old. I hold in my memory the teachings of elders the younger generation never knew. Dunlaing's advisors understand, they do. If I say a thing must be done, they'll do it." He chuckled. "And if I threaten a laird with a nasty curse, everyone believes it will come to pass."

Brocca laughed too, but Brigid couldn't help but be concerned. She asked again, "Will my mother and I need to gain audience with King Dunlaing, druid?"

Bram waved her off. "Nay. The messenger is just a formality, but I must see to it nonetheless."

Brigid took her mother's hand in hers, vowing to God that the king would never find her or her mother in the wilderness of Ireland, at least not if she could help it. Brigid embraced her mother, drawing in the aroma of charred wood and peat that had seeped into her hair. "We shall live together as free-women. Bram has also given me a cow so that we may survive."

The twig-like figure in Brigid's arms shook. The shaking gave way to weeping and the weeping erupted into laughter.

Brocca composed herself. "Bram, I will not forget my promise to ye. I will still go to the druid stone tonight on yer behalf."

Bram turned Brocca's face toward him. "No need. I can make the trip."

Brigid put her hands on both of their shoulders. "What are ye two talking 'bout?"

Bram patted her hand, and then drew it down to her side, keeping their fingers locked. "Yer mother, although she believes in only one god..."

"The True One," Brocca interrupted.

"The True One," Bram continued, "yer mother is trained as a druid."

Brigid dropped his hand and gripped her mother's shoulders, gazing into eyes echoing her own sea-green shade. "What does this mean, maither?"

The servants stopped working. Everyone was silent. They all knew things she didn't.

Brocca whispered into Brigid's hair. "'The meaning is that I understand these beliefs and can use them to teach the truth." She turned to Bram. "I will still go."

Brigid smiled. Perhaps in that company only she and her mother really understood. "Maither, Bram has allowed me to give butter to the poor. Will ye help me find them before ye must do this task ye promised?"

Bram laughed out loud, "It will not be hard. Follow the smell of the fires. They prepare food to appease the gods tonight and leave it outside their doors."

Brigid took her eyes off her mother for a moment and turned to him. "But I thought they were starving."

"Aye, perhaps. But better to have a rumbling tummy than to allow the Others to enter yer house looking for food."

Of course. The Samhain. She had forgotten about that belief. Cook had never allowed Glasgleann's maidens to follow the tradition, and when everyone woke up the morning after the

Samhain unharmed and without bad dreams, Glasgleann's young women grew to trust Cook and the True God a little more.

Brigid held her mother's hand and the two of them paraded down a dirt path toward the distance black flumes of the pagan fires. Her mother was freed. The two of them were off to minister to pagans. It was even more than Brigid had hoped for. God's love was for everyone, and now she felt free enough to take his love to the darkest corners of Ireland. If only they didn't have to participate in the Samhain before leaving Ennis Dun.

"Maither, do ye think Bram has become a believer?"

Brocca squeezed her tight. "He may be close. 'Tis so hard to amend old superstitions."

The day was overcast and biting. Brigid's woolen stockings needed mending. She had neglected them far too long. Thankfully, her leather shoes were still in good shape, because the festival marked the end of the warm months.

Brigid examined her mother's clothing as they walked. Her long tunic was trimmed in red embroidery. Her shoes bore no holes, and unlike Brigid's stockings, her mother's appeared new. "Maither, yer garments seem to be in fine shape. How is it that Bram provides for clothing but does not feed ye well?"

"Not feed me? Why would ye think that?"

"Yer as thin as meadow grass. I've seen ye eat no more than a field mouse since I've been here."

"Well, 'tis true I've had no appetite of late. But now that my daughter has been restored to me, I'm sure my health will return."

Brigid squeezed her mother's hand. She pushed away the thought that her mother's body might be invaded by some sickness.

Bram was right. The smell of smoke did lead them to the downtrodden. They approached a large outdoor fire and

149

Brigid smelled roasting boar. "Why do they do this, maither? Cook for the gods and not feed themselves?"

"'Tis their way. Perhaps our gift of butter will sweeten their meager meal of bland bread."

"Welcome, Brocca!" several people called. "Who's the fine lass ye've brought with ye?"

Brocca explained about their gift of butter, her newfound freedom, and the reunion with her lost daughter.

A gangly man nodded to a woman. "Let's celebrate the news."

The man's wife produced a bronze wine flagon with a base of twisted metal.

"Maither?" Brigid whispered into Brocca's gray-speckled copper tresses. "Are these people truly in need? Wine is a king's drink, usually taken in merchant ship raids. Why would the poor have it?"

Brocca whispered back, "I'm surprised ye know this. I suppose ye've spent much time at the seashore listening to stories."

Brigid had, but who were those people to own such things?

Brocca held her hand over her mouth. "They were probably given the treasure as payment for fighting in battle. Does not matter from where it comes. They are truly needy for spiritual guidance. We will join them for a short time. To refuse their hospitality would be rude."

They had to be polite to gain the people's confidence, but as the day dragged on, Brigid contemplated Brocca's appointment at the druid stone. Although she would have liked to skip the druid ceremony, Brocca had promised Bram she'd take his place. Brigid began to fidget, wondering if they'd return in time.

The sun dipped into the horizon as they left the woodsfolk to their evening preparations. Brocca had prayed to God and blessed the people. They truly saw her as a Christian priestess.

As they made their way back to Bram and the others, unanswered questions poked at Brigid like gnats. She could not shoo them away. Should she ask about Troya again or try to find out more about the druid stone? She imagined they'd have many hours to come in which to discuss the past, but the time of the Samhain was fast approaching so she decided to ask about that.

"Maither, what's to happen at the gathering of the druids?"

Brocca laughed and tugged at the flat tin brooch pinned to her cloak at her collarbone. "Most likely nothing, though they will all say otherwise. Some will offer sacrifices, some will interpret the ogham on the stone, some will toss their druid sticks in an attempt to gain insight into what the new year will bring."

The druid's estate was in view. Brigid whispered although no one was close enough to hear, "What will *you* do?"

"I will stand in for Bram, and ye'll go to be my eyes. Ye'll tell me what ye see and what ye do not see."

"And what of the ogham stone?"

"Ye'll describe the marks to me at midnight when a candle casts its glow on the writing. Foolish though that may be. I can feel the marks with my fingers. But we'll follow their instructions in order to do what we can to show people the truth."

"Ye know the writing?" The news delighted Brigid. She had wondered about the strange script ever since Bram had stopped at the stone and investigated it so carefully.

"Aye. Now come." Brocca pointed in the direction of the sleeping quarters. "Ye must help dress me in druidess clothing."

When Brigid left Brocca to take care of necessities, Brocca requested a private meeting with her master.

"What do ye mean, ye invited her to go with ye, woman?" The old man's voice was as stressed as the hide on a musician's bodhran.

"I know danger looms, Bram, but God has urged me to do this."

"I'll send a servant to guide ye."

"Nay. I want Brigid."

He tapped his druid stick on the ground and, as if he thought it worthless, tossed the wand into a corner of his sleeping hut. "I've told ye, I have, Brocca, that the gods spoke to me of danger lurking."

"She knows of Troya."

Bram grabbed her arm, squeezing too tight. "How does she know this?"

"She says Cook told her, although I don't believe she knows everything."

"And still ye choose to take her to the Samhain gathering of the druids?"

She wiggled free of his grip and then rose. "Oh, Bram. Don't ye see? I have to take her to the place of evil in order to protect her. We will confront it together, defeat it, and then go on to live in peace as freewomen. Besides, this is the perfect opportunity to teach about my God. Ye know that, aye?"

"I know that's what ye want to do. 'Tis no concern of mine that ye instruct 'bout this other god, 'tis not. But... " He grumbled and pointed to his fingertips. "The leaves speak danger. Brigid knows 'bout Troya. She fears a druid named Ardan. And the stone's message... "

Bram paced around the small hut, paused at the place where he'd thrown his druid sticks, then returned and put his hand on her shoulder. He lowered his voice. "If Brocca and her god can do this and succeed, then truly no other gods rival hers."

Brocca smiled and patted his rough, dry hand. She had expected him to rant and rave, to tell her how foolish she was. But somehow he understood. Brigid was God's blessing to Ireland and now was the time to prove it. With that accomplished, no one, not even the wicked Troya, would command enough power to harm Brocca's daughter. And all who observed the power of the One True God would give the Lord the honor.

Just before midnight Brigid and her mother approached the clearing where the mysterious stone stood like a grave marker. Brocca, though her robes hung on her skeleton-like body, looked lovely in the golden jewelry of a druidess. She carried a walking stick embedded with deep blue, green, and red stones.

Along the edge of the clearing, men and women dressed in white robes stood mute. No one was as exquisitely attired as Brigid's mother. Nearly barren trees with moonlight peeking between the branches, cast eldritch shadows on the ground. Although not the site of tombs, which pagans called passageways, the somber mood suggested such.

Brocca whispered, "When midnight comes, the moon will cast a shadow directly across the middle of the stone. Do ye have the candle?"

"Aye, but won't a torch do?" Brigid disliked carrying candles that dripped down her fingers.

"Nay, it must be a candle."

Brigid detested being present for the pagan ritual. If her mother could see the clearing, look at the solemn faces, she wouldn't like it either. "Maither, what if there had been no moon on this night? How would we know the moment of the supposed lowering of the veil between us and the Otherworld?"

Brocca smiled. "'Tis always a full, bright moon at the Samhain."

"How could that be?"

"Shush now, child. Tell me when the moonlight crosses the stone."

Everyone focused on the standing stone. Brocca was closest, allowed the position because she stood in for Bram, the most ancient of all druids.

The wind swirled around the clearing. The torch in Brigid's hand flickered. How would a lone candle stay lit?

The moonlight crept closer. Brigid tried to make out the faces of the people, but hoods masked identities. One figure directly across from her held his torch close to his face. Red and yellow light shone onto his robe, allowing Brigid a glimpse of a face she thought she recognized. *The beggar who had chased away the bandits?* She hadn't gotten a good look at the fellow, but he could not have been a druid. She tried to remember where she'd seen him before, but he pulled his torch back before she got a really good look.

A chill tingled at her neck.

Brocca touched her arm, making her jump like a frightened toad. "Where's the moonbeam now, daughter?"

Brigid glanced back at the stone. "'Tis nearly in place. What shall I do?"

"Light the candle. Stand opposite the mark, and hold the candle so that it shines directly on the mark I point to." Brocca strode to the stone as if she knew exactly where it was. She bent low and ran her hands from the bottom of the stone to the top.

The hooded audience closed in. Brigid wanted to run away. Why would her mother, a Christian, participate in a heathen rite? She must have a plan, but Brigid couldn't imagine what.

Brocca didn't need Brigid's help. Her hands read the marks for her and she spoke them. Brigid tried to discern the writing from her mother's interpretation, but it made little sense. She could make out something about holding the candle over the mark at midnight, and then the way becoming clear. There was also something about a birth being predicted.

154

"Now!" Brocca raised her voice for all to hear. "Hold the candle over the mark now, and we will know the way to the One."

Christ? Did her mother mean to interpret the pagan message to show the way to Christ? Brigid leaned across the upright stone and held the candle against the mark her mother pointed to. The moonlight seemed to push the candle's glow straight into Brigid's face. She felt its warmth and the peace of God. She would have stayed in that position for some time if the druids had not started such a ruckus.

"She is the passageway!"

"The druidess's daughter!"

They pulled at her like so many hungry people.

"Nay, nay!" Brocca called. "She can show you the Way, but it is not her."

Brocca's face disappeared in a sea of white hoods. Hands carried Brigid away. "Maither! What's happening?"

Then she saw his face again – that beggar on the road. He dropped his hood, exposing golden adornments. He was surely not a beggar. She saw that now. He was the first druid she'd ever met, Ardan.

CHAPTER

16

"SO, IF THE SON SETS YOU FREE, YOU WILL BE FREE INDEED."
JOHN 8:36

Ardan hadn't counted on the candlelight illuminating Brigid. Perhaps it was some trick brought about by her mother. Just before the commencement of the ceremony, he'd heard rumblings about a woman and her daughter standing in for the ancient druid. He couldn't believe how the gods had smiled on him and sent Brigid right into his grasp. He had thought he would have to go searching for her.

But even though she was in reach, stealing her away would not be as easy as he had hoped. Her mother was so revered among the people that she had been called on to replace a powerful druid.

He'd have to invoke his authority. The girl had seem him clearly anyway. Now was the time to reveal his superiority.

"Silence, brothers and sisters! I am the great druid of the king of Leinster, King Dunlaing."

Just as he hoped, the crowd drew back, leaving Brigid and her mother in the center. Those lower druids wouldn't know who to trust – the blind woman who had come in their leader's place, or a stranger. He'd have to tip the scale.

"I declare authority in this gathering."

One druid began to speak. A brother or a druidess? At first he couldn't tell in the dim light. "Bram's our authority and the priestess Brocca stands in for him this night."

Ardan nodded in the woman's direction. "She is less than perfect. Ye can all see that. Would the gods endorse an imperfect mediator?"

The frail woman turned full circle to speak to all. "I represent but One God and he accepts me as I am. He will accept you, too. Which one of ye has no fault, no blemish in yer heart?"

Ardan straightened his shoulders and stood over the woman, dwarfing her in his shadow. "Judge for yerselves, druids. Whom will the gods choose?"

The prophets and bards of the woods milled about, mumbling like a cluster of crows. No one ventured an answer. No one would admit their ignorance. Just when Ardan was about to invoke a chant to summon the wisdom of the Others, a wolf howled not far away, perhaps a sign from the gods.

The brotherhood scattered into the woods, leaving Ardan alone with Brigid and her mother. "There was no passageway open tonight!" they called as they drifted like fog into the dark forest.

Delightfully easy. Ardan had trained *his* followers much better than the old one had done with these in the western woods. If Troya were here, she would never have backed down so easily.

The girl stared at him. Her face was pale as seabird feathers. "Ardan, why do ye follow me?"

The girl's mother stretched her arms, grabbing at air. "Who is it?"

Brigid slipped her arm around her mother's waist. "He is as he said, King Dunlaing's druid. And Troya's teacher."

The one called druidess melted into a faint.

"Maither, hear me!" Brigid tapped her mother's pale damp face.

Ardan latched on to the girl's arm. "Ye'll come with me." He paused. Seeing the girl so exasperated, he thought it might be to his advantage to take her mother also. He muttered into Brigid's ear, "What is she called?"

Brigid jerked away and fell to her mother's chest. "She's Brocca of Ennis Dun."

Before Brigid could protest, Ardan slipped a pouch of sleeping herbs over her mouth. Brigid struggled in his grip, but as she drew breath to scream the odors from the toxic herbs filled her lungs, and she collapsed across her mother's body.

Ardan rode the bishop's horse and pulled a cart behind. He glanced back. He must have used more herbs than he thought. Brigid was still asleep in the back of the cart he had borrowed from common people celebrating the new year.

Commandeering the cart had been no trouble. People feared unfamiliar druids on the Samhain. Lugging the women the way he had, women who appeared for all the world to be dead, had frightened the small family he'd met. They would have given him anything, believing he was raised from the dead and roaming the surface of the earth.

Brocca, who had awakened almost as soon as they rode off, badgered him with questions.

"What know ye of Troya?" She tugged at the leather laces he'd secured to her wrists.

Brigid's mother was gaunt, spent like summer blooms. She might have been beautiful once, but now she was withered and fragile.

She spat dust from her mouth. "Tell me."

Demanding, she was. He almost pitied her.

Ardan kept his eyes focused on the road. The moon was

fading, and steering a cart in total darkness was a task he didn't relish.

The woman would not stop talking. Finally, hoping to silence her, he answered, "We have much in common, woman, but I'll tell ye nothing. I'll save my story for the king."

They both needed Brigid. Brocca was blind and dependent. The lass would stay by her mother's side. Holding Brocca hostage would keep Brigid compliant. The lass's love for her mother was her weakness. If druid training had taught him anything, it was to hold on to every advantage, just in case.

Ardan congratulated himself on his astuteness. Forcing Brigid to join with him, and using her mother as a hostage, would be an acceptable alternative should he later decide he needed one.

"Aagh." Brocca clenched her stomach.

Ardan pulled the horse to a stop. "Too much talking, woman. I'll need to tend to yer sickness."

The ill woman glanced toward him, her unseeing eyes bloodshot. "My reward is in heaven."

Ardan needed her healthy if he decided to let Brigid live. He'd make camp, scour the countryside for herbs, and wait for Brigid to fully recover from her unconscious state.

His plan did not unfold as he hoped. Brigid awoke and bolted from the cart. Ardan caught up to her and knocked her to the cold ground. She wiggled beneath him like an eel.

"Let go of me! How dare you?" Her elbow landed in his eye, sending him reeling backward.

She darted back to her mother. Ah, he'd been correct about her weakness. Ardan sucked in a breath and lunged after her.

Brigid struggled with the laces binding Brocca. Ardan grabbed her hair. "Ye'll not get away. Give up!"

Still she squirmed, as though she could free her mother while he yanked her golden locks out hair by hair.

159

The sick woman wailed, "Stop, daughter! Do what he says."

Brigid gave in, slumping to the cart floor.

Perfect.

The lass spat in his face. There was still fight left in her. "Let us go," she demanded. "If it's an honor price Troya desires, let her seek it from Dubthach."

Ardan dragged the lass to the opposite end of the cart and lashed her against the wheel, tying her wrists with strips of leather he cut from his bag. "She'll name her price in yer presence."

Brigid sneered at him. "Why are ye doing this?"

"Calm down, woman. All will be revealed in time. First, we must get yer poor mother well."

Brocca coughed. "Ye seek to poison me. I'll not help ye!"

He sighed. Why must he always be in the presence of irrational, emotionally driven women? "I do not seek to poison ye, Brocca. Ye want to help yer daughter, nay?"

Brocca nodded, shivering. Ardan pulled his wool blanket off the horse and wrapped it around her trembling shoulders. "There now. That's better, aye? Yer sick. Ye do not eat. How can ye help poor Brigid when yer weak?"

She shook her head and pinched her lips together.

"Don't hurt her!" Brigid called from her side of the cart. "Ye only need me, not her. Let her go."

He enjoyed the look of uncertainty on Brigid's face. With the help of his fire rock, he lit a torch the cart owners had left behind so could see her better – and she could see and fear him. He circled the cart slowly, watching her head bob like an owl. He stopped and snatched a lock of her hair in his fist. "Now, tell me, beautiful one, would it be kind to turn a poor, sick, blind woman out to the wolves?" He jerked harder on her hair. "Would it now?"

Brigid's eyes rounded. "Nay, it would not."

160

He let go, smoothing his hands down his cloak. "Druids have a code of honor. I could never do that. I will take good care of both of ye. When she's well, we'll go see King Dunlaing."

"What has Dunlaing to do with Troya's honor price claim?"

Brocca spoke. "He will decide whether to hear the claim. If he decides it has merit, he'll let the Brehons judge."

Ardan spun around. "Ah, yer right, blind one. Could it be true that the old one, Bram they call him, really *has* trained ye well?"

Brocca hung her head.

Before the sun rose, Ardan had started a small fire and roasted a small deer. Perhaps fresh meat would appeal to the sick woman and renew her strength. He prodded it with his walking stick. Almost ready.

He'd used a bag full of dried sweet herbs to make the flesh appetizing. Brocca would surely eat. Her nose lifted to the smell and her lips moistened.

How was this woman both druidess and Christian? If he allowed the women to continue with their questioning, he might find out. "We will talk while we eat. The feast is nearly ready."

He prepared the meat, chiding himself for not packing more herbs. The countryside had been racked by frost, and his search turned up no suitable plants. Perhaps if they'd camped near a stream, he would have found a few decent roots. For now he'd have to rely on chants and a hot meal to revive his patient.

He freed one hand of each hostage for feeding. Trust him or not, they were ravenous and accepted the food readily. He found it odd that they each uttered some sort of chant to their god before eating. The sacrificial offering was said before the animal was killed, not after. What kind of druid master would teach such things?

Brigid squirmed. "May we sit together? 'Tis awfully cold."

Indeed the north winds blew, so he laced the women together back-to-back while he fashioned a shelter from animal hides and sticks. Once they were all inside and covered with the single wool blanket, Ardan noticed color returning to Brocca's cheeks. "Tell me, woman, how long now have ye had no taste for food?"

"Until today, I cared for no food for six days."

Brigid tried to turn to look at her, but they were too closely bound. "Six days, Maither? Had I known, I would have given ye my share."

Ardan reached for his knapsack. "Are ye still famished? I've got a bit of bread packed."

"Nay. My stomach's a bit unused to the greasy meat. I need to rest now."

The two women worked together to lie down. Brocca closed her eyes, but Brigid glowered at him. "Have ye poisoned us, Ardan?"

He stroked her hair, knowing she'd fear he would tug on it again. "If that had been my desire, ye would be dead already. I told ye exactly what I planned to do. If yer mother has worms, however, I am without my healing herbs to help her."

Brigid squeezed her eyes tight. "God will help her. She needs yarrow tea with honey." She spat out her words. Her eyelids popped open. "Can ye do that, please?"

By the time the tea bubbled, Brocca had awoken. Ardan held a tin dipper to her lips and she drank with bright eyes. Though he wanted her well, Ardan began to fear the strength of her god.

In just two days the frail woman regained enough strength that Ardan thought it time to visit Dunlaing. He rehearsed his royal appearance in his mind, wondering if his words would be sweet enough to the king who still resented Brigid over the preposterous pet fox matter.

When they reached Cashel, Ardan left the women sitting in the cart, their hands tied to its sides.

"What's yer business?" the guard bellowed from atop a wooden lookout tower.

"I've come to see King Dunlaing. I am his druid."

The man disappeared and another guard opened the fortress door. He was taller than Ardan and quite chatty as he led the way. "So, druid, have ye spoken to King Dunlaing of late? I hear negotiations between our king and yours are going nicely. Seems there'll be sharing of grazing land without bloodshed."

Ardan halted. The guard continued talking and walking until he realized Ardan was no longer beside him. He chuckled. "Come along, man."

Ardan's blood rose to his head. He marched up to the tall guard and grabbed him by his leather helmet. "Do ye cower in the face of battle, warrior? Do ye fear fighting for King Aenghus of Munster?"

The man's teeth chattered. "N-n-n-no, sir."

Ardan didn't let go. "I see cowardice in yer eyes. Yer unfit for service. I'll see to it that yer king knows this." He patted the man's ruddy cheek while keeping a grip on his helmet with one hand. "Pity this head will soon be separated from these shoulders. No king can tolerate disobedience. Hearing about it from a visiting king's head druid... well, that would be an insult. Aenghus will likely order yer head sliced from ye this very day."

The guard's lips turned blue. "Oh, please, nay. What do ye want of me, druid?"

Ardan smiled and let go of the man. "Well, I suppose if yer king was not to hear of my visit today, I could be persuaded not to mention yer failings to my king. If King Dunlaing doesn't hear of it, yer king will not either."

The man bowed and scurried in front of Ardan as they continued down the hall. Ardan was let into a small room where he found Dunlaing laboring over a board game. His attendant sat opposite him on a low stool. Twin candles hung from the rafters, illuminating the activity while casting shadows around the game.

"I beg to enter the king's presence." Ardan stood at the room's edge. His escort had already left.

Dunlaing turned to look. The attendant's mouth hung open. He was young. Ardan didn't remember seeing him before. The lad probably had no idea who had entered the room.

Dunlaing shoved his chair away from the table. "Ardan, what brings ye here today?" His blue eyes appeared gray in the dim light, but the creases at his temples told Ardan the king was in a fine mood.

"I have a matter to discuss. Something of utmost importance."

The king joined him at the door and held out his signet ring, which Ardan kissed - a custom he detested, but endured. Dunlaing had no real authority in Ireland. Ardan was the one who spoke with the gods, who proclaimed curses when necessary, who won the heart of people. Dunlaing was just a figurehead.

Dunlaing put his arm around Ardan and ordered the young boy out. Just as the lad was leaving, the king hollered, "Bring us some drink, lad! Do ye not see my cherished druid has arrived?"

The boy disappeared down the corridor with a torch and Ardan sat down in a scrolled chair topped with a silk pillow.

Dunlaing resumed his place at the game table, scrutinizing the location of the pieces. "Excuse my new servant, Ardan.

He knows little. When I return to Leinster, I will obtain better attendants."

Ardan eyed the corners of the room. "It would appear the reigning king has set ye up in better comfort now."

Dunlaing flipped his bejeweled hand beside his head. "It will do. Now, what business is so important as to interrupt my leisure? I was winning the task at hand, ye know. Just like I'm winning with land negotiations, Ardan."

The king needed stroking. Ardan bowed his head. "Excellent, king. I'm glad to hear this news." He had to tolerate several minutes of hearing the king extol his successes.

The attendant brought in a two-handed vase. Ardan recognized the shape of its swollen belly and the carvings on the brass handles. "Does this king not offer ye hospitality that ye have to drink yer own wine while in another man's castle?'

Dunlaing chuckled, his blue eyes glinting in the candlelight. "Of course he has extended his best for me, druid. I will drink now with you from my own stores."

Dunlaing was keeping his best from his druid. The thought made Ardan grind his teeth. He sighed and took a sip of the cup. The taste of the sweet wine, a beverage Ardan rarely drank, was wasted on his lips. He took care to set his chalice down gently so as not to give away his annoyance. He needed the king's help to carry out his plan.

Ardan spoke his rehearsed words, raising his voice in just the right places and leaning his head closer to the king. "Troya was a devoted wife, fully unaware that her husband wandered like a wild boar, taking his pleasure where he willed."

The king looked away, likely reflecting on his own indiscretions. Ardan continued to play up Troya's right to have her honor restored.

The king made no comment, so Ardan spoke the name he knew would annoy the king most. "When Dubthach's maid ripened with child, Troya sent her away. But Dubthach later called for the child, a lass named Brigid."

Ardan took another sip from his cup, this time enjoying the experience. Dunlaing raised his eyebrows.

Ardan had woven the tale as though he were a king's weaver crafting tightly-bound cloth on a royal loom. Ardan was as talented in bending opinions in his favor as any bard.

Dunlaing made a declaration. "It shall be as ye said. We shall convene the Brehons here tonight in this room."

Ardan bit his tongue. "But, king, shall we not take the women back to Leinster first?" Ardan had heard rumor that the man called Patrick had converted the king of Munster to Christianity. He would surely be sympathetic to Brigid. Ardan's intimidation of the guard had hidden the matter thus far, but convening the Brehons at Cashel would require the presence of the reigning king, something that had to be avoided.

"I see no need for that." Dunlaing clapped his hands together, bringing several servants into the room. "By order of Dunlaing, king of Leinster," he instructed the young boy he'd sent away earlier, "the Brehons will convene tonight in my chamber. A matter of honor will be decided."

Ardan was losing control of the situation. "But, king…"

"'Tis the least I can do for ye, druid. And for that woman I previously believed was a burden. She shall have her complaint answered tonight, at long last."

"But she's not here, king."

"Ye'll stand in for her."

Rain sprayed from late-day clouds. The sky was fringed with shades of purple and gray. Although the shower would not last long, Brigid knew she'd be uncomfortably damp the rest of the evening – and so would her sick mother.

She glanced at the gray figure in the cart. There was not

enough daylight left to see her face. "Maither," she whispered, "how do ye feel?"

Brocca giggled. "Wet, I'd say."

"Aye. That wicked Ardan, to leave us here with no shelter. 'Tis getting dark."

"I know it is, darlin'."

"How do ye know, when ye cannot see the light? 'Tis always night to ye, I suppose."

Brocca leaned her head back toward Brigid. "Yer eyes have convinced ye they are the only tool ye have with which to learn."

Brigid shook the rain from her hair. "I don't know what ye mean."

"Daughter, think for a moment with me. Close yer eyes."

There was nothing to look at anyway but dark bulging rocks. "Aye, they're closed."

"Fine, then. Point yer head toward the heavens."

Brigid obeyed and blinked her eyes against the raindrops.

"Now, do ye feel the warmth of the sun on yer cheeks?"

"Nay."

"Be quiet. Do ye hear birds?"

"Nay. But, wait, I do hear something."

"I thought ye might."

Beyond the sound of rain pelting her back and bouncing off the road, Brigid heard squeaking.

"Bats? In the rain?"

"Ye can't hear them as well as usual, 'tis true. But they are in the trees, waiting for the rain to stop."

"That's amazing."

"We're not done yet, Brigid. Are yer eyes still closed?"

Brigid squeezed her lids shut. "I'm not looking, though 'tis too dark anyway."

"Fine. Now, with no sun, how do ye feel?"

"Chilled, maither. Ye must be too. I wish we could hold each other."

"Don't think 'bout that. Think only of the way the wind feels on yer skin."

Brigid held her face toward the sky again. The rain stopped. The breeze on her face was especially damp.

Brocca whispered, "With practice ye'll be able to tell the tingle of a night-time wind as opposed to the tickle of a day-time breeze, even if the day is overcast and bleak."

"Aye." Brigid wasn't sure she knew the difference, but she'd try to learn. Her mother still had so much to teach her.

"Maither, what sickness steals yer health?'

"Try not to worry, darlin'. I'm better. Let's talk of other things. We still have so much to learn about each other. I have missed ye all these seasons. Even though we know not what Ardan has planned for us, I cherish the moments we now have alone in this wagon."

"As do I."

"Is there anything ye want to ask me, darlin'?"

"Are ye sure yer up to talking, maither?"

A sigh rose from the dark mound where her mother lay with her wrists tied together and bound to the side of the cart. "I am much stronger than I was. 'Tis Troya ye want to talk about, aye?"

Brigid breathed in the evening mist. "I would like to know why she's concerned about me. And what happened before I was born."

"At first I did not want to tell ye, daughter. But the Lord whispered into my ear, telling me yer grown now and I *should* tell ye. If yer to meet her soon, ye need to know what evil yer facing."

"Evil? Is it proper to use such a word? Many people in Ireland are misguided by their fears, but not many are truly evil."

"Listen carefully, Brigid." Brocca's tone turned as quickly as Cook's had that day long ago when Brigid had asked about her mother.

"I will listen."

"I am sure I'm not a fair sight today, but ye probably noticed that I'm not many seasons older than ye. I was just barely turned a woman the night ye were conceived."

Brigid's throat tightened. Did she really want to hear the story?

Brocca whispered, "I was born a slave and sold into Dubthach's household. That's what Cook told me. I never knew my parents. Cook was like a mother to me."

"And to me."

"God is gracious even in the midst of dire circumstances, child."

Brigid longed to hold her mother, but Ardan's knots held firmly, keeping them apart.

Brocca continued. "Dubthach and Troya had a terrible fight one night. All the servants had gone to bed, but we could hear screaming coming from the master's quarters. 'Ye look at the young maidens with lust,' Troya said. Dubthach shouted back, 'I do no such thing!' And so the hollering continued."

Brigid tugged at the knots holding her prisoner. "He's a horrible man, maither."

"I have been over those events many times in my heart, daughter. My blindness has caused me to see with more than my eyes. I know now that at that time, Dubthach was not horrible. He was misguided, as ye say, but not evil. Not like Troya."

"He's disgusting!" Tears flowed and Brigid could not wipe them away. "He took me from ye. What more terrible evil could there be?" She felt sick, as though she had just eaten cabbage stew.

"Please, listen, darlin'. I hear the hurt in yer voice, but ye

169

must hear. Dubthach did a terrible thing to me that night, 'tis true. I didn't know what was happening at first, but by the time I figured it out, it was finished. He had planted the seed that grew into the lovely Brigid."

Brigid's voice choked with tears. "So Troya was right. He was lusting."

"He wept that night and apologized."

"Dubthach? Never."

"I heard it with my own ears. He said he had never done such a thing before, and would never again. In the years ye lived with him, did ye ever see him abuse a maid?"

Brigid wanted to say yes to prove that he was indeed a monster, but she couldn't. "He was gruff and stern. He never showed me any love, maither. He treated me like any other servant. He was greedy, too. Always seeking to expand his wealth."

"Aye, I will not argue that."

Brigid's stomach turned and though she heaved, nothing came up. That rotund man with smelly breath and yellow fingernails had touched her mother. How could she bear it now that she had seen for herself just how gentle and loving Brocca was?

"Shh, darlin'. These things happened long ago and God turned them into good. We are together and we are free. The Brehons are just. They will set us free."

Brocca's words were fresh green heather in Brigid's world of dry dirt. "I'm praying to forget, maither. We should plan for the future. We'll travel and preach, just like Patrick."

"I would like that, daughter. There are so many in Ireland who need the Light. We must carry on Patrick's work."

Brigid was reminded of Maire's words when she had asked Brigid to take Aine to Cillian. God indeed had intended for Brigid to minister to the lost. That's why he allowed her to perform miracles. She could now see why God had allowed

Ardan to bring them to the king. They'd be truly set free to begin their work. Her mother's fear of Dubthach's old wife made little sense. Perhaps she had been frightened by her because she was so young when she was sent away. Brigid wasn't afraid.

CHAPTER

"FOR I KNOW THE PLANS I HAVE FOR YOU,'
DECLARES THE LORD, 'PLANS TO PROSPER YOU
AND NOT TO HARM YOU, PLANS TO GIVE
YOU HOPE AND A FUTURE.'"
JEREMIAH 29:11

The women were quiet but soaked to the bone when Ardan returned for them. "We're going inside. Ye must be silent. The servants will provide ye with a warm meal and dry clothes, but ye must not speak. Not without *my* permission."

They were calm and cooperative, not at all what he expected. The gods were pleased with Ardan, the great druid of Leinster.

Before he left the women for the night, Ardan passed the head maid a silver coin to buy silence. He still feared the presence of the Christian king. He'd need a plan to budge Dunlaing from Cashel. He had previously thought he'd send for Troya, and have the matter settled before King Aenghus knew what happened, but he thought better of it. Troya was impetuous. Better that she stay in Leinster and he bring Brigid and Brocca to her.

Now, how to handle the Brehons? Dunlaing had already called for them. He sent his young attendant – of course! Dunlaing had said the boy was unreliable.

Ardan found the lad crouching in the dark threshold of

Dunlaing's chambers. He smiled at the pitiful creature. "Why do ye sit here?"

The lad held his head in his hands. "The king will be angry with me."

"Dunlaing? Why? Have ye disobeyed him?"

He turned his sad chestnut eyes toward Ardan. "I did not mean to disobey. 'Tis just that I don't know who to ask."

Ah, the boy's incompetence would serve Ardan well. "Do ye speak about the order to convene the Brehons, lad?"

"Aye. Can ye tell me how to carry out the king's wishes?"

Ardan glanced around them. The halls were quiet. He hadn't seen any of the reigning king's attendants since he arrived. Dunlaing occupied a separate wing of the castle. "I cannot. Have ye sought out the attendants to the ruling king?"

"That's what I intended to do. But they've all left."

Could it be true? "Explain, lad."

"The king of Munster and all his attendants. They're gone to the place of kings in the east. The guards will not speak to me, so I have no way of finding the Brehons."

Ardan would have danced a jig had he been alone. "I will speak to King Dunlaing on yer behalf. He'll not punish ye. He convenes the Brehons at my request. If I ask him to delay until we reach Leinster, he will, especially since the king of Munster cannot be entertained at the gathering here."

Ardan sent the lad off and hurried to speak to Dunlaing. He found him pacing the room. "Ah, Ardan. Have ye heard? King Aenghus of Munster, satisfied with our truce, has journeyed..."

Dunlaing seemed to be struggling with whether or not to tell Ardan the whereabouts of the king. He must not trust Ardan with that confidence. But Ardan already knew. The boy had told him. "To Tara."

Dunlaing's jewel-like eyes flashed. "That's right. My druid knows these things."

173

Ardan smiled. "Shall we convene the Brehons in Leinster, then?"

"'Tis too late. My boy has... unless he has failed me again."

"He has, king. The Brehons have not yet been summoned. But do not blame him. This has worked out for the best."

Dunlaing rubbed his fingers through his coarse hair and sighed. "I grant him mercy because he's young and still learning. We will leave for Leinster at the dawning of the new morn. I tire of this place, and it will be good to be home. Bring along the women, and my naive new servant. I will speak to the women after we arrive. If you also summon Troya, perhaps we will not need the Brehons after all."

Ardan made a polite exit from the king's presence and praised the gods all the way to his sleeping chamber. Now all he had to do was to convince Dunlaing that his plan was best for the kingdom, and Troya would take care of the rest.

Ardan disliked traveling with the women, but he dared not trust their care to anyone. When they arrived at Dunlaing's castle, he secured them in a cell and then steered the bishop's horse to the woodland home of his student Troya.

She welcomed him into her hovel.

The old woman cocked her matted head toward Ardan as he sat at her cooking fire. "She's here? In Leinster?"

Ardan wiped his weary eyes. "Aye, she is." He glanced around the woman's pit of a home. There was but one sleeping mat, but she had coated the floor with rushes in an attempt to make her dwelling comfortable. The walls were made of stone, an extravagance. Perhaps the home had been nice once, but no longer. The place lacked the amenities Ardan required in his own abode.

Ardan stared at his pathetic apprentice. "Did Brigid's friends give ye any trouble?"

Troya's toothless mouth gaped open. "Hah. No trouble at all. Cook and her young lad – Brian, is it?"

Ardan stirred the fire with a birch twig. "That's right. I've not seen them. Ye did well keeping them away."

Troya scrambled to a worm-eaten wooden cupboard and retrieved a stone canister filled with tea leaves. "They did come by. Cook ranted and shook her fist at me." Troya tilted her head back and cackled like a happy seabird. "I said nothing, though they thought they'd scared me stiffer than a crow on an ice-topped lough."

She sprinkled the dried tea into a cooking pot and stirred the concoction with a long-handled wooden spoon. She winked at him. "I knew ye'd take care of Brigid. That's why I let them think I was weak. And have ye done it, then?"

"Aye, King Dunlaing will hear yer request for an honor price in the morning."

Troya stroked a long fingernail across her crumpled chin. "This girl, does she own any property? Does her mother?"

"They say they own a cow, but 'tis in the hands of Brocca's former master. There's no proof they are anything but poor freewomen."

Troya stared at him with red-streaked eyes. "They are freewomen? How did this happen?" She stirred her pot of porridge and disregarded her own question. "'Tis better they are, aye? Their master cannot pay the honor price for them. They own nothing. So Brigid will pay with her life."

Doves from the rafters hummed approval.

Ardan knew at that moment, as if someone whispered in his ear, that ridding himself of the women would be much easier than convincing them to use their influence to advance his cause. He had to make sure the outcome was in his control. "Aye, so it would seem. But then... my sticks seem to say something different." He held out his druid fortune sticks for her to examine.

"Ardan! It cannot be. Is that truly how they fell?" She reached for them with fingers that had been burned and healed over and over – the hands of a woman who had stirred many cooking pots.

He jerked the wands away before she could look too closely and stuffed them inside his cloak. "I'm afraid so. Perhaps the gods are angry with ye." He knew she believed him.

Troya's chin quivered. "They're always angry." She held her arms over her head and leaned toward the floor. "No matter how much I sacrifice, no matter how many sprigs of mistletoe I cut from the oak with my golden sickle. Only human blood will end my suffering." She crept to her bed and lay down.

Ardan retrieved a bear pelt from a log seat by the fire. Troya was in the winter season of her life, and she had taken to carrying the bone-warming cover wherever she went, saying her scrawny limbs could no longer produce their own heat. In her misery, she had forgotten to bring the cover to her bed.

He draped it over her the way he'd seen mothers tuck in children at night. His gentleness would help her trust him. "There, there. 'Tis possible Dunlaing will not consent to the honor price, but do ye really need him, Troya? Do ye need me? Ye know where Brigid sleeps. If I should leave the key to her cell in yer cabin by mistake, no one would know."

She rolled over and wrinkled her pointed nose at him. "Ardan, ye would do that for me?"

"I hate to see ye tormented by angry gods, old one. 'Tis time ye had relief. Yer days on the grassy plains of Ireland have been overflowing with torment. I cannot bear to know ye'd have the same when ye pass below."

Tears streaked down her pasty face. "Nay. I want to live in peace. They speak to me day and night, like a banshee who never comes." She held her hands over her ears. "I cannot bear it."

He pulled Troya's arm away and pressed the key into her palm. "Below the king's great hall lies the cell where Brigid sleeps with her mother. If ye do away with them both, won't the gods be doubly pleased? Tomorrow night, after the sun sets. The castle will be feasting and no one will pay ye heed. Come before the moon rises. Come and take vengeance to please the gods and relieve yerself of their eternal punishment."

Ardan rode into the night on the bishop's horse he now called his own. Troya would kill both women. He would wait in the shadows until the act was completed and then call for the guards. But first, he would prophesy the event to Dunlaing at a banquet attended by all of Leinster's landowners who would be assembled to welcome the king home. When they saw how powerful he was, and noted the inability of Brigid's god to come to her aid, Ardan would grow in favor. It would not be long before Dunlaing was ousted and the great Ardan exalted.

Ardan returned to the castle serenaded by crickets. Candlelight glowed under the waxed wooden door of the king's chamber. He tapped his knuckles lightly on one panel. "King? 'Tis I, Ardan. If yer awake I have news."

The bolt slid back from the inside and the door swung wide. The king stood before him in a linen undergarment. The sudden clinking of metal meant guards were approaching from down the hall, their weapons clattering in their haste.

Dunlaing shouted toward the noise, "Go back! 'Tis only my druid." He welcomed Ardan into the room, which smelled of spice. "They want to watch over me in my chamber, but there's no need in my own castle. What news have ye?"

"The gods have spoken to me on the wind."

Dunlaing touched Ardan's white woolen cloak and rubbed his fingers on his walking stick. "Yer cold. Ye've been out long."

"Aye, king. I have walked among the oaks tonight and I bring ye the message."

"Speak it, then. The hour grows late."

"Tomorrow there shall be a large feast."

Dunlaing's face brightened. He had desired such a celebration back in Munster.

Ardan continued. "The gods want offerings in appreciation for yer alliance with the king of Munster. They do not blame ye for joining forces with a Christian king."

Dunlaing scratched his coarse graying beard. "Blame me?"

"Aye. They understand that ye did this for the good of yer people, King Dunlaing."

"That I did, and we will celebrate. 'Tis time all the lairds came to hear of my journey."

Ardan stood at the highest point of the castle and lifted his face eastward. Troya was approaching in the night – he could feel it. The guards would not detect her presence because he had instructed her on the fine points of moving about unnoticed. She was old, but still as crafty as a crow, and she was a crazy old witch. When Ardan had first discovered her living alone in the forest, he knew she would be of value to him someday.

He searched the sky for the first evening star. The heavens were orderly. Everything was unfolding as it should. He chanted toward the hills. The Others living there would hear his plea, take notice of his outstretched arms, and endow him with power. He closed his eyes and inhaled the night scent, breathing in the spiritual essence. His eyes popped open. Troya was nearly at the rear entrance.

Ardan threw off his white cloak and leapt down the steps leading to the dining hall. There was little time to waste. He slid into his place beside the king just as Dunlaing was finishing his tale of successful talks with the king of Munster.

Dunlaing pointed his cup toward Ardan. "Have ye a story to tell, druid?"

Perfect. "I do, king." Ardan rose and straightened his torque, which had shifted off-center in his haste to join the banquet. "There will be a murder tonight."

The feasters gasped and murmured among themselves.

The king hollered over the din. "Tell us! Who should be concerned for his life?"

Soldiers whisked out their dirks and pointed their spears at Ardan.

He held up his hand. "Not the king."

Relief washed over the crowd like a breeze on a hot day.

The king's cheeks flushed. "Who then, Ardan?"

Ardan enjoyed the anxious looks on the faces in the crowd. He prolonged the moment by staring back at as many as he could. When he deemed they'd suffered enough, he broke the silence. "'Tis no one here."

Another wave of sighs washed over the hall. Ardan closed his eyes for effect. "'Tis a young woman. Someone whose birth had been prophesied. I feel the time has come. I must go and find the murderer. Do not follow me if ye fear the banshee."

Ardan had never seen the fairies called banshees, the ones heralding death, though he thought he'd heard them at times. The mention of the spirit would be enough to keep anyone from trailing him.

He arrived at the women's cell just in time to see Troya enter ahead of him. She lifted her golden druid's sickle over Brigid's head. Ardan ducked away from Brigid's sight. He didn't want her haunting him from the other side, proclaiming that he had broken his druid code. He'd done nothing of the sort, of course. Still, one had to be careful with spirits.

A scream.

Troya.

The sound thundered in his ears. Good. The people would

179

believe the banshee had come. "Guards, come quick!" he shouted.

A voice rang out behind him. "I'm here."

The young lad, the king's incompetent, stood behind him. Ardan peered into the cell. Brigid and her mother clung to each other sobbing. Troya lay in the middle of the room with a spear protruding from the back of her head. Her white cloak was soaked crimson.

She was dead.

While Ardan had been congratulated for his keen senses, the young lad was lauded even more. The Christians had survived, and they praised their god for delivering them. As Ardan had imagined, many people believed Troya was the embodiment of the banshee. Unfortunately, they also believed Brigid's god had destroyed the evil fairy and delivered Brigid and her mother from harm.

Ardan was forced to resort to an alternative plan, although he wasn't precisely sure how to enact it. He escaped to his outdoor altar to ponder and seek inspiration.

The wind howled through leafless trees. Ardan flung the cowl of his cloak off his head and lit a candle with his torch. He was protected from the weather in his hollowed-out shelter beneath the roots of an ancient oak. He sought solitude and had ordered the other druids to stay away. He alone would seek help from the gods.

Ardan rubbed his hands over the earth. *Speak to me.*

Lightning flashed. A storm gathered. Ardan raised his arms to the heavens. "Come into me, powers, be ye dark or light. Any who help me obtain my rightful place in Ireland are welcome."

A tingle crept over him. Not from the cold, he told himself. The gods were present, and in that holy place they would hear him. They'd have to.

All night and most of the next day he took no food or water. He emerged from the tree shelter with a fresh idea.

The king was ready when Ardan entered the castle. Dunlaing extended his ring, as always, and Ardan kissed it – for the last time, he inwardly vowed.

The king twisted the ring on his finger. "This Brigid bothers me, Ardan."

"I understand, king. She has embarrassed ye, and now the lairds have witnessed her powers."

Dunlaing rubbed the embroidered edge of his royal robe. "There will be no hearing for an honor price against Brigid now that her accuser's dead."

"Aye, king." Ardan stood like a tree and he could almost feel roots growing beneath him, extending underneath the earth's surface and reaching the fringes of the Otherworld.

The king cleared his throat. "In spite of my misgivings, I shall grant Brigid the audience she has requested. That I must do." He stared at the floor and twisted his ring some more. "I do not wish to be made a fool. I will grant her whatever she wishes and set her free, be rid of her."

Ardan didn't like the sound of that. "But, king, do ye think this wise? She will expand her following. Soon the people will turn to her and reject the king."

Dunlaing's head shot up. "Do ye think it so, druid?" He slammed his fist down on the arm of his royal chair. "I brought them victory rather than bloodshed by allying myself with a neighboring king. This was not done easily."

Ardan bowed his head. "I understand, my king. And the gods are pleased by the treaty."

Dunlaing tapped his fingers on his knees. "What can be done? Exile her?"

Ardan knelt down, bringing himself eye-to-eye with Dunlaing. "If ye want to break someone's influence, ye have to remove what they cherish most." Ardan snapped his fingers as though the thought had just come to him. "Brigid cares not if ye banish her to the outermost wilderness. She wants to tell everyone 'bout her god and build her kingdom. If ye send her off, people will follow, and she will gather other clans together." He gazed into the king's puzzled face. "Ye know what would happen, don't ye? She'll build up an army against ye."

Dunlaing's fingers folded into fists. "What can stop her, druid? What do yer sticks tell ye?"

Ardan took the hint and pulled his wands from the depths of his cloak. He rolled them about in his fingers and then tossed them onto the stone floor in front of the king. The ruler of Leinster had no druid training and would trust Ardan to interpret the gods' message in the magical rods.

Ardan pressed his lips together and eyed the placement of the sticks. They seemed to be pointing to hope and patience, but it didn't matter. Ardan wouldn't be lying if he told the king what he really saw – a way to break Brigid's spirit.

"Hear her as she requested. Let her think her god will help her. Offer her whatever she asks, and let her live in peace for a time. When she starts to proclaim miracles, attributing them to her god, that will be the signal that the time has come to act. She will be the one humiliated, and you, great king of Leinster, will be honored."

Dunlaing straightened his back. "This sounds fine. How will it happen?"

"By taking from her what she cares most about."

"And that is what, man? I have little patience today for druid puzzles."

The time was not right to reveal his plan. He needed the king to depend on him for answers. "The magic druid sticks plead for patience, dear king. We will have the answers when the gods say the time is right."

CHAPTER

"A GENTLE ANSWER TURNS AWAY WRATH, BUT A HARSH WORD STIRS UP ANGER."
PROVERBS 15:1

Brigid woke in the middle of the night, sweating. The image of her father's old wife, a spear running through her skull, appeared over and over again in her mind. Somewhere she was certain someone was cooking cabbage. She found a bucket in the corner of the cell and vomited.

Brocca said nothing while running her hands over Brigid's damp hair.

The night continued on with the same events mercilessly following each other through her mind the way a dog chases its tail. At the first flicker of daylight entering through a slit of window high on the wall, the guard who had executed Troya came for them.

He was beaming, as though rather than murdering a human being, he had shot a prize buck for supper. "I brought boiled eggs and cream. C'mon, eat up. The ladies will be here soon to dress ye and take ye to the king."

Brigid wiped her mouth on her gown. "We will see the king, ye say?"

"Aye, just as ye asked. I suppose ye'll no longer be held

responsible for an honor price, seeing as the woman who asked for it is now dead."

Brigid felt sick again. Her mother didn't look too well either. The lad had saved their lives, but why had it come to this? Ultimately, Dubthach was responsible. He was the one who had caused Troya to hate them so.

The lad stared at them. "Did ye hear me?"

"Oh, aye. The king. We're to be set free, I suppose." Saying the words out loud helped Brigid realize there was much to do for the people outside Dunlaing's castle.

The guard brought hot water and cloths, and Brigid and her mother managed to scrub the grime from their bodies. They were given soft linen gowns and cloaks woven in many colors. Brigid placed one of the fine garments over her mother's shoulders and thought she stood straighter because of it. She pinned a silver brooch at one corner. "How does it feel, maither?"

Brocca patted the ornament and then ran her fingers down the cloak's gold-embroidered edges. "I much prefer this to the druidess costume."

"It suits ye far better." Brigid asked for her own cloak back. She preferred its thick black material to what the servants offered.

The young man reappeared when they were dressed. "'Tis time to accept the offering of the golden scepter."

This time Brigid knew what to do almost without thinking. She had appeared in front of the king before.

Dunlaing's brilliant blue eyes greeted her with no animosity. "I believe ye have been treated unfairly, Brigid."

Brigid touched the scepter and glanced at the floor. "I have. Troya's honor price should have come directly from the source of her pain. Not me, but my father, Dubthach of Glasgleann."

Brocca made a grunting sound in her throat and pulled at the back of Brigid's cloak.

Dunlaing waved his bejeweled right hand in the air. "I rid myself of this matter. I seek only to right the wrong that has been done to ye by keeping ye locked in my castle where ye were nearly killed with no means of escape. Please, tell me what ye want."

Brigid turned to her mother. "What shall I ask for, maither? What besides our freedom?"

"Only a place to lie our heads, darlin'."

She turned back to the king. "I ask but two things, sir."

He touched his fingers together and nodded.

"I ask that the freedom which Bram of Ennis Dun has granted my mother and me be made official."

"I shall order it into the Brehon records."

"Thank ye, sir."

She glanced around the hall, but saw no signs of Ardan. She turned to Brocca. "Maither, pray hard and do it now."

Brocca made the sign of the cross with her fingers.

Brigid bowed before the king. "I ask only for some land – for my mother and myself."

The king raised his eyebrows. "I see. And how much land do ye require?"

"Only as much as my cloak will cover."

He laughed. "And I suppose yer god will make yer cloak grow?"

Brigid narrowed her eyes. "Do ye mock the One True God, King Dunlaing?"

He stood. "I do not wish to look out my window every morning and gaze out on your small patch of land. Therefore, we'll ride a short distance where ye'll cast yer cloak."

Brigid led her mother by the hand as they left the hall. The chill of winter blasted from the north. Brigid did not relish removing her warm cloak. People poured out of the castle

185

– soldiers, maids, blacksmiths, and a handful of druids in white cloaks. They followed on horseback and in carts. Brigid didn't see Ardan, but she felt him watching her, from one of the wagons perhaps. They were driven a short distance until the castle could only be seen on the horizon.

Brocca sighed the entire way. "Brigid, was this wise? To put God to a test?"

Brigid circled her arms around her mother. "Maybe not. But God increased the butter I made. He blessed Dubthach's livestock so that they produced enough food for me to feed the woodsfolk. Who's to say he cannot do this? Dunlaing's pride will cause his fall."

A servant blew on an ox horn. The blast beckoned curious people from the woods. The horn blower took a deep breath and announced, "Brigid, formerly of Glasgleann, will perform an act in honor of her god."

Brocca whispered into her hair, "What have ye done, daughter?"

Brigid ignored her and focused on her cloak. The garment was generous in size, but if no miracle were performed, her territory would barely house a cow. Even so, a small still voice whispered, *Trust me.*

Brigid closed her eyes and held her cloak to the wind. The crowd grew silent. She prayed. After a few moments, she felt a tug and immediately opened her eyes. Her cloak was attached to another, and that one to another, and to another, as far as she could see. The wind held them aloft, making them appear as one large cloak. The woodsfolk had joined their meager clothing to hers.

The wind howled and blew her hair into her eyes, sounding like a thousand frantic boars trouncing down the hillside.

Dunlaing wailed. "Stop, stop! Put down yer cloak and I'll grant ye that much land. Please, stop now."

Brigid dropped her cloak. The wind ceased, and the tail of

black material floated down to earth. The poor folks shivered, shirtless. Had God snatched the clothes from them and added them to her cloak? Or had they willingly given their clothes to her? She was grateful, however it happened, and turned to face the king. Would he accept the elongated cloak or would he claim trickery?

Before she could ask, Dunlaing and his royal wagon were already disappearing down the path toward the castle walls.

Brigid dropped to her knees, feeling the wool of her cloak scratch her shivering skin. "A home, maither. We've a home now."

After winter had dropped its frosty hold on Leinster, Ardan left his druid shelter in the woods to visit King Dunlaing. He dared not go any sooner. He had assured the ruler that Brigid would not embarrass him any further. Ardan wished to give the king's anger time to abate.

"So, the great druid finally graces me with his presence." Dunlaing scowled at him from his scrolled chair. "I will ask that ye read yer news and leave me at once."

Ardan expected as much, so he had gathered men, fellow druids, to help him be reconciled with the king. Now, more than ever, he needed to be rid of Brigid. He wished he had bent the druid code, just a bit, and finished Troya's work for her that night at the castle.

"Today, dear king, I have brought a council of wise druids for the king's service." Ardan bowed and turned to the men. They each possessed talents in extreme measure – each different from the other. "I have convened a master of satire, a prophet, and a student of the stars. With such wisdom of the gods at yer hands, king, ye shall be rid of Brigid and her followers within one cycle of the moon."

The men dropped their white hoods and bowed deeply.

The corners of Dunlaing's mouth spread and his cheeks

glowed apple red. "A wise king always confers with advisors. I shall see what they have to say. But Ardan, I'm holding ye to what ye declared months ago. 'Twas seen in the druid sticks, nay?"

Ardan was pleased Dunlaing wanted to proceed. "Of course, king. In time, in time. When all the signs are right."

Brigid sat beneath an ancient oak tree, the spot where her trail of cloaks had come to rest when Dunlaing had challenged her God. The woodsfolk had insisted on building a shelter beside the tree, and it was nearly finished. How things had changed. Only one season ago she was homeless and facing death. Now a large wooden building was being constructed. She would live there forever with her mother.

The pagans chose the site, although the Christians felled the trees for it. The ill-advised declared her some kind of druidess and thus in need of a home beside an oak. Some even thought she was a goddess because of the power she displayed. She had much work to do explaining that her works were from God and that he used her to display *his* power.

"It was much the same for me," her mother had told her. "I tried to show the people God's Way, tried to show his love. But they called me a druidess. God found favor in me and allowed me to speak with them, just like he did with Patrick, though I, a slave, never reached as many people as he did."

Brigid had wanted to hear more about the gatherings with Patrick. She still didn't understand why Dubthach had allowed Cook to take her to the seashore. And why had her mother not come to her before she became blind? But the questions were unimportant really. She wanted to let go of the past, never again ask her mother what happened before they were reunited. They had a new life.

The poor starving folks living at the border of Dunlaing's castle needed much care. Brigid put aside her questions and kept busy blessing babies and producing large quantities of cheese and butter from small beginnings – God's doings.

Brigid gazed up at the spring green leaves above her head. God's hand had reached down to touch the tiny oak seed with life. Only the Master of all living things could turn a minuscule cold dark seed into a great immense tree, a vessel full of life. Pagans believed the tree was the god or that a god somehow inhabited the oak. She began to design a plan for presenting the Creator to the people. She wanted to persuade them to abandon the belief in a god who did not exist.

She'd need her paper, manuscripts. What was Cillian doing now? Maybe she could send for him, invite the monks to share the large shelter. They might refuse, choosing to stay secluded, but they could still assist her with manuscripts and she could send some of the faithful to Cillian for training. And, of course, Cook should come live with them. Brigid would see to that as soon as possible.

Brocca called to her from the building site. "Daughter? Come feast with us! A spring lamb has been slaughtered, and the earth's first fruits of the season have been picked."

Brocca was thriving. Whatever sickness she had suffered from left almost as soon as they took up residence on the land granted to them by the king. Her copper tresses were only streaks in her gray head, her illness had faded the color, but her skin was like milk and her smile as broad as the great river.

Brigid and her mother sat with the builders inside the roofless framed structure. Most of the men who worked there had converted to Christianity. Followers of Ireland's new faith seemed to cluster together now more than ever before. Smells of honey-sweetened bread and creamy cheese made the room seem that much more festive.

Pagans would be celebrating the new season that night with massive fires, but their activities could be no more joyous than Brigid's current gathering of friends in the Lord.

189

"How are the flock of sheep faring?" one fellow asked another.

"This one met a sad fate," another quipped, taking a bite out of a greasy drumstick.

Brigid enjoyed those people, even the unconverted ones. They were lighthearted, full of vigor and fun. Truly this was God's calling on her life.

Brigid's mother murmured into her hair, "Daughter, have ye thought of marrying?"

Brigid nearly choked on her creamed turnips. "Maither, why...?" The food burned as it slid down her throat. Brigid waved her hand in front of her mouth and blew puffs of air.

One of the men jumped to her aid, offering a tin cup of cool spring water. She accepted it, but didn't look him in the eye. Perhaps someone had a love interest in her, and she had never noticed. Having a husband would impede her work.

Brocca tugged at Brigid's sleeve. "I understand, Brigid, that ye labor for the Lord. That does not mean ye cannot..." She shielded her mouth with her hand to keep her words private. "Marry."

"Maither, shall we speak of this later?" Brigid cleared her dishes and headed for the solitude of the oak.

"Wait for me." Brocca followed, her bread still cradled in her hand. "We'll feed the birds together."

Brigid laughed. She longed to feed all of Ireland and her mother threw crumbs to the birds. Brocca didn't seem as driven as Brigid to touch everyone possible. Brocca was content in the space that she could cover with one swirl of her cloak. They were different in that way.

Brigid and her mother sat quietly, sometimes nibbling on the bread, sometimes tossing pieces to waiting sparrows. Perhaps they had run out of things to talk about.

When the time felt right, Brigid told her mother what was on her heart. "I'm praying that God will make me ugly, maither. So that no man will want me before I visit the bishop and devote my life to the Lord."

"Oh, nay, Brigid. Yer beautiful, even to one with no sight. And ye *have* given yer life to the Lord. Everyone knows that."

"'Tis not enough. I want to build a school of learning and place of worship here at the Cell of the Oak. That's what we'll call the place, maither."

Tears streamed down Brocca's face.

Brigid brushed them away with the back of her palm. "What's wrong? Why do ye cry?"

Brocca held Brigid's hand against her cheek. "For all these seasons I have never understood. Not until now."

"Understood what? Why I must become part of the church Patrick served and bring their teachings to the Cell of the Oak?"

"Dear one, I never understood the prophecy at yer birth. Do ye know 'bout it?"

Brigid patted her mother's hand. "We do not have to speak of this. We can just look to the future."

More tears spilled from the corners of Brocca's sightless eyes. "'Tis about the future."

"Very well. Tell me, then." Brigid lay down with her head in her mother's lap and stared up into the branches of the massive tree. Sparrows lingered, hoping for more bread.

"The day ye were born was much like this day, damp but sunny. It was a glorious day and I was so happy."

Brigid smiled as she watched the tiny birds hop back and forth on the branches like children at play.

"But the night before filled me with terror."

Brigid sat up. "Why?"

Brocca turned toward the sunrays piercing through the branches. She covered her mouth as though she was once again seeing the events she remembered. She flopped her hand back to her lap. "Bram invited a prophet from the woods

191

to visit. I had never seen him before. He stared at me like he knew me. Like he had come specifically to see me." She sighed. "I suppose he had. His eyes, deep like a peat bog, seemed to pierce my very soul. He declared that ye'd be born the very next day at dawn." Her voice choked back tears. "Half inside the house, half outside. And wouldn't ye know, that's what happened."

"What's so terrible 'bout that?" Brigid lay back down and covered herself with a plaid blanket, thinking a nap after the meal would refresh her.

Brocca smiled down at her. "Nothing's wrong with that. 'Twas not those words that frightened me. 'Twas the other thing he said, and also I was worried that Dubthach had sent him to snatch ye away at birth."

Brigid shivered and wondered why the horrible man hadn't done exactly that. He was loathsome enough to have done it for spite.

Brocca twirled a strand of Brigid's hair between her fingers. "The prophet said ye'd be either a curse or a blessing to Ireland. Don't ye see, dearie? What yer planning to do here at the Cell of the Oak will fulfill that prophecy. Ye'll be the blessing, and 'tis much more than my small mind could have ever imagined."

That night, while the pagans feasted and lit huge outdoor fires, Brigid dreamed she was alone in the forest. A fox came to greet her and did tricks, just as the fox in King Dunlaing's castle had done long ago. The creature curled up in her lap, and she stroked its silky bronze fur that smelled of spring heather. Suddenly the animal jumped up and nipped her left cheek.

She awoke with a swollen eye.

Brocca padded her fingers over Brigid's face. "Ye've gotten a sickness in yer eye. We must make a poultice."

They boiled some yarrow over the cooking fire and added several sweet-smelling herbs. The eye burned and itched.

Brocca fussed over her. "Don't scratch."

Brigid dropped her hand in her lap. "How did ye know I was going to..." She bit her lip. Brocca seemed to sense her every move.

"We don't want the other eye to gather the sick fluid and become swollen also."

One of the sisters in the Lord entered Brigid's sleeping chamber, toting more herbs. She dropped them to her feet and gasped.

Brigid hurried to scoop up the precious harvest. "What's wrong, child?"

"Brigid, yer face is so horribly swollen. Worse than when I saw ye this morn." The girl turned away from Brigid and busied herself at the cooking fire.

Later that day, even with her left eye covered with a bandage, Brigid's bloated face drew gasps and looks of horror from everyone she encountered around the building site.

Brocca stayed close to her side. Brigid reached for her hand. "It does not bother me much now. 'Tis good ye cannot see me or ye'd turn away like the others."

Brocca slipped her palm inside Brigid's. "Never. A mother's child is always beautiful to her."

Brigid's face was still puffy when a visitor came to see her, saying he'd arrived from King Dunlaing's castle. An odd fellow wearing a green tunic, he said he was a royal poet. In the evening people flocked to hear his stories while he strummed his harp. He spoke of battles fought long ago, of Queen Medb and her quest for a white bull, of monsters living in the lakes, of upcoming gatherings of Christians by the sea and, one night, he sang a song of Brigid.

Brigid happened to pass by on her way to fetch water

from a stream for the new morn's washing. She'd never sat in on such entertainment, just caught bits and pieces of the stories as she went on her way. This time the poet seemed to wait for her to pass at just the right distance so she'd hear him whisper her name.

She stopped, turned toward the assembly, and set her wooden bucket down at her feet. He never looked directly at her, but paced back and forth, looking every listener in the eye. He set the story of her unusual birth to song and told the people about her as if she were legend. How did he know about her? Had he, in his travels, visited Bram? She'd ask later.

The man's tone was enthralling. His words flowed in stunning waves of heart-thumping thoughts. His gift to the people was his voice and the melody of words. Such storytelling was the way of the people, Brigid knew, but she longed to write down the tales, the true ones, and teach people to read them, and God's Scriptures, for themselves.

The tale ended and Brigid continued on to the water's edge and dipped her bucket into the coolness of the spring. She hadn't brought a torch, but someone had left a candle burning at the base of two stone pillars. Were those pagan statues? She'd have to remember to order them removed.

The candlelight reflected in the water, casting a blurry image of her face – distorted, but clear enough to reveal the disfigurement. Brigid touched her fingers to her puffy cheek. Words, much sweeter than the poet's, drifted to her. She heard the Lord's voice in her head, the memory of what she had once written while living with Cillian in Aghade. She didn't remember exactly what she had recorded so long ago, but the meaning was unmistakable.

Favor is deceitful and beauty is vain, but a woman who fears the Lord shall be praised.

Praise from men wasn't important to her, but having God's favor was.

194

She hurried back to her sleeping quarters and peeled back the bearskin door. "I have to go see Bishop Mel, maither. At the seashore. The poet's songs say he will be there soon, so I must go. I will gain the blessing of the church from across the sea, and I will bring back supplies, everything we need to set up our center of learning and worship. When I return, I'll invite Cillian and his monks from Aghade." Breathless, she set the washing water down near the door and joined her mother on a straw-stuffed cushion near the now-cold fire ring in the center of the hut.

Brocca reached for Brigid's hand. "Then I shall go with ye."

"Nay, maither. I want ye to fetch Cook. I'll send men with ye so that Dubthach will not harm ye."

"He'll not harm me. He's terrified of suffering Bram's wrath."

Brigid gripped her mother's wrists. "Bram. Would he have known that poet?"

"The man visiting with the pagans and playing the harp?"

"Aye. Would he have knowledge of Bram?"

"Perhaps. A druid travels much. 'Tis possible. Did ye ask him?"

"I will when I have time."

Brocca laughed. "Daughter, calm yerself. Yer plans will succeed. There's no need to rush."

Brigid turned her mother's face toward her. "I'm leaving tomorrow. But I must know yer safe. Bram's threatened curse on Dubthach may not be enough to deter him. Grant me this, maither. Take an army of believers with ye."

"As ye wish, darlin'." Brocca reached for her healing herbs stored in a leather pouch around her waist. She untwisted the ties and slipped the purse around Brigid's neck. "Keep treating the eye with the poultice. Tell me ye will, child."

Brigid almost wanted the ailment to remain. No man

195

desired a wife with a hideous face, making her work much easier. But she did not want to lose her vision, so she agreed.

The sparrows and thrushes chattered at the first ray of light as Brigid prepared for her journey.

"Who will go with ye?" Brocca clung to her side and rubbed one hand against Brigid's cheek.

"I need no one. I'll travel faster that way. I expect to be gone no longer than a few days. Ye'll be back before I will, of course, but know we'll be together soon, with all our friends."

"And I shall kill a calf for yer return." Brocca kissed her daughter's right cheek.

The poet offered to ride part of the way with Brigid, saying he had to turn westward when they reached the wide river. Brigid didn't mind. She wanted to ask about Bram and hoped to teach this pagan poet about Christ on the way.

CHAPTER

Brigid packed a leather bag with only the barest essentials: a cooking pot, herbs for her eye, and some cheese and brown bread. She tied a dirk to her ankle the way she had seen Cillian do, but her knife would be only for cutting kindling and slicing her cheese. The ride to the river would not be far. From there they would board a boat and sail down the river toward the bay that emptied to the sea. Brigid remembered the place, though through a child's eyes. Even though Patrick would not be there, she looked forward to the gathering of Christians at the ath, the ford in the river.

The mysterious royal poet met her at the boundary of her property with his harp slung over his shoulder. He looked like a hunter bringing home a prize on his shoulders. "I'll part with ye at the ath. Immediately after I have a word with Old Conleth."

The poet's long black hair blew behind his grass-green robe in the stiff wind. Soon, Brigid hoped, she'd be able to ask about Bram.

The air smelled newly laundered, like a bolt of cloth fresh

from a drying rack. Brigid loved the spring season because it gave her a chance to sweep out the cobwebs in her dwelling as well as those in her mind. She was content with silence for the time being.

The poet hummed a tune. Now might be a good time to ask him about the song he had composed about her birth. He paused between notes.

"Poet, how is it that ye know the circumstances of my birth? Were ye there?"

He threw back his black mane and howled with laughter.

"What's so funny?"

He glanced only once at her and then stared down the road. "I must look older than I am."

She felt her face flush and her sore eye throbbed. "My apologies, poet. Ye must have heard 'bout it from someone." The man's eyes were concealed within his cloak. She couldn't judge his reaction. "Could it have been the druid of Ennis Dun, the ancient Bram?"

He resumed whistling and humming. Had she unknowingly asked him to break some kind of druid's code? She wished she understood these pagans better.

The grass in the meadow had sprouted the first green stalks of the season. The ground under the horses' hoofs was slippery. Old Geall had turned out to be a valuable gift from a poor woman, the one whose child Brigid had helped save. The animal served her well. God worked wonders.

Just when she thought the poet had dismissed her comments completely, Brigid heard Bram's name in the song he hummed.

Old Conleth sought the babe at the house of Bram,
Said she was special, of course.
Her birth would be blessing or curse, or curse,
Old Conleth said of Brigid's birth.

Brigid slowed her horse. "Ye *do* know Bram."

The poet paced his horse alongside. "We have never met."

"Then how is it that ye know this?"

He pushed the mossy-colored wool hood away from his head. "Old Conleth."

Dunlaing tore the flesh from the bone with one bite, waving away a servant who presented a knife. He chewed as though grinding the meat between his teeth would relieved his angst. The king wiped his mouth with a linen napkin and peered up at Ardan who stood still before him. No one had offered the king's chief druid a chair.

"Why have ye sent me these advisors? They bring no pleasant news."

Ardan squeezed his hands together behind his back. "Oh, king, I have yet to interpret their messages for ye. And we have not yet heard back from the poet who visits with Brigid."

Dunlaing swigged down his ale and glanced up. "I want to hear what the poet has to say, aye. But I heard the others well enough with my own ears."

Ardan's palms sweated and the collar of his linen tunic was strangely tight. "I will go to the oak sanctuary, king, and seek the gods' direction. They will speak to me."

Dunlaing's shoulders jiggled, and he spoke between bites of food. "Ye do what ye must, druid. Know this: the astronomer declares that the stars speak of a new king coming to Ireland, and the prophet foresees changes as well. Ye told me these men were masters, did ye not? What can ye say that's different?"

Ardan closed his eyes. He was a cauldron about to boil over. "The gods will speak, King Dunlaing. Ardan, the great master druid of Leinster, will receive their message and reveal to ye the path to overcoming these forces of change."

Ardan opened his eyes to find the king smiling.

Dunlaing pushed away his platter. "Then off with ye, Ardan! Do not make the gods wait."

Ardan flew out of the king's presence like a songbird freed from a cage. He passed the visiting druids in the corridor. "Go home, ye two. The king has no need for ye, and neither do I."

He pushed by their surprised faces and stomped out to the stable. He saddled one of the king's horses – why shouldn't he have the best? – and made for the sacred oak.

He leaned down to whisper in the horse's ear, "No one understands the gods. No one but Ardan the Great."

The late afternoon sun slipped behind clouds, and drizzle coated Ardan's hands and face and slid down his long cloak like raindrops on forest leaves. He dug his heels into the horse's hindquarters. "Faster, animal! May the gods curse ye if ye do not bring me to my sanctuary swiftly."

The massive tree reached out to Ardan like a mother's arms. He slid from his horse and tied him to an iron ring mounted on a stone pillar. The altar lay waiting with dozens of vessels holding candles. He pulled out his fire rock. "No one commands fire like I do. No one but the gods."

After lighting all the candles, he sat down on the dirt in front of the altar. He crossed his legs to make his body as small as possible and leaned so close to the ground that his nose nearly furrowed the soil. "Others, hear me now! I call down great curses on the woman called Brigid. May she have no more power to display. And may any king who defies Ardan the Great fall to the same fate."

He was pleased with the name he had given himself. The words rolled off his tongue sweeter than any poet's verses. He was great, as mighty as the oak he sat under. The gods were pleased with him, he knew. But he must not tempt them. He left the holy oak to seek a proper animal sacrifice.

The poet led Brigid to the home of the druid called Conleth. He lived alone in a rock house, a pile of boulders actually, in an area not far from the river. Brigid needed to get to the seashore soon, lest she miss the bishop and Patrick's followers traveling down from the north by way of the sea. Even so, this delay was necessary. She had to meet this man, this mysterious prophet her mother had encountered the night before Brigid was born.

Conleth met them outside and asked that they follow him in. He wore an unusual robe for a druid, embroidered with silk threads in too many colors to count. Brigid noted a pile of identical cloths stacked in a basket near the door.

The old man moved like a timid mouse, hesitating every few steps and gazing back at them. "I'm not used to entertaining visitors." He motioned for them to sit when they entered a main room furnished only with a few three-legged stools and a sleeping mat.

Brigid smiled at him and touched him gently on the arm. "We won't be staying long, sir. We are so grateful for yer hospitality."

He turned his slight frame toward her and cocked his head. He reached out his gnarled fingers and lifted a lock of Brigid's hair. "Poet, could it be ye've brought her to me at long last?"

Brigid stared into the druid's furrowed face. He was as ancient as Bram. She wanted to look away, but his gaze held her there. Her mouth went dry.

"'She's the one ye prophesied, Old Conleth." The poet picked up his harp and resumed the song he had been singing on the way to the cave.

Water in a cauldron blackened by age was boiling over a fire pit, but no one fetched it. Brigid gulped. Had they ensnared her? Did they wish her dead for some reason?

The old man released the strand of hair, letting it drop to

her shoulder. "Let me get the tea, child. Tell me, what happened to yer eye?"

She slumped to the ground. "A curse."

The old man shot the poet a look. "Has her fate been decided, poet? Does Ireland await a curse now?"

Brigid touched her bandage. "I will tell what happened to my eye, but 'twas I who did it."

The poet strummed his instrument, but ceased singing. He shook his black locks from his eyes to look at her.

Brigid gazed at the fire. "I want no man to desire me for his wife. I asked the Lord to take away my outward beauty until I make my vows in the presence of the bishop and receive his blessing. I'm on my way to the seashore now."

The old man poured steaming liquid into a mug and handed it to her. The tea's aroma soothed her. Old Conleth seemed gentle, and she no longer feared him.

He handed the green-cloaked one a mug. "'Tis good news ye've brought me, poet."

The dark one sipped and hummed.

Brigid's thoughts swam like a bowl full of minnows. "What does all this mean? Are ye the one who visited my mother the night before I was born?"

The old man's cracked lips turned upward. "I am."

"So yer a prophet from the woods?"

He lowered his body to his sleeping mat as though doing so caused him some pain. "I was. Now I am a prophet for the Lord."

She lowered her cup. "The Lord? Are ye speaking of the True God, the Creator?" She glanced back at the poet who, having traded his mug for his harp, grinned.

The old man refilled the poet's cup anyway. "Aye, lass. I was made a bishop by Patrick himself."

Brigid placed her mug on the dirt floor and clasped her hands. "Oh, praise God! 'Tis a church robe ye wear. Tell me, sir, what did ye mean by saying I'd be a blessing or a curse?"

The old man pointed to the poet. "I suppose that's why he brought ye here. So ye could discover the answer to that question. That so, poet?"

The younger man set his harp aside. "Ardan sent me to spy on ye, Brigid. He wrongly believed I followed his teachings. Ardan is a great sorcerer, but I never feared him. I was mentored by Old Conleth, and I do the Lord's work in the woods, with the common people who come to hear my tales."

Brigid had not expected that revelation. "But ye sing of legends, of gods, of monsters."

"Do I, now?" He accepted a biscuit from the old man. "Ye do not listen, Brigid. I tell the people the old stories, aye. But I tell them how the Creator is in them. The truth's what I tell them. That's all."

She had judged him too quickly. "Forgive me."

The old man twisted his stiff neck. "Ardan. He seeks to harm ye."

Brigid knew that. "Aye, he does. I know not why."

Conleth and the poet shot each other a look. The old man cleared his throat. "'Tis good ye seek the bishop. He will lay hands on ye and bless yer ministry. But having such a blessing will bring dark forces upon yer head."

Brigid rubbed her fingers over her chin, though it was her eye that itched. She considered the man's words. There was a force out there that disapproved of what she was doing. She must brace herself for spiritual battle.

The old man waved his arms toward bats snuggled above. "Poet here shall report to Ardan, truthfully, on what ye do while yer away. We walk in the Light. Is it not so?"

Brigid agreed and continued to sip her hot drink. She remembered the plans the poet had told her about and agreed. "I believe the poet desires to turn westward, however. He was not to accompany me to the gathering."

The old man blinked. "He will go with ye. He will see great things. And he will sing of them."

The poet's black head bobbed. "It will be as ye say."

The luxurious garments near the door caught her eye again. "May I look at those?"

The old man waved her on. She lifted them from the basket. They were, as she had thought, identical to the garb Old Conleth wore.

Bishop Conleth glanced at the pile of cloth. "Those are all the clothes I have. Given to me by the Roman Church."

Brigid held up one robe to examine its size. "Do ye know how much these could help someone? I have seen many people with short shirts and gowns who shiver in the cold."

The old man shrugged his shoulders. "Take them."

She carried the basket to the horses tied up outside. "Shall we go, poet?"

As soon as they left Bishop Conleth, Brigid tried to engage the poet. His reserved personality was frustrating. "Why do we call ye 'poet', rather than use yer name?"

"Because what I do is much more important than my name. Poet – 'tis who I am."

He trotted ahead. She caught up.

"Tell me, poet, 'bout this druid code. Do ye not betray Ardan?"

He studied some squirrels racing tree to tree. "I owe no allegiance to dark druids."

Bram had once said something similar.

They continued on until a wide expanse of blue water greeted them. They lodged their horses at a stable and paid the keeper with Roman coins the old bishop had supplied. They were given a boat for their journey.

Brigid spotted some children playing a game with rocks behind the stable. Their dirty faces matched the color of their ragged clothes. She interrupted the game to hand them the basket of robes. "Here is enough material to make ye all a fine set of clothes. And yer mothers and fathers also."

"*Brigid*," one of them whispered. "I heard the poet's song. Said she was coming."

Brigid shook her head and caught up to the poet just as he was about to launch their boat.

CHAPTER

20

"THEREFORE ENCOURAGE ONE ANOTHER
AND BUILD EACH OTHER UP."
1 THESSALONIANS 5:11

Brocca's chest tightened as the wagon neared Glasgleann. She had not been to Dubthach's estate since that terrible day when her only child was ripped from her arms. She was almost grateful she would not be able to look upon Glasgleann's wealth of cattle or observe the self-righteousness in her former master's cold dark eyes. She had forgiven him long ago, but memories could not be so easily wiped away.

She reached for the blanket she knew was somewhere in the wagon bed. Only one driver came with her, so she had to care for herself. Brigid had wanted a whole army, but that wasn't necessary. Brocca didn't fear harm, only her own resentment that threatened to rise up from her soul. She didn't want to hate Dubthach for what he had done, but she struggled with the temptation.

Heather and grass scented the open meadow as the wagon lurched upward. They climbed the rolling hills leading to Glasgleann. She thought about Cook, longed to wrap her arms around her.

"Almost there, Brocca! I can see smoke from the chimney," the driver called out.

Sounds of laughter drifted on the wind. There were children at Glasgleann, and they were happy. She used the blanket to wipe the travel dust from her face. "Stop at the kitchen, please."

The driver led her to the door. She held out her hands until she touched the smooth oak portal, weathered by years of northern exposure. It disappeared from under her palms when the driver swung it open.

A voice from inside greeted her. "Oh, dear me. Tell me that cannot be Brocca."

Cook's voice was harp music to Brocca's ears. She found herself smothered in Cook's hugs. Small children grabbed her legs.

Cook's voice rose among the others. "Blessed Lord, this is quite a surprise. I was just on my way out. Thought I'd see ye at the seashore and hoped ye'd know where Brigid..." Cook led Brocca to a wooden chair. The door creaked shut and the breeze it caused rippled the hem of Brocca's tunic.

Cook whispered in her ear, "'Tis true what Brian says? Yer master told him yer eyes no longer see."

Brocca whispered back. "Aye. Do not grieve for me. My life is good. And aye, I do know where my daughter is." Brocca reached for the woman's arm. "Cook. I am so sorry I have not come before now. Brigid is safe but fears a druid named Ardan. She did not want him to follow her here."

Pots and pans rattled nearby and chunks of turf thumped onto a fire, sending ripples of smoke to her nose.

Cook squeezed Brocca's hands so tightly they throbbed. "Oh, how my old bones have ached ever since I heard that druid had joined with Troya. Brian and I went to see her. Crazy old woman. She told us to stop looking for Brigid or..."

"What?" Brocca's question snapped like an iron trap.

207

Cook smoothed Brocca's hair from her forehead. "Oh, I was so frightened, though I pretended I was not. I put the fear of God into that one, I did. She seemed content leaving Brigid be so long as we never brought her back to Glasgleann."

"I understand. Let's sit and talk." Brocca reached for her silver brooch and unlatched it. The driver pulled her cloak from her shoulders.

Cook had been baking cakes and stewing fruit. Brocca turned toward the old woman's apple-scented breath. "What did ye know 'bout Troya?"

Cook's voice choked. "I knew she and Ardan were out to harm our sweet Brigid." Her voice choked. "Oh, dear Brocca, I failed to protect her! 'Twas all I ever aimed to do, but I could not, Lord forgive me. I had to return here, don't ye see?" Tears dropped onto their hands, intertwined on Cook's lap. "My daughter and my grandchildren, they greeted ye when ye came in. They live and work at Glasgleann. I couldn't run off and leave them, Brocca. I didn't know what to do. If my dear husband were still alive, he'd have gone after her."

Brocca embraced her old friend. "God cared for her, Cook. I'll explain later, but ye should not harbor any guilt. I know ye raised her fine. She has grown to be a God-fearing woman and has her own land where Christian brothers and sisters are building her a home."

Cook pulled back. "Glory! Could such a thing be?"

"'Tis so. She sent me here to fetch ye. She has named her place the Cell of the Oak and it is not far, just at the north end of the plains."

Cook sighed and moved toward the fire. "I am pleased. Ye'll never know, child, how much. So, you and Brigid are not going to the seashore? Dubthach, as always, has allowed me to travel there."

"I am not. But Brigid is there now. I would be pleased if

ye'd come stay with me until she returns. Where is the old man? Will he not allow that after all the pain he has caused?"

The murmur of children's voices drifted out the door. Cook had apparently ushered them out. She returned to Brocca's side. "I will go, but I must return soon."

Brocca patted Cook's hand. "He is still a hateful master. I am so sorry, Cook. God will reward ye for what ye've done for my daughter."

"Dubthach has been greedy, there's no denying. But hateful? Nay, no longer. He's not even residing at Glasgleann anymore."

"Not here? Where, then?"

Cook blew her nose. "My daughter and I manage Glasgleann now. Her family and the other servants still run things like always. Dubthach is still the owner, but he lives alone, sick and in despair."

"What a shame. Where?"

"Not certain. Somewhere in the woods. Shows up on the edge of the meadow from time to time. Brian meets him and carries out his bidding. The lad said the old man had grown thin, if ye can believe that. And his hair has nearly fallen out."

Brocca shook her head. "I do not understand. What brought about this change?"

Cook clicked her tongue. "He believes he received yer master's curse, and he hides from the gods so they will not take his cattle. He has believed so almost since he released Brigid."

Brocca relaxed her shoulders. She would not have to face the man after all. She prayed God's mercy on his soul. "Do ye think it best we tell him that Bram's curse was a farce?"

Cook handed Brocca a bowl of hot porridge and pressed a wooden spoon into her fingers. "I have tried, darlin'. He will not believe it. He clings to the old ways."

Cook's porridge warmed Brocca as much as her hug had.

She mourned for those like Dubthach who didn't know such comfort.

Brocca spent the rest of the day being introduced to Cook's family. She met Brigid's trusted friend Brian and his new wife and promised to bring back greetings to Brigid. In the morning, Cook joined Brocca for the ride back to the Cell of the Oak.

The showery day did not bother Brocca. She had her beloved friend next to her and she was on her way to her daughter again. God rewards those who wait patiently. She had waited, and now she had everything she had ever hoped for. "Cook, why must ye worry 'bout getting back to Glasgleann if Dubthach's not there?"

Cook leaned her face in close. "I am old, but not too old to understand my place."

"What do ye mean?"

"As sure as I'll be missing my grandchildren, I'll miss that old coot."

"Dubthach?" Brocca bolted back into the wagon's side as though a slingshot had struck her.

Cook sighed. "Aye. He's misguided, lonely, but not as cruel as Brigid thinks. At least not anymore. There was a time…" Her voice trailed off and Brocca allowed her friend time to collect her memories.

Cook swallowed. "There was a time we'd all be lashed with hazel branches. I wanted to wrap my hands around that man's throat, God forgive me. And for what he did to ye…"

Brocca held her fingers to Cook's lips. "Please, let's not…"

Cook pushed her hand away. "God is his judge."

They whispered quiet prayers. Without their faith to lean on, neither one of them would have endured what they had. Minutes passed like drops of water from a nearly dry spring.

Finally, Cook spoke. "Things changed when Brigid left. At first he drank himself into a useless state. Then one morning

I saw him pour his ale into the bog. Barrel after barrel of it. Brian asked him why and he said he had not built his fortune by being a fool, and he'd not lose it because he'd become one."

Brocca struggled against the wind to tuck strands of loose hair back under her scarf. "Dubthach said that?"

"Aye. Could hardly believe it myself. We thought that perhaps that was the time to teach him 'bout Christ, but he wasn't all changed. Was still as greedy and protective over his wealth as ever. Never whipped anyone again, but was far grouchier after he gave up his drink than before, if ye could believe such a thing so."

The wagon wobbled downhill. They would be at the Cell of the Oak shortly. Brocca didn't know when Brigid would return, but she wanted to understand what Cook was telling her before her daughter heard the confusing story. "What drove him to believe in the curse?"

Cook took a deep breath, seeming to prepare a long story. "One night, not long after the man disposed of all his drink, raiders struck Glasgleann."

"Oh, dear." Brocca knew that was what a cattle owner feared most. Dubthach did not employ enough men to rally a revenge raid. "Did he lose many?"

"Half a dozen, if I remember correctly. Then that very next night wolves ravished the barn, killing two more and a calf."

"I see why he thought the curse had come, but why would he move away?"

"Ah, that's the thing of it. He believed he'd wronged his daughter and the gods were angry with him. He thought he'd save his herd if he stayed away. When the gods came for him, they'd not find his cattle. In his small mind, Dubthach believed spirits would flee from him if they found him to be a poor man."

The lumpy ground under the wagon wheels caused

Brocca's head to bob up and down against the latticework sides. They would be home soon. "And have ye suffered any more raids, Cook?"

"Not a one."

"So, why do ye care if Dubthach finds ye've been away?"

"Because 'tis likely he thinks my God protects the cattle. Long as he thinks that, there may be a chance the entire house of Dubthach will someday follow our Lord."

Brocca clapped her hands. "Oh, how wondrous our God is! I wonder what he has in mind for us next?"

CHAPTER

21

"THE FUTURE IS NOT OURS TO KNOW, AND IT MAY NEVER BE. SO LET US LIVE AND GIVE OUR BEST, AND GIVE IT LAVISHLY."
OLD IRISH SAYING

"Ye've been here before." Brigid's statement sounded more like a question.

"Many times."

Brigid and the poet fell in line with other small crafts and waited to disembark. Crowds of people bunched together on the riverbank like wild berries. Brigid and her escort clambered out of their leather boat.

The poet chatted with some men and then fell in step with her. "The bishops from Patrick's church have traveled in large boats down the coast. We've arrived late. The boatman tells me the church leaders will depart tomorrow."

Brigid adjusted her outer garment on her shoulders. "Well, then, we'll have to find Bishop Mel right away."

A boy toting rolls of parchments pointed them toward a large tent. Its white sail-like covering flapped endlessly in the salty air. Inside, several men stood examining a scroll and speaking softly to each other. The men in long robes paused, looked at the newcomers, and acknowledged the poet.

The poet dipped low, brushing his green cloak on the

tent's sandy floor. He spread out his arm toward her. "Here is Brigid of Ireland. She has no clan, no allegiance to any place. She seeks to do her work all over our green isle."

He was right, although she hadn't thought of the difference her mission would make in her title.

The men waved them closer. The oldest and tallest stood in the center of the gathering. His robes were similar to Conleth's but graced with more embroidery. She wondered what the holy men would think if they saw little children at play wearing patches of cloth matching the bishop's robes.

The head bishop spoke. "I am Bishop Mel of Ardagh, but I too travel all of Ireland. I have heard of the wondrous faith of this woman." He smiled at her. "What is it that you seek?"

The room was as snug as any cabin. The cloth walls were anchored and did not give way when a squall from the sea struck them. Brigid plunged to her knees in front of the men. "I wish the church's blessing on my work. I devote my life to Jesus and become his bride only."

In the midst of the quietness, a low roar built, growing in intensity until Brigid cupped her hands over her ears. She huddled on the ground and never glanced up because the noise was in her head.

Gradually the rushing clamor ceased. The men's footsteps rustled and Bishop Mel spoke in Latin. He consecrated her as a bishop and asked her to rise. As soon as the poet extended his hand toward her, the men began bickering.

"She is a woman, Bishop Mel."

The bishop smiled at his counterpart. "I am well aware of that. What has happened, the Lord intended. Did ye not see the flame of the Holy Spirit rest on her head?"

The discussion continued. Brigid didn't know what to say or do. Did she have the church's blessing, and their aid, or not?

Finally, Bishop Mel held up his hands. "It is done." He studied her and cocked his head. "Sister Brigid, your eye is healed."

She touched her face. It was no longer swollen. She turned to the poet and pulled away the linen covering the wound. He laughed and smiled. It *was* true. Now that she had given her life wholly to the Lord in front of these men, God had restored her.

The bishop tapped her shoulder. "Where will you do the Lord's work? When you do not travel, that is."

"At the Cell of the Oak. Brothers and sisters in the Lord are busy building a house."

Bishop Mel's countenance beamed and her memory of Patrick's kind face seemed to merge into his, like shape-shifting. Pagans believed gods could merge from one being into another, from a man to a bird or some such thing. Brigid rubbed her eyes. There was a plausible explanation. Perhaps she *had* seen Patrick in him. They were related, she'd heard. There would be clan similarities.

She muttered a prayer. *Lord, have mercy.*

He waved his hand, and his silky robe brushing against her hair sent a tingle down to her toes. He remained a bishop, no change. *Lord, help me to think only of you and not of ridiculous superstitions.*

Bishop Mel sent his sleeve sailing over her head a second time. "Then you shall have the authority of bishop over the Cell of the Oak. It's God's will for you, Brigid of Ireland."

The poet plucked his harp and sang. They were escorted to another tent and supplied with food, quills, pestles for grinding ink, rolls of parchment, and a two-wheeled cart to pull it all home. The poet stored the bounty in his own shelter while Brigid found lodging with a family living along the banks of the river.

Once they were settled, Brigid's hostess, a kind woman bearing thirty summers, asked about her companion. "Dear Brigid, bring yer escort to sup with us. He must be very hungry."

The poet joined them at a long plank table for oats and

215

stew made with lamb's meat. Not long after they began to feast, the walls rattled and tin mugs danced on the table. The thundering hoofs of dozens of horses rang in their ears.

"Raid!" The host's son bolted from the table.

The residents scrambled to free themselves from the confines of the small room, sending ale and tea splashing across wooden plates of bread and broth. By the time Brigid joined them outside, the intruders had left. She heard them whooping amid the calls of the cattle they drove away.

"We'll be ruined!" the woman of the house wailed.

"We've nothing left but the food on our table and our mounts," another complained.

Brigid whispered to the poet. "We can catch up to them if we borrow horses."

Her companion didn't question her, though she wouldn't have blamed him. How could one man and a wisp of a woman call back those cattle rustlers? She held onto a thought: with God, all things are possible.

They caught up to the men as they were crossing the river. The cattle protested as they were driven into the water. Brigid, the poet, and her host who had ridden alongside them, watched. A small contingent of servants waited nearby.

One by one the men stripped their clothing and tied their garments and their shoes to the beasts' backs.

The poet chuckled. "Think that will keep them dry? Might as well see them all drown and then collect the cattle. The animals are smarter than the thieves who took them."

The raiding party managed to drive the cattle midway into the river when the beasts halted. The cows turned their heads in Brigid's direction and swam back. Once they climbed ashore, they stampeded in the direction of their owner's home, the naked cattle rustlers scrambling after them, trying to snatch back their clothes in vain.

The owner's workers held the men at spear point. Brigid

intervened. "These men should do penitence for their crime. Send them to the Cell of the Oak. There is much work to be done there."

The owner's head servant agreed to send for a wagon and drive them there as soon as they dried out.

Brigid and the poet continued their journey, this time employing the service of a large craft to carry all their supplies. After they crossed the river and collected their horses, the poet broke his usual silence. "'Twas wise, what ye did back there."

Brigid smiled and used her cloak as a shield against the evening cool. "Men may think cattle are their most valuable possession, but life should be cherished the most."

"There are some who think the punishment is not severe enough. Stealing cattle is a serious offense."

"The laird received his cattle back. The raiders have been humiliated, poet. To stroll stark naked among the people is indeed punishment. And now they must work for me. And hard they will labor, too."

They continued to travel along the riverbank until they reached the widest part where the poet departed from her. He called to her before she turned away. "I will report these things to Ardan, as I have promised to do. But do not fear, Brigid. Ardan has no power that is lasting."

She remembered what her friend Brian used to say. "I fear only one Master."

Brigid made the sign of the cross over her chest, and the poet bowed his head. He rode toward the sunset, his black mane streaming behind him.

What did Ardan have planned? *Oh, God, protect yer children and give us strength for whatever we must endure.*

Ardan spotted the poet approaching the castle. He had watched every night for the man, wondering if he was ever going to return from his visit with Brigid. He had begun to doubt his decision in sending the young poet, but the lad had finally returned and would now give a full report.

Ardan bolted from the castle's lookout tower and flew down the stone steps to the interior hallway. He snatched a guard from the king's doorway and pulled the man's ear toward his lips. "'Tis urgent to tell King Dunlaing that the poet has returned."

The guard's face drained of color, and he vanished inside the king's chamber.

If only they feared me like they do a poet of satire.

Moments later the man returned. "Fetch the other druids immediately," Ardan told him, thinking a council would be more persuasive.

Receiving the expected summons to the king's chambers, Ardan was followed by a cluster of men he'd hand-selected. Superior in spiritual insight, the group would speak the truth of what the gods were revealing, if Ardan asked them to, and the king would be impressed. The poet, a man who rarely spoke but rather sang most of his message, trailed behind. Rebellious at times, the man who would only be called "poet" chose a bard's green attire rather than the snowy robes of a priest. The poet was important, however. Ardan sensed the gods were with him.

Dunlaing hovered over a game board. The druid council was introduced, and the king dropped a game piece to the floor where it rattled around until coming to rest near the table leg. "Whatever Brigid is doing must be of utmost importance to disrupt me."

Ardan wished he had interrupted the king at some other activity. The man delighted in his amusement and would be distracted. Flattery might help. "King Dunlaing, I see yer intelligence has been too much of a challenge for yer opponent – once again."

The king turned toward the servant sitting at the game board. "'Tis true?"

The servant bowed his head.

Dunlaing grinned and flicked his hand at the servant who scampered off like a frightened mouse. "Well, Ardan, I suppose I can hear the poet now. It would not please the gods to ignore a poet, would it?"

Ardan sucked in air. "Nay, it would not."

The poet was announced and strolled into the king's presence carrying his harp.

The king extended his scepter. "What say ye, poet?"

The man bowed his dark head and then turned to Ardan. "I have followed the woman Brigid for many days."

Ardan could stand the suspense no longer. This young bard spoke so slowly, dishing out each word as though they were precious jewels. "Well, do the people follow her, poet? Do they bow to her king?"

Dunlaing jumped to his feet. "What king?"

The poet hummed and sang out, "They call him the King of the Jews, but he's King of the people everywhere."

"What is this?" Dunlaing's face grew red. He clenched his fingers into tight fists.

Ardan hurried to his side. "King, 'tis only what they call their god."

"Their god is their king?" Dunlaing glanced at Ardan and then the poet, his eyes searching first one and then the other. He seemed to be collecting all the messages the druids had delivered and setting them in place like game pieces.

Ardan drew his expression as stern as he could. "Aye. They will soon follow no other, I fear."

The poet sang of Brigid's exploits, of the healing of her eye, of a flame of fire that appeared over her head during the

219

blessing of a bishop. He told of naked cattle rustlers whom she helped catch. "And then," he sang, "I saw another miracle she did not see."

All of the druids had been mute during the meeting, but now one spoke. "Nonsense. No one does miracles they are not aware of."

The poet laid down his harp. "Oh, yer mistaken. On the way we stopped to see Old Conleth."

Ardan rolled his eyes. "What has this to do with Brigid?"

"Much. And I will tell ye." He spun around like a seanachaidh weaving a tale, engaging every listener. It was his gift, and he performed well. The poet pointed to his face. "I saw these things with my own eyes."

Dunlaing tipped his head to the poet. "Go on, then."

The poet paced the room, his earthy cloak swinging behind him with each step. "Brigid spotted robes given to Conleth by the Romans. He'd piled them in a corner. She thought they could be sewn into clothes for the poor, and he allowed her to take them. Thing is, poor Old Conleth had no other clothes, and no maids to sew him any either."

Dunlaing stroked his stiff beard. "Sounds just like that woman. Always taking to give to the poor. And here she has left a poor aging man without covering for his own cold body."

The poet retrieved his harp. "Ah, on the way back I returned to Old Conleth alone. As I reclined by his cooking fire, a wagon approached filled with robes identical to the ones Brigid had taken. They were given to Old Conleth, and what he'd donated to Brigid's cause was restored to him in full. And Brigid never knew this."

Another druid, this one sporting an old gray beard that curled on the ends, piped up. "A miracle? Nay. The church heard of his need and sent the clothes."

The poet wandered the room, speaking directly to each listener. "Call it what ye like, but the church's weavers had no time to replace such finely woven fabric, let alone sew new garments, in the few days between when she gave the robes away and when Old Conleth received them back."

Ardan addressed everyone. "'Tis nothing that any druid could not do. 'Tis of no importance."

The poet sang, "Building the Cell of Oak, they are, where all will come to learn of her Lord."

Dunlaing grabbed Ardan's robe and pulled him to his face. "And an army? Will these men form Brigid an army?"

Ardan flinched. The king's anger was good for his purposes, but he was uncomfortable being so close to the man's fury. "I do not know, king. But we must act right away."

Dunlaing released him and ordered the druids to join him at a table. A long silence passed before he spoke. Dunlaing shoved his chair away from the table and stood. "Wise men, we must crush the threat to my kingdom. Is there anyone among ye who thinks Brigid's god will not grow stronger in the hearts and minds of the people in the days to come?"

No one raised an objection.

The king continued. "Then, Ardan, I will hear yer plan."

Ardan resisted the urge to smile, though he was pleased. "Poet, does this woman value objects of gold or silver?"

He shook his black locks.

"Then cattle?"

Again the poet denied it.

"Is there anything man can buy that this woman cherishes more than her god?"

The poet stood. "Nay, Ardan. There is nothing, bought or no."

Ardan stood to look the young man in the eye. "Ah, but yer wrong. There is something she cares for dearly. Something, someone, she has worked all her life to have at her side – her mother, Brocca."

The poet reached for his harp. Ardan raised his palm to

him. "Stop, brother. There is no satire, no curse ye can compose that will change the truth."

Dunlaing turned to the young man. "Do ye agree?"

The poet sat. "I agree that the truth can never be changed. However, if Ardan seeks to turn good into something sinister, I'll not take part."

The other men mumbled to each other.

"Break the druid code of brotherhood?" Ardan was surprised the poet had suggested such a thing, and in front of the king.

The young poet turned toward the king. "Nay, to stand against what's wrong, that's no assault against the code."

Again the brothers whispered.

"Silence!" Dunlaing slammed his fists on the table. "If our kingdom is threatened, war is always an option. I will hear Ardan out."

It was the first time someone had mentioned war. The king was truly shaken by the mention of another king and Brigid's followers. Ardan would have to steer his ruler back to the topic at hand. "As I was saying, king, Brigid cares most about her mother. She draws her strength from Brocca. I am not suggesting a war against such a mouse-like woman, king." He glared at the poet, who stared innocently back. "We just take Brocca as a hostage. Hide her away. Then Brigid will lose all desire to build her kingdom. The threat will disappear like spring snow in the midday."

The brothers agreed and the poet was outvoted.

"'Tis meant as no offense," one druid told the poet. "What has been decided was fair."

The poet turned to leave. "None taken."

A sigh lifted throughout the room. No one wanted the poet to send dire curses their way. It would have been his right had he felt affronted.

After the others left, Dunlaing nodded to Ardan, pleased

with his druid. "This very night I will send my men for Brocca."

Ardan retreated to his room in the castle after volunteering to lead the raiding party.

Darkness fell before Brigid returned to the Cell of the Oak. A flicker of light in the distance became bright as a beacon as she rode closer, leading her home. In sight of the dwelling place, she saw that the frame of the great building had been completed in her absence.

She looped the leather horse reins to an elm near the house. Animal skins had been stretched over the doors, makeshift shutters covered the windows, and the roof was in place, awaiting sod. People inside were singing and laughing.

Brigid cupped her hands to her mouth. "Maither, I'm here!"

Deerskins parted and Brocca rushed out. "Daughter, I have Cook inside. Come join us for some refreshment. Haven't the men done wonderful work in your absence?"

Inside, barrels and logs served as chairs, and a peat fire smoked in the center of the room. Near it, cradling one of the worker's children in her lap, Cook sang with the merry crowd.

Brocca called to her. "Cook, Brigid has come home."

The old woman whispered something to the youngster, who sprang from her lap. Cook pulled herself up from the floor. She had grown feeble in the years they were apart. Brigid hurried to her side. "Cook, how fine to see ye!"

The old woman stroked Brigid's face with her dry hands. "They told me ye were terribly disfigured, but I see it is not so." She grasped Brigid to her bosom.

How magnificent it was that she was with Cook again, yet how sad that the woman had aged a great deal. "Cook, I've missed ye so."

"Ah, dear child. Ye've found yer mother and that's what ye

always wanted. It pleases me, it does, to see yer safe and to hear ye've dedicated yer life to yer Lord down at the seashore."

Brocca tugged at Brigid's sleeve. "Let me see." She ran her smooth fingers over Brigid's face and then touched her eyelid. "Ah, 'tis true. Ye've healed."

Brigid gripped both women's hands. "I'll tell ye everything that happened. Let's sit."

They laughed, cried, prayed, until all the others sought the refuge of their beds. After the excited chatter slowed, Brigid asked about her father – not to see if he was well, but to find out if he'd caused Cook any harm. "Tell me, Cook, how did Dubthach allow ye to come?"

"Suppose he thinks I'm at the seashore."

Brigid examined the freshly hewn beams in the ceiling. "Well, that evil old man does not deserve the labor of such a fine Christian woman." She squeezed Cook's hand. "Ye'll stay on here, with us."

Cook placed a withered hand against her cheek. "I have family at Glasgleann. Ye have yer mother now. Ye don't need me, Brigid."

"Don't need ye? I want ye near me, Cook. Bring the others here. I'll buy them from Dubthach."

Brocca put her arm around Brigid. "She wants to go back there, darlin'. Ye must let her be. People don't like change much when they're old. She'll visit."

Brigid whispered into her mother's ear, "Like ye said, maither, she's old. She'll not have many visits left. Dubthach owes us this for what he has put us through." She spat the words out like poison. "I'll convince him myself."

Cook grabbed Brigid's arm, pinching with more force than Brigid imagined the woman could muster. "Nay. Ye'll not go see him. He'll let me come when I wish."

Long ago Cook had grabbed her like that. Back when

Brigid had mentioned Dubthach's old wife. "Oh, Cook, don't ye know? Troya is no more."

Cook pulled her close. "Why do ye speak that woman's name?"

"She's dead. Did my mother not tell ye?"

Brocca reached for her. "Not yet. I did not yet tell her."

Cook let go and plopped back to her animal pelt cushion. "I'm sorry, darlin'. I didn't know. 'Tis just that I protected ye for so long from her." Cook's lower lip trembled and she tightened her mouth to keep from crying.

Brigid reached for Cook's hands. "And I thank ye, Cook. I thank ye."

Brocca patted the air. "I'll let ye two talk some more without me. I will see ye in the morn." She slipped back into a corner where the women slept together behind a curtain of ox hides suspended from the ceiling beams. The men occupied the opposite corner.

Cook smiled, her teeth still mostly white. "I have always known ye'd be a blessing. Despite what Brocca's druid feared."

"He feared I'd be a curse?" Brigid couldn't imagine kind old Bram thinking that way.

"He wasn't sure, child. That's why he was so cautious when arranging the seashore meetings. Pagans imagine all kinds of things. He said he felt powers unlike any others the day ye born."

"Brocca thinks he will accept Christ."

"He'd better hurry. Like me, time for him upon the earth grows short."

"Don't speak that way, Cook."

"'Tis not a bad thing, child. Death, 'tis part of life, not the end of it. If our Lord awaits us when we gasp our last breath, what shall we fear?"

Brigid leaned against her old friend and relished the security of her touch, her familiar scent of sticky bread dough and sweet apples. She gazed up into the old one's earthy eyes. "What shall we fear? Being separated from those who are most special to us."

CHAPTER

"YOU HAVE NOT HANDED ME OVER TO MY ENEMY BUT HAVE SET ME IN A SAFE PLACE."
PSALM 31:8, NEW LIVING TRANSLATION

The smells of the evening meal still lingered in the lodge. Brocca wished the windows could be flung open so that the grease and smoke would escape, but the night air was too chilly for that. She twisted her linen tunic back into position. The assault on her nose had caused her to wiggle in her sleep and entangle her legs in her covers.

She no longer heard Brigid's voice and assumed she and Cook had retired for the evening. The shelter was quiet. The hour must be late.

Brocca rubbed her nose with her finger. The irritating smells would not go away. She should open a window, just a crack. She'd never get any sleep if she didn't. Brocca tossed the woolen blanket off her legs and sat up on her straw mat. Rubbing her fingers along the ground, she found the corner where the floor and two walls met. The window, she knew, was not far up the wall and a wooden plank covering the opening was latched shut like a door. If she unlatched it, the resulting gap would let in just enough fresh air without waking anyone.

Brocca found the latch and slid it back. The window

shutter swung open too easily. She reached her fingers through the opening, frantically trying to find the shutter and close it before the night air woke everyone.

Fingers from outside grabbed her arm. The scream that formed in her chest was mute when it reached her mouth.

The intruder dropped her hand, and she heard the thump of his boots on the floor inside.

Everyone was awake now, screaming.

Torches... hot... crackling flames.

Fire!

"Maither!" Brigid's voice came from the other side of the room. "Here, come here!"

Follow the voice.

People stumbled into Brocca's path.

A sickening crack. Metal hitting flesh. People were dying.

Where are the walls? Bodies pushed and shoved her toward the middle of the building. Smoke clogged her nose, and she dropped to the floor, gasping for fresh air.

Who? Why?

A cattle raid perhaps. What should she do?

Brocca squeaked out some words. "The cattle are outside, the cattle are outside. Take them!"

Someone grabbed her by the hair and pulled her along. Night air tingled on her skin. She was outside. She was saved. Her lungs filled with fresh nighttime air.

"Ouch, you're hurting me!" The tugging continued.

"'Tis Brocca. She's the one." That voice. *Ardan.*

She was lifted and flung over the shoulders of a muscular man who whisked her away from the heat and noise. She gasped and coughed as she bounced about, the man's iron-like arms wrapped around her legs.

Suddenly, she was tossed to the ground and the jolt forced air from her lungs. Her ankles and wrists were bound. *Ardan again.* The way he flipped the leather strips around her hands and feet, the way he tied them so quickly she couldn't wiggle free – it was him all right. And his smell – like wet dog fur. She'd know it anywhere.

"In the boat!" he yelled.

She was stuffed into a vessel and felt the water give and bend around the leather-covered curragh.

"Help!"

A rag was stuffed into her mouth. It smelled worse than Ardan. Her head was as heavy as ten oxen. There was no mistaking it – she'd been smothered with the same herbs that had caused Brigid to sleep the night Ardan kidnapped them from the Samhain.

Brigid had not been asleep long when she found her newly-built home in flames. Cattle rustlers, thieves, the king's men perhaps? It didn't matter. Were her mother and Cook safe?

A figure, dark, coughing like a sick child, came at her with arms outreached. Cook. "I can't find her, child!"

"Go, this way." Brigid directed confused people toward the door while searching for the diminutive shape of her mother. Once outside, she turned each head toward her. "Brocca? Have ye seen Brocca?"

Frightened, wheezing – they couldn't answer. Everyone who could muster the strength ran to the spring with buckets to douse the fire. But what did it matter if the structure burnt to the ground? Her mother was missing.

Fear rose thick in Brigid's throat. She scurried to the spring. Was Brocca there? Her eyes adjusted to the darkness. Whoever had attacked them would flee in that direction.

She caught her foot on one tree root after another, sending shards of pain up her legs.

Maither, where are ye?

A rising moon shed a bit of light on the spring that glimmered down a trail of watery rocks. She scooted carefully along the water's edge. The stream spread wide, growing as it neared the river. She held on, tree to tree, until she heard the rushing sound of river water. In the distance, a light twinkled – the torches of the tormentors, devils – too far away to shout at.

Brigid's hands trembled. "Maither?"

She could no longer grasp the width of the birch she clung to, and she slid to the ground. Her fingers detected something metal and cold. She whisked away tree litter until her hands located the object, some sort of jewelry. She held it up to the moonlight. Brocca's brooch. Her mother had been kidnapped.

Brigid clasped the adornment so tightly that her palms bled.

"Child? Where are ye? Brocca?" Cook had found her.

"Maither…" Brigid held her fist, with the brooch locked inside, up to her mouth. She resisted Cook's attempt to move her.

Her mother was gone, snatched away from her like a fox's prey.

Cook summoned some men who half-carried Brigid back to the camp.

The others were pleased that they had extinguished the fire and that the building would be repairable. Brigid didn't care. Her heart was heavy, her head cloudy. Her mouth tasted like sour cabbage.

She stared into the distance, realizing that her actions appeared odd to the others, but knowing she was helpless to do anything else. Her mother, the one who loved her most, was ripped away, taking Brigid's very soul with her.

Days later – Brigid didn't know how many days – Cook managed to convince her to take some broth. The old woman whisked around the camp, assigning tasks and taking the situation under control. Brigid was thankful. Her sorrow shrouded everything, rendering her numb.

"Bear up, child. We'll find Brocca." Cook's dark eyes pierced Brigid's fog, bringing a fleeting moment of comfort.

"Do we know where to look?"

"Maybe. The men went to the king's castle to inquire. A fellow said he recognized one of the intruders as being the king's druid."

Brigid opened her bandaged hand and gazed at her mother's silver brooch. "Ardan." The name was flecks of burning embers, and she spewed it off her tongue. "Do ye think Dunlaing is holding her then?"

"We can hope so, child. Dunlaing will hear of this injustice and order her returned."

"If she's there, I've got to go to her." Brigid sprang to her feet and called for Geall. Night had fallen, but she felt an urgency to hurry to the castle. Too much time had already been wasted.

Cook motioned for Brigid's attendant to ignore the order. "There's no sense in rushing out. The men will take care of things."

Brigid scowled at the young man. "Ye heard me, man. Get my horse! 'Tis my duty. I'll take care of it."

Cook appeared hurt or worried, but Brigid could not tend to her. Brocca was a hostage. That had to come first. She marched outside to wait.

The servant delivered Geall and a torch for traveling. Brigid stroked the horse's nose. "Yer a good and faithful servant." She smiled at the attendant. "Thank ye for taking such good care of my horse. Although we've only just returned from a journey, he's been well groomed. Should harm come to me at the castle, this horse will be yours – for all yer good service."

"Glory, child." Cook emerged from the house. She pinched Brigid's arm. "Stop talking like that. If ye think ye could be in danger, don't go. I told the men... "

Brigid shooed her away. "Ye'll not order me as if I were

231

still a child. If my mother is in danger, my safety means nothing. I am nothing."

"Oh, nay, child. Ye don't believe that. Yer God's servant. That's not nothing."

Cook's objections did not dissuade her. She rode away as swiftly as Geall could carry her.

Brigid arrived at Dunlaing's fortress and noted the stillness. A calm permeated the area. She steered Geall close to the stone walls where torches blazed and huffed. Where was the watch? Asleep?

Still atop her horse, she rapped her knuckles on the thick oak door, the only portal in the fortress's outer wall. Her cold hands stung.

A voice called from the dark interior. "Who's there?"

"Brigid of the Cell of the Oak. I must speak to the king immediately."

"Yer servants have been here and left."

"Even so, I must speak to the king."

She waited. The surrounding woods were tranquil with only an occasional owl call.

Finally, someone cracked the door. "The king is sleeping. Come back tomorrow."

The door was let go to close on its own, but it didn't. Brigid dismounted, tied Geall to a post, extinguished her torch, and leaned close to the door. After she was sure the guard had disappeared back to his post, or to his ale possibly, she slipped inside.

She'd been in the castle before but didn't know where the king's sleeping chamber was. Removing her shoes would make her footsteps inaudible, so she slipped them off and tucked them inside the waistband of her tunic. Tiny pebbles encircled the path between the outer wall and the castle. She'd have to tiptoe through them, and then steal inside whatever door was unlocked.

Just like on the outer ring, torches hung along the wall, lighting her path. Brigid hugged the shadows underneath them, darting out to try the latch on several doors. Just as she was about to give up, one door nudged open a crack. She leaned all her weight against it until it finally pushed open, kicking up clouds of dirt underneath. The door obviously hadn't been used for some time and would be the perfect place to enter unnoticed.

She was wrong. It was nothing but a storage room with no inside door. Dusty, rusted spears and buckets made her sneeze. She scooted the door closed behind her in time to hide from soldiers padding by. She listened through a small crack in the panes of the door.

"See anybody?" a man's voice asked.

Another answered. "Nay, not me. Probably a cat. They're always roaming 'round at night."

"There was a lass by earlier. I sent her on her way though."

Geall! He was still tied up outside. What had she been thinking?

A squeal like a hungry babe took her breath away.

"Here's yer sneezer, Rogan. Take care of this cat outside."

Outside? Nay, dear Lord. Do not let them go out and see the horse.

The soldiers kept talking. "Don't be a half-wit. This here has become the king's favorite. I'll shoo her back to his chamber."

Brigid waited until she could no longer hear footsteps and then counted to ten before emerging from her hiding place. Down the darkened passage, the faint glimmer of the torch bounced. If she followed it, the soldier would lead her to Dunlaing.

Brigid again moved within the shadows of the outer wall. She encountered no one else. Once the torch light stayed

233

constant, she quickened her pace. An unarmed guard with red curly locks tumbling down his head unlatched a door and slipped inside. She followed and found herself in an interior hall. The guard marched along then stopped at a door. He shoved it open and pushed a cat inside. Brigid made herself as flat as possible against the wall and prayed he wouldn't look in her direction.

The guard retrieved a silver flask from his belt, laughed silently by pumping his shoulders up and down, and continued down the passageway, gulping as he went.

Brigid approached the door. He'd left it ajar. She entered. One lone candle flickered on the opposite wall. An enormous box bed stood in the center.

The cat curled itself around her legs and she instinctively picked the animal up and stroked it.

A figure sat up in the bed. Not Dunlaing, but someone smaller. A wife? A mistress?

The small shadowy figured stretched out her arms. "Here, lass. Bring the cat to me."

Brigid crept around the platform and leaned in toward the woman, allowing the cat to lunge from her arms.

The shadowy figure pointed to the door. "What are ye waiting for? Go now."

"I must speak to the king."

"What? Do ye know the hour? Go." She cuddled the cat and drifted back under the blankets.

Brigid sighed, too loudly. The larger lump under the blanket grunted. "Who's there?"

The woman in the bed groaned. "Just a servant bringing in the cat, love."

"Humph." Dunlaing rolled over. His black and silver hair floated down on his pillow like disturbed feathers.

Brigid tiptoed to his side. "Dunlaing, I must speak to ye. 'Tis urgent."

"What?" He boosted himself onto his elbows. "Who must speak?"

"Brigid of the Cell of the Oak."

He tossed his blanket over the head of his companion. "How did ye get in here? How many are with ye?"

"No one but me. Please, king, my mother has been kidnapped."

"Guard, guard!"

The door burst open and Brigid was yanked away. "Please, ye must help Brocca!"

She heard Dunlaing's voice before the chamber door crashed shut. "She's not here."

The guards dragged Brigid along the pebble path. Her knees ached as bits of stone cut into her flesh. "Help me, someone!" She glanced at the guard. "'Tis true that ye've no prisoner named Brocca?"

The red-haired one spoke. "We've no prisoner at all. No Brocca even visits."

They tossed her outside where Geall was obediently waiting. She reluctantly threw herself on his back. If Brocca was not there, then where was she?

The hostage had slept the entire trip. Ardan couldn't be more pleased. Soon they would approach Blackwater and head for the open sea. A tiny island at the southern tip of Ireland would be the perfect place to keep Brocca hidden away. He wouldn't allow her to be killed, of course. Having the lass know her mother lived would keep her under Ardan's authority.

The first leg of the journey, on land, had not been easy, but Ardan had employed the best guides. "How much longer?"

The driver turned to look at him. "Half a day, I expect."

"Could anyone have followed?" Ardan couldn't take any chances. There had been moments along the way when he had felt someone watching, but he'd seen no one.

"Nay, no one."

Ardan relaxed in the bed of the rig, using the sleeping woman's shoulder as a pillow. He called to the driver. "I'll pay for ye to stay and keep watch over my hostage."

The man behind the reins almost lost his grip and the wagon swayed recklessly. "Stay, ye say?"

"Watch yerself, man!"

The wagon steadied.

Ardan shouted to the front. "Aye. Guard her. But no harm shall come to her. I'll leave ye complete instructions."

The driver glanced over his shoulder. He was about Ardan's age and wore a red scarf tied over his head. "Where, Master Ardan, are we going? And for how long?"

"Keep going until I say to stop. I must return to Leinster, to the king. I have some matters to attend. Things ye wouldn't understand. Then I'll be back. Half a moon's cycle likely."

"She's blind?"

Ardan didn't like the sound of the question. "Aye, but like I said, no harm shall come to her. Ye know who I am?"

The driver stared straight ahead. "Aye, King Dunlaing's druid."

Ardan reached up and grasped the back of the man's neck. "I do not answer even to the king, man. I commune with the Others. They help me. They will know if ye harm her or if ye do anything whatsoever that does not honor what I ask." The wagon tilted, but Ardan continued. "Do ye know, man, what manner of curses I can call down upon ye and yer household for generations? The spirits will bring worms to eat yer eyes out while ye still live. And if that were not enough," he paused to chuckle, "on the next Samhain, I'll bring them to yer house. Where I picked ye up, where yer wife and children wait for ye. Only ye won't be there to protect them, will ye now? And the spirits will visit yer house – and do what they will." Ardan shook his walking stick at the man. "First yer wife will suffer

236

while yer children watch. Then they'll have their turn. One by one. Do ye understand?"

The man's shoulders shook. "Aye, Master Ardan. No curses, please! I'll be yer most trusted servant."

Ardan released his grasp on the man and returned to his reclining position. "Good. We understand each other."

CHAPTER

23

"DO NOT HIDE YOURSELF FROM ME.
DO NOT REJECT YOUR SERVANT IN ANGER.
YOU HAVE ALWAYS BEEN MY HELPER.
DON'T LEAVE ME NOW; DON'T ABANDON ME,
O GOD OF MY SALVATION!"
PSALM 27:9, NEW LIVING TRANSLATION

Brigid sped toward the spring where she'd found her mother's brooch. She looked for clues, a sign of where they'd taken her. The night air merged into early morning dew, wetting her hair and face. Somewhere, in some nearby home, someone was stewing cabbage. Why now? Where? She sniffed the sickening smell and her stomach turned.

Dubthach. After all these years, had he returned to take revenge? The arm of her cloak did little to wipe the moisture from her face. Dew had seeped into every fiber of her clothing.

Brigid reached the spring and pulled Brocca's brooch from a leather pouch fastened at her waist. She realized then that she still had her shoes stuffed inside her tunic belt. In her haste and worry she had not realized that her feet were naked, freezing, and sore. She dropped down from Geall's back and led him to the spring to drink his fill. The stones surrounding the spring felt like ice when she sat on them. She sucked in her breath and tied on her shoes.

Oh, God, why did this happen? What shall I do?

She examined the muddy ground near the spring and

238

followed footprints leading to the river. She already knew Brocca's captors had gone in that direction, but she slowly followed the path, leading her horse behind, hoping that some insight, some plan would come to her.

None did.

It was odd, those footprints still being there days later. None of her servants would have come this way. The path from the sleeping quarters to the spring was well worn, the path most took – not this way.

The river lapped in currents over small rocks, around bends of mossy turf, and off into the distant trees.

Brocca was gone.

No one knew where she was.

The thought which had come to Brigid earlier, about Dubthach stealing Brocca, was foolish, she now realized. Cook had clearly explained how physically and mentally paralyzed the man was, living alone in the wilderness.

Someone else had taken Brocca. If not random raiders, surely Ardan was to blame. He hated Brigid, though she didn't know why. His chin, jutting out like an ocean cliff, his eyes the color of hammered iron, his lips, thin ribbons spewing distrust, all told her that the man hated her. Why he hadn't tried to kill her when he had the chance was a mystery.

Brigid resumed leading her horse through the woods in no particular direction. Her mind was at work, trying desperately to find answers. She prayed for wisdom.

Druids. Brigid wanted to understand the pagans, but it was difficult. Especially since two she knew, Bram and Ardan, were so different. Yet, they both adhered to some kind of code. Was that why Ardan hadn't killed her? Was that why he had stolen her mother instead? But to what end?

The new morn's sunrays chased away the dark corners of the forest. She thought about returning to the Cell of the Oak, but could not see the purpose. She had no answers to the barrage of questions she knew would be thrown at her.

And Brocca would be notably absent. Brigid didn't think she could bear that. She could gather a search party and scour the woods, but the raiding party was half a day ahead. And in what direction had they gone?

She was weary, sickened by the smell of cabbage that would not go away no matter which way she wandered. She decided to seek shelter, to be alone, to think and pray. A small crack in a rocky outcrop west of the river suggested the presence of a cave shelter. She worked her way up, coaxing Geall along behind her, though he was none too cooperative.

She reached a narrow shelf near the opening and discovered she'd been right. There was a cave there, and it would be the perfect place to hide away and seek God's direction. After all, hadn't Jesus done that, hidden himself away in the wilderness for forty days? She should follow his example.

Inside, the dank darkness mirrored her mood. She threw herself to the ground and wept, not even bothering to tie up her horse. The stench of stewed cabbage had followed her. She held on to her stomach, willing the pang to leave, but it would not. With drops of sweat beading up on her forehead, Brigid ran out of the cave to empty her stomach. She cried and wiped her mouth with damp rhododendron leaves. *Oh, God, where are ye?*

She dragged herself back to the cave, embarrassed that she had allowed herself such thoughts and gotten upset enough to be sick. Geall had posted himself outside the cave entrance. She pulled a blanket out of the saddle pouch – someone had thought ahead to make sure she had sufficient protection from the weather. The wrap was thick and tightly woven. She swept it around her shoulders, imagining the warmth she felt was a hug from her mother.

Maither. She burst into tears again.

Days later, Brigid was still there, leaving the cave only occasionally to take care of necessities and to munch on a few wild herbs to settle her stomach. She prayed, when she could bring herself to, and recited Psalms that came to mind. Mostly, she wondered how God could have forgotten her.

After about a week of feeling sorry for herself, some woodsfolk discovered her.

"We've been looking for ye, Brigid. Are ye fine?"

Brigid peered out of the cave. The sun hurt her eyes, and she imagined an owl would feel the same way if someone stirred him from his home. "I am. I must be alone to meditate and commune with God."

A man with cheerful furrows fanning out from his eyes like a sunburst ducked his head inside the cave. "I understand. 'Tis like those monks. Especially those, I hear, who live out on the western islands."

She nodded and pulled the blanket up to her eyes.

An old woman, probably his wife, stepped in front of the man and held up a finger. "Before we leave, since we've come all this way just to check on yer wellbeing, might ye find some food for some hungry travelers?"

"Of course." Brigid snapped her hand to her mouth. What had she said? She had nothing. She cleared her throat. "God always provides, does he not?"

The old couple murmured, and elbowed each other. The man mumbled, "God provides for Brigid always."

"Give me a moment." Brigid searched the leather bag still attached to Geall's saddle. Nothing. She felt her pockets. Nothing. "Well, we'll have to look in the forest. I've no dairy here."

"Certainly." The couple followed her like baby chicks waddling after their mother.

Two pheasants were roosting beneath an elm. They would make more than a meal's worth of meat. Brigid felt she should pray, but no words came. Her heart refused. She hoped the pheasants would come willingly, but they did not, and she had no spear. She stood there, feeling the stares of the man and his wife on her back. The birds took flight.

She spun around and held her arms out to her side. "I'm sorry. I have nothing for ye, and nothing for myself either."

The couple was speechless, gazing at her as though they'd seen fairies in the trees.

She called toward their backs as they descended the cliff. "Please understand! I just can't help ye."

Never had she turned anyone away before. She should have felt grief over it, but she didn't. She had a hole in her heart that only her mother could fill. Without Brocca, Brigid felt unloved. And one who is unloved has no love to give. She was empty.

At night the cave was unbelievably dark. No firelight, no illumination from the moon, no distant torchlight from a settlement. The blackness was oddly comforting – until one night.

Brigid lay under her plaid blanket, dozing through unsettled dreams, when she felt a presence. She listened, hoping she could identify the sound. The object's shuffling through the leaves at the cave's opening gave the impression of mass. The thing, whatever it was, was large.

Brigid scooted back and leaned against the wall of the cave. Although she squinted, she saw nothing in front of her eyes. She remembered what Brocca had told her about being blind. *Use yer other senses.* But she was afraid. She couldn't see the thing. Where was it? Was it coming for her? Would she have time to react?

Brigid clutched the blanket's hem in her fists, willing herself to be calm.

Smell. What was that smell? A grunt told her – a wild boar.

She listened again. A short *snort-snort* came from the other edge of the cave. The animal hadn't detected her yet. She crept slowly, painfully, toward the direction where she'd heard the leaves shuffle – the cave's opening. She held her breath, then exhaled as silently as she could, blowing puffs of air through her teeth.

She hadn't meant to, but she let a cry escape. The thing heard and trotted directly at her. There was no choice now. Whether or not she trusted her senses, she'd have to take a chance and hope that she ran for the opening and not the depths of the cave.

Brigid flipped her arms from side to side and ran. Her feet hit the leaf carpet of the forest floor. She breathed in the forest smell. Still the boar pursued her.

Wailing, she changed directions, hoping to climb the cliff and thwart the beast. Her eyes gradually adjusted to the night, and she pulled on saplings, climbing higher and higher. Her legs ached and her voice grew hoarse. Brigid suddenly realized the boar was no longer near. She wept tears more bitter than tansy.

She scuttled under a bush and stayed till morning.

The sun's light brought little warmth. Shivering, she rose and returned to the cave to fetch her blanket. Fortunately, the boar had not returned and not left any excrement.

Brigid wandered farther from the cave, hoping to find some berries or roots. Today, this moment, was all she could manage to think about.

A figure in a dark cloak wandered near the river. Another beggar? She couldn't bear having nothing to give. She was as hollow as a badger's log home – and without meaning. The animals no longer obeyed her. She was worthless without her mother from whom she had gained strength.

A fast would be appropriate. She'd eaten little anyway, but if she avoided all food, perhaps then God would show up and aid her. And if she returned to the cave swiftly, the stranger would not find her.

She was only a few paces away from the cave when the man called out, "Hello, there! Might it be Brigid I'm seeing?"

She lifted her eyes to the ice-blue sky. *Why?*

He hollered again. "'Tis me, Brian of Glasgleann."

"Brian? What are ye doing here?" Her voice sounded foreign to her ears – scratchy and weak.

"Cook sent me. She's worried, she is. I've come to find out if yer well. May I come up?"

Brigid should have known Cook would send someone looking for her. She scooted to the edge of the cave's shelf and shouted down to him, "If ye'd please, Brian, tell Cook I'm fine! Tell her to return to Glasgleann. I must be alone, like Christ in the wilderness, to pray and meditate. Please understand."

Brian removed his hood. The morning sun shone on his copper-colored head. He raised one hand to his forehead. "How long?"

She bit her lip. What could she say to convince him to leave? She drew in the mossy air, collecting her composure. "Tell Cook that I'll return just as soon as the Lord gives me direction. I am safe. I just seek counsel with the Lord."

"I will tell her." He drew his cloak back over his head and mounted his horse.

She watched him ride toward the Cell of the Oak, and she wondered if she should have asked for supplies. No, she was fasting. She had wanted him to leave, but now she felt more alone than ever. No God, no God-fearing friends, no mother. Her fast would be of more than food.

The next morning someone or something stirred outside the cave. Brigid's sanctuary was not as secluded as she had first thought. Had Brian returned? She scooted to the opening and called out, "Brian, I told ye not to come back."

244

"Who's Brian?" Ardan, clothed in his snowy druid garb stood before her, smiling.

She was too weak to resist. "You? Where's my mother?" She pulled hopelessly on the edges of his robes. He stood stoic, more powerful and confident than she. Brigid flung herself back to her blanket bed.

"We will talk about Brocca shortly. First we have to do something about you."

She moved to the cave wall. "Would ye finally kill me, then?"

Ardan shook his head and his druid adornments clinked around his neck. "I would never cause harm, Brigid. I am a great druid."

"Not cause harm? What do ye call what ye did to my mother?"

"What is it ye think I've done, child?" He stooped at the cave's entrance and looked her in the eye.

"Ye've taken my mother hostage."

"Perhaps, but she's in no danger." He pulled the leather sack he carried from his back to his chest. He extracted a bundle of white linen and held it out to her. "Bread?"

Brigid snatched the food and consumed the soft oatcake before she realized what she was doing. The bread satisfied her stomach and seemed to clear her mind.

"Like I said, we have to take care of ye first, then we'll discuss Brocca." He glanced around. "No fire ring?"

She shrugged her shoulders.

"Lie down and rest. Ye look like a banshee, yer hair tangled and yer eyes sunken. I'll ready a fire."

Brigid woke. A ribbon of smoke tickled her nose. Ardan had started a fire. He was throwing bits of grass and twigs into it and hadn't noticed she was awake. Brigid watched him move. His torque of gold glowed brighter as the fire grew. His carved walking stick waited near his bulging sack at the cave entrance. On the ground next to his feet sat two sticks with the mysterious ogham writing – druid devices for supposedly foretelling the future. He fingered them the way a mother touches her child, or a husband teases a wife by stroking her curls. Those sticks were special to him. Pity he didn't understand how futile they really were.

The smoke stung Brigid's throat, and she couldn't muffle a cough.

"Ah, awake now." Ardan threw her a smile.

She pushed herself up on her elbows. "Now, what about my mother?"

He ignored the question. "Tell me, Brigid. Have ye cursed any more apple orchards? Tamed any more foxes?"

She turned away, but he continued badgering. "Miracles. Is that not what the woodsfolk call yer displays of authority?"

"Why do ye ask this?" She could not bear to look into his spiteful eyes.

"I see. Ye have not worked yer magic of late. Is that not true?"

"What does it matter? I demand ye return my mother. She is a freewoman."

"Demand?" Ardan's voice was louder than before. "Who are ye to demand anything? Look at ye, the mighty Brigid. Ye lie in a cave with no food, dirty, smelling like swine, living like them too. Yer nothing without Brocca, is that not so? Who will hear yer petition? Where is yer grand god now?"

She wrapped her blanket around her waist, freeing her hands so that she might gesture. No answer for God's whereabouts came to her. She tucked her hands back inside the wrap. It would be best to ignore the druid's accusations. "I'm sure King Dunlaing will listen..."

"The king?" Ardan laughed and tossed a thick branch on the fire. He worked to whittle a spit from another stick and spewed his words as though expelling flies. "The king has no power in this case, Brigid. I alone hold Brocca's fate."

"What do ye want from me?" She was afraid of the answer.

"I have seen yer powers. Heard tales of the wonders ye perform. I'd like ye to do these things for me, whenever I ask. In exchange, I'll reunite ye with yer mother."

His eyes were bloodshot and his pointed chin and thin nose made him look like a predatory bird. But he *did* have Brocca. Brigid felt she should at least hear him out.

She grunted the sleep from her throat. "Ye should know that my powers, as ye call them, are granted by God, and now he has seen fit to revoke them."

"Ah, a temporary occurrence." Ardan impaled a bird carcass on the spit and sent it sizzling into the flames. "I am sure that when yer in yer mother's arms, the spirits will be pleased to return your powers."

Something about his words rang true. The smell of smoke and mead filled her head. "I must think."

Ardan stood.

"Yer leaving?"

"I leave now, but will return in two days for yer answer, Brigid."

"But ye *will* return?" The thought of losing her only connection to her mother seemed unbearable.

"Aye, in two days." He wandered over to his belongings and retrieved his walking stick. He came back to her and tapped her head with it. "Ye have the gift of communing with the spirits, Brigid. 'Twas foretold before yer birth. Yer mother is a druidess with the respect of many people, but I see that yer much greater. Many more will follow you, Brigid of Ireland."

She flipped her head up to look at him. "Why did ye call me that?"

"What?"

247

"Brigid of Ireland. Why would ye say that and not Brigid of the Cell of the Oak?"

Ardan's broad smile made his eyes narrow. "Because, Brigid, if ye join me, ye'll have a following much greater than the little cell ye've built. Together we will command enough power to influence all of this great isle. Is that not true?" He winked at her. "Ye know it is. Think on this, Brigid."

He departed in a white swirl, leaving her to contemplate the coincidence that he'd named her exactly the way Bishop Mel had. Could it be true? Was it her destiny to become Ardan's apprentice?

Ardan found his horse where he'd left it, a fair distance from Brigid's cave. He hadn't wanted her to hear him approaching and run off, so he'd tied up his mount and tiptoed through the forest to where she was.

The gods truly were pleased with him. Although he'd learned from some wanderers that a woman named Brigid had concealed herself in a cave, sorrowing over the kidnapping of her mother, he might never have found her if he hadn't heard her wailing into the wind one night. The gods had seen fit to bring Brigid's sad song to his ears, and just like he'd hoped, she was alone in the cave.

His approach with her had worked. Fragile women had to be treated gently. He'd done so before with Troya. Now, by caring for Brigid's hunger, building a fire with the help of his special stone, he'd been able to win her trust. Once that was done, all he had to do was promise her the one thing her heart longed for.

Ardan laughed out loud, sending flocks of rooks streaming from the tops of the beeches. "Ah, gods, yer surely with me, and I will not disappoint."

He kicked his heels into the horse's haunches and headed

for Dunlaing's castle. A royal order would be needed. He'd have no trouble convincing the pathetic king of Leinster.

The forest gave way to rounded hills and in the distance Ardan spotted the stone pillars of the castle with its blue and white flag whipping in the wind like a lady's apron hung out to dry. The gusts brought the salty smell of the ocean to his nose. The sky grew purple. A spring storm was brewing.

"Faster!" He kicked the horse, one of Dunlaing's finest, and slapped him with his druid sticks. At least they were good for something. "I've no mind to be out here in the rain."

Thunder rolled, and Ardan thought about his own shelter beneath the oak. He never minded drizzle, but storms chilled him to the bone, blowing in sheets of rain and sometimes ice. Why was he content to live in the woods when an ineffective king slept dry and warm in a great stone house with a multitude of servants to answer his every whim? It wasn't right, and soon it would end. Ardan would replace that flag with one more suited to the gods, perhaps with the emblem of an oak leaf, and take up residence there. He could, he knew, with the help of a woman with spiritual connections – someone like Brigid.

He dismounted at the castle gate. Rain skirted his cloak, so tightly woven of the finest wool that even a decent shower would not soak through it. He rapped on the oak door.

"Let me in! 'Tis Ardan, the king's druid."

The door swung open and he pushed his way past the guard. "Does the king deserve such sluggards to serve him?"

Ardan stomped down the pebbled path, through the door to the interior hall, and continued until he reached his chamber.

A servant girl stood at the archway, ready to exit into the castle's main corridor. She lowered her head and whispered, "I've just finished readying yer room, sir. We did not expect ye back so soon."

Smart girl. She knew to revere him, respect his power. He

249

approached her and lifted her chin with his finger. "I appreciate yer work here. The gods will honor yer service to their chief representative."

The girl smiled without lifting her gaze. "There was another representative here. King Dunlaing allowed him to stay in yer room. I just cleaned up after him."

Ardan stepped back. "Who? Another druid ye say?"

"Aye, sir." The girl backed out of the room.

"Wait. Tell me about this person. 'Twas not an old man, was it? Tell me."

The girl now stood fully in the corridor. "Aye, very old. Bram, he said his name was. May I go now?"

Ardan waved her off. Despite being chilled by the spring rain, he was perspiring. He flung his cloak off his shoulders and glanced around. "Am I not the chief druid?" he said to the walls. "Why would Dunlaing allow another to sleep in my room?" He pounded his fist on the small candle table, knocking the flame to the floor. He stomped it out, kicking mud off his shoes onto the stone floor.

Lightning lit up the spaces under and around the window shutters. He paced, threw his druid sticks on the ground, and then snatched them up. "Nonsense! They tell me nothing."

He dropped to the three-legged stool near the fire ring and removed his soaked shoes. The cloak had kept him dry, but he really had to find someone capable of properly greasing an animal hide so he could make a new pair of shoes.

He tried to talk sense to himself. "Calm down. There's no need to worry. Brocca's druid has come looking for her, or perhaps for Brigid, but he'll never find what he searches for. And as for King Dunlaing, he will pay for not honoring my position."

He'd have to check his temper in order to proceed with his plot. He called the servant back and told her to request audience with the king for him at the earliest convenience.

Just before the evening meal, the servant came to Ardan's chamber. "Yer requested to approach the king's table." She bowed and disappeared down the hall.

Dunlaing had to be happy to see him to invite him to sup. Ardan dressed quickly and hastened toward the castle's main living area.

The dining hall was lit by dozens of flaming torches and heated by three huge fire pits. The smell of roasted lamb, sweet mead, and ale warmed Ardan and made him forget the storm raging outside. It was the way he always wanted to live.

Dunlaing held one arm out toward an empty chair and used the other to stuff meat into his mouth. "Ardan, come. I want ye to sit next to me and tell of yer adventures." With a mouthful, he ordered a servant, "Bring Ardan a full plate."

Ardan gulped the ale set before him. "We have much to talk about, king."

"Aye. I want to know, did ye capture Brigid's mother? She seems to think ye did."

"She came here looking for her?" Ardan dove in as soon as the servant placed a tin platter of food before him.

"That surprises ye, druid?"

"Nay, suppose not." He spat out a bone. "What did ye tell her?"

Dunlaing threw his head back and laughed. "She came in the middle of night. Woke me when I had company in my bed. There was a price paid by the night watchman, I tell ye." He took a long sip from his jewel-encrusted cup, and then slammed it down on the polished table. "I told her nothing, druid. Do ye think me a fool?"

Ardan could have strangled the man with his own hands. He tried frantically to swallow his hate along with his ale. "Brocca cannot be found, I assure ye. I have spoken to Brigid this very day."

The king turned his gem-toned eyes toward Ardan. "And is the plan working?"

Good. Ardan had the king's complete attention. "I can report that she is no longer performing wondrous acts. She has turned away those who seek bread."

The king wagged his head like a dog's tail and took a bite from a lamb chop. Grease dripped from the corners of his mouth. "I never thought I'd see the day. I always believed Brigid would give the last thread of clothing on her back to anyone who asked."

Ardan ripped a mouthful of bread from his loaf. The castle had the most excellent bakers. He licked his lips and turned to the king. "She's quite low right now, but if she should snap out of her stupor, we will need to motivate her further."

The king dropped the bone he'd been chewing and wiped his hands on a yellow linen napkin on his lap. "I like a man with a plan, Ardan."

There was still the matter of Bram. Ardan didn't like thinking Dunlaing might double-cross him. "I hear there was another visitor here, king."

Dunlaing nodded his head and chewed a mouthful of barley bread before answering.

"An old druid was traveling through. Is that of whom ye speak?"

Ardan regarded the king carefully. He didn't seem disturbed by the question, so perhaps giving shelter to the druid was all there was to it. "Did he say his name was Bram?"

Dunlaing called to his lady friend who was speaking to the bard organizing music for the king's pleasure. "Darlin', what was that ancient druid's name?"

The woman, several years Dunlaing's junior, blinked her dark feathery eyelashes and smiled with her lips closed. She tapped her index finger on her temple as though trying to remember. "Braun, nay, that's not it. Brian? Nay. Bram. Aye, that's it, Bram. Came from far off in the western hills, maybe the coast. Don't remember."

Clearly Bram had not made much of an impression on Dunlaing's house. He must have only been passing through.

Dunlaing blew the woman a kiss and then turned toward Ardan. "This does not concern the situation with Brigid. Now tell me, druid, what do the gods have to say?"

Ardan had only one druid stick left, having tossed the other into the fire in his room. He pretended to chant and then flung it across the floor. The other diners pushed their chairs back and gasped. Although this delighted Ardan, he had no time to waste. He retrieved the stick and returned to his place beside the king. He lowered his voice to sound as grim as possible. "We must speak in private, king."

The king's guests whispered together like a cloud of honeybees.

"Of course, of course." Dunlaing left the table and headed to the archway entrance of the hall. He waved his golden scepter at an attendant. "See that we're not disturbed."

Ardan paused to admire the stir he'd caused, and then followed Dunlaing to a private meeting room.

The king stood before a washing basin and cleansed the meal's residue from his fingers. He dried his hands on a crisp linen towel and hung it neatly on the washing bowl stand. He drew his palms across his gray-black hair, sighed, and then seated himself on a chair engraved with twisted knots and faces with huge eyes. "Now, druid, what is so important? Have the gods spoken or not?"

Ardan could not imagine why Dunlaing was not as nervous as the others who had witnessed his performance. "I assure ye, king, if the matter wasn't critical, I would have never requested ye leave yer feast."

Dunlaing closed his eyes and tapped his fingertips together in front of his lips. "Aye, aye, go on."

Ardan cleared his throat and found a stool. He paced around it, gathering his thoughts. "'Tis like I said before. Brigid may come to her senses and resume her ways. She'll lead all the people in yer kingdom to follow Christ the King and reject the edicts of King Dunlaing."

Dunlaing opened his eyes and leaned forward. "Aye, ye have said this. Stop yer pacing, man. On with it."

In all the years that Ardan had known Dunlaing, he had never thought the king impatient. He could grow angry, justly, but he was usually very accommodating. "Perhaps this is not the time to discuss a plan. Perhaps the king has grown weary after his meal. We could continue in the... "

"Nonsense." Dunlaing wiggled his fingers at Ardan. "If the gods see fit to replace me as king of Leinster, then 'tis not my place to argue. I care most about the people in my territory."

What had happened to the man? What had he discussed with Bram?

Ardan bowed his head, waited a moment, and then continued. "I understand, king. Ye *are* the wisest the territory has known. " The words wedged in Ardan's throat. "And the gods have been well pleased with yer leadership. 'Tis just that... there is a message."

"From the druid stick?"

"Aye, king. But I must ask first about the druid who visited ye last."

"Again?" Dunlaing stood, paced around his regal chair, wagged his finger at Ardan, and then sat again. "I told ye, he was just passing through."

"I understand. But if he gave ye a message from the gods... well, the prophecy may connect with mine in ways I don't yet know. I must hear his words."

"He said very little, really."

Ardan reached out his hand in a friendly gesture. "I must interpret the meaning, no matter how insignificant it may seem."

Dunlaing lifted his gaze to the rafters. "Let me think. Ah, that's it. He spoke about a god who will reward those who speak his truth. Do ye know what god he refers to, Ardan?"

Ardan twirled his stick between his palms. He gathered some stones he kept in his belt pouch, including the valuable fire stone. He stared down at them for so long that the only sound he heard was Dunlaing's breathing. He closed his eyes, pleading with the gods to give him the answer to Bram's riddle. *Reward.* How? *His truth.* About what?

Thankfully, Dunlaing waited silently.

In his mind, Ardan called on every god on earth, under the earth, in the sky and dwelling on the heavenly bodies there. Then, distinctly, Brigid's face appeared before him, not as he had left her, weak and ineffective, but bright and beautiful, the way she used to be.

"That's it!"

"What, man?"

Ardan hadn't realized he'd spoken out loud. "The message points to Brigid and the destruction that she may cause. Just like at the Samhain."

Dunlaing stared at him as though he'd lost his senses. "What are ye speaking of, man?"

"It's *her* god. 'Tis plain to me now." He tucked the druid stick into the embroidered folds of his tunic. "This will require an order from you, king, something ye command Brigid not to do."

Dunlaing snapped his fingers and ordered parchment and wax brought in. "I will only do what the gods insist, Ardan. I must trust ye."

Ardan flung his right hand over his heart. "King Dunlaing, am I not a trusted advisor? Did I not predict Troya's

255

actions and therefore save young Brigid's life? Do ye doubt my spiritual connection? Because if ye do, there's no limit to how the gods may punish... "

"Nay, nay, Ardan. I have trusted ye many years. But I must say this: If ever ye lead me astray, ye'll be banished. The same for any advisor."

Ardan tightened his abdomen and sucked in his lips. *This king will surely be deposed. And soon.* He tried to smile sincerely. "Have no fear, king. Now, to the matter." He turned to the king's scribe who had seated himself at a low wooden table next to the king's chair. On one corner of the desk a candle burned, dripping globs of hot honey-scented wax down its sides.

Ardan addressed the scribe. "Be it known that from this day forward, Brigid of the Cell of the Oak shall not instruct any inhabitant of the land called Ireland to follow her god, the one called Christ the King. Further, she shall not declare that any works she performs are done in that god's name. Failure to comply will result in indenture and torture for herself and anyone found following her god, by the order of Dunlaing, king of Leinster."

Dunlaing removed his signet ring, and then paused. "Druid, why must the order include all the people of Ireland? Should it not be pronounced only in my providence? And torture? Really, is that necessary?"

Ardan rose and touched his torque as a reminder of his position. He hadn't realized Dunlaing had grown so tender and inept. "The gods command it. We may not understand. We are mere mortals."

The explanation was enough. Dunlaing sealed the order and commanded readings to commence throughout Leinster.

"Is there anything else, druid? I'd like to return to my guests. As ye hear, the music has begun."

"Only one thing more I require. Grant me a copy of yer order, so that I also may declare it wherever I travel."

Dunlaing knew that Ardan traveled a great distance. Certainly he'd not object.

Dunlaing cocked his head. "Very well. A copy will be delivered to yer room tonight."

Ardan bowed and headed toward his chamber amid tunes of tin whistles, harps, and bodhrans. He was in no festive mood. Bram had probably already found Brigid. He'd need to hurry just as soon as the scribe delivered his copy of the order.

Ardan stopped by the scriptorium to inform the servant that he'd carry the parchment unfurled. That way he would not be delayed waiting for ink to dry.

CHAPTER

"WHERE THEN DOES WISDOM COME FROM?
WHERE DOES UNDERSTANDING DWELL?"
JOB 28:20

After Ardan left, Brigid went about caring minimally for her needs. She had no desire to starve herself, but had little motivation to do anything beyond that. She ate a few berries and crumbs of bread that Ardan had left, washed her face in the frigid waters of a stream, and returned to her cave home to pray.

She wasn't sure if she was truly fasting to obtain spiritual guidance or if she refrained from nourishment solely because her stomach cramped every time she smelled cabbage. Even if the stench was only in her mind, she could not will it away.

Deciding that they hadn't done her any good, Brigid abandoned her usual spoken Psalms and praises which she'd learned from the monks and began to plead her case before God. She plopped down on the cave floor and lifted her hands. *Yer just and mighty. Ye know that what has happened is not right. Teach me, Lord. Somehow, teach me what ye would have me do now.*

Brigid moaned, frustrated that her prayers were inadequate. In the semi-dark edges of the cave, dimly lit by rays of sun filtered through the head of the shelter, bats winged

258

about, annoyed at her outburst. Even the wild creatures despise her.

She cried aloud. "I'm being punished! Why?"

"Because yer human." The voice came from outside the cave.

"Ardan? Back so soon?" She scrambled to her feet.

A figure, too small and bent to be Ardan, appeared at the cave's opening with the sun behind him. He wore a white cloak, but Brigid could not make out his face.

"Who are ye? What do ye want?"

"Don't ye know me, Brigid?" The man lowered his hood and blinked clear blue eyes at her.

"Bram!" She ran to him and threw her arms around his neck.

He did not return the embrace but kept his grip on his walking stick. Afraid that he was so fragile she might cause him to collapse under her hugs, Brigid stepped back. "Oh, how I've missed ye! I should have come out to Ennis Dun, but... well, so much has happened. We were kidnapped, my mother and I. Ye must have wondered why we didn't come back after the Samhain."

Bram stepped lightly into the cave and found a rock to use for a seat. "Hush, now, child. I know quite a bit, I do."

Brigid could not keep still – perhaps because she'd had little company. She hadn't realized how much she had missed the kind old druid. "Ardan took us away. Said that Brocca owed a woman named Troya an honor price."

Bram raised his hand to stop her rambling. That was when she truly looked at him. In only a few months he seemed to have aged greatly. Every slight move seemed to cause him pain and a gurgled cough stirred from his lungs.

"Bram, yer not well! How did ye ever make yer way up here? And why did ye come?"

Bram shook his head and ran his wrinkled fingers across

his forehead. "Brigid, please give me a moment to catch my breath."

"I'm sorry. I've gathered herbs for tea. Have ye a pot about ye?"

He pointed to a leather sack he had dropped at the cave's opening.

"Rest while I prepare it."

Bram pulled his cloak back over his head and closed his eyes, still coughing.

Brigid trembled. God himself had to have sent the old druid to her, for care, or perhaps he came because he bore a message.

She gathered the herbs she had stored in a leaf pocket and stashed behind a rock. Then she went to Bram's sack and pulled out a round tin cooking pot, just the right size for brewing tea. Before she left to collect water, she threw a few sticks and dry leaves on her fire and coaxed the old man to lie down next to it. "I'll be back soon." She darted out into the forest.

Spring was in full force, having driven away enough cool breezes that the wildflowers were free to bloom. She stopped when she spotted miniature star flowers. The tiny white blossoms poked their faces up against large green leaves that cupped the blooms like little hands. She gathered a few. Perhaps she'd find some watercress near the stream. With those ingredients, she could make a remedy for Bram's cough.

She returned with the water and plants, sprinkled fresh herbs into the pot, and then set the mixture over the fire to brew. She crushed the star flowers and watercress to form a poultice.

Bram was asleep, but when he woke, she would spread the mixture on his chest, cover it with a cloth warmed over the fire, and bid him to sit with his back against the rock. She'd seen the monks do this, and many people recovered after such treatment. She might not be blessed anymore to perform miracles, but at least she could do something.

The next day, after benefiting from Brigid's care, Bram seemed better and eager to talk. "Tell, me now. If 'twas Ardan who took you and Brocca hostage, why do ye look for him to return here to the cave? Do ye not seek to escape him?"

After explaining all about Troya, Brigid's miracle with her cloak that forced King Dunlaing to grant her land, the building of the Cell of the Oak, and how she had taken a vow before a bishop, Brigid told her trusted friend about Brocca's latest abduction.

"And ye think Ardan is responsible, do ye?" Bram sipped tea and shared barley bread from his bag.

"Absolutely. He as much as told me so when he visited me just two days earlier. In fact, he promised to return today, and he wants something from me."

Bram gummed the bread. His front teeth were gone. "Ah, he surely does. And something that will benefit him, no doubt."

Brigid scratched her head. "Bram, ye once said Ardan was not part of yer druid brotherhood."

"Aye, he seeks spiritual powers for his own benefit, be they good or evil. He does not care as long as he gets the esteem and power he covets." He washed the bread down with a swig of tea.

Brigid could not remember Ardan ever saying he sought things for himself. He wanted the honor price paid for Troya, not for himself. And now, he recognized her as Brigid of Ireland, helper to all those living on the isle. The druid might be misled; but like Bram, he could come around. He seemed to want to help people, and besides, he held her mother. Brigid had no choice but to trust him if she wanted Brocca back.

Brigid leaned in close to whisper to Bram. "Ardan may seem untrustworthy, but I have seen another side of him, a side that wants to help others. He's going to reunite me with my mother."

The old man raised one wispy eyebrow. "That so? And after he took her hostage?"

"I know it sounds odd. But I've no other choice. Perhaps he had a reason to take her. Perhaps he was protecting her somehow. There were other strangers at the Cell of the Oak that night."

Bram struggled through coughs to speak. "Brigid, yer speaking nonsense. Yer trying to make what is into what you want it to be."

She refilled his mug and encouraged him to sip the hot liquid and let it soothe his throat. "I have to find my mother. Ardan may worship gods who have no voice, but…"

"No voice. That's how it is?"

Brigid patted the old man's hand. "I meant no offense. 'Tis just that he… well, he'll come around to being as nice as you are."

Bram narrowed his eyes. He shifted a bit until he found a comfortable position. "And yer telling me, then, that the crafty self-serving fellow does not require anything of ye to restore yer mother?"

"Aye, I suppose he does. But don't worry, Bram."

He leaned forward, coughed softly, and then raised his shoulders while chuckling to himself. "There's much ye don't understand, Brigid. I have lived long, learned much. Ye'd be wise to heed my words."

Ashamed, she stared at the dirt under her black feet.

He stood up with the help of his walking stick. "Pray for knowledge. I'll pray too. But first, I must hide from his sight."

She went to him, feeling his limp body lean on hers for strength. The thought of someone depending on her, a small woman who had not had proper nourishment for days, seemed foolhardy. He settled himself into a dark corner on top of two blankets he'd had her claim from his traveling sack.

"How is it, Bram, that ye come to me, here in this lonely place, and you in such poor health?"

"I am old." He puffed between words. "But that does not mean my spirit is not strong and willful. Now," he cleared his throat, "pray to yer god while I listen."

She wished he hadn't asked. Brigid wanted Bram to believe in her God more than she could tell. But, her heavenly Father was far away from her desolate cave. No signs, no visions, no small still voice. He wasn't there. For her old friend's sake, however, she would try.

Folding her hands, she bowed in reverence. "Father, God, Creator of all things, please hear yer servant. Come to us in this place. Speak to us." She was begging. She couldn't help it. "Give us wisdom to do yer will." What else? She was anxious to end it and made the sign of the cross on her chest.

Brigid left Bram to snooze and climbed out onto the cave shelf. The sun streamed through trees that had not yet fully birthed their leaf canopies, warming her for the first time since she took up residence there. Not even the fire that Ardan built had reached her soul like these solar rays. Soon she was asleep.

In the first dream she remembered she was a wee lassie on Cook's knee. Cook was young with much less gray hair than now. The woman instructed Brigid, asking questions.

"Who created the sun?"

Brigid gazed up at her. "The One True God."

"How do we know this?"

"Because the Holy Scriptures, given to us by saints of old, tell us."

Cook grinned and wiggled her fingers through Brigid's hair. "And how do we know what the Scriptures say, Brigid?"

Young Brigid passed a finger under her nose and wrinkled her forehead.

"Come now." Cook tilted her chin upward. "What's the

man's name? The one who came across the sea to tell us 'bout those Scriptures?"

"Patrick?" The young girl sounded unsure.

"Aye, Patrick. And one day ye'll meet him. And then ye'll understand."

Brigid dreamed more.

Brocca sat in a fluffy cloud field of meadowsweet and yarrow. She turned toward Brigid, her eyes wide open as though she could see. Her lips formed words with emphasis, as though she was afraid Brigid might not understand. "I'd rather be a slave for my Lord than be a free woman belonging to a sinful world."

Brigid reached out her hands, but all she grasped was flower petals. Drifts of pollen floated off her fingertips toward the heavens.

She awoke then, her heart pounding. Had she received a vision and was her mother now dead? Somehow, sleep came again.

Brigid dreamed Bram was healthy again, with straight, strong legs, just like the day she'd met him. "A druid makes a pledge," he told her, his blue eyes bright again. "Like the pledge ye spoke to the bishop and yer god. A druid pledges to commune with the spirits and minister to the common people. In doing so, he or she vows to cause no harm with the powers granted. 'Tis a great responsibility, Brigid, it is." He wrapped one white wool-covered arm around her, an arm much sturdier than the one she'd felt earlier. "To whom much is given, much will be required."

She awoke, puzzled by all her dreams, especially the last one. Why had Bram, a pagan man, recited a Scripture verse in her dream? Dreams often contained messages from God. What did it mean?

Late in the day, after the king issued his order, Ardan received a copy. The parchment would dry on the way, secured to a pole like a flag. He hoped he wasn't too late. Ardan mounted his horse and galloped toward Brigid.

"She'd better still be there." He hit open meadow and prodded his horse until he soared with his face in the wind. "God of the air, grant me speed."

Before the sun set, Ardan spotted Brigid sitting on a ledge outside her dwelling. "Ah, fine, she's still there." He curled up the parchment proclamation and stashed it under his tunic belt.

Since he knew she hadn't left, Ardan could take his time. He collected a handful of dry grass, strung a long blade around the whole bunch, and secured it with a leather thong. Taking another strip, he attached the bundle to a stick. Satisfied with his torch, he sat down on a stone and struck a fire with the help of his fire rock. At the top of the rock wall where he'd seen Brigid, a lone blackbird sat, pruning his shiny feathers. The lass was no longer in sight, but the faint flicker of a fire told him she had retreated into her cave to sit at the fire ring.

He patted the official papers at his waist. She'd accept the deal he offered. And when she did, there'd be no one to hinder him. Even if that ancient druid was in there with her, he'd be no problem. The gods had ordained Ardan's task.

He paused. *The gods.* Ardan could take no chances. He'd need to offer a sacrifice before he visited Brigid. He stuck the end of his torch into the ground and crept through the forest, holding open an empty linen sack. He searched for a small animal to capture and held the sack out, planning to throw it over the creature. Normally he'd hunt in daylight for a proper sacrificial animal, but he hadn't planned ahead. He had to resort to bumbling around the woods like a lad trying to snare a fairy.

"God of the simple-minded fowl," he called out, "hear yer

servant! Send to me a proper sacrifice for the Others." He hoped the god would hear. The Others, living in the seas, lakes, and under the rocks, had to be appeased if Ardan wished their help. His ultimate prey, Brigid, was a powerful woman. One who required the spell of the Others to subdue her.

Hours later the forest was completely dark, save for the light given off by Ardan's torch. No birds of any type lingered where Ardan could snag one. Near a pile of branches, a pair of eyes flashed. *Badger!* Ardan was off and soon bagged the fellow, suffering wounds to his forearms in the process. But the linen bag did not hold the animal's diggers – he escaped, scampering off and slithering beneath brambles.

Sweating, with blood dripping from elbow to wrist, Ardan retrieved his golden sickle, used for spiritual sacrifices, from his travel bag. A small animal was not a worthy sacrifice anyway. He eyed the horse. To sacrifice him, Ardan's transportation, would surely be a worthy and acceptable offering.

Ardan lifted his arms to the stars, little pinholes of light in the night's blanket. He chanted holy words known only to druids, and beckoned the Others to draw closer to him and help with the task. And to help him possess the power that Brigid had.

The sharp blade of his sickle sliced into the horse's side, and Ardan felt detached, as if someone else was performing the ritual. Ardan chased after the injured animal, shouting praises to the gods. Pools of blood gushed out as the horse whimpered and collapsed near a stream. The tributary changed from dark and moist to thick and sluggish – red with sacrifice. The offering was poured out directly to the Others under the river.

Ardan stripped off his clothes and bathed in the stream. After most of the blood passed by him, a light rain fell.

"Pleasing, aye, it was. The gift was received." He laughed

out loud, pulling his chilled body from the water and grabbing onto the torch that sizzled whenever a raindrop struck it.

A twig snapped nearby. Ardan waved the torch in all directions but saw nothing. A red deer or a boar perhaps. Whatever watched, be it earthly or otherwise, seemed to have vanished.

Ardan left his white robe behind. The garment was no longer worthy of a great druid as it was no longer pure white. He dragged his leather traveling bag a distance from the slain horse until he found shelter under a hefty hawthorn bush. After dressing in a linen tunic and a thin black cloak he used for traveling, he remembered the golden sickle. He'd left it at the site of the sacrifice. The tool was more valuable than druid sticks, and he'd need to retrieve it before visiting Brigid.

CHAPTER

25

Brocca was relieved that Ardan had left her. His continual questions and taunting were nauseating. She would gladly put up with him, however, if it meant he would stay away from Brigid. Brocca had no idea if he'd return.

The island where she was held captive was small enough that she heard waves pound on all sides. Even at night, while she was bound to her sleeping board, she heard the tide, knew the ocean was near all around.

Ardan had sailed days ago on a rudderless boat, heading east to a harbor near the river leading back to Brigid. She'd heard him say Brigid's name just before he left. "Curse!" he had wailed again and again until the sounds of the ocean birds grew too loud for her to hear him any longer. What had he meant? Perhaps he called down a curse on Brocca and her daughter for refusing to yield to his power.

As she sat alone on her bed, her guard gone to fish for breakfast, Brocca recalled the miserable nights she had spent listening to the druid condemn her beliefs before he left.

"Yer god," he'd said, "he is not here on this island, aye?"

She'd answered surely. "The One True God is here and everywhere. No one can hide from him."

"If yer god is here, why does he not free ye? Why does he allow *me* the power to hold ye?"

"I will wait upon him for deliverance."

Ardan huffed, paced the tiny hut, and then sat down close enough for his damp dog smell to permeate her nose. She smelled it still. "Ye'll die first."

"Perhaps, but still I wait."

Her answer had surprised him. He paused and cleared his throat. The druid's voice lowered. "What good does it do ye? Ye'll wait forever, and still he will not come. I am a great druid. I commune with spirits great and small. Because of this, all people will revere me. Ye cannot do this, Brocca."

She had wondered then how Ardan had come to be so arrogant. Bram never put himself ahead of people, even those he considered not spiritually endowed. He believed himself their servant.

"I serve the God who is the Creator of all," she had replied.

Brocca heard the sounds of Ardan packing a bag. She was pleased he was leaving.

Suddenly, his hands were at her throat. She tried to push them away, but he held her legs still with his thigh. She couldn't draw a breath, and still he taunted her, whispering in her ear that she would one day serve him and not any other, not even a god.

Just as she was about to faint, he let go, spilling her back onto the solid wood sleeping board. Her head pounded the board so hard her teeth rattled.

He snarled like a mad dog. "Just remember what I told ye."

She sensed someone else in the hut at that time – the driver who was now her guard.

Ardan whispered, but since Brocca had lost her sight, she

heard things others didn't. "I'm taking the small craft. I'll sail up to Hook's Head then take the river back to the settlement."

Ardan then raised his voice to the man, and Brocca heard the thud of a body hitting the wall. "Remember what I told ye."

The driver's voice cracked. "Aye. Ye can trust me."

Since that day, the guard said little. He cared for Brocca, bringing her fresh roasted fish and allowing her privacy when needed. She could not escape, and he knew so too because he tied her only at night.

At first she had feared what he might do to her, the two of them on a lonely island; but he never touched her improperly, never spoke a harsh word.

One evening on the beach, over a supper of scallops, Brocca probed for information. "What are we doing here?"

He sucked the flesh from a shell and answered with a mouthful. "Don't know."

"Then why don't we leave?"

"Can't."

She sighed. Why wouldn't he talk to her? Ardan could not overhear. "Don't we have a boat?" She knew they did. She could hear the ocean rocking the wooden vessel. It was tied up on the south side of the island.

"Aye, we do."

"Then let's go, before Ardan gets back. Surely ye have a family to return to."

He coughed, gagging on his food. "What know ye of my clan?"

"Nothing. I just figured a young man like you had some-one waiting for him."

He scooted closer, sand grinding under his weight. She had the sensation that he was holding something in front of her.

"Can ye see this?"

"Nay. I see nothing."

"Ye don't know what it is I'm holding in front of ye?"

"I told ye I cannot." She threw her empty shells in the direction of the water and wiped her hands on her tunic.

"How do ye know if I'm young or not? Ye can't tell by my voice, now can ye?"

"Sometimes ye *can* tell, especially if the speaker is quite young or quite old. But I can tell in other ways with you."

He laughed. His voice moved farther away. He was putting the cooking fire out. Grains of sand hit logs.

He mumbled, but she heard him. "'Tis getting dark. Let's be off to bed."

After she had retired to her sleeping board and he had wound leather strips around her ankles, a nightly routine, he spoke to her from the other side of the hut. He'd never spoken to her so much in one day in all the time they'd been together.

"How can ye tell my age, then?"

She shifted to her side even though doing so caused the ties to cut into her skin. She could hear him better if she faced his voice. "Will ye tell me yer name?"

"Suppose there's no harm. 'Tis Erc, though ye'd better not be speaking it when Ardan's about."

Ardan! May he stay away. Brocca drew a deep breath and answered. "Ye work hard, always chopping wood or hunting, so yer not too old, but old enough to know the value of a good day's work – something sometimes lost on the young."

"Is that the way it is? Ye could be wrong."

"I could be, but I'm not."

He groaned as his large frame plopped down on his sleeping board. "What makes ye so sure?"

"I hear ye speak to yer lass in the wee hours of the morning when ye go outside, though she must be far away. Only a young man in love would do that, rehearse what he'll say to her and how he'll make up his time away. I hear ye say ye'd

271

protect her and yer children with yer own life. Such are the heartfelt words of a young man who has not yet been separated from his mate for long periods."

She heard his feet hit the dirt floor. He was sitting up.

"How could ye know that? Yer tied up in the cabin in the early hours of every new morn. Magic! Yer a witch for sure."

"Nonsense, man. My ears are keen. I hear things ye ignore because ye have eyes to depend on."

Erc was quiet for a long while. When he spoke, his voice was choked with tears. "Yer right. I have a young wife and two daughters, twins, born two summers ago. I have not been able to feed my family properly. Desperate as I was, I accepted employment from Master Ardan. Bevin, my wife, begged me not to. She feared Ardan." He punched something solid, his board perhaps. "But my lassies, they cried for bread, begged for cream – and we have no cow. So I went. But, ah, she was right, that woman. I should never have done it."

He was opening up. Maybe he'd let her go. "Then why don't we leave tonight, go and return to Bevin and the wee ones?"

"Can't."

"Why?"

"I've said too much." His voice echoed off the wall. He had his back to her.

Brocca's night-time discussion with Erc was a lone occurrence. He returned to his usual silence, feeding her but otherwise ignoring her. Brocca pleaded with God to end her isolation.

Brocca was almost asleep one evening when she noticed that the salty breeze brought another smell, a strong greasy smell. She tried to imagine what it could be. *Smoke.* She called to Erc, "There's something out there!"

"I hear nothing."

"A smell. Like burning grease – fish flesh."

272

"Like whale blubber?" He threw back the window shutters. "By the gods! Raiders! I've seen them before, I have. They burn whale blubber in barrels for light on their ships and attack seaside settlements at night."

"Will they kill us?"

"Might." He untied her. "I'm not waiting around to find out."

He led her to the door.

"The boat's not far," she said.

"No time. They've seen it, that's why they're coming. Only chance we have is to hide." He pulled her, first one way, then another. They seemed to be headed toward high ground in the center of the island.

"Where will we hide?" She tried to catch her breath. They had been climbing for some minutes.

He tugged some more. "There's an abandoned cabin up here."

"Won't they find us there? Maybe we should greet them instead. Plead for mercy."

He squeezed her hand. "Foolish, that. There's a hidden room in the cabin, beneath the floor. Found it when I was hunting. 'Tis our only chance. I see the lights on the beach. They're in our old hut."

She heard a door squeak open, and he pulled her inside. The cabin was musty and smelled like rotting wood. She bumped into something. Furniture?

Erc nudged her elbow. "Careful. Come this way."

She heard a creaking sound. They dropped to their knees.

He stretched her arm out for her. "There's an opening here. Feel for the ladder. It leads to a hollowed-out room."

Brocca did as he said, feeling along the cold earthen floor until her hands hit empty space. She wiggled her fingers until she hit upon the ladder.

"Hurry, now!" He was right behind her as she descended.

Brocca hesitated. "Are there rats down here?"

"Don't know. But rats follow people, and from the looks of things there's not been anyone human here for a long time."

Her feet hit solid ground, and Erc drew the trap door closed. Bits of dirt showered her, landing in her hair and stinging her nose.

She shook the soil from her hair. "Will they not see that door, like you did?"

Erc rubbed stones together and sparked a fire. Snapping and popping sticks meant he'd lit a torch.

"And won't they see that light?"

"Hush, woman. I'll put it out soon. Got to see what's down here with us. Hmmm. How about that?"

"What do ye see?" She pulled on his sleeve.

"This place used to hide thieves, I'd say. Though likely in a time even before my seanathair was born. Crafty fellows they were, those old ones. We're well hidden."

She felt along the wall and down to the floor until she was satisfied that she'd found a safe place to sit.

Erc continued hmm-ing and clicking his tongue while he moved about. "Well, the dust has not been stirred, not even by animals. There's a chest over here with a lock on it – some ship's chest, I'd say. There's some holes here..." He grunted as though moving something. "Holes in the wall for air. When I shove this stone in front of them, we're sealed off. I expect there's another to cover the trap door. Be right back."

He grumbled some more from overhead. She heard the sound of rock grinding against dirt and then more soil fell on her head.

He grunted. "Clever bunch, them that built this. Seems the trap door swings from either side."

She sneezed and coughed, and he offered her water from a sheepskin flask.

She swallowed and then turned to him. "Who's to say the raiders aren't of the same clan who built this place?"

Erc sat beside her and stomped out the torch. "Can't say. But 'tis our only chance."

Brocca prayed. "For in the day of trouble he will keep me safe in his dwelling; he will hide me in the shelter of his tabernacle and set me high upon a rock."

Erc made his own plea for deliverance. "Whatever god yer praying to, may he hear us and not Ardan."

Brocca reached for his hand. "Why do ye say that?"

He didn't answer, but sobbed softly, as though trying to hold back.

"Erc, what are ye talking 'bout?"

He sniffed. "It's not the time to talk."

She listened instead, into the darkness, remembering how long it had taken them to get there, imagining where the intruders might be at that moment. The smell of burning whale blubber was stronger. When they made port, they kept the fires burning. Or was it torches she smelled, bobbing up the hill in the hands of violent marauders?

Brocca was acutely aware of her breathing, and of Erc's. She tried to match his rhythm, thinking they'd be less likely to be heard that way. But the young man's breaths were shallower than hers.

Godless people have no hope. She longed to tell him of her faith, but like he said, they could not talk now. Reaching out her hand, she met his touch and he latched on. She felt his fear, his trembling.

She tried not to let it feed her fear. All she could think about at that moment was her daughter. If death found them in their hiding place, would she have done enough for Brigid? Their time together had been so brief. *Please, God, don't let it end this way.*

Men's voices, faint but growing louder, drifted from

downhill. The raiders had not yet ascended to the refuge where Brocca and her captor huddled, afraid to breathe.

Surprisingly, Erc spoke. "I must guard yer safety above all else. If they come down here, I'll fight them, and ye must escape."

"But how?"

"In front of ye there's a tunnel. I know not where it leads, but it must be a way out. Directly in front of ye. Hear me?"

"Aye." She wished there were another way. *Please, God, don't let them come down here.*

The voices were near now. Brocca couldn't make them out – a strange dialect she'd never heard before. Shouts rang out. The men had found the cabin.

Just above their heads feet pattered back and forth. The furniture she'd bumped into earlier was thrown about, some of it shattering against the cabin walls and clattering to the floor in bits. Another sound, quite unexpected, rose above the din. A harp, and then someone singing in Latin. Were they planning on staying? Setting up there for the night? Brocca put her hand over her mouth, muffling her gasps.

A sickening sound came next. The stone covering the hidden door slid across the dirt-packed floor. Brocca's heart nearly pounded free from her chest. Erc urged her forward toward the tunnel. She heard his knife sliding out from its sheath.

Tears streamed down her cheeks as she reached out her arms, feeling for the tunnel opening. Erc gave her a push and she landed inside what felt like a burial chamber. She froze, not wanting to continue scurrying down the tunnel like a frightened badger. Erc was in mortal danger.

The trap door flew open and a voice called down, first in Latin, then in Irish. "'Tis safe to come out! The others have left. I won't hurt ye."

Then Erc's voice. "Ye'll have to come get me."

"Come now, man. I've said I won't hurt ye. I'm a bard, a royal poet, and a Christian."

Brocca crawled back out and bumped into Erc, hitting her head on his hard knee.

"Get back!" he barked.

She called up, "I'm Brocca. A follower of Christ."

The man answered back. "Brocca? Mother of Brigid?"

Somehow she managed to push past her guard and clamber up the ladder. "Aye, that I am. Who are ye?"

A gentle hand reached down and pulled Brocca up into the cabin. "I am a royal poet, as I said. My name is not important because it does not say who I am. Poet, that's what people call me."

Erc joined them. "I am her protector, servant of Master Druid Ardan."

The bard strummed his harp. "I've sent the others off. They seek treasure not murder. I assume ye harbor no gold."

Brocca thought about the locked chest in the chamber below. "None that we've seen, poet." It was true. The chest could be full of mouse droppings for all they knew.

"Then they'll not harm ye. I'll join up with them tomorrow and tell them that yer my kinsmen and I'm now traveling with ye. 'Tis not a lie." He touched Brocca's hand. "We're brother and sister in Christ."

She patted his hand and then he withdrew it.

"How do ye know my daughter Brigid?"

"We've much to talk about. Let's get settled in here and then we'll get acquainted."

Erc cleared his throat. "They'll not wonder where we hid?"

The poet strummed his harp again. "Not that smart, that bunch."

That night in the cabin as the bard spoke, Brocca realized how he knew Brigid. He'd accompanied her when she traveled to the seashore to seek the bishop and speak her vows.

Brocca lowered her voice toward the ground. "Poet, 'tis no coincidence, ye finding us?"

He squirmed on a rickety chair. "I am a friend to yer daughter, bard to King Dunlaing. I knew Ardan was after ye. I alone had this knowledge and planned to warn ye. I suppose Ardan knew the trail to the Cell of the Oak better than I."

Brocca slumped back on her wooden chair. "I don't understand."

The poet leaned close to her. "Ardan got there before me with men and weapons. At first I was going to help the others douse the flames. Then I spotted him dragging ye off. I followed to the river where I saw him take ye into a boat. I followed on foot as best I could. Each day the distance between us grew, but I dared not stop and loose the trail."

No one but Brigid had ever cared so much for her. Brocca's eyes stung with tears. "Why, man? Why would ye do this?"

His voice choked. "There was no one else. No one saw what I did. Ardan is the king's head druid. I'd get no help from the castle. God chose me for the task." He swallowed hard. "I knew he'd make it possible."

She reached out until her hands met his clean-shaven face. "And he did, man. God is good."

Erc shuffled nearby and cleared his throat. They'd left him out of the conversation.

"Dear man," the poet said to Erc, "if ye guard this Christian woman for the druid named Ardan, then ye do not protect her as ye claim to do."

"Ye do not understand." Erc's strained voice shook. "If I do not return her to Ardan, he'll visit my family with horrific curses."

That was the truth he'd kept from her. Brocca turned toward him and cupped his hands in hers. "He has no power to do that which he threatens, Erc."

He pulled away from Brocca and stood. "He's a great druid. Surely, poet, being in the king's service, ye know this."

Brocca reached for his legs, and when she located him, she got to her feet. "Nay, Ardan's power is useless."

The bard plucked his instrument and sang, "Ardan follows darkness, the poet follows the Light. He who knows the poet's God will overcome this night."

"Listen." Brocca reached for Erc's face. "Ardan seeks to control people for his own purpose, not to appease any god. And even when he sacrifices to his gods, it's futile. They command no authority over what the One True God created."

"No authority?" Erc pulled away and trudged to the door. "Someone must control the forces of nature. May the gods have mercy on me, I cannot let my family be harmed."

Brocca pleaded. "Ardan can cause no harm with curses. Do ye not hear the bard? Do ye not believe, as all the pagans do, that the bard's songs are true?"

"'Tis not my wish to contradict a bard."

A boulder-size weight lifted from her shoulders and she breathed deeply. The smell of whale grease torches was faint in the distance. "Good. Poet, shall we collect Erc's family before returning to the Cell of the Oak?" She whispered, "Or do ye think we must hurry back? Will Ardan threaten my daughter?"

The poet strummed his harp one last time before she heard him tuck it away in a bag. "He'll not harm Brigid. He seeks to control her powers by holding you, the one she cares most for in this world, hostage."

"He cannot do that. Brigid's powers are not hers. They are given to her by God."

The poet snapped his fingers. "Aye. We've time to help this man."

CHAPTER

26

Dunlaing paced the length of his chamber. Even as the candles burned to stubs, he could not sleep. He hadn't told Ardan all that the old druid named Bram had told him. How could he? Ardan had been a trusted advisor for many years and he could not reveal any doubt he might have about the druid's integrity lest he turn against him.

The king turned to his disheveled bed. Silk wraps and pillows stuffed with swan feathers were scattered across his mattress. He hadn't been able to sleep. He had not allowed company. He was troubled.

Next to his bed sat a carved wooden box. He lifted the lid and gazed at the signet ring nestled in purple velvet lining. Had it been impetuous to give the order constraining Brigid? He snapped the box shut. A king's decree could not be revoked save in the most extreme circumstances. Otherwise his words would be as gnats, something better left ignored.

Dunlaing knew the old druid's name, though. He had pretended he could not recall it. Bram had brought troubling news. Even Ardan seemed to think so and insisted that the gods named Brigid's god the one who would lead the people away from Dunlaing. When Bram had spoken of a false god, Dunlaing at first believed he referred to the one called Christ. He was no longer sure.

Dunlaing threw himself onto the pile of silk linens. Perhaps he had let jealousy obstruct his judgment. Bram had not mentioned Brigid. He had not said the false god bore the name Christ. He'd only stated that false gods would threaten to destroy the reign of Dunlaing, king of Leinster.

Which gods were false?

He closed his eyes and pictured the old druid who had visited. He was an old sage, and had studied spiritual matters for more seasons than Dunlaing had lived.

"I speak with my heart," the one called Bram had said. "And from the heart of my spiritual brothers who passed the truth on to me."

Dunlaing had thought at the time that the old man was speaking about tradition, beliefs that Ardan proclaimed. But after the old man left, saying that he had more wisdom to pass on before his bones became dust and melded back to the earth, Dunlaing thought the old man might have been speaking of a new way, one which Ardan would never accept. That was why Dunlaing had decided to be vague about what the old visitor had revealed.

Then Dunlaing had gotten befuddled, slipped back to a comfortable place. He trusted Ardan because no affliction had come into the kingdom since Ardan claimed to protect it with his sacrifices and spiritual communion with the gods. Dunlaing had believed that Ardan's prayers and chants had helped the negotiations with the king of Munster succeed.

A soft knock at the door stirred Dunlaing from his thoughts.

"Do ye require anything, king?" a small voice whispered through the lock.

"Nay, nothing."

He watched the light fade away from the bottom of the door until he was satisfied that the servant was gone, taking his torch with him. Then the king tossed all his blankets on the floor and lay exposed on his platform bed, watching the candles flicker until they had no more life in them.

The next day Dunlaing urged his servants to dress him as quickly as possible. There was much to be done. "Bring me my most trusted spy," he ordered.

When his shoes were the last piece of clothing awaiting him, a willow of a man entered.

Dunlaing ordered the others out of his chambers with one clap of his hands. "Galvin, I've got a special task for ye."

Galvin bowed low. "I am at yer service, king."

Dunlaing wondered if he left the spy kneeling on one knee how long it would be before the man tumbled over. Galvin was reed-thin but healthy, with ruddy cheeks and milky skin. Some men are bred by the gods to perform certain tasks. This man was naturally light on his feet and as invisible as a deer in the woods while gathering sensitive information about Dunlaing's enemies.

Dunlaing held out his ring for the man to kiss. "C'mon. Up, man. We've matters to discuss."

They wandered to a table and chairs positioned at the south end of Dunlaing's chamber – a spot where they could soak up the best light from the windows. Dunlaing seated himself and pointed to the other chair. Galvin sat, crossed his legs at the knees, and bowed his head again.

"This is not a military mission, Galvin. But it does concern the future of my reign as yer king."

Galvin glanced up at Dunlaing, barely lifting his head. "I assure ye, king, I will consider the mission critical and will perform whatever ye ask to the best of my abilities."

Dunlaing stared out the window. "I want ye to follow my druid Ardan. Report what he does in the woods. Ye know, who he visits, what he talks about to those he meets. And tell this to no one but me."

"I will do what ye ask." Galvin sealed his promise with another kiss to Dunlaing's ring.

Dunlaing didn't say another word. Galvin rose, bowed his stick-like body, and left.

Three nights later a small rapping at Dunlaing's window woke him. Thinking a mouse was scurrying about, he called for a servant. Sometime later the man returned to report that the guards had checked thoroughly, but no mouse, indeed no creature at all, was found.

But after the servant left, the noise returned. "What *is* that? Can't a man sleep in his own bed without disturbance?" Dunlaing went to the window and threw back the shutters. Nothing. The night was nearly spent but dawn had not yet arrived. All was still. He attempted to close the shutters, but they stuck. He glanced down at the sill. A fist blocked the way.

"What?" Dunlaing jumped back.

"King, 'tis Galvin."

He looked down at the spy planted so flat against the wall he looked like he'd been run over by an ox cart. "Why are ye lurking about my window? Ye scared me to death." Dunlaing stuck his head out the window and glanced in all directions. The guards had not spotted him. Galvin was truly a master of his occupation.

"May I enter?"

"Aye, enter."

Galvin slid his small frame through the window and seated himself on a chair, dusting grime from his gray and brown stripped tunic.

"Have ye news, man?"

"Aye, I do have a report, and since ye said this was sensitive information, I came to ye at night."

"Good, good. What is it?"

Galvin tapped his branch-like fingers on his knees. If Dunlaing didn't know better, he would have thought Galvin was a shape-shifter merging from tree back into man. "Master Ardan. I found him offering sacrifice in the woods, near a river."

"What of this, man?"

Galvin grunted and blinked his eyes. "The animal he sacrificed, king, was one of yer horses."

Dunlaing joined Galvin at the table, sitting directly across from the spy to gaze into his eyes. "Are ye quite sure?"

"Aye, I'm sure. 'Twas the king's high druid dressed in his white cloak embellished with fine gold thread, a golden torque at his neck and a shining sickle in his hand. And 'twas one of King Dunlaing's sable stallions." Galvin pulled a shiny object from an ox hide sack he carried on his back. Round and glistening, with blood stains and horsehair stuck to its blade, Ardan's sacred sickle was in the spy's possession.

Dunlaing's head grew hot. "So he destroys my property for his sacrifice without my knowledge! What else?"

Galvin laid the sickle on the table. "He waved his arms in the air and then dropped them to the ground, calling to the Others to hear him."

Dunlaing straightened in his chair. "The Tuatha De Danann?"

"Aye, sire. He called to them in the sea, under the rocks, and under the rushing water. That is why he performed the sacrifice at the river, I believe."

"And what did he ask of them?"

Galvin's eyes focused on Dunlaing's. The spy wrinkled his eyebrows until his forehead furrowed like a newly-plowed field. "He asked for their power to help sacrifice the large animal and also..."

"Go on."

"He asked for the Others to help him capture the power Brigid has for himself to use."

Dunlaing gripped Galvin's bony shoulders. "For himself? He asked nothing for the kingdom of Leinster?"

Galvin shook his head.

Dunlaing squeezed his fingers into the man's collarbone. "Be sure, man. He must have petitioned on behalf of the kingdom."

Galvin didn't flinch. "Nay, king. Ardan petitioned only for Ardan."

Dunlaing let go and focused on the spy's last words. *Only for Ardan.* A wave of regret washed over him. As ruler, he was sworn to be protector of the people. He'd once understood that well. Believing Brigid had tricked him, he felt personal insult over all else.

Dunlaing let out a breath and glanced at the ceiling. Was Brigid's god the false one? Were all these thoughts put into his head by devious fairies seeking to mislead him?

He turned to his confidant. "Galvin, I do not know who to trust. Is Ardan doing what is required to protect my kingdom? Or is he not a true spiritual leader, but rather an evil self-serving deceiver, and I am the one who has been mocked?"

Galvin studied at the floor. "I am not worthy to advise the king on such matters."

Of course he wasn't. What had Dunlaing been thinking to spill his innermost thoughts to this man? "Galvin, did ye happen to see this young woman whose god-given talents Ardan covets?"

Galvin raised his eyes. "I saw only Ardan. He spoke to no one but the Others, and he slept in the forest under a hawthorn."

Dunlaing snapped the spy a look. "A hawthorn, was it?"

"Aye. As I said, he converses with the Otherworld and he stayed close most of the night. I observed him for a long while. I could have stayed with him, but since the king said this was an urgent matter..."

"Aye. Ye did well, Galvin. I'll see to it that yer rewarded. Keep yer eyes and ears open and if ye hear that Brigid resides anywhere in my kingdom, inform me at once."

Galvin bowed and slipped out of the chamber.

Dunlaing opened the window shutters wide and shooed away the servants who had come to investigate the chatter. Ardan would not know of the king's suspicions until Dunlaing was sure. But if Ardan could not be trusted, where would Dunlaing find proper guidance? The council Ardan had brought to the castle had returned to the woods. Dunlaing would send for them and probe for information without mentioning Ardan's name. There was one man in particular he should speak to – that mysterious bard, that poet who had followed Brigid at Ardan's request. Surely he had more to tell.

Dunlaing stayed at the window until the sky dawned pink and clear and stretched forever. Dunlaing stared at its emerging blueness, wondering where one should look when pleading with the god whom the king of Munster called the Creator of all.

Morning rays lit his face and made his beard itch. All the spiritual advice he'd ever received had told him the sun was central to life. Dunlaing stepped fully into the warm morning beams bathing the limestone floor of his sleeping chamber. "God of Patrick and Brigid, if ye hear me, endow me with wisdom in this matter."

286

CHAPTER

"TEACH ME YOUR WAY, O LORD; LEAD ME IN A
STRAIGHT PATH BECAUSE OF MY OPPRESSORS."
PSALM 27:11

Ardan woke with great anticipation. Never before had he been so invigorated by a sacrificial ritual. He rubbed his hands through his hair and glanced around. He'd fallen asleep under a thick bush, staying for the most part dry while the rest of the woods were damp and dappled with sunlight. He recalled the previous evening's sacrifice and remembered that he still needed to retrieve his druid sickle.

Ardan retraced his steps toward the stream. The smell of the dead horse was unmistakable, as were the calls of scavenger birds. The royal horse lay on the bank with most of its internal organs spilled. Ardan had offered the animal's heart to the Others – he remembered that. But he'd taken a vessel of mead into his woodland shelter and the beverage had caused the evening's events to grow fuzzy in his mind. He tapped his forehead. Ah, the sickle. That's what he'd come for.

Ardan's head ached from overimbibing. The dead animal's stench made his stomach turn. Now where was that sickle? He searched up and down the carcass, shoving the animal into the river to examine the ground underneath. The sickle was gone, stolen. Why had he been so careless?

Ardan looked toward the rocks where he hoped Brigid was still sleeping. He'd worry about the sickle later.

Brigid's naps outside the cave had not brought much rest. The ground was hard and ravens preferred to perch there. They tried to convince her to leave and she'd finally relented. She had wanted to curl up next to Bram for the night, but he insisted she stay away, wishing to stay hidden when Ardan returned. So she slept next to the fire ring until the morning light filled the cave's opening.

She glanced at the druid's sleeping spot and found him awake. "Shall I find breakfast?"

He whispered from his dark corner. "Nay, Ardan approaches."

She frowned. "He'll hear yer breathing anyway. Why not come out and take nourishment? He'll not harm ye."

"I do not fear the druid Ardan. I seek only to listen to what he will not say in my presence. I want him to speak freely to ye, I do. And... I do not desire food."

Brigid held her hand over her mouth. Bram was nearing death's door and she wished it wasn't so. He was such a dear friend, and one who did not yet know Christ as Savior.

Rocks plummeted down the side of the cliff. This time Ardan would not arrive unannounced. They heard him coming.

"Hello, Brigid?" Ardan called from somewhere outside.

Bram whispered, "Go now. And give his words careful thought, Brigid."

She crept to the edge of the rock shelf. Ardan, dressed in a common black cloak, climbed up.

She called down to him. "Why don't ye go round to the side of the hill and approach that way? Would be much easier."

He wasn't far away, his face sweating and red, his arms taut, grasping first one rock and then another. "Would it be now?" He tilted his head back and laughed. "I wanted to come the quickest way possible. Yer anxious 'bout yer mother now, aren't ye?"

Brigid folded her legs underneath her and curled up to wait. He drew himself up to the shelf and plopped down on the dusty ledge, drawing in air. A raven tried to light on his shoulder then thought better and flapped away.

Ardan pulled a sheepskin water bag from his belt and gulped from it. "That was a more difficult climb than I thought. I should have circled back and approached from the other side like I did before. Yer a smart one, Brigid of Ireland." His dark eyes smiled, giving her a chill.

She kept focused. "My mother."

"That's why I'm here, to talk about the terms of her release."

Brigid scooted back as far as she dared. "A ransom? I have no silver, no gold."

He laughed again, tossing his faded black hair against the wind. "I do not seek riches, lass. 'Tis an agreement I'm after."

"Ye want me to become yer apprentice, like Troya. Well, I cannot…"

"Silence!" He held his hand in front of her face. The man who had only moments ago laughed like a child had become oppressively frightening.

Seeing her fear, Ardan drew his frown up and softened his demeanor. Shape-shifting – the ability of people or gods to transform themselves from one entity into another – Ardan's rapid mood changes were the closest Brigid had seen to such a thing.

"Shall we move to the fire ring and share a bit of bread?"

Bram!

Ardan stood up, and she tugged lightly on his cloak. "I prefer to stay outside, in the warm sun."

"Very well." He grunted, pulled a piece of flat oat bread from his pocket and offered her a portion.

She wanted to refuse – it carried the faint aroma of cabbage – but she dared not insult him. She nibbled in silence as he attempted to retell the kidnapping of her mother in a more favorable light.

Ardan wiped his chin with the back of his hand. "I tried to stop the men, but they were drunk. I accompanied them to assure Brocca's safety. I promise ye, Brigid, no harm has come to her."

"Where is she, then?"

He swallowed his bread and held up a finger. His nails were rimmed in red – blood. She bit the inside of her cheek. *Please, God, don't let it be so.*

He noticed her staring and plunged his hand into the folds of his cloak. "I cannot tell ye, not yet. I have an order here from King Dunlaing."

"What kind of order?"

Ardan pulled a rolled-up parchment from underneath his cloak. He smiled as he read. "Be it known that from this day forward, Brigid of the Cell of the Oak..."

"I can read." She snatched it from his hands.

They stared at each other for a moment. She was just as surprised as he was, and swallowed hard. "I mean, I'd like to see for myself, if ye don't mind."

Ardan tipped his chin forward.

She read silently, her mouth dropping open. "Is this to say that I cannot invite others to my Lord's table?"

He jerked his head. She realized he didn't understand.

"I mean, this seems to say that I can no longer ask anyone in all of Ireland to accept Christ as Savior nor perform any miracles in his name."

"Aye, that's what it says. Sealed with Dunlaing's mark." He pointed to the waxy seal.

She continued reading, and then looked up at the druid. "And if I disregard this order, I am to become a slave again?"

"Aye, that's what it says."

"Why would Dunlaing order this?"

Ardan stood up as though he were leaving.

"Wait." Stunned, Brigid struggled to her feet. "Ye said ye wanted an agreement. Is there more?"

"There is."

"Please, sit. Tell me."

"I will offer ye something in return, Brigid."

"My mother."

He smiled again. "Simple proposition, really. If ye do not wish to yield yer powers to me..."

"And I won't, Ardan. I can't."

He cleared his throat. "If ye do not wish to do that, then there is another way to get yer mother back. Just agree not to do the things Dunlaing forbids and I will return her."

Brigid opened her mouth. She wanted to agree, to feel her mother's arms around her again. But no sound escaped her lips.

"Think on this, Brigid. I will return at sunset."

Ardan left, and Brigid hurried to Bram's side. "Ye heard?"

"Aye, I heard everything."

She escorted him to the smoky fire. "Oh, Bram. I know that to you this seems like a simple choice to make."

"Ye know how it seems to me, do ye?" He held his fingers over the fire.

"Well, I know 'tis not simple at all. I am the Lord's servant, but I would be required not to ask anyone to come to him. There are so few followers of Christ in Ireland. How can I turn my back on what I was destined to do?"

Bram pointed to the cooking pot at the fire ring and Brigid poured him some tea. He sipped slowly. "'Tis true that yer destiny was foretold before yer birth. Yer to be either a blessing or curse to Ireland. The time has come for ye to choose the path." He pulled himself to his feet. "And 'tis time I left ye to yer thinking."

"Nay, Bram. Please, don't go! I have no choices. I'm helpless." She wanted to pull on his arm but feared she'd cause him to lose his balance. She watched as he crept out of the cave.

He called over his shoulder. "Do not let Ardan convince ye there's only one answer. There's always the choice of doing what's right. And when ye follow that path, it always leads to good. Make him keep his word."

"Don't go, Bram!" Tears dripped from her chin. She dashed to his side.

"I must go. Duty calls and a druid must travel. Ye know this."

She wept freely into his sleeve. "Nay, wait. If I make this agreement, I can never... "

Bram pulled away and didn't turn back. He wandered around the trees on the sloping side of the cliff until Brigid could no longer see him through her tears.

Oh, God, what do I do now?

No one answered. She was alone, dreading the arrival of the dipping sun.

All day Brigid waited, but the king's druid did not return. She prayed, pleading with God. Her sobs exhausted her, driving her into a fitful sleep. In her dreams, she heard Bram's voice. "Doing what's right always leads to good. Hold Ardan to the agreement."

She awoke with a start. The fire was nearly extinguished. She smelled smoke – a blazing fire. Ardan's torch? She strained her eyes in the dark cave.

A flicker of light glowed from the entrance. She heard the druid's voice. "I must have yer answer, Brigid."

The fog of sleep clouded her head. Was she still dreaming? Had Bram actually encouraged her to accept Ardan's demands?

She rubbed her eyes. "Ardan?"

She heard the shuffle of his robe and the clanking of his gold adornments. "Aye, 'tis me." The torch grew closer.

"Yer answer?"

"It will be as ye said." The words grated her throat like grains of sand.

CHAPTER

"LET YOUR GENTLENESS BE EVIDENT TO ALL. THE LORD IS NEAR."
PHILIPPIANS 4:5

Brigid traveled back to the Cell of the Oak with the eerie feeling that someone was watching her. Ardan indeed was watching, or would be, though she knew not when or where. He'd promised to observe her, or send someone who would. Odd that while once she'd felt horribly alone, now she felt more exposed and examined than when she was a slave. She had to be diligent. If she passed the test, her mother would be freed.

A gathering of ravens, sparrows, and finches frolicked in the trees above her head. Brigid was reminded of the Scripture promise that God, who cares for the wild birds, the creatures with no worry, will most certainly care for those he loves. Had she betrayed him?

She barely recognized the settlement when she arrived. In her absence, her followers had rebuilt the large house. Not only that, she counted four other structures: a barn, a blacksmith shed, and two other storage buildings. Tears streamed freely down her face. While she had taken leave of them, her brothers and sisters had continued their work.

"Sister Brigid!" Fiona, one of the faithful – a girl who

desired to devote her life to the Lord's work – met her. What would she think of the changes Brigid would have to live by?

The lass, younger than Brigid, slipped her arms around Brigid's neck. "Have ye found yer mother?"

Brigid stiffened. "Nay, but I have received assurance that she will return soon."

Fiona stepped back. "That's wonderful. Ye've worked a ransom?"

"Aye, a deal has been made." Brigid tilted her head to peer around the lass. "Ye've done a wonderful job here."

Fiona took Brigid's hand. "Let me show ye."

They explored the grounds, a handful of women joining them, praising God for Brigid's return.

Brigid searched their faces. "Cook?"

Fiona pulled her aside. "She's returned to Glasgleann, but she said to send for her when ye came back. Did ye not send word that she should go?"

Brian. She'd forgotten she told him that. "Aye, that's right. Is all well with her, Fiona?"

"As I hear, it is."

"Good. Then there's no need to send for her. She's got her family to care for."

Brigid's hands were shaking. Perspiration coated her collar, and she itched as though an army of lice populated her undergarments. A bath would revive her and also provide the solitude she'd come to crave. "I must bathe."

Fiona tipped her head. "Of course. I'll fetch fresh clothes and meet ye at the spring. Ye'll be pleased to know that the pagan statues have been removed, just like ye asked."

The others drifted back to their chores. Brigid cherished the solitude. She dipped a toe into the spring. Chilly, but Brigid needed some kind of discomfort, a penance, for making a deal with the evil Ardan.

She shed her clothes and stepped into the pool. When her

shoulders sank under the water, the cold shock made her suck in her breath. Her fingers and toes were numb. She ducked completely under and opened her eyes. Blue and green shapes fluttered at the surface. Someone was standing over her. She emerged and spat water from her lips.

"Oh, Fiona, 'tis you!" She slapped her hand on her chest to calm her thumping heart.

"Aye. I told ye I'd meet ye here. Truly, Sister Brigid, I believe yer time in solitude has made ye jumpy as a toad." She handed Brigid a thick sheep wool towel.

Brigid accepted the fleece and climbed out of the spring.

Fiona gasped. "Brigid, yer undergarment!"

She'd forgotten to leave it on. "I'm sorry, Fiona. I suppose I grew accustomed to being alone." She snatched the clothing Fiona had brought and slipped behind a pine to dress.

Brigid peered through tree branches to keep her eye on the lass. Fiona held her hand over her mouth and pretended to stare at the ground. She'd probably never seen a naked body before and was sorely offended. Brigid would need to do more penance for that mistake.

Brigid called to her. "Fiona, there is much the sisters should know. There may be strangers about."

Fiona shrugged her black-cloaked shoulders. "Aye, Sister Brigid, there have been many people stopping by to seek Christ's charity. And some have even converted."

Brigid emerged wearing a white mantle and scarf. "Fiona, why did ye bring me white?"

The lass wore a colorless dress beneath her cloak, but Brigid's garment was much more exquisite, plain but better woven and bleached to the color of summer clouds.

Fiona smiled and her cheeks flushed like wild rose petals. "I made it myself, Sister. 'Tis the color of a druid cloak, but made for our Christian spiritual leader. All the others approved. I hope it is acceptable."

Feeling humbled, and not nearly worthy enough to be called a leader, Brigid remembered her vows at the shore. She had pledged to uphold Patrick's teachings, and more importantly, Christ's teachings. She once was filled with desire to reach all the pagans she could for Christ, and now she felt like a failure.

"Oh, Fiona, I fear I can never be a leader. I failed to convert my dearest friend, and now I must go about my work without speaking God's words or delivering miracles. Is such a thing possible?"

Fiona half-smiled. "Oh, Sister Brigid. Ye've just been away far too long. Ye need rest." She gathered up the dirty clothing and held onto Brigid's elbow, guiding her to the main house. "There's a room where ye won't be disturbed."

Brigid stopped. "Just one thing, Fiona."

The girl blinked her dark eyelashes. "Of course."

"I expect there will be spies, coming to check to see if I've paid the ransom. Tell the others. Warn them not to talk about me to anyone."

Fiona cocked her head in a way that suggested that Brigid's words were nonsense to her. Brigid wouldn't blame Fiona if she thought her leader was mad. First she'd absentmindedly exposed her nakedness, and then she rambled about strangers. But this matter was too important to have the lass believe she'd lost her mind. "'Tis important, child. Promise me."

"Aye. I'll see to it."

After the first day, Brigid found her return to the settlement not nearly as awkward as she'd imaged. As long as she kept to her tasks of copying scrolls loaned by Cillian and supervising the dairy work, she could avoid thinking about her higher mission, that of converting the pagans of Ireland. Her plan worked for days, until she was unable to avoid the pleading eyes and empty hands of children who pulled at her skirts.

Usually Fiona and the others tended to them, leaving Brigid to the solitude they assumed she sought. She could never tell them the details of her promise to Ardan. How could she defend what she'd done?

But one steamy summer morning, when Brigid left the dairy barn, a youngster emerged from the trees and called her name. Two others followed the young lass.

"Fiona!" Brigid called toward the barn. No one answered. When Brigid had left the dairy, all hands were busy tending the cattle. No one could hear her.

With little hands pulling on her cloak, Brigid glanced about the settlement. Where were the men? Of course. They were on the hills with the sheep. Cook? Surely she could feed these children. Brigid slapped her hand to her forehead. She was panicking and must have forgotten where she was. She was at the Cell of the Oak and Cook wasn't there. She had gone back to Glasgleann. Fiona and the other sisters cooked the meals. Brigid's head whirled like a sinkhole. She was trapped.

Brigid knelt down. The children's faces were dark and muddy with eyes shining with hope, as only children's can. "Come, young ones, I'll find something for ye in the kitchen."

Brigid gathered the group like a mother hen with her chicks and nestled them in a corner of the kitchen. She pulled a chunk of cheese from the pantry. "Ye'll not be feasting in here with hands so black," she told them.

A servant girl entered with two buckets from the morning's milking.

Brigid stopped her. "Would ye be fetching some water from the spring for the children?"

The girl soon returned with a bucket of cool water. The young ones sneered.

"Has yer mother not taught ye to wash before eating?" Surely even poor pagans knew better than to blacken their cheese with dirty hands.

The tiniest, a lass no more than two summers old, began to weep. Her brother, a lad of about ten, spoke. "Our mother's dead, Sister Brigid. That's why we come here for food."

Her heart melted. Why had she been so distant? Feeding the starving had not required a miracle. Filling their tummies would not require a discourse on faith. Though she could not tell these children to believe in the One True God, she could feed them.

And feed them she did. When they were scrubbed, she requested the servant girl to prepare a roasted bird while she sliced cheese and fed the children hard pieces of yesterday's brown bread. The children said they lived with a foster father nearby, so when they had their fill, she sent them on their way with a basket of brown eggs for supper.

Brigid returned to her work in a round hut with a large smoke hole that let in plenty of light for writing during the day. Winter would require warmer lodging, but for now, she loved the small quiet space for its simplicity. Having no distraction meant she could focus on reading and writing the Lord's Word. That work brought her peace. One day she'd teach the others to write and illuminate the parchments as she did. But for now, while her mother was still separated from her, she'd dwell in the solitude and enjoy God's Word alone.

Brigid retrieved a rolled parchment from a basket under her work table and unfurled it. Cillian had sent it to her just yesterday. She was eager to see what it contained. The words were Latin, though the brown writing was difficult to read. Settling herself on a stool, she studied the script and began to formulate a plan for how the words would appear on her own paper.

"Sister Brigid?" a voice called into the hut.

Brigid squeezed her eyes tight. *Why now?* Could she not enjoy one moment alone with her work?

"Sister Brigid, a man has come to see ye." Fiona stooped to gaze into the room.

Brigid rose from her stool. "I told ye to avoid strangers asking for me, Fiona. What did ye tell him?"

"Only that yer here. He's waiting in the big house."

Brigid cleared her throat and rolled up the Latin text. "His name, darlin'. Did ye ask him his name?"

"Aye. Said he was Ardan from King Dunlaing's castle."

Brigid quickly joined the lass outside the hut. She probably should have given Fiona more information. The girl was naive about the danger this druid could bring. "Has no one told ye who was responsible for my mother's kidnapping?"

Fiona backed away. "Nay, Sister. Should I have sent him away?" Fiona's eyes were wide and her mouth hung open.

Brigid had failed her again. Learning to be a mentor as wise as old Bram would take practice. Like he'd always said, there was much she did not know. "Nay, child. Ye did fine. We'll talk later. But now, tell me, did he ask questions? Did he ask about miracles? Anything?"

Fiona stuttered. "Why... nay, Sister. He asked only to speak with ye. I wish I had known what to say. I would have sent him away, Sister, if ye did not want him here."

Brigid touched the young girl's arm as they made their way toward the Cell of the Oak's largest shelter. "Forgive me, child. Ye did nothing wrong."

They ducked their heads under the arched doorway. Ardan's white-cloaked figure was seated at a long table, the gathering place for the Cell of the Oak's inhabitants. No one else was about. The faithful were hard-working men and women and would not be found lounging about at the midday hour.

Brigid's voice echoed off the house's wood and stone walls. "Leave us to our business, Fiona."

The girl whispered into Brigid's hair, "Are ye sure, Sister? Ye seem bothered by this man's presence."

"Aye." Brigid raised her voice. "I fear only the One True God."

Ardan laughed at the statement as he rose from the table bench. Fiona hesitated.

"Go on," Brigid told her.

When they were alone, Ardan stepped toward Brigid, tapping his long fingers together and holding his walking stick under his arm. "There is something else ye fear, Brigid."

"There is not." A lumped formed in her throat.

"Let's not squabble." Ardan walked in a circle around her. "Fine white garments ye wear, lass. Much more regal than the rags I found ye wearing in that cave."

"State yer business." She wished he'd leave and not return until he brought her mother.

"I plan to depart tomorrow to fetch Brocca. I've only come to see if ye kept our bargain."

She wrinkled her nose. "Ye know I have."

Ardan huffed. "Ye think I've been everywhere watching?"

"Ye haven't?"

"Perhaps I have, through the eyes of others. And now I came to see for myself."

"And what do ye see, druid?"

"I see ye keeping your god's words to yerself in that small hut. That pleases me."

She forced words out through her teeth. "Then send my mother."

He reached his hand toward her, but she backed away. He tucked his arm under his white cloak. "Ah, Brigid. I will return Brocca, but I'd much prefer ye'd use yer skills to join me in my work. What good can ye do alone?"

"And what good can be done if I work with you, Ardan?"

He raised his hand to heart as though wounded. "Brigid, ye speak as though I want to harm people. I only want to help them, like you do."

301

"True bread comes from heaven, from my Father. That's what will truly help the people."

He swung his head like a cow's tail. "Such nonsense. Foolish talk does not give the people what they need."

Brigid bravely took one step toward the large man. "And *you* know what they need?"

Ardan closed the space between them and towered over her. "I am the great druid of King Dunlaing's castle. I commune with the spirits. The common people cannot do that. They *need* me."

"They need Christ."

He returned to the table and sat down. "Perhaps yer right. But whatever spirit they need, one thing is certain, Brigid of Ireland. They do not need *you*."

Ardan's words echoed in the depths of Brigid's mind. They didn't need her. That was true. God didn't need her either. But Brigid needed her mother. Because of that, she was at this man's mercy.

"Yer business. What do ye want?"

"Ah." He sat up straight. "My golden sickle. I would like it back, please."

"I have no such thing."

"I warn ye, Brigid, I'll not feel compelled to keep our bargain if ye have stolen it from me."

"I have stolen from no one."

An expression crossed his face as though he realized his error. "Very well. I'll be on my way and return to ye in six sunsets."

Brigid was running low on patience. "See that ye do or our bargain will be void."

He was silent for a moment. "A druid always keeps his word."

"So I've been told."

Dunlaing called once more for his spy Galvin. He ordered all his attendants away so they could speak privately. He put his hand on Galvin's shoulder. "Come walk with me in the rose garden."

The morning dew had laid a blanket on the flowers, but now the sun peeked through clouds and the moisture would soon evaporate. Midsummer was Dunlaing's favorite time of year, a season of fairs and traveling musicians and good times. At least it had been in the past. This summer he was haunted by his order to silence Brigid and no amount of food or tunes would calm him. He must find the bard and discover the truth.

"Galvin, I desire to speak to the royal poet whom Ardan brought to me earlier. He has returned to the woods, but I must speak with him. Find him and there will be silver for ye."

Galvin bowed low and departed, worming his way through bushes of pink and red roses.

CHAPTER

29

"AND YE SHALL KNOW THE TRUTH,
AND THE TRUTH SHALL MAKE YOU FREE."
JOHN 8:32, KING JAMES VERSION

Hiding Erc and his family away had taken many days, days that might be crucial to finding her daughter. But Brocca couldn't take the chance that Ardan's threats against Erc's loved ones were shallow. He might not be able to call down curses from nonexistent gods, but he had evil intentions and was crafty enough to enact them in other ways.

The young family had trusted her, and when she and the poet found a distant clan willing to take them in, she was relieved. They would now not starve. To be sure they'd accept Erc's family, the poet had given the clan the treasure trunk from the hidden room on the island.

Now they were finally headed in Brigid's direction. Rumor among the woodsfolk was that kind Brigid had left her friends and hidden herself away. When they got closer, Brocca was sure the woodsfolk would be talking about Brigid, the one who did miracles in the Lord's name. Someone would know how to find her.

Brocca reached for the poet's hand. "Is it far?"

"At least three days' journey. Praise God we were able to obtain a horse and wagon."

Brocca was amazed at the young man's ability to speak the truth of God and get people to listen. A royal bard always drew a crowd of listeners, of course. But this man lured people with songs of hope and truth. So hungry were these people for encouragement that they provided for every need she and the poet had.

On the third day, they traveled until the sun was high and then stopped for a meal of oatcakes and cheese. They were eating in the wagon bed when a man approached. Brocca was startled. She always heard people approaching, even those trying to hide, but this one had escaped her notice.

The man whispered, "I hear ye look for Brigid."

Brocca heard the sound of the poet's drinking gourd hitting the wagon floor. His voice was tight. "And who, sir, are you?"

"I hear ye look for her. Maybe I can help."

The poet jumped from the wagon. "I cannot answer, sir, if I do not know who ye are or who sent ye. Can ye answer at least one of my queries?"

Brocca scooted to the side of the wagon to hear the response.

"I can tell ye that I believe the one who seeks Brigid could be the one I seek."

"Oh, and who might that be?"

"The royal poet. The one who uses no name. The one brought to King Dunlaing by the druid Ardan."

Brocca coughed – a piece of cake had stuck in her throat. She scrambled around the wagon bed until she laid hands on the sheepskin water bag. She drank and dislodged the crumbs in her throat and then struggled to hear the rest of the conversation.

"And what if I can tell ye where that poet is? Can ye then

help me find Brigid? Word is, she's isolated herself some-where."

"I can help ye."

The poet grunted. "Well, then. First tell me what business ye have with the poet."

The other man lowered his voice so much that Brocca had to lean far over the wagon to hear. She might have been obvious in her eavesdropping, but they seemed to ignore her.

The stranger's voice was as light as wind. "I must take the poet to see King Dunlaing at once."

The poet cleared his throat. "The king requests his presence?"

"He does."

"Why?"

"I am just a messenger, sir."

"Tell me, man. Would this have anything to do with the druid Ardan?"

There was a pause. Finally the stranger spoke. "I can only speak of this matter with the poet. But..."

Brocca wondered if the man had guessed the truth.

The stranger continued. "I can assure the poet's safety, under the king's protection."

"Well, then. Here I am. Take me to him."

Brocca discovered that the stranger was in the wagon bed with her and the poet was already driving toward the north winds, so she scurried up to the reins and joined him. "Why are we going to see the king? Will he lead us to Brigid?"

"I believe so."

"And just why do ye believe so? Have ye not considered that Ardan may have found us out? That this could be some sort of trap?"

The poet laughed and tapped her hand. "Brocca, I have done nothing wrong to merit punishment from the king. Do not forget that pagans fear my words. While I do not desire to use their fear to my advantage, I do use it for the Lord's advantage. And there's something ye missed."

"What's that?"

"A wink. Clever man knew who he was speaking to."

Brocca turned her face to the stiff breezes and prayed silently that God would protect her daughter.

At nightfall they arrived at the castle. They were escorted to the king's large dining room where a meal awaited. The smells of roasted venison, smoked salmon, and honey-sweetened porridge awakened a hunger in Brocca she hadn't realized existed.

A servant pulled chairs back from the table, scraping the legs against the limestone floor. "Please, sit and eat."

Brocca found one and the poet helped scoot her close to the food.

"We will give thanks to God *first*." He put such emphasis on the word "first" that Brocca reasoned the stranger must have been helping himself to the meal.

The poet strummed his harp and sang a song of praise. His music brought people into the room, laughing and talking. When he finished, Brocca savored the food but was anxious for the king's appearance. Would he know where Brigid was? Should she ask or trust the poet?

While she thought on those things, a servant blew a horn, signaling the entry of the king. Brocca accepted the poet's hand and they stood until they were instructed to sit and resume eating.

It didn't take Brocca long to get her fill, but the others continued feasting for a long while. Much later a servant whisked them away to a quiet room.

"Touch the scepter," the poet whispered.

With all the noise and movement, Brocca had gotten confused. She hadn't realized they were finally in the king's presence. She reached out her hand and touched the cold surface of the king's scepter.

"We have met before, woman. Have we not?"

She recognized the king's voice. "Aye, King Dunlaing. My daughter and I were guests in your castle some months ago." Prisoners was more like it, but she didn't want to sound disgruntled.

"Aye, Brigid. I'm surprised my servant found ye in the poet's company. I'm told ye were taken hostage in a raid."

"That's true. The poet rescued me."

"Well, I shall like to hear that story sometime. But first, I have other matters to discuss with the poet. Would ye mind if I confer with him first? Then I will address yer concern."

The poet whispered into her hair. "I told the servant ye wanted to ask about the whereabouts of yer daughter."

She nodded without speaking and was led to a chair.

The king's voice was emotionless. "My man Galvin has done well. I told him I must speak to ye."

The poet answered. "Aye, king. I am at yer service."

"I would like to know about this god, this new one the Christians speak of. Do ye know of him?"

"I do indeed, king."

The poet reached for his harp and sang a song about God's deliverance. Brocca had never heard such a beautiful melody and wondered if King David had sung similar tunes. The Scriptures revealed the ancient king's lyrics, but the tunes were left to the imagination.

The poet finished and the king wept. "I have betrayed Brigid and this God. Is there no salvation for my kingdom?"

"Aye, king. There is."

Brocca gasped. Had he caused her daughter harm?

The poet carefully explained the Way of Christ to King Dunlaing, and Brocca heard it all from her chair. Tears streamed down her face as she realized the significance of yet

308

another Irish king turning to Christianity. But her joy was tempered by a fear of what it might be that the king repented from.

Dunlaing called for Brocca to approach and she fell at his feet.

"In my greediness, I have sent out a royal order restricting Brigid from spreading her faith in my territory. I now regret that decision, one that was made selfishly and not for the good of the people. I was deceived by Ardan, aye, 'tis true, but I am responsible for this terrible decision. I'm afraid it gave Ardan the influence he sought to control her, and it sent her into exile. My servant searches still for her." He pointed his words at the ground. "The false god I had been warned about was not Brigid's God – 'twas Ardan himself. I fear he believes he is a god, and by fearing his powers, some of us believed it too."

Brocca bent her face toward his voice. "Brigid? Do ye believe she still lives?"

There was silence. The poet touched her shoulder.

Finally, the king cleared his throat and spoke. "I have had no word that she does not. Truly, woman, if her life had been taken, all my kingdom would be buzzing with the news. The people love her for her charity."

The poet spoke. "Listen to his wisdom, Brocca."

She thanked the king and accepted the poet's invitation to stand.

King Dunlaing's voice softened. "There is hope that Ardan may be discouraged. My spy has retrieved Ardan's golden sickle. Ardan believes it's central to his power, but here it is."

Brocca heard others gasp and knew that the king was holding the druid sickle in the air. She couldn't believe what she heard. First her daughter was separated from her, and then she was forbidden from carrying out her mission. *A curse.* Could that be what Ardan had referred to when he left her on that island? Had he been trying to force the curse? She remembered what the poet had said earlier. Ardan sought power for himself. He must have deemed Brigid a threat.

Brocca's mind whirled with thoughts, and she felt as though an undertow would pull her away. She covered her face with her hands. *Oh, God, I remember the prophecy. Brigid will be either a blessing or curse to Ireland. Please let her be the blessing ye intended her to be.*

"Has yer spy checked for Brigid at the Cell of the Oak?" a voice from the back of the room called out.

She knew that voice! The guard who had saved her from Troya. The lad must be a servant of God, maybe even an angel.

"Come," King Dunlaing ordered.

The voice moved closer. Brocca heard the clanking of his spear against the stone floor. She scooted to the king's side to allow the guard to approach.

"I heard she has returned to her settlement where she lives among believers. She feeds the poor, but not by miracles. I hear she has not broken the king's order."

Brocca rose to her feet. "I must go to her now."

The king's silk robes rustled. He was standing. "Wait. You shall be reunited, but please, allow me this chance to make amends. I will visit her myself first. With no royal bodyguards or kingly robes. I want to speak with her as a fellow believer."

The poet strummed a new tune and sang about the king's conversion. Brocca nodded and heard the king's silky garments whisk along the floor and out the door.

CHAPTER

"... THE MIRTH OF THE WICKED IS BRIEF, THE JOY OF THE GODLESS LASTS BUT A MOMENT."
JOB 20:5

There was no fire, no sound. Where were they? Surely he'd scared that simple-minded man enough to keep him from fleeing with Brocca. Ardan kicked at the sand on the beach. The small craft was gone. That man was going to be sorry.

He gathered all the driftwood he could and sparked a fire with his special rock. *The gods will hear of this.*

In a rage, Ardan marched to top of the highest hill. A few wild goats grazed there and he snatched one, tying its feet together with the leather straps pulled from his shoes. Satisfied that the animal would make an excellent sacrifice, he started downhill. A small shack caught his attention and he went inside. The place was abandoned, but footprints in the dust, and ashes scattered about, told him someone had been there recently. Where were they now?

After he returned to his sacrificial fire, he remembered he had no golden sickle. A darkness gripped him. He feared the gods would not accept his sacrifice. And if he didn't please them, Brigid would get her mother back. And if she got the source of her strength back, well, all her power would slip out of Ardan's clutches. He planned to tease Brigid with her mother, let her see Brocca but then snatch her away until Brigid agreed to share her power with him.

He fell on the beach and panted for air. The sun dipped below the horizon, but still Ardan stayed there, holding on to his goat. A strange smell made him rise just as the sky turned black. Off in the distance, a large sailing vessel rose and fell on the waves. Fires burned onboard, the source of the awful smell.

He stood and pulled a dirk from his waist bag. Ardan feared no one. He was dressed in his druid clothing, holding a sacrificial animal. The intruders would respect him and perhaps give him passage to the river where he'd travel back to King Dunlaing.

He waited. A drunken chorus drifted to his ears. He didn't understand the language. The boat thumped against choppy dark waves. "Oh, gods!" Ardan called out. "Aid yer servant Ardan. Give him power over those who approach."

His pulse pounded in his neck. The ship neared close enough for him to see the crew's faces lit by the onboard fires, and he shivered. *Raiders!*

Ardan dropped the goat and ran, trying to remember the way to the shack. Scraggly bushes scratched his legs and without their laces, his leather shoes fell from his feet. The chanting strangers came closer, their voices filling his heart with terror. He reached the shack and fell into its darkness. He stumbled. There was a hole in the floor and he fell into it.

Ardan awoke aboard the smelly ship. His legs and hands were bound, and he sat with his back against a wooden crate. He squinted his eyes in the sunlight. They were out to sea. His head hurt, but other than that, he was whole.

"Ah, you have come to your senses." A man stood over him, shadowed with the sun behind him. His words carried a strange lilt and his Irish was broken. He was a foreigner.

"Where are we?"

"On a boat. Have you never sailed?"

Ardan gritted his teeth. His mouth was coated in sand. "My father was a fisherman."

"We're going to the land of..." The man paused, seeming to look for the right word. "I believe you call it the land of the Picts. That's where we're off to, man."

"I'm a hostage?"

"Could say so. Though you are more important than all that."

Ardan spat dirt from his mouth. "I'll say I am. I am King Dunlaing's royal druid."

"Are you, now? That means nothing to these men. You are the keeper of the treasure."

"What treasure?"

The man offered Ardan a drink from a gourd. A charm dangled from his neck. "The treasure that was for many generations kept on that island."

"I saw no treasure."

The charm was a cross. Ardan had seen it before on Christians.

"Well, that does not matter to these men either. They found you in the place where the treasure was supposed to be so you are now a hostage."

Ardan squinted. His head ached. "Are ye a hostage also?"

"Definitely not. I am sent by the church to convert these people. Because I speak your language, I am assigned your care."

Ardan stared at the wooden cross pendant. There was a silver figure of a man stuck to it. He didn't know what it was, but on the beach he had cried out for help. Brigid wore a similar cross. Perhaps her god was the one he should pray to. He pointed to the man's pendant. "Tell me more about this god ye serve."

313

CHAPTER

"BECAUSE OF GOD'S TENDER MERCY, THE LIGHT
FROM HEAVEN IS ABOUT TO BREAK UPON US,
TO GIVE LIGHT TO THOSE WHO SIT IN DARKNESS
AND IN THE SHADOW OF DEATH, AND TO
GUIDE US TO THE PATH OF PEACE."
LUKE 1:78–79, NEW LIVING TRANSLATION

The sun's rays summoned the mist, and the morning dew settled like glittering jewels scattered across a green carpet when
they came for Brigid.

A stiff gale whisked its way into the meeting house she
shared with her sisters in the Lord, propelling four visitors
through the door. Brigid nodded, though they spoke not a
word. Pulling her cloak around her, she followed them to a wee
stone house. The four men, small in stature, left her standing
outside while they scampered off, east, west, north, south.
They vanished so quickly she feared what might be inside.

The door wailed and creaked, leaving no chance she'd
enter unnoticed. At first the single room appeared deserted,
but then a faint call drifted from the damp walls.

"Water, lass? A wee bit of water for my parched lips?"

The droning came from a mat in a corner, opposite a lone
pantry. A stool was positioned beside the ill fellow, but clearly
those who had cared for him had handed the task off to her.
Brigid removed her cloak and stepped closer to have a look.

The man lingered at death's door.

She spoke softly. "Aye. Water for a thirsty soul. I'll return."

Brigid took a small wooden cup from the cabinet in the room and donned her cloak once again. She left the house to fetch water from the well and heard the man's soft wails floating to her on the brisk air like a whisper. It wouldn't be long before he succumbed. The cool water from the well would be the last he'd taste, replaced by the blazing fires of hell, if she didn't help save him before he died. But she could not disobey the king's order and hope to see her mother again. What could she do?

Brigid scooped a cup full of water from the well's bucket. *The water of life*, she thought.

Walking back to the minuscule house, she thought about the men who had fled from the sick man's door. It was common for pagans to abandon their dying brothers. What a pity for the departing to be abandoned.

The bleakness of the situation was heavy, yet it was a burden she bore gladly. Had she been there when her Lord died on the cross, she would never have left him. Not having that opportunity, Brigid would serve the sick and hungry as though she served Jesus himself. Serving – it was the only thing left to her now.

She whispered a prayer. "Do not hold their abandoning against them, Lord. They were frightened, for sure."

The sick man had probably been delirious with fever, causing his clan to believe he'd been possessed by an evil spirit.

He might be yet.

Brigid quickened her pace. She heard a small voice whisper in her ear. *Hurry now.* That fellow, a pagan, would be doomed for all eternity if Brigid didn't minister to his soul. But she couldn't carry him to heaven herself. He must take up his cross. She'd have to think of something to urge the poor man to come to Jesus on his own.

The sweet smells of the peat fire greeted her when she

returned. But as she closed the door, shutting out the misty breeze, she noticed a putrid odor. The smell of impending death.

She hurried to the man's side. "A drink, sir?" Brigid drizzled a few drops into his mouth. A stream ran down his chin, and she wiped it away with the shroud-like linen sheet covering his fragile body. She didn't know the man, but yet he seemed so familiar. There were many like him – pagans without hope.

The hours of the man's life dropped off like petals in a windstorm. She kicked at the reeds covering the floor, trying to form words that would speak to the man's heart yet not betray the promise she had made. The thin reeds, scattered in the room to add cushioning to the dirt base, gave her an idea. She gathered a few and sat on the three-legged stool beside the pagan man's mat.

"What is it that yer making?" He tried to raise himself onto bony elbows.

"Oh, not much. Here, let me boost yer head with a pillow." The straw-filled sack crunched softly under the man's thin white strands of hair.

His eyes, dim and cavernous, strained to see what she had in her hands. "Please, tell me what it is yer doing with that grass?"

Brigid ignored him for the moment and twisted the reeds until she formed an odd-shaped square with four stems sticking out in all directions.

"Oh, just passing the time, and as I worked with these reeds, I started thinking about the cross Jesus died on."

The man licked his cracked lips. Puffing out his cheeks like a piper, he let out a breath. A nearly toothless grin crossed his creased face when he spoke. "Why was he killed?"

"They thought him a king who would someday rule over them all. They didn't want him to have so much power."

"Was he a king, then?"

316

She paused, weaving a bit more before answering. "A King he was. But ah, not the kind they expected."

"A kind king he was?"

"Kind, gentle, forgiving. But fierce when people broke God's laws knowingly." She continued weaving the reeds, back and forth, her hands trembling when she remembered how little time she had. Was someone listening outside the door? Ardan perhaps?

The old man raised a bony finger. "Why would they kill a man like that? Did he try to escape? Did he not have friends to rescue him?" The man seemed to have been given a reprieve, fortified by a hunger to hear about Jesus.

"Aye, he had many followers. But he went to his execution by his own free will, telling his friends, 'He who lives by the sword, dies by the sword.'"

The man drifted back to lie on his mattress and stare at the rafters.

Brigid followed his gaze to two doves scurrying back and forth, making a nest. *Some die, others are born. God's plan.*

The man rubbed his thorny whiskers. "Aye. 'Tis true. I have seen that myself."

She held the finished cross up for him to see. "That's not the entire story."

"Nay?" His eyes grew large as bird eggs.

"I have not told ye the best part." She leaned in close. "I said he went willingly, remember?"

"Now why would anyone do that? Every man wants to save his own life. Was he a wee bit deranged, then?"

The question made Brigid chuckle. "He was God's Son."

The fellow bent his wooly brows. "If he was the son of a god, woman, why did he not save himself?"

"The best part. Now we're getting to it." She laid the cross on the man's chest and gripped his pale hand in hers.

"He took our punishment – for all our sins. Yers, mine,

those who lived back then, and those who have not yet been born."

"And yer god accepted his blood sacrifice? For all them people?"

"Aye."

"How do we get that for ourselves?"

Brigid sighed deeply. Perhaps her message had reached his heart in time. But now what could she do to lead him? She glanced at the door. Even if no one was listening there, she could not break a promise. She would not tell this man to accept Jesus, but she'd tell him how it was done. Perhaps that would be all right. "Ye pray."

"To yer god?"

"Aye. The One True God. And ye ask him to forgive ye for all yer wrongs and accept ye as one whom Jesus died for."

Tears streamed down the old man's face. "What happens then?"

"Then he takes ye to heaven to live with him when it's yer time to go."

"Let me see that cross ye made."

She held it up, allowing the sunbeams from the window to glow through the spaces between her weaving.

"Is heaven a good place? Better than here?"

"Ah, man. 'Tis a far better place. Ye won't be sick there or sad or lonely."

"Jesus is there?"

"Aye. Those who accept him will be there with him."

Brigid thought she'd have to pray with the man, and she was prepared to, realizing that obeying God, not man, was her true duty, but to her surprise he folded his hands around the cross she made and uttered his own awkward but sincere offering.

"Ah, God. I just heard 'bout yer Son. I want to be with ye when I die. Please take me to heaven and accept Jesus' sacrifice in my place for all the ill I've done. Thank ye for letting him die for me."

"Aye." She agreed. Tears streamed down her face.

Brigid sat with the man the rest of the day, only rising on occasion to fetch more water. The man accepted baptism and Brigid's prayers, and she no longer feared giving them. King Dunlaing could arrest her if he wanted. There was surely another way to free her mother.

The old one seemed at peace and asked no more questions. The cool breezes of evening squeezed their way through a crack under the door, and the man inhaled deeply. Then, sighing, he pushed the air back out of his weak lungs. He did not take another breath.

With the help of her sisters in the Lord, Brigid buried the man under a grove of ancient oaks near her home. She left the cross entwined in his fingers, but she wove another to place on top of his stone-covered grave. When she turned to leave, she saw a man approaching.

Brigid reached out arms she hoped would offer comfort. "Are ye related to the departed?"

"Nay. I must speak to ye, Brigid." He lowered his cloak and she recognized his sapphire eyes.

"King! What are ye doing here?" She glanced around, expecting to see armed men who had come to take her away for violating the king's order.

"I have not come as king." He smiled and reached for her hand. "I have come as a fellow believer."

Brigid gasped and held a hand to the wooden cross around her neck.

"I have rescinded the royal order. There are no restrictions on your work, Brigid."

Brigid's knees shook. "Oh, thank ye, King Dunlaing! I must find my mother now."

"She is at the castle."

Brigid raised her cloak above her ankles, preparing to run toward the horses, but he blocked her way.

"One moment. Do ye know who it is ye've buried today?"

"Oh." She made the sign of the cross over her chest and turned to the mound of dirt speckled with stones. The reed cross still rested on top. "We would have sought a burial tomb, but the man was poor and sick. A pagan – at least he *was*. He accepted the Lord before departing. His family abandoned him during his last hours."

"Ye do not know his name, then?"

"Nay, I'm afraid I do not."

"Let me tell ye. I know his name."

She studied his expression. What could it matter? The sisters buried unknown people all the time.

Dunlaing lowered his gaze to the ground and spoke in whispers. "I have very capable servants, Brigid. While looking for ye, they discovered the identity of the man ye ministered to in his dying moments."

"Who is he, then?"

Dunlaing placed a hand on her shoulder. "Brigid, the man in that grave is yer father, Dubthach of Glasgleann."

Brigid turned from the king and returned to the gravesite. She covered her mouth with one hand and bent down to retrieve the cross with the other. Tears dripped onto the woven reeds.

Regret? Pain? Sorrow? They blended so that she could not tell one from the other. Had she known it was him, would she have been so willing to share the story of salvation? She would never know, God help her.

The poor will always be with us. Brigid clutched the cross to her chest and hurried back home, not because her mother would soon be there, but because God had always been.